And Then There Were Three

Drexel M. Johnson

DellArte
PRESS

ISBN: 978-1-4501-0012-0 (sc)
ISBN: 978-1-4501-0011-3 (e)

Dellarte Press books may be ordered through booksellers or by contacting:

Dellarte Press™
1663 Liberty Drive
Bloomington, IN 47403
www.dellartepress.com
1-877-217-3420

Because of the dynamic nature of the Internet, any Web addresses or links contained in this book may have changed since publication and may no longer be valid. The views expressed in this work are solely those of the author and do not necessarily reflect the views of the publisher, and the publisher hereby disclaims any responsibility for them.

This novel is a work of fiction. Any references to real people, events, establishments, organizations, or locales are intended to give the fiction a sense of reality and authenticity. Any resemblance to actual events, locales, organizations, or persons, living or dead, is entirely coincidental and beyond the intent of the author or the publisher.

Printed in the United States of America

Dellarte Press rev. date:03/29/10

This book is dedicated to
the memory of my devoted grandparents.

Thank You.

"Luck is preparation awaiting opportunity."

-- Oprah Winfrey

Military basic training or "boot camp" is designed to transition one from the *civilian world* to the rigorous life of the military. Among other things, new soldiers will not be identified by their first names or even nicknames. Doing so breeds familiarity and that leads to a breakdown in authority. Until the time one is discharged, military personnel will be referred to by both rank and last name or simply by last name.

PROLOGUE

Preacher really didn't want to attend this party but he had promised Sergeant First Class McCullen that he would attend. He had a lot of school work to finish prior to the next night of class. He hoped this party was worth an early departure from the library. The work was just getting interesting.

It wasn't often that certain unit members and their friends got together and besides, Johnson was ETSing. The drive from the base was a brisk, cool one. One unlike any other this time of year. The chilly night was confirmed with a frigid breeze coming down from the distant snow-capped Pikes Peak.

Preacher turned off Academy Boulevard and was blocks away from the party. He had only been here a couple of times to pick up Sergeant McCullen, mostly when his wife wasn't able to take him to work. At other times too, when the unit had a rare field exercise that usually ran late and McCullen didn't want to inconvenience his wife and kids. Besides, Sergeant McCullen's apartment wasn't that far from his.

After arriving in front of the house, Preacher could tell that a party was in the area. Cars were parked along both sides of the street. If it wasn't for most of these apartments and houses having their own parking areas, the civilian police would have paid a visit to the McCullen residence.

Preacher parked on the next block over. Upon his successful maneuvering of the car, he exited and locked it. He walked to McCullen's residence. The half-a-block walk gave Preacher time to notice the star-blanketed sky. *What is a black man doing in a state like this?* Away from the military community he could count the number of black people on one hand. After a playful ponder, reality kicked in and he said, "The U.S.

Army sent me here to this god forsaken place." That statement put a smirk on Preacher's face. It was quickly replaced with another expression when he saw a shooting star streaked across the dark sky. Astronomical forces never cease to amaze him. *Damn.*

Preacher's thoughts were interrupted with Keri Hilson's *Knock You Down* when he made it to Sergeant First Class McCullen's place. He quickly walked up the ten steps of stairs. Preacher started to knock on the door, startled when it opened. It was then that the smooth flow of Maxwell's *Sumthin' Sumthin* escaped the confines of McCullen's apartment. Not only was the music flowing, but the current residents appeared to be in the groove as well. At first glance, he estimated twenty people were in McCullen's apartment, all of them enjoying the music.

Specialist Four Petersen was leaving in a big hurry. She was looking rather radiant this evening in her black, skintight "hoo-chee mama" outfit. She was definitely showing enough cleavage and the garment just barely covered her butt. Despite the little ghetto girl's taste in clothes her curls looked really great. She apparently didn't have a whole lot to do with that. Her stylist did a good job.

Petersen was approaching Preacher to pass when a hand, then a whole arm came out of the doorway grasping for Petersen's arm. "Get the fuck off me!" Petersen shouted without even turning around to see the grabber. It was then Preacher saw the face that was responsible for the offending hand. It belonged to the most irritating, shortest, loud mouth and sex deprived person in 4th Finance battalion: Private First Class Folster.

He would have made a second attempt if it weren't for the "don't mess with me" stare Petersen gave him. It was then, Folster decided that maybe it's not worth it. "Get out of here bitch," Folster told her in the most disappointing tone. Petersen lifted her middle finger.

"You sure do have a way with women," Preacher told him.

"Malcolm, you made it. A lot of people were not even sure you would come with your stuck up ass," said Folster.

"You are looking quite nice today Petersen," Preacher said, ignoring his last comment.

"You too Malcolm, even in your uniform."

Petersen's strapless purse slipped from her hands while standing on the steps. When it fell Preacher bent down to get it for her. Petersen saw Preacher reach down and she did so as well. She put her hand on Preacher's while he held her purse. Folster noticed as her skirt crimped up her firm body. She gazed into Preacher's eyes when he looked at her. "Help her," she whispered.

Preacher stared at her, puzzled. "What are you…"

"If ya leaving bitch, then leave," interrupted Folster.

"You are truly an asshole, Folster," replied Petersen, now standing and tugging on her skirt to bring it back to its original uniformity. Petersen glared at Preacher again as she went down the steps toward her car. She had a blank look on her face. Folster watched as Petersen walked down the sidewalk. "All I asked is just a chance with that ass," said Folster, still glaring at her butt. Preacher wasn't positive but he was almost sure he saw dribble at the corner of Folster's mouth. Preacher's thoughts went back to Petersen. Maybe Folster finally got to her. But he doubted it.

Preacher entered the apartment trying his best to ignore Private Folster as best he could, leaving him to close the door behind him. The usual crowd from his unit was there. But it appeared that some guys from 3rd Brigade 29th Battalion (3-29) Field Artillery and 1st Brigade 12th Battalion (1-12) Infantry Regiment were there too. Most of the guys seemed lined up against the living room wall as if it needed to be held up. All of them appeared to be glaring at the two couples dancing on the living room floor. Occasionally, the guys on the wall would start up a conversation among themselves about some event that occurred earlier in the day on the base. But for the most part they just stood there looking glassy eyed. A couple of them had glasses filled with a brown liquid in hand.

In addition to the living room floor, a few people would enter and exit the kitchen to retrieve their choice of munchees and drinks. The entire apartment smelled like weed. Preacher remembered that there were other occasions when one could cut the smoke with a knife.

"My boy-eee, you made it!" shouted Sergeant First Class Randall McCullen, as he quickly shut a door from one of his rooms down the hallway. For reasons unbeknown to Preacher, Sergeant McCullen smoothly raised one hand and spread his fingers as if to signal "five" to one of the guys standing along the wall as he passed them. The recipient of the signal nodded his head in acknowledgement. "I thought you were going to be tied up tonight?"

"I thought so too, but I decided to take a break from studying and come to the 'Party of all Parties,'" Preacher said as he raised up two fingers on each hand. "That was the statement you made, right?"

"Yes, I did and it is my man."

"Yeah, I can see that," said Preacher, looking around the sergeant at the statues along the wall. Sergeant McCullen must have caught what Preacher was referring to. "What are you drinking? *Miller Lite*? *English 800*? Vodka?"

"You know I don't drink alcohol."

"Yeah, that's right. I forgot," he lied. "What about some *Perrier*?"

"That would be great. That's just what I need."

"I will get it for you."

McCullen walked to the kitchen. Before he even reached the area, he noticed one of his infantry buddies helping himself a little too much with the liquor. "Don't stand there drinking up the shit. We have other guests if you haven't noticed!" shouted McCullen.

Preacher decided to maneuver his way to a fellow unit member sitting on the sofa. He appeared to be rocking to the music while stuffing his face with nachos. He noticed Preacher heading his way and immediately reached for a napkin nearby.

While chatting on the sofa, Malcolm Preacher noticed that the door to a room down the hall opened. One of McCullen guests exited the room and before the door closed, another one entered. "What's going on back there?" Preacher asked.

"I don't think you really want to know," said the nacho-eating associate. Preacher was about to tell him that he had a couple of crumbs around his mouth but he evidently sensed it and swept them up with his tongue.

"Sir, can I get you anything else?" said McCullen in his worst waiter impersonation.

"McCullen, what's with that room back there?"

Sergeant McCullen appeared to have been taken off guard. He glanced at the person setting next to me and nodded his head sideways to signal me to take a walk with him. Preacher rose up and said his good-byes to his fellow guest. Sergeant McCullen and Preacher zig zagged back to the front door.

"I have a hard core freak down the hall, Malcolm," said Sergeant McCullen with a glow in his eyes before reaching the door.

"Civilian or military?" Preacher asked.

"Military."

"Who is she?"

"You know the new private who came in a couple of weeks ago?" Preacher thought about his question and all the new faces he had encountered the last couple of weeks. Then he realized that that was hopeless considering his unit's job pertains to meeting and processing newcomers to the post. "No, I don't recall seeing anyone new."

"You got to stop studying so late and coming to formation half asleep and pay more attention to the honeys." McCullen spoke passionately for someone who appeared to be happily married with one child. But he could be right, thought Preacher.

"What does she look like?"

"She's just out of high school. I think in the south some place. I believe in Mississippi. She's about 5 feet something, cinnamon brown skin, baby face, laughs a lot, long hair, high yellow and naive as hell. Gwendolyn, that's her name, loves to hang out at the Enlisted club. I would bet that she came from one of those strict church families that kept their kids on a leash or some shit. Then once she graduated and broke free. She just got buck wild." They both started laughing at the last statement, especially when McCullen started motioning his hips back and forth.

"Petersen said she can't tell sometimes if she is just extremely naive from being sheltered or just plain stupid," continued McCullen. "Both of those ho's was at a club off the post and met these guys, OK. Petersen said if it weren't for her that naive hafa' would have left with one or all of those guys despite only knowing them for ten minutes. Petersen thought she was going to have to cut somebody after they told her to mind her own business." Pause. "The bitch should stay out of people's business anyway."

The two couples on the dance floor now had some more company as more people arrived. With the addition of more females, the hard heads against the wall didn't stand out as much. Sergeant McCullen apparently saw someone in the kitchen he had missed when they arrived. "Malcolm, I want to hook you up with something later. Don't leave without seeing me first, OK?"

"No problem, sarge," Preacher replied.

More and more people arrived, singles and couples. For the most part, the crowd was primarily military with a couple of civilians. Preacher could always tell the military type from the civilians. He didn't know if it's the way that they talk or their demeanor. But military personnel seemed to stand out in certain climates. He had to chuckle at the thought.

What wasn't unusual was the ethnicity of Sergeant McCullen's guests. Like in all areas of the civilian sector, people tended to work together despite their differences but after work they went their separate ways. McCullen's world was no different. He could work with just about anyone and for anyone but he prefers to party and relax within his own race. This is one of the points where both McCullen and Preacher agree. There aren't many of them.

One would say that this is a form of prejudice. It could very well be. One could also guess to some extent we all have some form of prejudice in us. For most of us, having different skin color also determine where you grew up, what friends (not just associates, but true friends) one had and what type of job you have. In places such as the small town Preacher grew up in, southerners tell you what's on their mind. None of this covert stuff that you sometime encounter outside of the south. People are either for you or against you. Southerners tend to make that very clear. Over a period of time, one will develop a form of prejudice. How far they take it, that's up to them.

"Wes' sideeeeeeeeee is in da house," barked a group of guests as they open the door and entered the room. Startling most of the other room occupants including myself. This group was greeted by another calling from the other side of the room. "Eas sideeeeeeeeee is already in daaaaa house." "You got that right my brothers. Let them know where they're at," shouted McCullen, a New York native. After the two familiar groups of guys and McCullen acknowledge each other with a forward two-finger peace sign, the newest arrivals made it for the kitchen to douse their apparent thirst. The other guys and McCullen went back to their conversations.

After mingling with a few associates from Fort Carson, Preacher decided to make his way to the back hallway. Whatever the activity was, its appeal was apparently drying up. The number of guys along the wall was now down to two. McCullen, Preacher thought, always had something unusual at these gatherings.

As he made it to the hallway, Preacher greeted the two young gents waiting anxiously for something. Preacher didn't recognize them at a distance, but now he realize they are the two new finance specialists that had just arrived in our unit from Fort Gordon. They soon recognize me. "Waz up specialist?" They could have been brothers. Both were wearing almost identical denim shirts and kaki pants with loafers. Since they were not twins, it was almost funny. Hell, it was funny. They probably went through basic training together and been inseparable ever since. "It's your world, guys. You two staying out of trouble?" "Oh yes," they replied. "Have Sergeant McCullen been taken good care of you guys?" They looked at each other and nearly at once started smiling. "Yes, he is," replied both in unison. Preacher didn't know what that was about but at the moment he didn't care. Preacher proceeded to walk to the room where the activity seemed to be in.

Before Preacher even reached the doorknob of the room, one of the privates interrupted me. "Excuse me specialist, but would you please wait your turn?"

Preacher turned around. "Wait my turn for what?" It was at that moment the door to the room opened.

Almost startling him again, Preacher turned around and immediately got out of the way so the former room inhabitant could leave. The stocky brotha was very pleased about something. He was showing all of his teeth. With the view unobstructed, Preacher positioned himself to look into the room. He couldn't believe what he was seeing. The rectangle room was dimly lit. At the far end directly opposite of the door was a bed. On the bed appeared to be a black female, naked from head to toe. She was spread eagle on her back with her feet toward the door. The bed itself appeared to be ruffled, with a pillow under the butt of the female. She didn't move at all even after the door was opened. She looked asleep but no one could be in that deep of sleep, Preacher contemplated.

The thought of her being drunk also entered his mind but that didn't fit either. "Damn, she's fine," said one of the "denim" brothers. Preacher wasn't the only one who caught the view that was before him. He had passed by him so fast he didn't get a chance to see which one of the "twins" it was. The youngin' Preacher saw wasted no time. Upon entering the room, he proceeded to unbuckle his pants and unbutton his shirt. He wore no underwear. When he got to the foot of the bed, he whipped out his dick with his back still to the door and us standing just outside it. He turned his head to the side. "Do you mind? You will get your turn soon." It was like stepping into another world.

An arm reached by Preacher swiftly. In seconds, the door was closed. Sergeant McCullen had returned. This time, he had his annoying sidekick with him. McCullen put his right arm around Preacher's broad shoulders. "Let's take a walk for a minute my man." As they approached the living room, heads were nodding in unison as D'Angelo serenaded on the box. The dance floor was full of brothas and sistas. This whole time a few of Preacher's boyz were getting their freak on with a freak. This night was getting interesting.

The way McCullen ushered Preacher back to the living room got him thinking. "What's up, McCullen. What's going on?" Once they got back near the front door out of ear range, they stopped next to the wall.

McCullen slid his arm from Preacher's shoulders and proceeded to talk. Preacher actually had his back on the wall while McCullen stood in front of him leaning against the wall with one hand next to Preacher's head. "Check this out. We're into something you may not be down with. I want you to know that you can simply turn around and walk out—no sweat, my man. I'll just know better next time." Pause. "Oh don't get me wrong, whatever happens tonight as far as I'm concerned--you were never here. Like I said, if you're not feeling the situation I understand but I wanted it to be your choice."

Preacher thought, *cut the damn drama and get to the point. I know if it's that bad (especially criminal), I'm fucked, most black people I know just can't keep a secret. It's almost like it just kills them to keep their damn mouth shut.*

"That hafa' in that room." Preacher nodded in acknowledgement. "Well, she's not exactly herself tonight."

"I would say so. How much did she drink?" Just like the guys, the girls in the military were known to handle their fair share of alcohol. Some handled it better than others.

"She drank some but that's not what got her knocked out--"

"Then what did ... What do you mean, 'knocked out?'" Preacher demanded, almost not catching that last statement.

"I had Folster give her a dose of *ruffies*." McCullen said that like Preacher was supposed to know what that was. Apparently, McCullen noticed the puzzled look on his face and went in closer to Preacher's ear. "'*Ruffies*,' '*roche*,' '*rope*,' or otherwise known as the '*date rape*' pill." You know what it is now?" Preacher stared at McCullen and tried to get his composure together and prevent any outburst of emotions. Preacher couldn't believe this career-minded "family" man could put himself, not to mention everyone else, in this position. An illegal position, at that.

"Are you out of your mind, Sergeant McCullen?" The room was definitely thumping. If it weren't, Preacher would have certainly been heard. "How can you put everyone here in that situation?"

McCullen knew that Preacher was pissed off despite his mild tone. They had worked too long together for him to not notice. "It's only a situation if it gets out, Malcolm." Preacher didn't want to tell this man in his own house what a complete dumb ass he really was. One day he would figure that out for himself.

"Of course it's going to get out."

"What do you mean, Malcolm?" asked McCullen in a worried tone.

"Relax, McCullen, I'm not going to the police. At least not yet," he told him sarcastically, now looking at the dance floor in disgust. At this point Preacher wished he had never come here tonight.

"McCullen, do you honestly believe that these 'hard heads' you currently have here boning her are not going to open their mouths?" Before he had a chance to open his mouth and reiterate his lack of intelligence Preacher started again: "You've been in this man's army longer than I have. These young soldiers talk about any sexual conquest they may have made to anyone who will listen. Take Folster for instance, if some 'chicken head' would give it up to him he would be talking."

The blank expression on his face and a certain eye movement told it all. Foster probably got his turn on Private Muse long before the line even started. "You have a problem. A big problem. These guys may not talk tomorrow or the next day, but they will talk. Like the rest of us, McCullen, you were young and dumb once." Preacher only threw himself in the equation to help make his point. "But I was never this stupid," he added.

"Didn't you tell the first person about the first girl you boned?"

"Yeah, Malcolm I see your point." Making sure he didn't lose focus, "Now what are you going to do about it?" "I don't know yet." McCullen stopped leaning against the wall and repositioned himself where he too had his back on the wall. Apparently, what Preacher said was actually absorbed. He seemed to be thinking about his (correction) their predicament. While resting along the wall, he was tapping his fist (raising and lowering from the elbow) in a rhythm and staring at the dance floor. He had finally realized the gravity of the situation. Preacher guessed he didn't have that much to drink after all. He had not committed a childish prank, but done something possibly illegal. And to one of his own soldiers.

While still distantly staring at his guests, he responded, "Fuck it."

"What?" Preacher asked.

"I said, fuck it. Nothing has changed. This party will continue as scheduled," he replied, with more enthusiasm than before. He even had a gleam in his eyes.

McCullen removed himself from the wall, looked at Preacher and said, "As I said before, you should walk out if you're not feeling it." Preacher certainly didn't expect that response. He really wasn't sure what, but certainly not that kind of response. "I need a drink," McCullen added. He left Preacher's company and headed for the kitchen. Upon arriving, he clearly didn't agree with his own selection of spirits on the counter and reached for a cabinet door above. *Kentucky Bourbon* was what he needed for the occasion to come.

McCullen poured himself a heroic-size glass of bourbon, splashed in some tap water, and swigged deeply. The bourbon flowed down as smoothly as it had looked. He felt the glow of the amber-colored spirit immediately, and, as he did, he saw again in his mind the image of Private Muse's cinnamon-brown nude body lying on his bed. He took another long mouthful of bourbon and announced to the empty kitchen, "I'm coming, bitch."

Preacher stood there still wondering where he lost him. Usually *Someone to Love* by Jon B put Preacher in a serene mood but not this time. Stupidity, whether committed by a stranger or a relative, really pissed Preacher off. It hurt even more when he was involved and he couldn't do anything about it. Or can he?

Sergeant McCullen had drank enough of the bourbon. Whether it was to drench his thirst or build up his nerves, he had plenty. McCullen placed the remainder of the spirit back in the cabinet and closed the door. After welcoming and showing guests the variety of beer and liquor in the area, McCullen decided to reenter his guest's bedroom.

As expected, another male also occupied the room. He was startled while on top of Private Muse. He looked around, "What the fuck…" Then, saw that it was McCullen. The young man slowly withdrew from inside of Muse. He repositioned himself on his side next to her still keeping McCullen in view. With the exception of a silk shirt clinging to his sweaty body, he was naked and apparently quite comfortable with his body. He didn't attempt to cover himself. "Waz up sarge?"

"I need you to vacant the premises," demanded McCullen.

"But sarge," he responded looking back at the dazed young girl, then back to him. "Ya' kidding me, right? … I haven't even gotten a 'nut' yet." While still on her back, Private Muse would moan something unrecognizable from time to time and even gracefully move her head from side to side."

Unknown to the private, some of her previous visitors literally left their marks upon her. Teeth mark impressions could easily be seen on both her breasts as well as a number of "hickies" on them and her neck. All living out their wildest fantasies on her and she was powerless to stop them. McCullen also noticed a large number of wet spots on the old navy blue sheet he had laid on the bed prior to bringing the young female private in the room. Not everyone used a condom, he thought. This as well as other things would have to be cleaned up before his wife arrived in town. McCullen only stared at the young man with glassy eyes. "PUT YOUR DRAWS ON AND GET YOUR ASS OUT ... PLEASE!" barked McCullen.

As far as the young man was concerned, the conversation was over. He not only saw this command coming from an asshole, the owner of the house, but from a non-commissioned officer as well. Unconsciously, he was still a soldier. "Fuck it," he angrily replied. He rose up from the bed and dried himself off as best he could while McCullen stared at his athletic body up and down. He also noticed McCullen's stare. The young guest 'eyed' the Sergeant who now had a sly grin on his face. The young man shook his head slightly and quickly turned around while he maneuvered his rod and pulled his Jockey underwear and pants up.

After watching his guest vacate the room, McCullen proceeded to get to business but another detail had to be taken care of. He exited the room as well and started to look for Folster who just happened to be coming his way down the hallway. Probably to get another peek at Muse, McCullen thought. "Folster, I need you to do something for me."

"Sure McCullen. You want me to start charging admission to the 'show'?" Folster glanced in the direction of Muse's room.

McCullen wasn't sure if this idiot was kidding or not. "No, stupid. I need you to keep the area outside of the room clear for a while."

"No problem."

With that said, McCullen reentered his guest's room, closed and locked the door. Folster returned back to the end of the hallway and leaned against one side of the wall. He was now into the beat of Fabolous' *Throw It in the Bag* coming from the speakers.

McCullen wasted no time and proceeded to strip himself of his clothes. First his shirt and then his loose carpenter jeans, he was now ready for Muse. Using a loose piece of the sheet dangling on the edge of the bed, he wiped what appeared to be cum spots on Muse's nude body. From head to toe, she does look fine as hell, he thought. Too bad she put her own self in this situation. Upon finishing the cleanup, he grabbed Muse's right shoulder and upper thigh and rolled her on her stomach. Now he repositioned her body to center it on the bed.

While still on the bed, McCullen reached across Muse to the handle of a drawer. With some fumbling around he was able to finally detect what he was looking for. Upon grabbing the toothpaste-type tube and a small foil package, McCullen closed the drawer. He repositioned himself where he was able to get between Muse's legs. The whole time he was positioning Muse and himself, she did little more than mumble some inaudible words before silence reentered the room.

Muse was now spread eagle on her stomach. Again, McCullen admired the view. From her pinned hair bun to her painted toenails, McCullen loved what he now saw. Her high-yellow complexion looked especially good in the dim light. Her shoulders, firm butt and calves were smooth and beautifully curved. His dick was now harder than ever. McCullen squeezed some *K-Y* jelly from the tube to the fingers of his right hand. Using two of his fingers, he inserted the jelly and greased beyond the opening of Muse's anus. The cool feeling of the jelly inside her was enough to acquire another wail from Muse's conscious state. After rubbing in the remainder of jelly from his fingers, McCullen wiped his hands on the sheets.

He then grabbed the foiled package and removed from it the yellow, ribbed condom. When the condom was properly fitted, he moved into position above Muse's hard butt. While propped up using his right hand, McCullen used his left to spread Muse's cheeks. After careful probing, McCullen was able to enter.

Despite the chilly air, Preacher was relieved to be standing outside on the steps taking in the fresh cool air. He was sure that it wasn't anything in the air inside but after the weird talk with McCullen, Preacher needed to get out for a while. He didn't know if his conscience was bothering him concerning Muse being taken advantage of or just that a soldier in his squad was being hurt no less by one of their own. Since he didn't recall meeting Private Muse, it must be the latter.

In many ways a lot of these new recruits came into the units "virgins" by their very name. They were impressionable from the start of military life. The system was design for, among other things, to allow all recruits to be patterned and nurtured by their chain of command. Not mishandled by it. Preacher knew what needed to be done so he went back inside.

Folster, being McCullen's obedient lap dog as usual, appeared to be casually manning his guard post at the hallway entrance. When he saw Preacher approaching, he rose up from against the wall and stood at the center of the hallway pretending to be into the pulse of the music. "Where's McCullen, Folster?" Preacher said.

"Ah ... I think I saw him go outside. He should be back shortly."

"I don't think so. I've been outside for the past fifteen minutes or so," Preacher retorted, "Why don't you try again?"

Having been caught in one lie and apparently unable to think of another one on the spot, Foster said, "Look, I'm not his keeper. If you…"

"No, you're not his keeper but you stick around him like you're his woman," Preacher said.

"Fuck you too, Specialist. Look for him ya' damn self. If you weren't…" At that moment, they both heard it. Both of their heads turned in the direction of that bedroom down the hall.

"I think I found him." Preacher's only concern now was getting Private Muse out of there. Preacher wasn't sure what would happen afterwards but he'd have to cross that bridge when he come to it.

Preacher started walking past Folster, who grabbed him by the arm, "McCullen asked me to keep everyone away from there." Preacher looked at his arm somewhat surprised of his actions then looked at Folster with a less than pleasant expression on his face. Folster with his femininity about him wouldn't give most females a good fight much less Preacher. Preacher had a good 60 pounds on him easy. "You can leave it there and end up in a fetal position or remove it."

Folster let go. "McCullen gonna kick your ass if you go in there," he said, having put some distance between him and Preacher.

"It won't be tonight," Preacher said. "Maybe one day, but not tonight." As he walked closer to the door, the screams increased.

The easy flowing and smooth voice of *Erykah Badu* was in the house now. A lot of things were bouncing around in Preacher's head as he stood in front of the closed door. Under normal circumstances he would feel bad about abruptly entering a host's closed door without notice but this whole situation wasn't normal. While attempting to turn the knob and pushing the door at the same time, Preacher almost broke his wrist. The door was now locked.

Not a good sign so far, he thought. He actually expected Sergeant McCullen to shout out something but that didn't occur. Maybe he thought it was Folster attempting to tell him that a certain brand of beer or bourbon was getting low or even out or something to that effect. In any case, Preacher heard nothing coming from the other side of the door. Not a good sign.

Preacher then realized that his rigid U.S. Army-issued I.D. card was in his upper-left breast pocket of his ACU top. He retrieved it and simply inserted it between the bolt and the strike plate. Fortunately, this interior door didn't have a dead bolt lock on it. The construction of the interior within this apartment was very similar to the whole subdivision. Most of the apartment complexes reminded one of those fancy dollhouses that you sometimes see in fine catalogs. Once the bolt was clear of the strike plate, Preacher was able to open the door. The stench of sex and sweat filled the room.

McCullen must have noticed the sudden rush of music enter the room because that's when he turned his head Preacher's way. McCullen was on top of Private Muse abusing her. Part of a pillow was in her mouth as she lay on her stomach apparently to dampen any screams even in her sedated state. Preacher closed the door behind him.

McCullen was not pleased with the interruption. This, Preacher could determine from his facial expression. This Preacher expected. What Preacher didn't expect was Private Muse being able to turn her head around and look in his direction. Preacher had never seen anyone with a look like the one she had on her face. It was both a look of terror and one of a battered wife or girl friend. It was like footage you would expect to see on the eleven o'clock evening news. Sex wasn't the only thing that Sergeant McCullen got off on. It was also a look of helplessness. Preacher saw her attempt to say something, now free of her pillow. She struggled to position her lips. Trying as hard as she could, she blurbed, "Hap... me." Once again after a short pause: "Help Me," she murmured as loud as she could muster.

Not only did this surprise Preacher but it surprised McCullen as well. His dose of ruffies was now losing its effect. Private Muse was still a little dazed. Without uttering a word, McCullen turned back to Private Muse and grabbed her hair from the back of her head. The tight hair bun that was a trademark of Private Muse came loose. "You chicken head bitch, turn your ass around!" commanded McCullen. He pushed her head into the pillow and proceeded to anally rape her. His biceps would tighten up as he appeared to use her head and neck as a brace for his assaults. About every other stroke of his hips, he would glance back at me with a look of determination and arrogance in his eyes. It was an "I dare you to say something. We're in this together," look. "If I go down, so do you."

To see Private Muse being brutalized like an animal was a little too much for him to handle. Seeing this young girl in such a vulnerable position made Preacher almost sick to his stomach. At that moment, the only person in the world that could help her was him. Lying there beneath that bastard was somebody's daughter, sister or possibly girl friend. If it were Preacher's sister, he would want somebody to help her if they could.

Sergeant McCullen still assaulting Private Muse, didn't see Preacher as he approached him from the side of the bed. He also didn't see Preacher's right fist approach the left side of his head. What Preacher thought was a solid blow sent the sergeant tumbling to the other side of the bed and to the floor with a thump. Almost instantaneously, Preacher grabbed what little clothes Private Muse had laying on the other side of the bed. Laying them on the bed next to her, he rolled Muse on her back.

She looked at him with a dazed look on her face. She didn't know if he was there to ravish her or help her. She quickly brought her hands and arms to her breasts and curled in a tight fetal position opposite of me. "Pleaseee! Pleaseee! No!" she cried.

"Look, you don't understand. I'm here to get you out of here," Preacher said. "Here are your clothes, get them on in a hurry." He wasn't sure if McCullen was still out of it or not.

Amazingly in her "drunken" state, she managed to put her black satin blouse and *Apple Bottom* jeans on while still on the bed. The specialist had her sit on the bottom edge while he looked for any shoes she might have. Preacher lightly but repeatedly padded both sides of her face. "Are you still with me?" He wanted to make sure she was as woke as she possibly could be in her condition.

"Yes. Yes. Stop hitting me," she managed to say drunkingly.

Preacher let her go while he looked for her shoes. McCullen was still holding his head on the floor. He was shouting his fair share of "mother fuckers" and "goddamits." Preacher saw some black, ankle-length women's boots next to the door behind Preacher. Whether they were Muse's or McCullen's wife, Muse was putting them on. Preacher grabbed them and turned around just in time to see Muse fall back on the bed. That was an image right out of a comedy or something involving a drunk. If the situation weren't so serious it would have been funny.

The specialist put each boot on and grabbed her by the hands. He pulled her forward to raise her on her feet hoping she could stand, or better yet, walk. But looking to his right Preacher knew this would have to wait. He let Muse go again and stood erect and motionless facing the direction of McCullen. To his right, he saw McCullen rise up and stand on his feet. "You mother fucker," he said. "You think you're gonna come in here and jump me?" Despite him approaching Preacher sluggishly, Preacher felt he could take him. The specialist had one thing to his advantage. He was half drunk and Preacher wasn't. Preacher had to slow him down enough to get Private Muse and himself out of this apartment. Within six feet McCullen drew back his right arm and while lunging forward, threw his right fist towards Preacher.

Using a classic basic training defense, Preacher blocked McCullen's right arm with his left one and sent his right fist into his gut. This instigated a loud, rush of air with some spit from McCullen's mouth. He staggered back, balls dangling. Preacher needed to buy himself some time. He wasn't about to fight his way out of this apartment. He took one step forward with his left foot and shot his right foot out. The hard combat boot made contact with McCullen's *privates*. He made that squealing noise right before he hit the floor in anguish. Now it was McCullen in the tight fetal position.

Preacher went back to Muse and raised her up from the bed. Surprisingly, she had laid there, head to the side watching the whole thing. She looked at him with a blank stare on her face but probing him with her normally pretty and bright eyes. Preacher was sure there was a "thank you" in there some place but she said nothing. That would have to wait for now. "Let's go."

Preacher wrapped his right arm around her back and they both proceeded to the door. He started slowly. He could imagine the pain she must be in just to walk. For someone who experienced what she went through she verbally said very little as an indication to any discomfort. But the expression on her face said it all. Preacher took it easy as best he could.

Preacher opened the door and they both exited the room. No one was in the hallway but Folster, still somewhat manning his post. The opening of the door must have caught his attention. Surprisingly, he stood there in shock as he saw both Muse and Preacher. With Preacher's assistance, the two kept walking along. As they passed Folster, he stared at Muse and she stared at him. It was a stare not of disgust for what he did but simply an unexpressive one. Almost as if she felt sorry for him. Preacher couldn't tell if Folster's look was one of sorrow to see her bruised and swollen face or one of regret.

When they reached a common area, the two were in view of all the guests in the apartment. As Muse and Preacher caught their attention, everyone stopped what he or she was doing as they saw them limp across the room. Drinks that were previously being raised stopped, people who were dancing slowed to a stop and laughter went to whispers. "*Oh fuck. What happen ta' ha'?*" "*Somebody whipped da' shit outta that sista.*" "*What happen to da' ho?*" "*I would smash windows and slice some tires if my man did* some shit like that to me." "*I hear ya' girl friend.*" The only thing that kept its pace was the music.

Preacher kept a steady step to the front door. Muse kept looking forward. She appeared to be keeping her head held high as if she had to. It was crowded in that particular area but a path was cleared as people instinctively made way for them. Almost to the point of one of them having some contagious disease or something. A young brother still in uniform like Preacher but with a "forty" in his hand opened and held the front door for them. He too had the same expression on his face as Folster. They walked past him and were soon outside. "Take care of her my man," said the young soldier. Then the door was closed behind them. At that point, Muse released a sigh as if it was finally over.

"How do you feel?" Preacher asked. It was actually a stupid question, he thought to himself. How would he feel if he'd went through what she went through? But it was the only one he could think of. "Not good," she muttered. "Soon you will start feeling better." He wasn't sure about that either but once again it sounded right.

They cautiously but steadily proceeded down the steps. Muse tried to shake off the drowsiness. Her legs were like rubber. She also began to feel sharp pains coming from her anus and vagina. Noticing something was wrong, Preacher paused so she could catch her breath. "Take it easy. I'm not going anywhere," he said as compassionate as he could. Preacher really felt remorse for her. It was there on the sidewalk that he noticed what appeared to be vaginal bleeding on her jeans. Muse noticed it as well. After looking at herself, she looked at Preacher.

Unexpectedly and in a child-like voice, she cried out, "They hurt me! They hurt me!" Then her cheeks were covered with tears.

Preacher held her in his arms. Preacher's eyes were almost watery as well in the cool air. He tried his best to prevent it from going any further. He wasn't about to let Muse see him go into tears as well. "I'm going to get you some medical help," he promised her.

After a couple of minutes, Preacher retrieved his full composure and she recovered as best she could under the circumstances. They both turned in the direction of Preacher's car when he thought he'd heard someone call his name.

"I think someone is calling you," whispered Muse. Preacher stopped and maneuvered both Muse and himself in order to see who was calling him. A few cars down, the silhouette of a black female dressed in a black mini skirt-like outfit was getting out of a vehicle. "Preacher. Muse. Wait a minute," she said again.

"Yeah. Who is it?" Preacher replied, annoyed.

"It's me, Petersen." Specialist Petersen approached them at a fast pace. Despite now having a thin sweater over her shoulders she was still a little underdressed on this chilly night. "How is she?" she stated rather worriedly.

Muse and Petersen actually arrived together for Johnson's party but for whatever reason Petersen was able to escape the madness. Petersen felt some regret and a little responsible for the young girl despite being told to "chill out" when she tried to intervene on Muse's behalf in earlier encounters with McCullen and his boyz. "Petersen, I'm not dead or anything. I'll be OK," responded Muse. The optimism on Petersen's face when she approached was replaced with worry when she too saw the blood on Muse. It confirmed what she already knew at that point, what had happened.

"What can I do to help?"

Muse and Preacher turned around and proceeded to walk towards his Cavalier. Petersen walked along side them. "For starters, Petersen you can get my keys and open the door for us," Preacher said. He fished in his left pants pocket and retrieved his keys. Slowly but surely the trio arrived at Preacher's car. Preacher gave Petersen his keys and she opened the front passenger door. Afterwards, he got Muse closer to the front seat and positioned her so she could settle in smoothly. After getting her comfortable and inclining her seat, he looked at Petersen. "I got to get her to a hospital."

"Civilian or on post?" asked Petersen.

"Penrose is closer. I would appreciate it if you would come with me," he told her. "Muse may need some emotional support and all. It may be a little easier for her if it comes from another female. Besides she doesn't really know me too well."

"OK, of course."

"Thanks," he replied.

They got in the car and he proceeded to Penrose Community hospital as fast as he could without getting all of them killed. This night was bad enough as it was. Muse seemed to be dozing off. Preacher looked in the rearview mirror, Petersen had a "worried sister" appearance on her face. She wasn't looking hysterical or anything but just worried about her young friend. She wondered if there was anything she could have done. Maybe, maybe not.

As Preacher drove down Academy Boulevard they were all thinking what each of them could have done different. Petersen felt she should have been more persistent with Muse, Muse thought she should have listen to Petersen since she was the new kid on the block and all and Preacher should have went home. Period. What happen to Muse tonight would eventually affect a lot of people in ways none of them thought. The response from the military establishment would be direct and firm.

CHAPTER ONE

Three months later...

Despite having very little use for an alarm clock, Malcolm would set it to go off religiously at 0400 hours. Malcolm's biological clock would always wake him somewhere between 0315 and 0345 hours every morning during the workweek. In the military the workweek is technically Sunday through Saturday, 24/7. But unless he had duty of some sort, Malcolm usually worked Monday through Friday like most of the military personnel.

Malcolm was already in the bathroom wearing only his black sweatpants with U.S. Army stamped on them and socks on when he heard the alarm go off on top of his bed's headboard. After three more strokes of his toothbrush, Malcolm leaned over and spit into the sink. With the toothbrush still angled in his mouth, he then walked into his bedroom and turned off the alarm. He continued his brushing as he reentered his bathroom. Standing in front of the mirror, Malcolm checked his hair to determine if a cut was in order this week. He could handle trimming his own mustache and sideburns but the rest he left to the professionals. Malcolm knew a lot of his unit buddies who were coordinated enough to cut their own hair with strategically placed mirrors, Malcolm knew he wasn't one of them.

He also checked out his upper body. He turned around using several poses to see himself at different angles in the mirror facing him. Malcolm appeared to have a build that was a cross between a runner and a quarterback. The 22 year old had a 30 inch waist, medium height, short hair, 5'10" in height, tight abs, toned but developed legs and arms, caramel complexion and brown eyes.

Malcolm knew he wasn't always this fit. The Arkansas native and graduate of Hamburg High wasn't exactly the star athlete growing up. In fact, high school gym class was as close as he got to participating in high school organized sports. Malcolm's keen interests were in organizations such as the school's Future Business Leaders of America (FBLA) and the Coin & Stamp club. Outside of school, sports consisted of small game and deer hunting. Small game involved mostly cottontail rabbits and squirrels. Whitetail deer hunting in his small town was like a major holiday. The first day of the hunt, usually in November, was a school holiday. His northern cousins would find this whether funny and odd. He would often hunt with his uncle and other relatives. Occasionally after school he would go by himself.

Malcolm started to gain weight and toned up during the first few weeks of basic training. Initially because of the shouting from the drill instructors, the running and weird wake up times; Malcolm wasn't sure if he would survive it at all and had eventually realize that this may not be for him. But one day after not exactly completing a 4 mile run with the rest of his unit, something occurred. A black drill sergeant pulled him aside from the rest of his unit and told him in the most adamant tone, "under no uncertain terms will you drop out and quit this man's army. All of this is just a 'big' head game. Once you get through this phase the rest is a piece of cake. Now get back in formation and start producing like I know you can, Private."

Malcolm wasn't sure if it was just the way it was said, who was saying it or a little of both. But it worked. After that day, Malcolm performed his duties just as good or better than most of the recruits he was with.

Malcolm finished brushing his teeth and started to brush his hair while he mentally reviewed his check list of gear that he would be taking with him this morning. He would typically shower, dress, and eat breakfast on post after physical training, or PT. He would avoid making an extra trip back to his apartment just for that. It just wasn't time efficient to do so. The trip from the base back to his apartment was not long but one which could easily be avoided with the proper planning. Besides, it'd been a long time since he forgotten something and had to make another trip from post back to his apartment.

He didn't think it would be a big problem for him if he had to come back but he also didn't want to push his luck. Specialists with his time in rank and service was given a little more slack than personnel of lesser rank. Besides both the officers and non-commissioned officers, well, most of them anyway, within his chain of command respected Malcolm as well as his peers especially those of lesser rank. Partly due to his skills as a 25 Bravo. That is the army's official designator for Malcolm's Military Occupational Specialty: Information Technology Specialist.

After double checking his face for any remnant of *sleep* in his eyes, Malcolm went back to his bedroom to put his army-issue gray sweatshirt and his Nike shoes on. Sitting on the foot of his bed, he tried to concentrate on a local morning news show to get any traffic updates prior to hitting the door.

NBC-TV 5 showed a clip interviewing some soccer mom who somehow found the time to bake between her kid's workouts and games and won some baking contest in Denver. The camera person was so close during the "close up" Malcolm could almost taste the icing on those gourmet cinnamon rolls they were showcasing.

I hate it when Ken and Barbie have a segment like this knowing a lot of people have to get to work in a hurry and they see something like gooey pastries on TV as they head out the door. That just makes you start the morning all wrong, Malcolm thought, with a chuckle. Malcolm would often think of the Ken and Barbie dolls whenever he see these stereotypical scenes of a blonde, white male and female duo in the anchor seats of some of these shows.

When he was finished, he grabbed the remote and powered down the TV. He glanced at the bathroom to make sure that all lights were off and headed to the door. Next to his front door was a coat tree. In addition to his field jacket hanging on it, was his freshly iron and starched army combat uniform (ACU) on a hanger. He had prepared his uniform last night. With the exception of special military ceremonies, Malcolm insisted on ironing and starching his own clothes.

His black gym bag sat on the floor beneath his hanging ACUs. It consisted of his toiletries, combat boots and wash clothes. This too, he would get ready the night before a PT day. Malcolm unlocked his front door and cracked it. He reached over to grab his gym bag and pressed camouflage uniform. After making one more glance behind him, he closed the door.

At 0430 hours, Malcolm soon found himself merging into the Academy Boulevard's military rush hour on a fine Wednesday morning. Traffic at this time on this main, long stretch of highway running parallel to

Interstate 25 outside of the heart of Colorado Springs was at its peak. The traffic was primarily due to large numbers of military personnel headed to their various and respective posts, installations and bases around Colorado Springs.

To the north of Colorado Springs just off Interstate 25 was the United States Air Force Academy, south was both North American Aerospace Defense Command or NORAD and Fort Carson Army Post and to the west of the city was Peterson Air Force Base.

Malcolm knew this morning's PT run, probably a four miler, would be a chilly one. *All of us lined up in formation standing still for thirty minutes or more of attendance taking, inspections and other pleasantries. All of this before we do our first warm up exercise,* He thought. *Why come we just can't show up at a particular time, whoever isn't there, just discipline them later like professional adults and proceed with the PT session. No. That makes too much sense. The military wouldn't be the military if they couldn't mess with one's day.*

The traffic, though steady but still congested, snaked its way around past Pikes Peak Community College. A few miles past it, the traffic lightened up as the Fort Carson-North Gate exit appeared. Some of the other Fort Carson traffic continued on to enter the Main Gate but that was no concern to Malcolm.

Fort Carson, the "Mountain Post," was located just south of Colorado Springs at the base of the Rocky Mountain and about an hour's drive south of Denver.

Fort Carson was bounded on the east by I-25 and on the west by Colorado Highway 115. The fort extended from the main post, which was just south of Academy Boulevard, to its southern perimeter, which was just north of the communities of Pueblo West and Penrose.

All told, Fort Carson consisted of 138,523 acres including the cantonment area or the main post, and training areas down range. The areas included a wide variety of different vegetation types. There were open prairies and heavily forested areas. There were lowlands, wetlands, and creek drainages as well as mountainous and hilly areas.

The weather in the region was not as harsh as people often believe. The Colorado Springs area had a mild year-round climate. In January, the coldest month, temperatures averaged a high of 43 degrees and a low of 23 degrees.

But believe it or not, August was the warmest month coming in at an average high of 84 degrees and a low of 61 degrees. The area has about

42.4 inches of snow annually. Up until around June, Pikes Peak was very likely to have snow on its cap.

The Colorado weather could also be erratic. Mountain passes were frequently closed due to snow and ice or mudslides--even in the summer. During winter months, storms could suddenly occur trapping unprepared travelers. Those who frequented to and from Denver were usually prepared to spend a night in the host city--whereever that was--due to bad weather.

But for all new arrivals to the area, specifically to the Mountain Post, there was another concern: the elevation. Fort Carson's elevation is above 6,000 feet and some newcomers experience slight fatigue at first. Because of the high elevation, all new personnel are allowed 30 days to get acclimated and to reach the Fort Carson fitness standards.

Some have seen the elevation as an advantage. Located in Colorado Springs was the home of some of the best amateur athletes in the country: the Olympic Training Center. The elevation gave them the additional cardiac resistance they often strode for.

The post had a very diverse military and civilian population. Over fifteen thousand soldiers and thirty one hundred civilians have been assigned to the post. The military units assigned to the post included a mechanized infantry brigade, a Special Forces group, an armored cavalry regiment, and an area support group. Many other smaller units also called Fort Carson home.

Malcolm exited off to enter Fort Carson's North Gate as always. Patiently waiting his turn, he slowly approached the military police or MP checkpoint. *FORT CARSON MILITARY BASE. RESTRICTED AREA -- NO TRESPASSING BEYOND THIS POINT. PHOTOGRAPHY IS PROHIBITED.* This sign was posted prominently at this checkpoint and could be seen by all who past through this and most military checkpoints. Its purpose was primarily to deter anyone from following his or her plans of spying, theft, or just having no official business on the post. The military establishment passes through these gates every day and probably couldn't remember seeing the sign or couldn't tell you even part of what's on it. They saw notices like these each and every day in their structured and disciplined lives.

A paved area to the right of the checkpoint traffic in both lanes was reserved by the MPs to pull over suspicious vehicles. This morning, like most times, there were none. Then even if you did see some vehicles pulled over it was usually a tourist requesting permission to drive onto the post or some other civilian type needing some other help.

Malcolm almost forgot another important task as he approached the checkpoint and its lone MP this early in the morning. He reached for his switch and killed the headlights. After waiting for the car ahead of him to clear, Malcolm's Chevrolet Cavalier approached the MP's guardhouse. A rather youthful MP who couldn't have been out of basic training a good six months stood erect in his clean, sharp ACUs. Malcolm stopped the Cavalier.

After appearing to look serious and faking a visual vehicle inspection, the young MP snapped a salute. Malcolm could now proceed onto the post. *Stop faking it recruit*, Malcolm was thinking to himself. *If there was a problem, what could you possibly do by yourself?* The guard shacks had at least one MP manning it at all time, 365 days a year, 24 hours a day. Realistically, you would need a minimum of two MPs to man checkpoints at entrance/exit gates on this post. One MP for each lane of a two-way road. Two would constantly occupy the guard shack while the others would monitor traffic for the entry and exit lanes.

But despite being alone at the moment, help was only a radio call away at the Post's Provost Marshall office. *This post couldn't have anything of great importance on it or one of its heavy traffic gates would have more than one MP posted. This post like so many government installations does more for show and than for substance*, Malcolm thought. *Sustaining normal traffic flow and the occasional surprise contraband/stolen property checks, the MPs initiate near these gates are about as busy as these guys and gals get.*

The scenery and activity on his way to his unit's PT area was usually uninteresting and uneventful. There was no greenery this time of the year since here in the Colorado Springs area like every other city in Colorado now, water didn't last long. It contained mostly a lot of dry, brittle, harsh-looking grass and the occasional tumbleweed rolling across Barkeley Avenue on the edge of garrison or the main post area.

In southeastern Arkansas this time of the year there was still green grass, bushes, and some trees. Malcolm often dreamed of the days he spent growing up in Arkansas especially this time of the year. Down there, now, the people he grew up with and his relatives would be attending to their daily business wearing mostly summer attire. Not now, of course, at this hour they would be in bed.

The post traffic, though not as heavy as in the city, was still congested this time of the day. A mix of personnel reported to their unit's regular duty shift and physical training sessions. And that's just the military personnel. Fort Carson also had a large number of Department of Defense civilians or employees who support the mission of Fort Carson. These people performed functions ranging from janitorial services at some buildings, secretaries, plumbers, counselors, and to highly classified weapons engineers.

Upon entering the main post area, the cavalier made a right on O'Connell Boulevard. At about 500 feet, Malcolm approached a rather large unit of troops running in unison on the right side of the street. The men, all dressed in black T-shirts with "U.S. Army" stamped in bright yellow letters and black ACU pants, were very distinctive looking. It wasn't just their PT uniform either. To the left of their PT formation was a lone soldier running alongside his troops matching their pace and steps. He had the job of motivating and maintaining order by singing cadence during the runs.

Two old ladies were lyin in bed.
One turned over to the other and said.
I wanna be an Airborne Ranger!
Live that life of blood and danger.
Airborne Ranger.
Blood and danger.

I wanna be a paramedic.
Pump that funky anesthetic.
Paramedic.
anesthetic.

I wanna be a mountain climber.
Climb those mountains higher and higher.
Mountain climber.
Higher and higher.

I wanna be a scuba diver.
Jump right in that muddy water.
Scuba diver.
Muddy water.

Saw an old lady walkin down the street.
She had a ruck on her back and jump boots on her feet.
I said hey old lady where you goin' to?
She said US Army Ranger school.

I said hey old lady now ain't ya been told,
Ranger school's for the brave and the bold.
She said hey young man, I'll do just fine.
I maxed my test and I'm ninety-nine!

Cadence calls, in general, truly had a purpose. How it was sung told everyone when they should be on their left foot while running. This was what kept everyone in uniform. Most civilians found little tidbits of information of this type absolutely interesting. Unless told, no one ever knows how everyone is kept in unison. These calls or songs changed over the years to be politically correct and all. Particularly, with the All-Volunteer army and a large influx of females and gay soldiers. The purpose was still the same. Until a couple of years ago, even the cadence calls with anti-gay tones were tolerated. The murder of the gay soldier at Fort Campbell changed all of that. The investigation of that case pointed out that the unit command may have contributed indirectly in a small part by allowing its non-commissioned officers to sing cadence calls that were demeaning and described harming gay soldiers.

On the head of all these soldiers sat a green beret. This alone sat them apart from any soldier in the United States military arsenal. If that wasn't enough, a soldier running twenty feet ahead of the main group was holding a unit guidon or flag. The unit emblem consisted of two crossed arrows with the words *De Oppresso Liber* on a green background. This emblem was assigned to the Green Berets of the 10th Special Forces Group who was also housed on Fort Carson.

It was unusual for them to even run within garrison. They had a reputation of not doing a lot of intermingling with the *regular* soldiers. They were after all, different or "special" and they made sure everyone knew that.

At the rear of the running formation, another lone soldier trailed it. He too was an elite soldier. He was wearing a bright orange safety vest like those similar to what highway construction crews wear. Per orders by the Commanding General of Fort Carson, all units running in a PT formation had designates wearing safety vests. Obviously, this was for the safety and well being of the troops.

The soldier wearing the safety vest saw Malcolm's car approach and he quickly motioned to Malcolm to slow down. This was only out of habit. Malcolm, used to the habits and regulations that came with being in the U.S. Army, had already slowed down. He has seen too many times where someone was reported to their command for vehicle violations. Regardless of whether they actually sped near a formation or just got too close to one, if it was reported by a high-ranking officer then it was "true"--period. It may not be fair but that's the way things was in the military. Good order had to sustained at all costs.

Malcolm knew there were vehicles approaching ahead of the running formation in the other lane. They too were given the signal to slow down. Once the vehicles passed, Malcolm was able to go around the soldiers and proceed along O'Connell Boulevard. He then made a right turn on Wetzel Avenue. Within 400 feet of Ellis Street, the vehicles as well as the soldiers walking were familiar now.

Malcolm reached the corner of Wetzel Avenue and Ellis Street. He also saw several people, officers and enlisted, whom obviously arrived early doing their various warm up routines of stretching in advance of the start of Headquarters and Headquarters Company's morning PT session. This unit's function was to operate the post's Replacement Detachment and Inprocessing Center. Like everything else on a military installation, the Inprocessing Center had a building number. It was designated: Building 1218. The Inprocessing Center, like the name implied, was the first place all incoming personnel visited when they arrived at Fort Carson. The center operates 24 hours a day. When new arrivals reported in they were given a Post Inprocessing appointment. On this date, soldiers would attend a series of meetings with soldiers responsible for the various areas that all soldiers would eventually interact. A soldier will hand over their medical, finance, dental, and personnel files to the respective departments. Issues that can't be resolved at this level will be taken care of after he or she reports to their unit.

When a soldier reported to the center, he or she was quickly evaluated to determine if housing will be at the Inprocessing Center, at temporary facilities on post or at a hotel/motel in Colorado Springs. A Staff Sergeant or below who was unaccompanied or single, received temporary housing at the Inprocessing Center. The accommodations were nowhere like a hotel, but the old-style, long hallway, bunk bed barracks did provide a free place to lay your head during the brief inprocessing period. Depending on your rank and whether your files are in order, 2 to 4 days was usually the norm for inprocessing. Most soldiers used this time to both take a breather and relax from Basic/Advanced Individual Training, if a new soldier, or from their wife and kids.

Malcolm maneuvered the Cavalier around to the back lot of the Inprocessing Center. This area consisted of a parking lot and basketball court with hoops on each end of the course. It also served as a hard surface formation area for attendance call before the start of PT sessions and during non-PT duty days. After parking his vehicle, Malcolm noticed that a group of co-workers were standing around the corner of the center. Still seated, Malcolm double-checked himself to make sure that he was in the proper PT uniform. Everyone, with the exception of the HHC commander or CO was in similar uniform. The CO was in his regular duty ACUs. He possibly may have had an appointment with the battalion commander.

Malcolm would often find himself outside of the Orderly room, the administration room of the unit, for some reason or another and overhear things. Among the items of great importance that could be heard were the CO and our First Sergeant, highest ranking enlisted person in the unit, joking about how out of shape our battalion commander really was.

It wasn't unusual for the battalion commander to hold meetings, coincidentally of course, during the early morning hours during PT. He had good reason to. The battalion commander would often find himself at the end of the PT formation at the start of a run. Then, when he ran out of breath about halfway in the run, he could just stop and turn his butt around and start walking back to his car. This was another example of the differences between the regular soldiers and the Special Forces. The latter, generally speaking, led by example.

The U.S. military, like the rest of society, had their problems with the battle of the "bulge." These officers would be allowed to take it upon themselves and at their convenience to exercise. Officers were given a lot more latitude than enlisted in this and other matters. That's how things always were and will be for a long time to come. Even though it happens, officers are rarely kicked out due to merely for a weight problem. Take the former U.S. Gulf War General H. Norman Schwarzkopf, for instance. Enlisted, well that was another story.

The pre-PT meetings or *bull shit* sessions that routinely preceded most PT meetings were about to come to an end. First Sergeant Brackett had vacated his office and had exited the center's rear door. No announcement, as usual, was made to indicate that all were ready. Just his presence told everyone that the PT sessions were seconds from starting and all smoking would cease.

Even though the CO was officially in charge of HHC, historically and even now--the First Sergeant was the man. He or she was personally responsible for the enlisted men and women under him or her. These men and women were also the backbone of any army unit. They were the ones who actually made things happen in wars. Under the guidance and orders of an officer, of course. The First Sergeant often had the most experience and time in service than any other enlisted person. In most cases, most commissioned officers as well.

It had always been the basis of respect that all First Sergeants received from enlisted as well as officers. Officers and other enlisted would rather "back slap" their wives and children before playing mind games with higher ranking enlisted personnel. They simply were in the Army too long. First Sergeants always knew what to do and when to do it.

The First Sergeant was walking down the long sidewalk to the formation area where we would all be standing. For an old redneck of fifty, he was in great shape. He didn't have a body builder's physique but he had little or no body fat on his five, eleven frame. He had a solid chest and developed legs.

It suited Malcolm just fine. Normally he wouldn't mind hearing some of Private Folster's wild tales to the other Privates and Specialists of what he planned to do when he was discharged in a couple of months but this morning it would just be irritating. He had been "passed over" for promotion to Specialist Four or Spec Four so many times that the Army is not allowing him to reenlist.

Malcolm knew this as well as most of the people in HHC. To keep from hurting his feelings, most didn't mention to him his shortcoming. Not to mention a widely known legal matter that he was involved in. He would be allowed to be discharged or ETS upon being cleared by the Judge Advocate General or JAG. If this was not done prior to his ETS date, he simply would not be let go. Period. Somewhere in all that fine print of that very long contract that all soldiers must sign, it states that. It may not be in plain English but its there. Malcolm was certain that the JAG lawyers have explained that to him or at least tried to to his dumb ass.

Malcolm normally would be with some of the specialists and sergeants in the morning but got maneuvered to the present group with a series of work-related questions by some other specialists who worked in his section. Malcolm always tried to learn something new and beneficial everyday whether in his work environment or in conversations. And Private Folster and his crew certainly didn't provide an environment for this.

Like the hens and roosters that Malcolm observed as they reacted to their masters, my grandparents, when they approached the enclosure growing up back home. They too would stop their chatter, stump out the cigarettes, for those of them who had them, and proceed to the formation area as if a bell that only they could hear had reverberated.

To the outside, non-military observer, HHC company personnel would appear to be a bunch of people trying to find their rightful place within the unit's large formation. Soldiers would strategically go from left to right of a person as though not sure where to fit in, eventually finding his or her place in the arrangement of personnel. To the contrary. Prior to the anticipated command, soldiers found their rightful place within formation by platoon, squad and rank. Within his or her own platoon and squad, a soldier determined his or her own place in this small segment of society. Rank.

Standing alone approximately five steps in front of each platoon and centered is the platoon sergeant. He or she is responsible for making sure that the platoon has a 100 percent accountability of its personnel prior to the company's physical training. Sergeant First Class McCready, like most platoon sergeants merely glance at his squad leaders and each of them would nod to assure him that they have fulfilled their duties. The platoon was ready.

The other platoon sergeants and their soldiers looking ahead stood in formation at parade rest. The first sergeant gracefully proceeded to the front of his formation and stopped approximately five steps but centered. He looked staunchly to the left as if to give a quick inspection of his troops and then to the right. After breathing in a quick gulp of air, the old man gave the command that would officially put us at attention and officially start our day. *"FALL IN."*

CHAPTER TWO

The cool morning air that was no doubt sent by Pikes Peak reminded them all that we are in mountain country. It was now being felt through his PT uniform. Despite having ran 5 miles and topping it off with a series of cool down exercises, his body was quickly returning to its old self. It usually doesn't take long for Malcolm to cool down. Not sure if that's bad or good, he thought. In any case, Malcolm was ready for the shower.

It would be nice to just take a nice long quiet shower by himself. But that was not an option at the moment. After a long hot run like they had this morning a lot of sweaty and funky guys and gals had one thing on their mind: shower. Unfortunately, the soldiers of today and tomorrow had to do what soldiers of the past had to do: share a shower by utilizing the company's shower stalls. HHC had two shower stalls. One for the females and one for the "hard heads." Each stall had five shower heads.

Because of the number of soldiers within the company, one could rarely just walk in and proceed to take a shower. A line was always formed outside the latrine leading to the shower stall. It wouldn't be too many guys. Anywhere from two to five just waiting to get in the stall. This would no doubt leave Malcolm and others just like always with no hot water by the time they finally got to the stall.

Due to the substantial number of soldiers who lived in base housing whether alone, mostly the sergeants, or with their families, the line wasn't really that bad. Those soldiers who did live on the post went home as quickly as possible to perform the 3 Ss: *Shit, shower* and *shave.*

Malcolm retrieved his ACU and other gear from the car and proceeded to the Inprocessing Center's barracks area. Immediately after walking through the rear door, he passed by the NBC or Nuclear, Biological and Chemical room. The sergeant sat at his desk.

As to whether or not all that gear including the gas mask with filters actually work, well, no one really knew. To Malcolm's knowledge, none of that stuff was ever actually field tested with the real thing. Not even during Desert Shield, Desert Storm or the Iraq war. Yes, the troops routinely wore the gear over in Saudi Arabia and Iraq, but never in an NBC-contaminated area. Well, at least it wasn't reported. This was the same gear that CBS's *60 minutes* did a piece on and determine that the whole NBC suit with mask may be inadequate for what confronts soldiers today. Israel even decided not to use the type of NBC mask we currently use.

Based on his uniform and the Puerto Rican sergeant's settled appearance, he had been in his office for a while. He, for whatever reason, did not attend the company's PT session either. Still walking without changing his pace, Malcolm said, "What's up sarge?"

"From what I hear, Preacher, you're the man. I'm a sergeant and I don't have nowhere near the clout you pull around here. Shit, the first sergeant treats me like one of his kids," he responded with his Brooklyn twang. "I'm just a very, very small squirrel just trying to get a nut around here."

"Yeah right," Malcolm said, still walking.

"Stop by sometime this week. I need to run something by you."

"No problem, sarge." By now Malcolm was several feet down the long hallway. Now to the left of me was the Retention or Reenlistment office. At this time of the morning that office was closed. But it wasn't like that office was getting a lot of traffic in and out anyway.

Every Reenlistment office within the typical army unit would be run by both a Reenlistment NCO and a commissioned officer. In most cases, the officer would be a low-level one such as a second or first lieutenant. Lately, it had been tough for Reenlistment personnel to meet their quotas in most units.

The Inprocessing Center's interior was not unlike most buildings on the post built during the post-World War II/pre-Vietnam era. They all had long hallways and plenty of room space and one large latrine. One on each floor if it's a two-story. Buildings of this type were most likely used as office space for some function. Since then some of the buildings on post like this one were converted to unit space equipped with barracks for the troops. There must be regulation on what color the walls and tile floor must be because someone or some agency was definitely in keeping with the color scheme. Most, not all building of similar type and use are painted a pale eggshell with a light or dark gray floor tile. The colors couldn't have been selected better than if an insane asylum director had picked them his or herself. Obviously no one in the Department of the Army had read any of the studies that concluded bright colors contributed to one's mental attitude.

Malcolm proceeded down the hallway. He could hear the floor buffer running. No unit would be without one and one was required in order to maintain the shiny tile floor. From the time one enters the army as a fresh recruit to just before you got your sergeant's stripes, one get to know the floor buffer really, really well.

Malcolm remembered when he first arrived in boot camp a few years ago. Among many unforgettable memories there, he remembered his first introduction to using the buffer. It was about his second or third night there in the barracks at Fort Jackson, South Carolina. They had just wrapped up a full day. It was now 1900 hours or 7 PM. Keep in mind a full day in the army during boot camp meant from 4 AM or 0400 hours to about 6 PM or 1800 hours. Malcolm's drill sergeant / platoon sergeant decided they needed what he called a "bull shit" session in order for everyone to get to know each other a little better. A few of them had already proceeded down that path and gotten to know each other a little more.

That evening they all got in a circle on the pale but somewhat clean floor around their drill sergeant who stood. Like most supervisors and new employees, they got to the moment where they went around and stated their name and, in their cases, their hometowns. There was no need to indicate rank at this point since with a few exceptions, they were all E-1s or simply privates.

The exceptions were those 2 or 3 individuals who were either "prior service" or "reprocessed." Prior Service personnel were those individuals who were previously in the army or another branch of the armed services and decided to reenlist or enlist if they were from another branch. Reprocessed personnel were just another term given to those who, for whatever reason, did not initially fulfill his or her obligations during the nine week boot camp period. An injury during one of the long hikes like a sprained ankle or death in the family while in boot camp could get you excused and once your injury or family affairs were in order, you could return. As to what point you start back up at in the nine weeks was determined on a case-by-case basis.

When the drill sergeant was ready to talk about himself he gave them the spill about how long he has been in the army and how much he enjoyed it. He even broke the ice with a comment about he's so devoted to the army that he didn't even talk to his mother because she's a civilian. That got a chuckle from everyone. From the time they got off the green school buses from the airport to the training center, they had been bombarded with tasks and interacted with either their drill sergeant or one of his co-workers in a less than genial manner. An outsider would consider most of the interaction between a recruit and the drill sergeant as hostile. In fact, if some mothers saw how the drill sergeants were talking to their sons and daughters and practically bringing tears to their eyes, one or more drill sergeants would surely get his or her ass whipped. The drill sergeant reminded Malcolm of the legendary World War II General, George S. Patton. He certainly had the features. Malcolm was not talking about just attitude, but he could pass for a brother if not a close cousin. Sometimes Malcolm wondered if he knew this.

After the drill sergeant had finished talking about himself he asked if they had anything else to add before he dismissed the meeting. All of the class quickly glanced at each other then responded with vigor like they had been drilled to in the last day or so:

"NO DRILL SERGEANT!"

Then as quickly as he had changed his stripes for the meeting, he changed again. The drill sergeant got to the position of attention and shouted, "ON YOUR FEET!" Temporarily startled, the group had regained their senses and did as they were instructed. In a split second, not only did he physically change but he did a mental switch as well. As they stood there apparently frozen in time the drill sergeant barked some orders to them about cleaning up "his" house. He wanted it "white glove" clean from top to bottom. When he said top to bottom he meant it. He went rambling on about getting rid of all dust and dirt from the light fixtures on the ceiling to being able to see his face somewhat clearly on the tile floor.

Among the many things that ran astray through their minds was how they were gonna get that dull floor to shine. Clean was one thing, but to produce a shine was another. Apparently the drill sergeant picked up on this as well and offered to demonstrate one of the ways in which to polish and buff a floor without burning the barracks down.

He pointed out that you should make sure that the floor is properly clean first. Then he told them how to prepare the wax. He had instructed a white guy that was standing near the front to go retrieve a wire coat hanger, one small can of floor wax, and the floor buffer from the utility room. He even described the floor buffer just in case the guy was confused once he got there. Upon retrieving, the drill sergeant got the wax and the hanger first from the private. They watched him remove the lid from the can and wrapped the coat hanger around the can but snug under the top lip.

After making sure the makeshift coat hanger handle was secure around the can, he retrieved his Bic lighter from his right breast ACU pocket. For a second they could see the top of what apparently was a cigarette pack. He, like 50 percent of all military personnel, was a smoker. He lit his lighter, tilted the wax can slightly, and slowly brought the flame to the brown wax. Like all flammable material of this type, it created a slow but steadily larger flame. Instinctively, we all took a step back. The drill sergeant saw this and with a sharp grin on his face he said, "Relax ladies, this is not going to hurt you." After about a one-minute burn, he took the lid again and slowly slid it horizontally over the can and you could see the flame slowly extinguish. Once the lid was completely over the can and the flame was out, a small tail of smoke was produced.

The drill sergeant removed the lid that was only resting on top of the can to show that the flame was really out. What was left of the flame was a layer of hot, liquid wax. He tilted the can from side to side a little and lowered the can to the floor. Being careful not to put a drop on his spit shine jump boots, the drill sergeant tilted the can slightly and poured a moderate stream of wax between him and them. Afterwards, he returned the open can of wax with the lid to the private and instructed him to secure the lid on it.

He retrieved the buffer and made sure that the round brush underneath was firmly attached. Slowly our drill sergeant put the buffer along top of the stream of wax and in about 5 minutes that area of the tile was as close to a mirror shine as you could possibly get considering it was old tile.

Momentarily, he stopped the buffer and the humming noise was replaced with one of a much higher pitch. He stood there and barked out at them on how clean his house better be when they were. Upon successful passing of his inspection and only at that time, they would be released for the evening in order to get to bed. It was now 2000 hours or 8 PM.

He also pointed out that the U.S. Army in which we all volunteered for is only obligated to give you 4 hours of sleep. Not the *New England Journal of Medicine* recommendation of twelve, not six but 4 measly hours. "And ladies, those four hours go by really, really fast. So it's to your advantage that when you start this thing. Commonly referred to in this man's army as a 'G.I. party.' Yes, a party. Get used to it because there will be many of them for a lot of you. You do so quickly but effectively and the one way of assuring this is done right is working as a team," he shouted, with a cynical smile on his face. "Squad leaders, take charge!" With that inspiring speech, Malcolm attended his first "G.I. party."

A few more paces down the hallway, Malcolm took a right turn and immediately saw the buffer and its handler going along the recently mopped floor. By the smell of the hallway, one would guess that someone reused some water from some place. The floor had a faint musky smell to it. Either the mop itself needed replacing or someone should have used more cleaner in the water.

The buffer's handler and the one responsible for the musky smell was a private first class Malcolm knew in the Inprocessing Center. His name was Grissom. Matthew Grissom. He too was a man of the south. Alabama to be exact. They worked in different sections though. Despite being real close to Sergeant First Class McCullen for whatever reason, Grissom and Malcolm got along pretty good. Mostly on a professional level.

Malcolm could tell by the expression on his face and his red eyes that he had a long night. Not a party or anything but he was wrapping up a Charge of Quarters shift, CQ duty for short. Basically, it was an after hours shift that started when the company commander and the first sergeant have left for the day. Because someone must be in charge of the unit during the evenings, the CQ took over.

"Man, you look like you had a rough night," Malcolm greeted him.

"Shit, you got that right. Sarge kept me awake most of the night talking and shit. I don't know, he must have something against getting some shut eye. If he wasn't an E-7 I would have just told him to shut the fuck up," Grissom responded. He did so in a low tone. Malcolm gave him his props.

There were times when Grissom would have told sergeants, regardless of rank just that. Coming out of boot camp, Grissom had a serious attitude problem. He was cussing people left and right when they told him to do something, then wouldn't do it. But he eventually came around shortly after disrespecting the wrong people. The stockade could do that to a person. It was after 1700 hours. Grissom, not knowing that the first sergeant was around the corner from his barracks room one day was overheard making some not so nice comments to his supervisor.

Immediately afterwards, the first sergeant politely put PFC Grissom, later Private Two (PV2) Grissom, in check as how to respond and how not to respond to an NCO. That and the stockade time instituted a good attitude adjustment. He had changed a lot. But a lot of people including himself also wondered how did someone like Grissom even get through boot camp. Since that is the place to assist those with bad habits, he should have been weeded out. Perhaps the military now was really desperate for personnel right now, Malcolm thought.

Ready and willing to take just about anybody. Malcolm remembered when the army would not accept you among their ranks unless one had a high school diploma. Now if you got a GED or not, you're in. Then again like the rest of them, maybe those drill sergeants with Grissom saw what we saw as well but for whatever reason decided that Grissom like the rest of them deserved a second chance in life. Who knows, maybe the military was his last resort as far as trying to make something out of himself.

Perhaps his supervisor thought the same thing as well. Malcolm knew their unit is not exactly viewed as the first to go in a war or even a conflict. But the personnel within it, particularly the senior NCOs, come there mostly from combat arms units. A more relax life may have prompted the career change to a job with HHC. Despite any of the good that Grissom's supervisor, another SFC, may have saw in him. He too got the wrath of the first sergeant in that hallway as well and later in his office. You might even say that the first sergeant bit out a little of his ass.

But that was it for him. The first sergeant wanted to make sure that he made his point to the enlisted ranks that his senior staff would be respected and everyone conduct themselves in a professional manner. In the end, neither Grissom nor his supervisor saw the first sergeant again on that matter.

After hearing Grissom's last remarks, Malcolm couldn't help but laugh. But he also realized that as one of the senior specialists here in the unit, some of the privates and even other specialists looked up to Malcolm. He had a responsibility to try to keep those personnel who were responsive to his assistance "in check."

"Now OK Grissom, soon you will have your spec 4 or specialist four rank. Everyone is behind you, including the first sergeant." Malcolm removed the grin that was on his face and replaced it with one of a serious expression. Just to make his point. In a "in your face" kind of way, but tactful. Malcolm told him, "Don't mess it up! OK!" After making sure they had eye contact, Malcolm gave him a pat on the back and proceeded past him.

Grissom was actually cleaning near the main entrance way to area-2, the second half of the Inprocessing Center. The center was basically one long building with various blocks of rooms branching out along the way like the re-enlistment and NBC offices. Area-2 was designated for the staff personnel's barracks areas, administration including the offices of the company commander and the first sergeant. Area-1 on the other side was designated as a barracks area for those individuals not requiring other residential accommodations such as a motel for the family while inprocessing takes place.

There was a red line about a ½ inch in diameter that goes across the hallway separating the two sides. It's there primarily to make sure that those personnel that was inprocessing do not enter the residential areas of the HHC staff. They simply had no reason to. Their barracks, all preliminary meetings, and their assigned coordinator, one who make sure that everyone gets to their assigned appointments on post, are all on Area-1.

Some of the administrative staff was going in and out of the main doorway this morning. Standing next to but barely out of the way was the CQ. Though tired from the night before, he greeted all who passed him. Malcolm knew CQ duty could be rough but most people's uniform is not as wrinkled as this one. He looked like he used his whole uniform as a pillow.

With the shower stall still calling his name, Malcolm shook his head and entered the latrine, thinking he may be the first to arrive before the stampede appearing. Malcolm was disappointed to see two guys, one Malcolm knew, already waiting on the wooden bench with a towel wrapped around their waist and soap in hand or in a waterproof toiletry bag. "Good morning gentlemen," Malcolm stated, while proceeding to the other end of the bench to lay his gear and hang up his uniform. Despite the humidity and the obvious fogging of the windows and mirrors above the row of sinks, Malcolm was confident that the starching he gave his ACU would hold. Malcolm didn't get a response to his earlier greeting. Then again he could imagine why. By the look of their faces, both had a good weekend. Both appeared either extremely tired or drunk. Malcolm couldn't tell which one, but he would probably guess the former. After that run, any alcohol would surely be pumping out of those pores by now.

By the time Malcolm was settled on the bench and waiting for his turn, the two guys before him were now heading for the two available stalls after the previous occupants vacated them. They briefly visited the sinks to tidy up a bit and left the latrine upon getting into their uniform. Now, still somewhat unusual, Malcolm was alone in the open area of the latrine. It was so unusual for the latrine to be nearly empty this morning

Malcolm was thinking whether or not he had missed another formation upon getting released from the PT session.

Two minutes would passed before there was any activity to or from the shower stall. A white guy, who Malcolm had not seen before in the unit, probably new, had exited the shower only after being there for a couple of minutes. He, like the two guys before him, proceeded to the sink, then got dressed and soon left the latrine area. Malcolm quickly noticed that steam was still coming out of the shower area.

Now ready for his hot shower, Malcolm got up with his nice thick, cotton towel wrapped around him, shower shoes on, and toiletry bag in toe. Malcolm approached the main entrance to the shower stall and stepped through the shower curtain. After assuring the gray, government-issued curtain was restored as before, he proceeded to one of three shower areas. There was only one person there already.

Specialist Four or SP4 Clarence Hodkins, one of the two guys waiting, was just leaning forward towards the wall with his back to the front when Malcolm arrived. The brotha from Louisiana had his legs spread apart and the palm of his hands on the wall while the hot water stroked his back. He stood there with his eyes, apparently closed as if in a state of thought.

SP4 Clarence Hodkins was Preacher's best friend, confidant partner in crime and occasional *fooling around partner*. These two had towed the long road for the past four years while in HHC, and it had indeed been rocky. At first they hadn't really gotten along. Preacher was quiet and somewhat standoffish, while Hodkins was popular and always the center of attention. Sometimes, Hodkins truly believed he loved Preacher, but Hodkins believed Preacher was confused with his sexuality, and often times would clam up or completely shut off when the two were alone. But, when it came to being a friend, a shoulder to lean on and a confidant in which to confide, Hodkins knew he couldn't find anyone better than his "Preach." Preacher was an inch shorter than Hodkins, and about the same complexion. Hodkins had bright, brown eyes, which were sometimes hidden behind stylish, silver-rimmed spectacles. These were only for cosmetic appearances since he didn't need to wear glasses or contacts to see. He dressed rather conservatively; one should think "Gap" when thinking of Hodkins. This, Preacher liked. He had a short fade, and a thin moustache.

"Man, you must have had a great weekend. You got to stop trying to juggle three women at once," Malcolm told him.

Seconds went by, and then the dead spoke: "You got that shit right. I'm not as young as I use to be."

"Nigga, please. You're only 20 years old. Face it. You just can't hang like the grown ups." They both laughed. Malcolm was very conscious of what he said to other brothas around people of other ethnic groups, when it came to using words such as nigger or nigga. Malcolm knew he shouldn't use it at all but like the word "ain't" it might as well be part of the Merriam-Webster dictionary. And he believed it was. But he didn't want the white guys to think that it's ok for them to say it.

"You know Malcolm, that white boy got in here and he might have stayed a good 3 minutes. That's barely enough time for the water to roll off your ass."

"Yeah, I noticed that too."

"Some of these motha fuckas, mostly white I might add, just don't like to be in water," Hodkins murmured, while still leaning against the wall. "You know Preacher, white people can say what they want about how bad some of us may live but when it comes to cleaning our asses we don't mind the water. That's why when some of us go get an apartment, one of the first things that are asked is whether the heat and water is included." They both laughed again but in Malcolm's opinion Hodkins was right on the money.

Malcolm Preacher and Clarence Hodkins, both single, were of the same age. Specialist Hodkins stood 5 feet, 11 inches and weighed 185 pounds with a washboard stomach above his 31 inch waist. The water appeared to bead down his medium built, caramel body as it flowed from his short, wavy hair to his developed calves. This did not go unnoticed by Preacher.

Preacher intermittently stared at his buddy next to him as though in a stupor then shook his head and continue to lather down. Hodkins would notice the next time. With his eyes still closed, Hodkins stood upright and slowly turned around to allow the hot water to directly pulsate on his back. He leaned his head back slightly to wash his hair and brought it back forward. Then Hodkins opened his eyes and saw Preacher gazing at him.

Preacher quickly turned his head back to the shower head. He could have literally kicked himself in the ass for letting himself get caught. He knew better and still, it happened. He hoped that Hodkins would not react to the stare and go on with his shower. Preacher turned around back to Hodkins while he made sure the suds covered his body. Trying to be as casual as he could, he glanced at Hodkins when their eyes met. "It's ok Preacher. You wouldn't be the first to want to catch a glimpse at this. You're not the first or the last." Hodkins was now standing there under the shower slowly stroking his dick, which was now almost covered with lather of its own. Preacher appeared to be surprised of the action but certainly not startled. He looked back up at Hodkins as if to say something but didn't. Instead, he slowly moistened his lips as if in slow motion and slid the tip of his tongue along the bottom of his lip. *Well I be damn. The guard comes down after all*, Hodkins thought.

It was at that instant the door to the latrine opened and the voices of HHC personnel penetrated the unusual silence of the moment. Hodkins responded by slowly nodding his head and whispering, "Bet that..." The two men retreated from their moment and allowed the water which was now turning cool to wash the suds away. They exited the shower stalls one at a time about 1 minute apart, greeted their fellow soldiers, made sure they were properly dressed in uniform and vacated the latrine without saying another word to each other. It wasn't necessary. Each man knew just what took place a few moments ago.

Unlike Hodkins, this was the first time Preacher let his guard down among his co-workers and left thinking. *Did I make a mistake in doing so? How will I react around Hodkins again? How will Hodkins react around him now?* Preacher had always suspected Hodkins of being bisexual but never asked him. He wasn't sure why. Perhaps he didn't want to hear the answer. He wasn't concerned about Hodkins telling anyone about the intense look because they were close enough to trust one another with almost any secret. They were almost as close as brothers but this was one matter Preacher really wished he kept contained.

CHAPTER THREE

Malcolm couldn't wait till 1700 rolled around. The day seemed to drag by. He had guessed that he didn't do a whole lot today. Because usually the time would seem to fly by. But, in his case, he was headed out the door. Malcolm poked his head into some offices to wish a few folks mostly NCOs and warrant officers a good evening and off he went.

He opened the two gray government-issued main doors that kept the worker bees housed in the 13th Finance Group building. It felt great! Even though he went out for lunch earlier, the sun's rays felt like it had been two days since he had been outside. Nevermind really do need to start taking my breaks outside more, Malcolm thought.

He made sure his black beret with unit insignia, was mounted on his head as he proceeded down the front concrete steps. Malcolm was in such a good mood, I even snapped a regulation salute to a captain that was visiting the 13th Finance Group. It was done so fast and steady that he apparently caught the officer in some sort of a daze and startled him into quickly returning back his own brand of salute. It was terribly executed for an officer, funny to see. He evidently was a product of Army ROTC and not of the United States Military Academy at West Point, New York.

As Malcolm was headed towards his car, getting himself ready mentally to go into the afternoon rush hour traffic along with everyone else, he saw Specialist Petersen walking out of the side door of the building with two of her girl friends. She glanced over at him. "Preacher!" she called out. "Wait up. I need to talk to you." Hesitant, he slowed his pace as he watched her get closer and closer.

For months, he tried to avoid contact with Specialist Petersen, which also included avoiding the subject of PFC Gwendolyn Muse and what occurred to her that cool night. One could only imagine the trauma one went through after seeing something like that, much less be a victim of it. Malcolm imagined seeing one of his own close relatives through her and how an assault such as that would affect his family. Then there was the TV coverage, both local and national. You know when you are a part of something big when it makes the first fifteen minutes of CNN's *The Situation Room with Wolf Blitzer*. Probably tipped off by the civilians. Then the military investigation took place.

Since the rapes that took place at Aberdeen Proving Ground, Maryland with that drill sergeant and his female soldiers, the U.S. Army was trying to crack down on all sexual misdeeds. For the better, Malcolm thought. Malcolm knew there would be some females, both enlisted as well as officers, who would try to take advantage of the current climate and use it to their benefit, making false accusations against another male soldier because she didn't get the promotion she thought she should have. Perhaps because the male soldier turned down her advances towards him and she felt insulted or embarrassed. In a lot of these cases, they mirrored the same problems that occured in the civilian world. But by and large it was something long overdue in this man's army.

"If I didn't know any better, I would think that you were avoiding me or something," stated Specialist Petersen, while they both walked to his car.

"Of course not, why would I do that?"

"You got me. Why would you have to, Preacher?" You don't have to avoid me. You did nothing wrong unlike some of the others that were there that night. In fact, you were a hero that night. The only hero, I told the investigators. Not that many people would do what you did that night."

"Maybe, maybe not," Malcolm replied.

"Shit! Well, I know. That poor girl would have been his sex slave that whole night if it weren't for you. No telling what else would have occurred. If that wasn't bad enough for her."

"Perhaps," he muttered.

"Preacher, what the fuck is wrong with you. Did you hear what I just said?"

Preacher really didn't feel like talking about this right now. "Petersen, I really would prefer not to talk to you about this."

"Preacher, relax. The investigators told me that McCullen and some of his boys are about ready to go to trial and all appear to be an 'open and shut' case against the motha fuckas. Every last one."

"That's not it."

"What's the problem then?"

Preacher looked at Petersen for a minute. One could say he stared. Then as though out of his trance, Preacher said, "Petersen, please get in the car. I will take you to the barracks."

Specialist Petersen really didn't know how to take that statement. Neither she nor any of the other females ever saw Preacher with another female. There were even rumors circulating among the enlisted female ranks that he may be gay or bi at the very least. But whether or not he was, chances were he was safe to be with, she thought. What happened to PFC Muse shook her up as much as it did Preacher.

Specialist Petersen turned around to view her girlfriends who were immersed in conversations of their own. "Go ahead without me. I will catch up with you later," she said. The two looked at each other for a moment and responded, "Are you sure, Petersen; it is a good walk back to the barracks from here?"

"Yes, ladies, I'm sure." A smirk was planted on her face by then. The ladies caught this and thoughts immediately swamped through their dirty minds.

"OK sis I guess you are really OK now," one of them stated with a seductive tone and a wink of the eye.

Preacher was a little ticked by now. He rolled his eyes slightly. "Yes, ladies she is safe."

Preacher couldn't help but laugh as he opened the driver's side door to electronically unlock the passenger door. "Why is it so hard for some people to grasp the idea of a man and a woman being just friends?" he asked. Preacher inserted a CD in the player while he waited for Petersen to get settled in and secure her seat belt.

Petersen thought about what Preacher said about her being a friend and all. Was it his choice of words at the time or did he mean what he said about that? Petersen noticed how clean his car was when she was buckled up. It was almost clean to perfection other than what appeared to be some school books, a suspended plastic hangar above one of the rear windows, a gym bag and a yellow legal pad on the back seat. Unlike some of the cars of other guys, Preacher didn't appear to leave any trace of him lying in the car. His car interior even had a neutral smell to it. *A neat freak!* she thought.

Then there was the person. Preacher, she saw up close and personal, was very fit and kept a neat appearance. Hair was close cut and his ACU, including boots, were ironed and clean, respectively despite a day of work. But she did really notice something that only Petersen would see. Preacher's finger nails. Without staring and making it obvious, she discreetly looked at them closer. They looked bitten. She knows of relatives that do this but wasn't really sure what made people do it. She thought maybe it was a nervous condition or something. This apparently perfect person had a flaw.

Preacher noticed again how "healthy" Petersen was. There weren't too many people he thought who could *fill out* an ACU particularly the pants considering how they're made and all but she sure did. A swift of perfume was lingering from her body as well. He wasn't sure of the brand, but his nose told him that it wasn't cheap. Her uniform caught his attention as well. He wasn't sure if it was a woman thing. But in general, regardless of what the military day brought on, females would always keep a better than neat appearance regarding their uniform.

Her uniform appeared to be machine pressed or ironed. Obviously it went to the Army & Air Force Exchange Service (AAFES) cleaners on a regular basis. Going well beyond what was in *Army Regulation 670-1, Wear and Appearance of the Uniform*, her shirt and pants creases looked like if you touch it you would cut your finger. One could probably take them and stand them up based on their own starch. This observation greatly clashed against everything he had heard about her, most of it being how *sexually free* she was. Preacher also knew that the way barracks gossip was there wasn't really no way of knowing what's true and what isn't. He wasn't even sure how everyone felt about him personally. He had a good idea about things professionally, but *personally* was another thing.

Without her knowing, Preacher really did notice how fine she was. Her bronze complexion, high cheekbone and full lips were complemented by her soft, shining black hair. Though nestled under her beret, Preacher could tell her hair was lengthy. He thought it was absolutely amazing how much hair one could stuff under those black berets. Even in combat camouflage, women could look good, he thought.

Petersen was now settled in and after looking around the interior of the Cavalier, she was now motioning to Preacher that she was now ready. After a few seconds, Petersen wasn't sure if he had caught the hint and let out a sigh.

Preacher closed his eyes and leaned back his head and allowed it to rest on the headrest. He appeared to allow his mind and body a chance, though momentary, to cycle down from the strain of the past work day.

"Preacher, waz up?" After several seconds had passed, Preacher opened his eyes.

"How is she doing?" he asked.

"How is who doing?"

"Muse. How is she really doing? I know that you see her from time to time."

Petersen let out another sigh.

"I know what the CO and the first sergeant are saying publicly to the rank and file, but I'm also getting conflicting rumors around the company of how good Muse is really doing. I'm not one to constantly listen to gossip, but sometimes the grapevine is just as reliable, if not more so, than official channels. You and her are somewhat close, right? ... I figured if anyone knows how she is really it would be you."

"Well, we talk but I wouldn't exactly call us close. Basically between some others and me I'm her choice for a soul mate. More of a sounding board than a real friend. Keep in mind, we all is a long way from our families," said Petersen. She had a point. Preacher couldn't think of another profession that was demanding and would often separate you from your loved ones than a military career.

"The hospital that we took her to, a social worker there referred her to a clinic in the Springs. The Rape Crisis Center, I think the name is," she said.

"Oh yeah. I'm aware of that clinic," replied Preacher.

"You are?" said a surprised Petersen.

"Yes, it was one of the clinics that I requested sexual assault information from while preparing for a class I was scheduled to give on one of our training days. I actually didn't give the class. I'm not sure if I was relieved or disappointed. Normally I don't like giving classes I'm not qualified to give, but in this case reading the information and knowing all the help one gets from these type of clinics opened my eyes. I have a whole new respect for social workers as well as the victims and what they must go though. I was definitely ready for that class."

Petersen was once again surprised how passionate he spoke of these clinics. She didn't see or hear stuff like that either in her work section or in the barracks. But she never had to use their services either. Most of the guys she was around didn't see any need for a woman to get help, other than medical for scars and such, after being traumatized like that. She assumed as much still after the Muse incident off-post. That was the talk of the post for a while. With the new and enhanced emphasis of antisexual harassment announcements being made throughout the Army, she wasn't hearing or receiving blatant verbal abuse herself but more of subtle tones. This bottled tension among some males, obviously not all, may have contributed to Muse being assaulted.

"Maybe it should be you who Muse should be talking to," declared Petersen.

Preacher raised his head from the headrest and looked at Petersen. "I don't think you heard me too good. She should be seeing someone who does that kind of thing for a living."

"I don't mean professionally. I mean socially. Other than a few people, she doesn't talk to too many people in the unit. She is a total 360 from who she use to be. From bubbly schoolgirl to a secluded hermit. Neither female nor male enlisted would carry a lengthy conversation with her. Not necessarily being mean. Mostly due to not really being sure what to say to a rape victim. And she has to notice this. That must be really tough on her. With the exception of her supervisors mostly watching over her and making sure she has everything she needs *per* the Fort Carson commanding General--she is basically by herself. Everyone seems to mean well for the most part. The unit, as you know, allowed her to go home to visit her folks without using her own leave for a few weeks."

"Yeah, right," said Preacher sarcastically. Now looking straight ahead to the front.

"Once again, that came from the very top. This case got so much publicity the last thing the Fort Carson Post Commander, much less the unit wanted was that poor, young girl being heard and seen on CNN that the U.S. Army wouldn't even let her visit her mama. That would have been very bad PR on somebody's part. You can bet that despite the assault happening in Colorado Springs, just outside the gates of Fort Carson. It might as well happen on post because everyone from the post commander on up to the Secretary of the Army was watching how this was handled. No one wanted this to happen. The army was still feeling the repercussions of the Aberdeen Proving Ground assaults." Preacher said all this with authority in his voice.

"To properly answer your question Petersen, I would do so when she is ready to talk to me. Besides I really don't won't her to think she owes me anything because she doesn't."

"I'm sure she don't see it that way," said Petersen.

"Good. Then do me a favor please. The next time you see her, let her know that if she would just like to talk she can do so anytime on or off post."

"I will do that Preacher. I'm sure she would like that very much," Petersen said happily. "I think Preacher that that clinic is helping a lot." Preacher was still looking straight ahead in his car. He was watching as vehicle after vehicle left the parking lot carrying its passengers away from their workplace for the day. Some vehicles, military as well as civilian, were still there but that wasn't unusual. Despite the slow promotions, long hours, fair share of the daily bullshit and meager annual raises, U.S. military personnel were among the most dedicated and hardest working people in the world. The individuals that were still in the building were no exception. For reasons entirely their own, some 13th Finance Group unit personnel were still hard at work.

"Initially I noticed that Muse was fearful of being alone, afraid to trust people--even me--and very, very concerned of how her parents may feel about her situation prior to going home."

"If I recall, that is not unusual behavior for a rape victim," stated Preacher. "I found out while preparing for my class that that is just part of the rape trauma syndrome. This syndrome is comprised of three parts: trauma, denial and resolution. What you described earlier were part of the trauma."

Petersen looked at Preacher again and arched her eye brows.

"But after talking with the folks at the clinic she is opening up more. She's not back to her old self but she is definitely making progress."

"I wouldn't give them too much credit. You obviously helped a lot as well. She at least had you to talk to and she will see you around a lot more than those social workers or doctors. Petersen if you're her friend or soul mate or whatever you want to call it, you can do the following to help her: listen to her, be attainable, and let her know that she is not the blame, be patient and understanding and don't be overly protective."

Petersen nodded in agreement as she looked down fondling with her fingernails. She had found a hangnail.

Preacher caught the body language as well and he reached for his keys and upon inserting them, started his car. Relieved that they were moving out of the parking lot and headed for the barracks for a much-needed rest, Petersen's thoughts were upon McCullen now.

"I am sure glad that Muse pressed criminal charges against McCullen, I hope his ass get at least ten years behind bars for what he did."

30

"That may not be a problem. Muse's assault was reported to civilian authorities initially as a matter of routine. From there the civilians could have handled the criminal proceedings as usual. But in this case, according to news reports, the U.S. Army Judge Advocate General here requested that they handle things. The Colorado Springs district attorney's office was more than accommodating to Fort Carson. One, they have enough work of their own much less handle soldiers through their judicial system. Besides, with the potential of this case having a national spotlight at that time, the DA's office didn't want to create a situation where the local taxpayers would have to pick up the tab for matters that routinely accompanied big, high profile cases. Take the O.J. Simpson trial and the city of Los Angeles, for instance. Not to mention Michael Jackson.

"Two, civilian prosecutors knew that with the Aberdeen Proving Ground incidents and most recently, the assaults at nearby Air Force Academy, the U.S. Army would like to show that this type of assaults are not tolerated anywhere. They will show this by prosecuting the case to the fullest and handing out sentences much more severe than anything the accused would get in the *civilian world*."

How could the Army be so sophisticated when it comes to race and yet so backward on gender? Preacher thought.

The efforts to assimilate women have benefited from a technique learned from the Army's attempts to get blacks and whites to function together: stamping out offensive behavior, instead of trying to change soldiers' underlying attitudes. That way, soldiers at least act in a civil manner--even if deep down they feel uncomfortable. Now on bases and posts around the world even innocent words that could carry sexual connotations, such as "stud" or "studette," are forbidden on Army time. So is swearing. Sergeants who bark out motivational cadences when units do their morning runs are no longer allowed to use popular chants now deemed sexist.

Punishment for these violations can be severe. One soldier who saw a bee buzzing near a female colleague's waist commented, "There must be something sweet between your legs." The female soldier complained, and following an investigation the soldier was issued a formal letter of reprimand--effectively killing his chances of ever being promoted. Perhaps because of such ardent enforcement, battalion commanders, who were in charge of six to seven hundred soldiers, say they typically get only a handful of substantiated sexual harassment complaints a year.

Petersen and Preacher were cruising past a number of buildings on post. Among the many buildings that got its fair share of patrons after hours were the clubs, both officer and enlisted, and the AAFES shoppette stores. While Petersen wrestled with her recently discovered hangnail, Preacher observed how much traffic one AAFES shoppette was getting while approaching a yellow traffic signal. As he sat at the intersection, he noticed the number of people exiting the convenience store with cigarettes and alcohol, mostly beer. Occasionally he would see someone with hard liquor. Preacher wondered if there wasn't anything else for them to do but drink and smoke.

Of course there was.

Most of the soldiers he viewed were minorities. Blacks, Hispanics and even one or two individuals that appeared to be of American Indian descent could be seen walking out of the store with their own brand of poison.

After getting the green light, Preacher gassed it through the intersection. Petersen had a look of satisfaction on her face as she sat straight up after taking care of her finger. "What are your plans tonight, Preacher?" she asked.

"Take off this uniform and relax a little before I have to study before class tomorrow," replied Preacher. "Where do you go to school? Is it on or off post?"

Fort Carson contracted with a few schools to offer classes in some of the old post-World War II buildings at one end of the post. The colleges and universities placed signs in the front yard of the white buildings they occupied. You have to look for the signs because the buildings look like white cheap row houses with the same architectural design. The school signs were the only things that differentiated one from the other. Obviously not all the local colleges and universities had these branches on Fort Carson, for whatever reason. Some schools still must be attended on their campus. Petersen Air Force base or Pete field also located just outside of the Springs have similar arrangements with the local academic institutions.

"I go to Regis University at their Colorado Springs campus near Manitou Springs."

"Oh! Let me guess. You are taking some computer-type course, right?"

"You got it," replied Preacher with some enthusiasm despite a long day. The western sun was noticeably dropping from the sky to indicate that this day was approaching its end.

"Obviously since you're going to school, you're not planning on staying around here are you?"

"No, Petersen I'm not. I thought about this for a long, long time and I think the best thing for me to do is just leave when my discharge date rolls around."

"I bet you could make sergeant really fast with all those college credits," said Petersen.

"Yes, I could ... and I have--in a way," said Preacher.

That last statement peaked Petersen's curiosity. She knew promotions for specialist fours didn't happen that often. Years could go by before specialist fours in a finance unit saw anyone promoted to sergeant.

"What do you mean?" she asked.

"What?"

"What do you mean about you have?"

"You mean you don't know about that."

"About what, Preacher?" Petersen was getting somewhat irritated with Preacher now.

"I was sure everyone in the unit knew about me turning down the sergeant promotion," replied Preacher. "Oh, you're the one," said Petersen like a schoolgirl who just got her first kiss from a boy in class.

"What do you mean by 'you're the one?'" he asked.

"I overheard some sergeants during PT talking about someone who had made sergeant but because he did something that the first sergeant didn't like, was denied ever getting his *stripes*."

"Well, that's not exactly true." Petersen sat there giving Preacher her undivided attention, oblivious to the good looking male soldiers whom were skirmishing to their respective destinations on the sidewalks.

"It's really no secret what actually happened," he added.

"A few months ago I had the number of cutoff scores or promotion points needed for sergeant. For each college credit you have in your education file that too equals a promotion point. Well, that particular month's promotion list went from battalion, to the CO, the first sergeant and eventually my supervisor. The first sergeant, after a review of my personnel file, recognized that I needed to take the Professional Leadership Development Course. Thinking that all little E-4s wanted to grow up and become E-5s, he scheduled an arrival date for me to attend PLDC."

Petersen still sat there looking content with a half smile on her face.

"He then called my supervisor with the congrats and notified him that I had made E-5 but needed to attend PLDC. My supervisor realized this may become a problem since I had already expressed to him that I was leaving the army when my ETS date rolled around. But I'm sure he was hoping that upon notification that I could be promoted, I may change my mind. Well, that obviously didn't happen.

"We had a chat about it, but in the end I made it clear that I was not interested in becoming sergeant. He understood, but he was certain the first sergeant wouldn't."

"What were your reasons for not attending the school and just get the stripes until you leave?" Petersen asked.

Still looking at the road in front of him, Preacher said, "Why?"

"Well, the money for one thing."

"Okay, young lady listen up." Preacher made a sigh and moistened his lips. "The aggravation that comes with being a sergeant in this unit as well as attending PLDC isn't worth the little money you get. Sure, there are some perks that come with the rank like order the subordinates around, walk around with your coffee cup looking important while everyone else works, and just merely go about like you have no boss. But there are just as many negatives as well."

"Such as?" interrupted Petersen.

"Well, like ... ah." Preacher was a little caught off guard by Petersen. "Such as, baby sitting."

"Baby sitting! What do you mean by *baby sitting*?"

"We have soldiers here who clearly have alcohol problems and probably dealt into other things as well, if you know what I mean. They may be a little young and dumb but that doesn't entitle them to call the unit when they go to jail for DWI or beating their spouse on a given night. Then, the first sergeant who eventually gets notified calls *little Johnny's* or *Sue's* immediate supervisor and he or she has to go to the police station in the middle of the night to get them out of jail. That, in my opinion, is absolutely ridiculous.

"Most people enter the U.S. Army at least age eighteen. That, in my book, makes them an adult, who should be able to face up to any mistakes they may make while growing up. And if they're not able to then one can also question why are they're even able to function in the military. *Pause.* One can say that's part of being a unit. And yes, they would be partially right but it is competent, adult soldiers who make up a unit, a professional fighting force, if you will. When you don't allow people to mature to a point where they are not allowed to stumble, dust themselves off and proceed through life whether in or out of the military, you prevent or slow the process of an individual achieving his or her maturity as well as the competency that comes with it. Therefore, you have a unit, if you will, that is not as strong and cohesive as it could be."

Preacher paused for a second again then looked at Petersen with a smile and a seductive wink. "But that's just my opinion."

Petersen swung her head to her passenger side window and grinned. *He does have a point*, she thought.

They were approaching the driveway of the unit and Petersen would soon be in her room. Preacher turned off the boulevard and after a few swerves and stops for pedestrian traffic, he entered one of the first parking spaces near the entrance door of the building.

"We are here and you are in one piece," said Preacher.

"So I am. Thanks for the ride." Preacher noticed again how smooth her voice was.

"You're welcome." Petersen reached over to pull on the door latch and after opening the door she paused and looked again at Preacher. "We must continue our chat sometime very soon, OK?"

Preacher wasn't really sure how to take that, so he said, "OK."

Petersen exited the vehicle and proceeded up the sidewalk with her hand purse in tow. Preacher watched her do so like he was on some sort of surveillance. He watched her hips in perfect unison with the swinging of her arms. Even at this distance Preacher noticed she had very good skin. He realized he had gotten a better view of her body when she was at McCullen's house party.

Petersen eventually disappeared behind the doors of the barracks and Preacher came back to reality. He started the cavalier, but it wasn't done fast enough. Private First Class Hammond, the supply clerk for the unit, apparently saw Petersen depart Preacher's car and came out to inform Preacher that he saw it. He was barely out of the door before he started shouting.

"Player! Player! I thought we were friends. You didn't even tell me you guys were seeing one another. You always have to keep an eye on the quiet ones. You just never know what they're up to."

Preacher placed the vehicle in gear after backing up and simply waved his left hand from outside the driver's side window. He even giggled to himself. He didn't feel like denying or confirming PFC Hammond's remarks right now. He just wanted to get home.

After exiting the parking lot and eventually the Fort Carson military reservation, Preacher found himself like others on Academy Boulevard with the Colorado sun to his back. Tomorrow will be another day.

CHAPTER FOUR

It was quite possible that Petersen had beat Preacher to the punch as far as achieving serenity. She and her roommate had already gone over to the mess hall for dinner. Petersen was now in her bright, yellow bathrobe; Winnie-the-Pooh slippers and a pink scarf wrapped around her head. She was now lying stretched out on her bed watching Black Entertainment Television's *College Hill*. She had watched this show only once before on BET and thought it was interesting to see these three black divas with their own talk show. The thick, green wool G.I.-issue blanket with accompanying white sheets were replaced a long time ago by a Martha Stewart collection. Even the plain G.I. lamps were replaced courtesy of a visit at Wal-Mart. Those personal touches made the barracks a little more homey and bearable.

The ladies' assign room within the barracks area on the second floor was much like the guy's. Each room, painted a pale white, came with government-issued or G.I. white blinds with accompanying drapes. Both items looked from a rummage sale. It also came with radiant heat and a small "college dorm"-type frig. The floor tile was definitely "government." It was a dull gray, but was recently polished. The females had a definite knack for keeping their floors shiny.

Each occupant had his or her own locker to store their personal belongings as well as a desk and chair. The three appeared to be a matching set because all had similar imitation oak stain. On the left door of the locker was an official diagram of how the items within it as well as in the desk should be stored and displayed. It seemed somewhat anal, and most soldiers did not follow the diagram to the letter except during inspections.

36

Once you got to your permanent duty station after AIT, life in the army was more relax than in basic training.

Petersen had planned to take a shower down the hall in the latrine but decided she wanted to rest a little in front of the TV. Her roommate, also a specialist, had already decided she needed a shower and had left a few minutes earlier.

The viewing of the show wasn't quite keeping Petersen's attention. Her mind wondered back to moments earlier. Seeing her roommate prepare for the shower wasn't always been the easiest thing to handle. But somehow she did.

Petersen grabbed the remote and turned the tv off. She rose up from the bed and went to her assign desk. From the lower drawer, she retrieved her diary and immediately went to the page marked by a bookmark. She then went back to her bed and propped her head on two fluffy, goose feather pillows. That too was not G.I. issue. She then proceeded to read.

July 15, 1998

It was a summer evening in July of 1993 and hot; I'm talking muggy with the humidity percentile way up there. Sweat dripped off your body just from breathing too hard. Or though it seemed. I arrived home early, totally disgusted from my evening with my man. I'm going to drop his tired ass any day now. Well maybe in another month cause the dick is good and he can eat a pussy so good I swear I was having seizures.

"Fuck that trifling nigga," I said to myself and head for the showers, the third one of the day for me. I'm the type that perspires a lot and can not stand being sticky unless it's due to a sexual exertion if you know what I mean?

Felicia was in her bedroom that adjoined mines. We could literally pass through one to get to the others. Only thing separating them was this makeshift divider which was crafted out of this afro centric beading and dense mesh which hung to the floor. It added a funky authentic blackness to an otherwise white wicker flavor we had going on right out of Better Homes and Gardens. Shit, I like that spacious uncluttered look but the bead thang stood out and made a statement for which I am not quite sure what that was suppose to be... LOL.

I stroll into the bathroom, dripping, (what's the point of trying to dry off when I drip faster than I could pat dry with my towel) so I just came out all natural. It's only Felicia and I and it's not like we haven't seen each other before. So I'm in my bedroom and I'm looking around for something, anything that won't stick to me five seconds after I put it on. Looking through the drawers I hear this soft moaning from just beyond the beaded-thick mesh divider. I pause, listen, and it comes a little louder. It's definitely a moan and not a moan of someone in pain. So I ease on over as quiet as I can and peek through the beaded-thick mesh and see old girl sprawled out on her back.

Her eyes are closed, legs spread eagle and two fingers are working deep inside her pussy while the fingers of the other hand is tugging at and rolling her nipples moving from one tit to the other and back. Instantly I feel a deep pulsing within the walls of my own pussy and my nipples rise up stiff and throbbing as if to say "hello I want some of that action." Seeing Felicia getting her groove on has got me horny, jealous and needy. Feeling very bold and thinking if I'm ever going to get something going with Felicia I better make my move now while she is too engrossed and too hot to care. I step behind the beads and stand silently watching as Felicia raises up her hips from the bed, those luscious ass cheeks clutch tightly as she grinds in a circular motion driving her fingers inside her sex in long, leisurely strokes.

I watch her roll two fingers over her clit. My tongue darts over my lower lip in anticipation of what that tiny erect bud peeking out from the hood protecting it and the moist, pink inner lips of her vagina clamped around her driving fingers, would taste like as I suck, lap and nibble drawing them within the liquid heat of my ravishing mouth. Absentmindedly I begin to play with my own pussy wiggling two fingers in a V-shape between the sleek inner lips shuddering as they slid back and forth causing moisture to gather at my aching opening. Biting down on my lower lip, I guide one, then other finger inside, struggling not to cry out as I penetrate my hot, damp core. Eyes fixed on Felicia gyrating with her ass high above the bed, nipples standing stiff and dark calling to me; I can no longer hold myself from what I seek. Stepping towards her until I am close enough to reach out and touch her, my eyes crawl over her beautiful, naked, thrashing body and a loud groan breaks my lips that I could not restrain.

Felicia's eyes open and roll back in her head. For a second, I'm uncertain if I should make a dash out the room or stay. Slowly they rest upon my face and focus. Within them I see the fear of discovery and the anguish for release. I smile down at her trying to communicate with my eyes, my smile that its okay and I want what she wants. To receive pleasure. After coming to her I lowered myself to the bed, my hands tenderly sliding along her hips watching them jerk under my touch. They move over her tart belly, ribcage and higher till they are caressing the sweet undersides of her 38D's. Enclosing those tits within the warmth of my hands, pinching the nipples possessively between my thumbs and forefingers, Felicia arches her back, head moving from side to side while her eyes roll back murmuring unintelligibly.

Lifting and pressing her breasts together, squeezing them at the base till the nipples stand out plump, I lean forward, tongue snaking out and curling around those mocha tips. "Oh fuck!! Shit baby" she shouts shivering from head to toe each time my tongue strikes out and captures her dark peaks with its wet firmness. I continue my oral seduction licking, flicking, curling and stroking at her nipples with an aggressive tongue. Felicia's back arches even higher pushing her tits further to my lips. I take her round offerings with a greedy mouth that sucks deep and strongly at each nipple gathering as much areola between my lips as I can while nibbling at the nipples when they pass over my tongue. "Oh yeah. . ah yeahhhh" she hisses. I begin to work her nipples with my teeth pulling at the throbbing, sensitive knobs drawing louder cries from her lips. Sensing Felicia's release is not much further off and waiting my mouth upon that sopping wet pussy at the delicious moment of climax to drink up all her sticky warm juices, with my palms rolling over her nipples in a circle teasing them, I kiss down her slim, mocha form.

Swirling my tongue over her stomach, dipping it into the hollow of her belly button, I hear Felicia gasp. Snaking it along her hipbone and onward till it works into the crease between her upper thigh and crotch area, Felicia lifts her lips whimpering "Please baby, oh please taste me. I need it so bad now...now." Her eyes staring down at me hard and dark with hunger. Keeping my eyes locked on her tense face, beads of sweat rolling off both our bodies. My pussy grows wetter and wetter throbbing fiercely needing to cum badly. My tongue glides through the soft thick hairs that cover her mound. "Jesusssss" is all she can manage grinding her crotch against my mouth. Closing my lips over the soft, slippery vaginal lips, tongue flat, I drag it up between the pink folds lapping along them with a slow pull of tongue. "Damn baby damn" Felicia growls grabbing handfuls of my hair pushing my head firmly between her outstretched legs. Pressing the tip of my tongue hard against her clit, I begin to strum it back and forth, concentrating just the tip in a maddening flicking and stroking at the tiny bud.

My scalp hurt as she continues to wind my hair around her fingers. I answer her demands with a harsh penetrating tongue that seeks her hot, dripping depth with quick jabs plunging between her pussy lips driving in as far as it will go then licking back out to the entrance lapping at the opening to once and driven hard and fast into her pussy. Felicia rides my tongue screaming like a woman possessed. Her cries are all I need to send me over the edge. Trembling, the pressure in my pussy intensifies. The powerful currents of pleasure crash against my inner walls and erupt, flowing strong out of me gushing my juices out and trickling between my strong thighs. With lips buried to her sex, I suck and drink and swallow eagerly taking all that Felicia has to offer which is considerable as her body convulses violently. Removing my hands from her tits, I bring them to her pussy and spread it open with my thumbs and starting licking the deliciously sticky residue of her cum cleaning her thoroughly. We were still panting and our breathing unstable. Gazing up at me with contentment dancing over her face, with shaky hands, Felicia reaches out for me. I move into her embrace and lay out flat upon her sprawled form gently grinding my hips against hers.

That was the first time and regrettably, the last time Petersen was intimate with another woman. A month later, Felicia would move out stating that her lame-ass boyfriend finally got that job that could easily pay the rent on a crib they were looking at a few weeks earlier. To smooth things over between them, Felicia said it was only fair that Petersen keep the place and her share of the security deposit considering they had a two bedroom apartment, with terrace, washer and dryer for under fifteen hundred dollars in a trendy area of Baltimore. It was insect and rodent-free in a decent neighborhood close to everything. Petersen reluctantly went along with the idea. She would have preferred to stay there with Felicia.

Petersen, to this day, had no hard feelings for the sista but wished things had proceeded a little further. But Felicia, she thought, had to do what she had to do.

Petersen missed her, even now. Petersen closed the diary and laid it by her side on the bed. She just eyed the pale white ceiling for a few minutes until the day's work had caught up with her. She drifted off. After about fifteen minutes in her dream state, the room door was closed shut again. Her roommate had returned and was the signal, she thought, for a cool shower. Petersen missed that hot, summer night and she could still close her eyes and smell Felicia, taste her, feel her and crave her.

As usual, Preacher awoke at 0430 hours without the assistance of his alarm clock. After rolling over on his back he reached to turn off his alarm clock. The only reason it was even on was just to serve as a back-up just in case he had one of those extremely rare days when he was dead tired and his biological clock fail to kick in. After rising from his bed, Preacher hit the lights and proceeded to make up his bed by tucking in and folding the sheets and the blanket just right. Last but not least, he laid out his checkered burgundy and blue comforter. If his grandparents taught him nothing else, it was that you need to get your butt out of bed in order to make the most of your day. Preacher had found out early on when he lived with his grandparents that it was always something that needed to be done whether you work inside the home or outside. This, among other things stayed with Preacher. It also didn't hurt that the military had similar philosophies too.

Preacher always liked to sleep warm and comfy in the fall and winter. The bed and the temperature in his apartment were indicative of that. The temp usually hovered between seventy-five and eighty degrees. Preacher was not fond of the Colorado weather, but he was used to it. The weather in the region could be brutal when it wanted to particularly with an artic blast. But most of the time during the fall and winter months it was just cool to cold with the occasional snow fall. The mountain range which includes the Pikes Peak area prevents the Fort Carson/Colorado Springs area from getting substantial snow fall. Soldiers were expected to wear summer gear until ordered to switch to winter gear.

Preacher's b ball and unit buddies would often come after work or on the weekend and would make a statement referring to the heat setting he would have on. Preacher's response would be, "If you feel uncomfortable, leave because the heat stays." He would say it with a smile but they would know he was serious. Preacher liked his apartment off post. He treasured his privacy, but he didn't always have it.

Preacher was very relieved to find out about a year ago that all senior E-4s and above that currently in the barracks would have the opportunity to live off post if they desired. This was due to the barracks being fully occupied and no room was available for the lower ranks especially those arriving from AIT. With the exception of a couple of E-4s, all took advantage of it. The unit grapevine affirmed that the ones that didn't were already having some financial problems and didn't want to compound it by living off-post.

Everyone in the military got free or almost free housing. How the military chooses to provide this to you depends mostly upon your marital status, or your rank. If you are married and living with your spouse and/or minor dependents, you will either live in on-post housing, or be given a monetary allowance called BAQ or Basic Allowance for Quarters to live off-post. Those that are single and below the rank of E-6 usually reside on-post in the barracks.

The "free housing" could be anything from an open-bay barracks, a large room with twenty or more bunk beds, with a central bathroom/shower facility or latrine to a two- or one- person room with a bathroom/shower shared with the room next door. Some rooms, depending on rank, offer a private bathroom/shower. One could usually have a small fridge, coffee pot and a microwave. Hot plates and other cooking appliance are normally not allowed in barracks. Most barracks rooms, at least in the States, have cable and phone jacks, but recruits had to pay for services.

For the privilege of living in the barracks, everyone was expected to do their share of the barracks' duties, which means keeping the common areas: hallways, outside area, day rooms clean and tidy. Even those of the ranks of E-5s and above who stay in the barracks had to participate in some way. However, if there was an influx of E-5 and/or E-6 personnel, that would obviously get any E-7s off the hook of such menial duties. The E-5s and above wouldn't do the dirty work but would just supervise. At times, barracks occupants will be subjected to the classic G.I. Party in which the commander and/or first sergeant would get all the "barracks rats" together to clean up everything. These usually preceded the Battalion Commander's inspection.

Preacher also had another motivation for moving off-post. Shortly after arriving at Fort Gordon, Georgia after basic training to attend his AIT course: Information Technology Specialist (25B10), he had an incident.

It was at Fort Gordon, the Home of the U.S. Army's Signal Corp., that Preacher trained and received his first Military Occupational Specialty or MOS.

Preacher was assigned to a two-man room in one of the dorms nearby. The dorms looked very much like those found on college campuses. His roommate like Preacher was from the south. Austin, Texas to be exact and he liked the room cool for whatever reason even in the winter.

After attending a *Database System Design and Development* class as part of the 25B10 curriculum, Preacher arrived back in the room. He had made a detour to the post's department store or Post Exchange (PX) prior to arriving back, which gave his roommate time to settle in after classes. It was his first time visiting a main PX since entering the army. Upon entering the room he immediately felt a cool breeze hit him in the face. Preacher wasn't too thrilled about it and immediately asked the Texan to close the windows since it was cold in the room. The Texan stated that he would in about ten minutes. Preacher wasn't pleased but decided to just wait it out for ten minutes or so. He just figured this guy had some issues or something. But still they should try to get along during the duration of their stay.

After about twelve minutes, the Texan still had not budged from his bed where he laid listening to his iPod. Preacher couldn't take it anymore and closed both windows. In a tone and demeanor inappropriate for the circumstances, the Texan started shouting, "Guy, you didn't have to do that! I would have closed it eventually. You people think you can just run over whomever you want." Preacher thought it was always interesting the way some people talked to others depending on their upbringing. The Texan kept calling him, "Guy," as if he wasn't around blacks or any other minorities.

Being taller and heavier than the Texan, Tex said and did everything except attempt to approach Preacher or say the "N" word. Preacher had noticed during their stay the uneasiness he had of him. The Texan just would not accept Preacher winning this round and decided to bring in the CQ to resolve the matter-- hopefully in his favor. It didn't happen. The CQ, an older white guy, decided to prevent this from escalating any further and made a "Command Decision."

Immediate arrangements were made for the Texan to move in with someone of his liking. Preacher even got the room to himself. Problem solved. Preacher, as well as the Texan, successfully completed their AIT and eventually went to their respective initial post assignments. According to the official roster that was posted, the Texan got Fort Greeley as his first PCS assignment, an Alaska location. Opening the windows there may not be necessary.

Preacher would later find in the U.S. Army that issues that could potentially flare up from a possible racial episode were often handled in a similar tactful fashion.

CHAPTER FIVE

Preacher continued his morning ritual and was currently brushing his teeth. In the middle of the scrubbing, he stared at his body. The six-pack was not as defined as it once was. It would appear that more gym time might be in order, he thought to himself. He posed side ways from left to right and back again. He even did a muscle pose and he came up with the same answer: more gym time.

The Iron horse gym, the Fort Carson main gym, was a facility housing equipment very similar to a civilian gym minus any juice bars but also had an outside jogging track. Preacher mostly frequented the gym after work on a non-school night. There were less people to deal with and he had more equipment available to utilize because of it.

Preacher wrapped up his morning beauty regiment and decided to fix a quick fried egg sandwich with the customary mayo and American cheese before getting dressed for the new day. Preacher first entered his kitchenette and started boiling the water in his glass cafe to really get things started. Since joining the army, Preacher had become quite fond of his morning cup of java, usually limiting himself to a cup a day or maybe an additional one if it was a cold day at work.

He didn't always drink it. It all started upon joining the military and being introduced to the monthly guard duty and CQ rounds.

The late nights of just sitting or walking around, in the case of guard duty, could be very uneventful and sleep can easily creep up, especially on one-man shifts.

One night Preacher was pulling guard duty while in basic training, a fellow trainee had offered to bring him some coffee to fight back the sleep.

Preacher hesitated but decided otherwise considering he could feel that his body needed it and took the trainee's offer.

Preacher had always liked the taste and smell of coffee ever since he would wake in the mornings before school at his grandparents' house in Hamburg, Arkansas. His grandmother or, as he called her "Big Momma," would always rise in the early morning hours to fix breakfast. It would be the usual items of white steamed rice with butter, country sausage patties or hot links, homemade buttermilk biscuits with Hersheys hot chocolate (not that instant stuff but the one in the black can). That was a typical breakfast in the Fall and Winter unless someone wanted an egg or two. The south Arkansas family was not too keen on eggs unless it was for the homemade corn bread. Preacher really didn't start to eat eggs until he enlisted.

Included with that, Big Momma would make a cup or two of *Folgers* instant coffee for his grandfather or, as he called him, "Big Daddy." It always looked and smelled so good. Whomever Preacher would inquire to about getting a cup the usual reply would always be, "*When you get grown, you can.*" Preacher would always leave it at that. His grandparents always protected him. In this case, for whatever reason they weren't encouraging him to get started with coffee. They knew how addictive it could be.

It could be worse, thought Preacher as he sipped the hot liquid that cold night. He could be taking something harsher such as *No Doze* or something like that. Preacher decided that if he was going to use any drugs to stay awake it might as well be caffeine and nothing drastic.

While the water was getting prepared, Preacher quickly entered the living room to turn on the TV. Still in his pajama pants and beach thongs, he sat back to watch the two *Fox 21* anchors listen to a military consultant discuss the military's justice system: Uniform Code of Military Justice or UCMJ and how it affected, what was now dubbed the "Fort Carson Rape." "Ken" and "Barbie" listened intuitively as the consultant, probably a former U.S. Army officer, explain in layman's terms UCMJ was, differences between it and its civilian counterpart, as well as how it would affect the young lady's accuser.

"*The UCMJ or the Uniform Code of Military Justice is the foundation of military law. The UCMJ is a federal law, enacted by Congress. The UCMJ resulted from the desire for uniformity amongst the armed services,*" replied the figure still wearing a military hair cut but in a neat, sharp black civilian suit. The gentleman sounded off with authority in addition to an in depth knowledge. Perhaps he may be a former U.S. Army JAG officer, thought Preacher. The gentleman looked straight at his anchors as he spoke, not into the camera.

He was about to continue his primer until the female of the team interrupted him, "*Excuse me but where is the sergeant first class being held now, if at all, and how is pretrial confinement different from our civilian system?*"

"*My sources tell me that Sergeant First Class Randall McCullen is being held at the Fort Carson stockade or military jail. Depending on the services and the various bases and posts around the world it could also be called the 'brig' or 'confinement.' To be frank, I'm not surprised he was immediately confined even for the military considering all the press this case has received. The U.S. Army has yet another sexual assault on their hands. Certainly not on the scale of the Aberdeen incidents but one getting a lot of publicity never the less.*

"*Pretrial confinement in the military is similar to the civilian system in some respects and different in others. In the civilian community, police arrest serious offenders and take them to jail. In military cases, 'apprehended' or arrested has a different technical meaning in the military, you see, and service members are typically turned over to a member of command authority. The command then decides whether to confine the member in a military jail. The command may also impose pretrial restrictions instead of confinement. For instance, the servicemember may be restricted to his post or base, pending trial. That obviously did not happen here.*"

The military consultant shifted his body slightly in his high, swivel chair to continue talking apparently to the male anchor, not wanting to appear to leave out the other anchor in the conversation.

"*Before any servicemember is confined or restrained, there must be 'probable cause'--a reasonable belief--that the service member committed an offense triable by court-martial and that confinement or restriction is necessary under the circumstances. In addition, like a civilian policeman, any military officer can order an enlisted servicemember to be confined. The decision to confine a military member is the subject of several reviews. The military justice system follows the civilian requirement that a review of the decision to confine the person be conducted within forty-eight hours. Within seventy-two hours, the military member is entitled to have his commanding officer review whether his continued confinement is appropriate.*

"*Thereafter, a military magistrate who is independent of the command must conduct another review within seven days. Throughout the confinement review process, a servicemember is provided a military lawyer, at no expense, to assist him or her."*

The male anchor interrupted, *"You mean the tax payers would be footing the bill during this particular process?"*

"That is correct. Like many other things a soldier is provided during his or her tour in the military, legal representation is one of them. Even in the military, one is assumed to be innocent until proven guilty."

The consultant wasn't sure if the journalist really didn't know and was just asking a question that one of his viewing audiences would ask as well or whether he was just trying to create his next story by getting as many people upset about their tax monies being used on this accused rapist. In any case, the consultant, possibly someone who spent time in the military himself, underscored that soldiers need to be adequately represented as well. On that point, he continued: *"These reviews must confirm, in writing:*

One, that there is probable cause to believe that the servicemember committed an offense triable by court-martial."

His fingers to better emphasize his point.

"Two, there is probable cause to believe that confinement is necessary to prevent the servicemember from fleeing or engaging in serious criminal misconduct.

Three, there is probable cause to believe that lesser forms of restraint would be inadequate."

The consultant then proceeded to eye each anchor intermittently as he spoke: *"When and if the sergeant first class' charges are 'referred' or presented to a court-martial—and it does appear likely—the confined servicemember may ask the military judge presiding over the court to review his pretrial confinement again. According to my sources, there is no indication that the sergeant first class has done so or even plans to."* Pause. *"If rules were violated, the military judge can release the servicemember, and he or she can reduce any subsequent sentence, giving additional credit for inappropriate confinement. This may be a high profile case, but even the newest JAG officer will make sure that all the t's are crossed and i's are dotted. Not doing so would be career ending for that lawyer."*

"J.A.G. Officer?" injected the female anchor. "I'm sorry, J.A.G. stands for Judge Advocate General's office. It provides the legal support as well as the legal training for the Army." The analyst continued, *"In most cases, imposing pretrial confinement 'starts the clock.' After imposing pretrial confinement, the command must usually bring the case to trial within one hundred and twenty days, or risk having the case overturned on appeal.*

"In the civilian community, people accused of crimes that might flee or commit other crimes may also be confined prior to their trial. A civilian magistrate must review this confinement within forty-eight hours. In many cases, the magistrate will require confinees to post bail to ensure their return for trial. While awaiting trial, a civilian confinee usually does not receive pay and may actually lose his or her job. Servicemembers do not have to post bail, receive their regular military pay, and do not lose their jobs while awaiting trial."

The interview was winding down. The military expert was now talking about the options or lack thereof that was available to SFC Randall McCullen within the UCMJ. The gentleman finished up with his views and insights on the matter. From the quick eye glances the female anchor made to the side of the live camera indicated by a red light, she was getting the "time out" signal from someone in the vicinity. *"And on that note that will be the last word. I want to thank our guest for joining us this morning and hope that you will return as this case moves forward,"* she stated.

"Glad to be here," responded the consultant and after he nodded, the camera focused on just the two anchors. The two continued to read from the teleprompter on other stories of the day.

Despite being in the military himself, Preacher listened with interest to the man. Fortunately, Preacher like most soldiers in the military had very little contact with the UCMJ system. Like the criminal justice system on the civilian side of the house, it's not something anyone really want to get involved in.

Preacher thought back for a moment and realized there was one occasion he sought the assistance of the Judge Advocate General's office for a matter.

About a week after arriving to Fort Carson, Preacher received a letter from a civilian law firm in Detroit, Michigan. It was representing a young lady who was requesting child support for her kid. Preacher read the letter and soon determined that it simply was a miscommunication on somebody's part. Preacher first checked the name of the person who was being represented and it wasn't one that was familiar.

He remembered a very intimate incident with a young lady while he was in high school, but that was years ago. She didn't live in Detroit now nor did her first or last name match that which was in the letter.

Preacher was seriously considering responding to the letter personally but decided against it. He quickly realized that there weren't too many employers who would "foot the bill" and represent one of its own. But the military would. Since it was a legal matter he wanted the military legal "eagles" to handle it. And they did.

After a visit to the Fort Carson JAG office for a preliminary meeting with one of the lawyers, a letter was sent off to the Detroit law firm. It generally said that they sent the letter to the wrong "Malcolm Drexel Preacher." The young, white female lawyer who looked like she had just returned from a *Miss America Pageant* and slipped on an ACU assured Preacher that he would probably not hear from them again. She was right. That first letter was the only letter he received.

Preacher jumped from the sofa and entered the kitchenette to respond to the whistling that was coming from the café. Preacher poured the hot water in the mug with the coffee bag. While it brewed, he went back in the bedroom to retrieve his ACU, underwear and green army socks. After laying the items on the sofa, he went back to his coffee to finish prepping it. On the oak, farmhouse kitchen table was a container of apple turnovers that he had picked up from the post commissary night before last. One of these with some cold cereal would be his breakfast for the day.

Preacher grabbed a turnover, a bowl of *Sugar Bear,* and his mug and went back to the living room. After setting his breakfast on the glass top coffee table, Preacher proceeded like most mornings: to get dressed, eat and get caught up on some national news.

Preacher continued to listen to the broadcast until the weather report wrapped up. Afterwards, he reached for the universal remote to turn off the set and turn on his Sony system. Jamming 92.5 out of Denver would do for now since they were playing *Beyonce's "If I Were A Boy."* The radio would be less of a distraction than the TV, therefore allowing him to finish getting dress and ready to hit the door sooner, the gym bag still where he left it yesterday after work, would remain there today. He wouldn't need to change clothes again since he would not go to the gym today nor was this even a PT day. Today, would be a typical duty day.

The traffic on Academy Boulevard was as expected, heavy again during this time of the morning. Preacher wasn't late therefore he took the stop and go traffic with ease. What was surprising as he got near the post was the backup he saw on the approaching exit to Gate 4 to Fort Carson. He wasn't sure if there was an accident up ahead near or on the post or perhaps the military police were conducting a vehicle inspection this morning. The latter wouldn't make much sense since it would be more practical to do it after normal business hours as people left the post. That way half the post personnel, both military and civilian, would not be late while trying to report for duty.

He took no chances on being tied up in traffic just because somebody wasn't paying attention to the vehicle in front of them. Preacher decided to bypass his usual exit ramp and proceed on to Highway 115 where he would enter the post via the main entrance gate or Gate 1. Like most cities and communities, military installations usually have several means to enter them.

As he had hoped, the main entrance gate was virtually clear with the exception of three vehicles waiting to be cleared by one of four guards there. Fortunately, no vehicle inspection was being performed today or at least not this morning. Ninety seconds after arriving in the area and waiting in line, Preacher was at the entrance. The military policeman saluted the vehicle and allowed Preacher's Cavalier to proceed onto the post. The vehicle rode down Wilson Boulevard. There would be no delays as far as troop formations on this morning. Most troops like Preacher and his unit would be going straight to their respective units to attend their first formation of the day. Like his unit, other support units observed PT days on Monday, Wednesday and Friday.

After a little weaving around the garrison area of the post, Preacher arrived near the HHC area. He saw that the front parking lot was full and proceeded around to the rear parking lot. After having found a parking space, he double-checked his uniform while seated to ensure that all was in order. Preacher placed his keys in one of four pockets of his ACU field jacket and exited the vehicle.

By his watch, he had about ten minutes before "FALL IN." Preacher briskly walked from the lot across the street into the rear door of the unit building. He knew the barracks guys and/or the CQ were on top of things this morning. The smell of wax and bleach bombarded his nostrils. Fortunately he would not have to endure it much longer down the hallway approaching the front. He, like all the rest would soon find themselves not lingering inside on this chilly day but standing outside. Preacher greeted some senior NCOs as he exited through the main front doors of the unit from the inside.

Preacher barely had time to greet some of the soldiers in his section when he and the rest saw the first sergeant breach the building and proceeded to take his rightful place in the front of the formation. Before long and without saying a word like all other times the company of soldiers, mostly enlisted, were standing in front of the first sergeant.

The formation was brief, not a whole lot of activity taking place in the unit at the moment. There were some personnel temporarily assigned to some field units while on training exercises "down range" in Pinon Canyon but those were very few. Some people would say that a unit like HHC was a typical "rear line" unit. Meaning--in time of war--the unit would be so far to the rear about the only thing that could touch it would be some long range artillery round or nuclear explosion.

Up until Desert Storm a lot of people thought that very same thing. That was until some rear soldiers including Air Force personnel behind enemy lines were awakened to the impact of Scud missiles. Some of them even made direct contact with their sleeping quarters killing a few. And more recently the 507th Maintenance Company out of Fort Bliss, made known by names such as PFC Jessica Lynch and SP4 ShoShawna Johnson, was ambushed by insurgents during Operation Iraqi Freedom. Since then some soldiers' perception of a "rear line" unit like theirs has changed but not by a lot.

The formation area in the front of the unit building, usually plush green in the summer time, now appearing somewhat brownish from a combination of the bitter cold and the boot traffic of the troops hammered upon the grass was a lot more scattered now. All parties were now dismissed and reporting or should be reporting to their respective sections to start the busy day. The lower enlisted would do one of several things: Finish up any "details" or duty that wasn't accomplished prior to the company formation, go to the mess hall for breakfast or "chow" for those who had the time or simply go to work. Upper enlisted may do all of the above with the exception of the "detail" work.

There were some who would simply meet up at a nearby AAFES snack shop, similar to a coffee house or coffee shop, to shoot the breeze with each other before kicking off their work day. Some of these guys could stay there for hours killing most of their day before going to work. These were mostly "fuck ups" whose supervisors really didn't want them around anyway out of fear that they would mess up something. A lot of these guys, mostly E-6s and E-7s, throw-a-ways from the Combat Engineer and Infantry units due to mental or physical limitations, were just happy the army didn't kick them out and glad to be in a support unit to relax in and retire from. The majority of the ones, at least in HHC, were fortunate enough to leave more than adequate supervision of their respective section at the Replacement Detachment & Inprocessing Center.

Preacher now had started to slip on his field jacket immediately after formation. He cursed as he did so. He thought after all these years a better system would be worked out that would allow soldiers to wear their cold weather gear--whatever was appropriate--when the environment dictated it. "Maybe next year," he said.

Preacher headed to the Replacement Detachment & Inprocessing Center, building number 1218, in his vehicle. The distance between his unit headquarters and his workplace was about two to three miles. After parking his ride, Preacher retrieved his headgear and gloves and even grabbed a stick of spearmint gum from the glove compartment prior to leaving. He couldn't stand being caught with bad breath. Preacher learned early on in middle school that it wasn't a nice feeling for someone to tell you that you might want to switch mouthwash. Then again he wasn't sure which was worse. Some philly straight up telling you that or trying to carry a conversation when you noticed that her nose is inching up and her eyebrows are arching. That happened once and once was plenty.

He put on his black beret and gloves as he approached the main doors of the Replacement Center. He looked down the bright-lit hallway of yet another post-Vietnam era building and as usual the gray floor was shining. Twenty yards down the hallway and just after the sergeant major's office which housed the most senior enlisted person in the building was the door to Preacher's section, Personnel Automation.

The Replacement Center consisted of various operations to assist all new soldiers arriving at Fort Carson in the processing of themselves and as well as their family, when applicable. A *Personnel* section to handle new addresses, updating other records, insurance, emergency contact data and, if necessary, a new ID card. A *Medical* section to screen records for immunization, hearing tests and dental examinations. *Army Community Services* or ACS to provide welcome packets, information on counseling and citizenship requirements for family members. A *Housing* section provided a complete listing of available off-post housing. Those eligible may be placed on a list for government quarters at this time.

The *Transportation* group was responsible for making sure that the soldiers' household items from their last duty station was transported to their new housing. The *Finance* section was one most soldiers looked forward to seeing the most. If a pay advance was wanted or reimbursement for travel costs to Fort Carson was warranted then this was the section to process it. But, for any reason, if monies were due to the U.S. Army then it would be taken at this point as well. A section for bank representatives for anyone to open a new bank account.

Preacher fought the urge to go straight to the break room to get a cup of coffee as well as any pastries that someone may have brought in. This was usually the place where some who do arrive in the building early will meet to "bullshit" with each other until the first batch of soldiers are due in.

Men and women, mostly men, reminisced about the good "ole" days or the "old army" as they called it. There were few differences between the army of today and that of yesterday. You had a different uniform now than you did back then. There were different and newer equipment available.

Determined to make that one cup of coffee he had this morning do, Preacher removed his head gear and approached the secure door to Personnel Automation or PA. A military installation was full of offices, compartments and safes that had various means to access them. PA was one of those areas that had something other than a conventional lock to enter within. Indicative of the importance of what's inside was the large metal plaque that was prominently displayed to the right of the steel door.

THIS IS A RESTRICTED AREA -- NO TRESPASSING BEYOND THIS POINT. PHOTOGRAPHY IS PROHIBITED...

Slightly below Preacher's eye level and to the left of the door was a black five by ten inch square with buttons on it. The electronic keypad is designed to be easy to use while providing a high degree of security. One merely stands in front of the pad and after keying in there personal pin will enter the area within.

The numbers, three rows of three buttons, appeared on the keys using a light-emitting diode display. The numbers were not fixed in natural order—one, two, three on top, four, five, six in the middle and so on. The display could be scrambled every time the pad is used. The "one" may end up in the lower right hand corner, or the "nine" may be found dead center. Each user approached the keypad to find the numbers in a different configuration.

This scrambled effect combined with horizontal and vertical polarizing filters—to hamper side viewing of the display—made it virtually impossible for a person standing nearby or a potential intruder with long range detection equipment to capture an access code.

Preacher stooped to the same level as the keypad and slowly entered his pin. Two seconds later, he heard the locking mechanism release.

The Personnel Automation section consists of a number of people, commission and noncommissioned officers as well as lower enlisted. The duties of the section are simply to support the technological needs of the Replacement Center. These duties range from acquiring hardware and software based on the needs of its clients to programming and supporting the Replacement Center's Intranet and Internet web sites.

In a large secure room about the size of two double house trailers, the crew consists of one major, one lieutenant, one sergeant first class, one staff sergeant, two specialist fours and three privates ranging from pvt to private first class. Everyone with the exception of the commission officers have their own cubicles. The officers, of course due to their status and supposedly to better enhance the unique work that they do have actual offices. The SFC as well as the SSG does not have offices, but they do have enclosed cubicles with doors. This too was to allow the supervisors to be more productive but also due to them being supervisors they should also have some sort of privacy for personal conferences and personnel evaluations.

Each personal area comes equipped with a PC networked with the rest of the building. In fact, the administration of the main computers or servers as they call them is also performed by the staff. In particularly, it is the job of Information Technology Specialists who are solely responsible for this task. SPC Hodkins and Preacher have this particular MOS.

The interior of the Personnel Automation section was already fired up. The lights were on and all of the computers' cooling fans were humming. At the helm, this time of the morning, like most mornings, was SSG Hamilton. SSG Hamilton was originally from South Carolina and a divorced father to a high school-age son. The balding, white, forty-two year old, son of the Deep South pulled a few strings to somehow get assigned to this unit not to mention this section. SSG Hamilton's MOS was 92G-Food Service Specialist-- a cook. Preacher initially springed to the conclusion when he first got wind about the SSG coming to the section that he must be someone very bright or simply another big "fuck up." Units just didn't cough up their cooks like that unless they were "top heavy" with senior enlisted 92Gs. Preacher assumed the latter.

As it turned out, Preacher soon realized that the SSG was a computer geek "want to be." Not that Preacher or anyone else in the section considered themselves the stereotypical computer geeks. SSG Hamilton, who arrived in the section to fill a computer operator slot, had a strong interest in programming despite having little or no formal training in the field. Not even a one-day continuing education course was under his belt. He was simply an Army cook. One who lost interest in a profession that he held for twelve years. He simply couldn't see himself in the field and perhaps in the army for that much longer.

Preacher contemplated the plan may be that somehow if he could get into a marketable field he could easily disseminate into the civilian world in a family-supporting job and not flipping burgers some place. Preacher didn't see the SSG in the army that much longer either since it was not clearly known at least by the lower enlisted how a cook arranged to get in an automation section in the first place. Again, just another stop-off point.

Preacher thought maybe that that idea as well as it affecting his future well-being was always on Hamilton's mind. Preacher helped the SSG learn his operations duties within the section as often as he could. Then when he had the time, Preacher assisted him with picking up one or two programming languages. Despite the SSG out ranking him, Preacher discretely assigned the SSG projects that would normally go to Hodkins or himself to better enforce Preacher's tutoring. The SSG despite the workload was very appreciative.

In time, not only was the SSG handling his computer operation responsibilities but was also performing quite well on his assigned programming tasks. The section received the normal user comments and questions pertaining to the applications created by the SSG. The number of complaints concerning an application was always a good measuring stick to how good it was designed, coded, tested and presented to the users of it.

As the SSG worked on his projects, he couldn't help but notice how little or no calls, Preacher received concerning an application he worked on. Less than SPC Hodkins, too. The SSG was truly impressed with his tutor. He didn't see a lot of black men like Preacher and Hodkins where he grew up.

CHAPTER SIX

Preacher entered the cool interior of the closed section. This restricted area was the only section in the whole building that had air conditioning. The cool air was for the comfort of the servers. Of everything in the room, some people would include the personnel as well, the servers were the most important asset. They processed the data in and out of the center and when they or their software did not perform, PAS would know about it.

SSG Hamilton apparently heard the main door open because Preacher abruptly heard a chair move across the floor. "I know you're a sleep in here, sarge. I didn't mean to wake you up," shouted Preacher.

"Yeah, yeah, yeah!" replied the SSG. "I need to be sleep. I sure didn't want to come in this morning."

"I know how you feel, sarge." The two carried their conversations without yet seeing each other. Their line-of-sight were blocked by the cubicle walls and interior columns situated within the room.

Preacher proceeded down the short path, passing cubicles as he walked until he had reached SSG Hamilton's cubicle. "Well good morning, specialist," said the SSG while still looking at his monitor and keying in some commands at the keyboard.

"Morning, sarge." Pause. "You know that you were really downloading porn when I walked in the door just now. Now you're trying to pretend like you're working."

The two laughed at the statement. SSG Hamilton turned around in his chair and looked at Preacher. "You know that's really not a bad idea. I haven't been laid nor had a decent date in six months."

"Gee, I bet you're about to explode right now then?" asked Preacher. He had barely got the words out of his mouth without laughing.

"Not quite but I'm getting close."

Preacher cut short the morning pleasantries by asking the SSG how everything was running right now. Preacher liked a good joke like everybody else but he tried his best not to cross the lines between respecting and having a good professional relationship with his supervisors and being too personal with them. This included not socializing with any of his supervisors off-duty. It was easier for Preacher to have a mere professional rapport with them this way. In addition to creating and maintaining a good understanding with his supervisors, it made things a lot easier if he had to file a complaint on someone over a matter he thought warranted taking something to that level.

SSG Hamilton picked this up. He often invited Preacher to various hunting outings but Preacher always declined them. The SSG thought it was something related to race even though he never noticed him cling to other personnel. But his supervisors later told him the reason. The lieutenant told him that Preacher and he were talking about him attending night school to finish up his bachelors in Management Information Systems when the subject of Preacher not having a lot of free time to party came up.

The dimmed street lights of the post appeared to just fly by the outside of the late model Chevy blazer. Despite a lack of sleep and the feeling that the volcano in his stomach created by the drinking which started the night before would abrupt at any moment, Specialist Four Clarence Hodkins gave the appearance of being his usual vibrate self. He had to. It was amazing what a long, hot shower and some mouthwash could do. He certainly didn't want to come to work looking like he was drunk, raising suspicion and giving someone a reason to test his pee.

Just hours before, he had left his favorite off-post club with one of his companions and went home to hopefully catch an hour or two of sleep. Unlike Preacher, Hodkins depended a great deal on his alarm clock. Despite having a family with a strong work ethic and like everyone else had participated in the nine-week boot camp, Hodkins just hadn't been able to condition himself to awaken at the right time. But he also knew that staying out all night certainly doesn't help his cause in achieving it.

Like Preacher, Hodkins lived off-post as well, opting to leave the restraints of the post barracks for more freedom. He lifted his heavy foot and the vehicle appeared to Hodkins to just crawl. He won't have to endure it much longer because he was approaching the Replacement Center. Hodkins didn't know the consequences of him missing company formation this morning. If past history was any indication, he would merely be placed on some dirty work detail replacing another specialist or even a private on latrine duty for one or two days after everyone else left for home.

Eventually his absences got to the sergeant major's ear and punishment was handed down. The sergeant major of the Replacement Center was responsible for the operations of the Replacement Center and soldiers ran the Center therefore he has some say involving the troops. To keep the appearance that there was some type of order behind the secure door of the Personnel Automation Section and order and discipline weren't lost, Personnel Automation Section management somehow found out before the Sergeant Major did and by the time he catched wind of it, Hodkins' supervisor had already taken disciplinary action. It didn't take away the severity of Hodkins' actions but it looked better upon the section. And sometimes looks are everything.

Hodkins thought as he was approaching the parking lot that he shouldn't push his luck so. The excuses he has given were old and to his supervisor, they were irrelevant. If everyone else could make it to formation, so could he.

Both Hamilton and Preacher heard the main door open and close. "Wassup sarge, wassup Preacher," greeted Hodkins, still trying to act as alert as humanly possible despite what his body was actually telling him. SSG Hamilton and Preacher were immersed in a conversation going over the to-dos of the day.

"It's about time Special--ist four Hodkins, soon to be Pri - vate Hodkins," replied SSG Hamilton, emphasizing the word: private.

"Well, you know sarge, some of us have it like that," responded Preacher immediately making a sucking noise to imply that Hodkins sucked butt. Hodkins merely gave a pat on the back of the staff sergeant who was still seated in front of his PC and gave a hard but friendly stare at Preacher as he walked past the two of them. Even though there was plenty of room, somehow he managed to brush up against Preacher as he went down the hallway to his cubicle. This caused Preacher to stumble back.

"Excuse meeee, Specialist," said Hodkins. The SSG looked at Preacher and Preacher looked at him and they both started laughing.

"If I can be of any assistance to anyone I will be at my desk, working," said Hodkins. After hanging his field jacket on the back of his chair he logged on to the computer system and proceeded to work. The SSG and Preacher continued their chat.

The comments made to Hodkins by Hamilton and Preacher weren't true. Not that Hodkins cared. There were no discussions, as far as the two of them knew, of Hodkins being busted down to *Private* status. Nor did Preacher really believe that Hodkins, out of all people, brown nose to anyone. He certainly had his ways but he was a superb analyst and even with some rough edges, got along with his colleagues especially his supervisors.

His only major problem as far as Preacher saw was his tardiness. Hodkins and Preacher talked one on one about it especially when Preacher heard things in the grapevine but Hodkins would give his usual response of: "Fuck it!" and "If they want to kick me out, they can go ahead. I'm about tired of this shit anyway." But despite Preacher hearing the same old stuff from Hodkins he never got a sense that he meant it.

Hodkins "soldiered" just as hard as the next guy and played even harder during his off duty time, according to the women. He had "career" soldier written all over him. He could have a temper when he wanted and he could be very blunt at times to enlisted and officers alike but with the exception of some of his absentee justifications he would always tell the truth. He had a tendency to joke from time to time, but when it comes to knowing the army regulation related to a task. He would be right on the money. Particularly when it came to security regulations.

He would often frustrate officers who would try to intimidate him with their rank and position to gain computer access that wasn't necessary. That attempt on their part would be futile. Hodkins would quote a regulation to back up his argument and they would sometimes tell Hodkins to show them the reg and he would.

Out of frustration some officers would immediately storm out of the office. Others would try to seek atonement by going over his head and talking to his supervisor. Usually no relief would come from them either. His supervisors would often wish he would use a little tact but the outcome would still be the same. To make matters worse, sometimes the last face the officers would see is the smirk written on Hodkins' face. It would be one not of smiling but not a serious one neither. Hodkins would have the last word.

Sort of. Preacher would notice the visual exchange between some of the officers and Hodkins and he would later tell Hodkins that he needed to be careful. "You're riding a fine line." But he seemed to shrug it off.

At one time he told Preacher that he should be careful too. "You know some of them think that we all look alike anyway." The two got a big laugh out of that one. That statement wasn't a whole lot from the truth. There had been occasions when one of the officers called him or responded to Preacher as if he was Specialist Four Hodkins. They would later try to clean it up by saying that it must be the hair cut.

All soldiers had a nametag with large letters on the front of their uniform shirt. The perpetrators of this act usually had one thing in common as far as Preacher knew: they grew up in a sheltered environment. Or, at the very least, didn't grow up around many minorities.

SP4 Hodkins pecked at the keyboard and maneuvered his mouse as he tried his best to wrap up a personnel reporting project he was given last week. Considering he only received one phone call from one of his female friends and minor disturbances with his stomach that required a quick trip to the latrine, he made great progress with it. He wanted to wrap it up so he could have more play time. This was assuming he wasn't placed on some work detail like latrine duty or some odd and dirty job for being absent this morning. Officially it was Absent Without Leave or simply AWOL if someone really wanted to push it that far. He couldn't imagine that coming from anyone in this section but certainly from outside it. He knew that he had his fair share of "pay backs" in the unit and some were outside of it.

Hodkins rubbed his pinkish, irritated eyes. Tired of the current task at hand, not to mention staring at the monitor for a while now, Hodkins stopped. He sat, his face in the palm of his hands with his elbows rested slightly at an outward angle on the desk. His eyes were now closed and therefore provided a trigger for his brain to drift back to a time when his life was a little simpler.

Hodkins was from Clinton, Louisiana, a long way from Colorado. Like a lot of young boys in the hard working neighborhood where Hodkins grew up in, he was the product of a single mom household. His mother raised his younger brother, Chip and himself during the majority of their lives.

Their father, who left their mother when the boys were very young, lived in another city nearby but would call the boys about every two months or so. Other than small birthday gifts, the boys and mother received almost no financial support from their father. For whatever reason their mother didn't push for child support.

Growing up, Hodkins didn't quite understand why so many single mothers would not try to get monetary support for their children from the fathers. He always thought that the more money you had the more you could do for your children. But whether the request for support was coming from the mothers or from the government one was bound to get something eventually, no matter how small it was.

The contact that Hodkins and his little brother had with their father was apparently enough for them because neither of the boys growing up expressed any desire to visit since their first visit with their father.

That visit was more like an introduction to the rest of the family than a "let's get to know you" meeting. Their father was more interested in making sure that the children knew each other than him. There was no real discussion about how was your mother, what did they like to eat, what subjects in school were their favorite, etc. None of that took place. Even though his wife and their daughters—Clarence and Chip's half sisters, all three of them--treated them well, they felt uncomfortable at the picnic, like outsiders and had no desire to repeat it. For a long time all contact with their father and his new family was by telephone and by mail.

The boys had discussed their discomfort with their grandmother-- on their mother's side--and she talked their mother into not making the boys visit their father. "They need to do that on their own conditions. When they're ready to see him. They will, but on their own terms," their grandmother told their mother.

"What did he expect to happen when you leave your family like that," she snapped. "This is not *Burger King*, he can't have it his way." They both had to laugh at that one. "Unlike a lot of young boys they at least know where he's at," she continued.

Hodkins was only an average student at his high school, East Bayou High. About the only thing he really did well in was track & field. He broke several of his school's track and field records such as the 100 meters and even competed at State competition. Even though quite good, he really didn't see a future in track. He really didn't see how it could take him away from the town he grew up in. Although a nice place to raise a family, he thought there had to be more in the world than working at two of Clinton's largest employers: Dixon Correctional Institute and Hawco Manufacturing Company.

Hodkins had no desire to ensure the local criminals were fed, tucked away in their beds or risk getting shanked by one of them. Nor produce industrial buckets. But this was what Clinton of East Feliciana Parish had to offer. Hodkins wanted to see a little of the world, its people and possibly learn a marketable trade. After a long discussion with his mother, grandparents and even his little brother, Hodkins contacted an Army recruiter.

"Wake up over there, Hodkins!" shouted Preacher over several cubicles. "I hear you picking on the keyboard but I know you're faking it. You couldn't possibly be working on anything of great importance." Preacher paused as if to hear whether or not he had broken Hodkins' keyboard stride. "No one would trust you to work on any of their important projects."

Despite everyone knowing that Preacher was joking about his friend, laughter broke out. That created a nice mental break before lunch. After a few more insults being tossed around from nearly all of the enlisted personnel, the last one was again to Hodkins. It was graciously returned with a single, reverse finger by Hodkins. Everyone within PAS then prepared for lunch.

"Anyone needs a ride to the mess hall?" barked one of the specialists. After seconds of silence, the specialist exited the door alone. The only enlisted personnel left were a private who desired to skip lunch, Hodkins and Preacher. Preacher rose up from his own desk and after retrieving a report from the printer, he grabbed his own jacket getting ready to exit for lunch. He saw Hodkins still at his desk and proceeded over there.

"Hey man, are you going to lunch?"

"Yeah dude. I need to finish this reporting module while everything is clicking together for me. If I don't and I come back from lunch all those good, intelligent thoughts may just go away."

"Yeah, I know what you're saying," replied Preacher. "I've had times like that myself. You either use it while it's there or risk losing it forever."

"You got it my man." He turned his head and looked at Preacher, declining Preacher's offer for lunch if, in fact, that was one.

"OK, I'll catch you la' ta' my man." With that said, Preacher departed PAS.

Looking above the cubes, Hodkins watch Preacher as he exited the section and entered the main hallway of the center just before the swinging door severed his view.

Hodkins liked Preacher a lot. Probably a lot more than Preacher ever knew. Or did he? What was that scene in the shower stall about? Was that a stare or was it something Hodkins wanted it to be? As tired as he was that morning, he wasn't sure what if anything happened between Preacher and him.

Preacher never struck him as being gay or bi. No, he wasn't displaying the classic, stereotypical signs of being gay. You had to look for a lot more than the limp hand, the high pitched voice or the switching of the ass in this day and age. Especially if you wanted to stay in "this man's army." This Don't *Ask, Don't Tell, Don't Pursue, Don't Harass* policy was indeed a joke. Hodkins *had* the friends to show for it.

Upon getting caught up in a sting set up by the Army's Criminal Investigative Division or CID, a couple of Hodkins' friends were caught by undercover investigators at one of the enlisted clubs. They supposedly tried to come on to the investigators. That was a big No, No.

"Don't Pursue" was intended to stop the infamous witch hunts against lesbian, gay and bisexual service members. Commanders' inquires, not criminal investigations, were supposedly the preferred method of handling allegations of homosexual conduct. Commanders began inquiries only if they had credible information that a basis for discharge existed. Inquiries had to be limited to the allegations that have been made, not used as an excuse to launch fishing expeditions into every aspect of service members' private lives or to seek out other people who might be gay, lesbian or bisexual.

The "Don't Pursue" provision was the least well understood in the field, so the witch hunts continued. Some service members were even threatened with prison if they did not name names or confess to being gay themselves. The military was allowed to discharge people even when military investigators violated the current limits on gay investigations and conduct an improper witch hunt. Violating the policy, officially called the Department of Defense Homosexual Conduct Policy, constituted dereliction of duty. That was a crime punishable by confinement of up to and including six months, a bad-conduct discharge, and reduction to private and forfeiture of two-thirds pay for six months.

The Pentagon recently expanded harassment to include verbal and physical assault, military cadences or jody calls, anti-gay graffiti, comments and slurs. Those who harassed and those who condoned harassment *should* be held accountable under current policy. The service members who reported harassment to the proper authorities within their chain of command and who did not reveal their sexual orientation when doing so *should* not be investigated.

Preacher could be bi or gay, right? Hodkins kept trying to convince himself but to no avail. He hoped that his friend was but he was sure that Preacher wasn't. He and many others could put a lot of people on that list of possibilities and Preacher would be dead last on it. He neither had the look, the demeanor or the character. He realized that wasn't enough to come to a final conclusion but Preacher didn't give him a whole lot to work with. He was usually a very private person. Friendly, but private. He could very well be on the "down low," Hodkins thought.

It was definitely lunch time. The stampede of officers and enlisted made their way to their cars to eventually be part of a larger group of people waiting their turn in lines at their favorite restaurant, shoppette or mess hall on post. Regardless of the post or base whether it was an Army, Air Force, Marine or Navy installation, there simply weren't enough eateries during chow time.

A lot of people lived off post so the breakfast and dinner crowd is a much different than the lunch crowd. Not a whole lot of people chose to make the round trip trek to and from their off-post homes just for lunch unless they were leaving early anyway.

Preacher had made it through the main doors and was headed towards the front stairs when he saw Specialist Four Petersen standing by herself at the right corner of the building with a bottle of water in her hand, taking a break and soaking up some rare sunlight. Looking at her facial expression, it would seem she had a lot on her mind.

Preacher normally ate lunch alone, with the exception of the rare occasions when he may go with Hodkins or someone else in PAS. But today he didn't feel like eating by him and decided to ask Petersen if she would like to have lunch with him.

CHAPTER SEVEN

It was all very odd, SFC Randall McCullen thought as he looked at the Class A uniform his wife had delivered to him to wear to his preliminary hearing. In the past, the "monkey" suit was just something he had to wear while traveling and during inspections. Most soldiers scorned them, possibly due to the irregularity of their wear. Like a kid only wearing a suit to Sunday school, he didn't feel comfortable wearing it despite it making him look whether nice looking.

With the Class As, just like in Sunday school, if it didn't look just right, the discrepancies would be pointed out. There was a whole manual, believe it or not, covering the wear and appearance of that uniform and others. It covered everything from the haircut to the shoes. His wife knew this too. In addition to the clothes, she also delivered his shoe and brass polishing kit. The brass insignias and array of service medals and ribbons that were often fitted on the chest of the jacket were considered part of the uniform. If it was in your personnel file, then it was part of the uniform. Period.

He wasn't really sure how his wife was dealing with the situation. His wife, in the past, would take him for his word assuming that these females that her husband interacted with at work were simply jealous, not to mention under-educated.

"'Till death do us part,' right Randy?" she would say.

"Till death do us part," he would acknowledged and that would be that. The last time she said that, SFC McCullen noticed it was said with no emotion.

When caught red handed with other women, those words were so comforting to him. A confirmation that he got away with his mischief. But could his wife, a smart and beautiful lady who gave him one wonderful child, be that naïve all this time? He knew the answer to that. She had to know.

Now he was counting on his Class As to at least make him appear like a proud human being. Not to mention a disciplined soldier. To somehow dismiss what the mass media had played him out to be: an animal. He would love to walk into the courtroom with his lovely wife by his side and just say that the young lady has made a mistake that it wasn't rape but consensual. The latter would initially be hard for his wife but at least he wouldn't be in prison. Or at least, not for long. But that would not happen, at least in whole. Unlike a civilian proceeding, he would come in the courtroom alone and face the judge.

It was never supposed to be this bad. McCullen took off his prison uniform and started putting on the Class As.

He had made up his mind what he was going to do, what he had to do, and he had plenty of time lately to think about it. He needed to because he didn't want to break down and cry if he tried nothing and went to prison for a long time because of it.

Nor did he want to look over and see his wife there, a look of pathetic, disgust on her face, as if she was questioning why she had ever involved herself with him in the first place. That is if she even showed. He had spoken to her on the phone the other day, apologized and told her what he had decided. She didn't respond to what he was saying, as though she wasn't even listening, disconnected from events.

"I'm sorry about what happened," he said softly. "I was just... just..."

"Don't worry about it, Randy," she said. She didn't say much else. She told him she wasn't sure if she would come or not, then she hung up, simply hung up as if he were not in jail but at one of his boys' place and could call her right back. It must be all that media that's getting to her, he thought. That had to be it.

He pulled the trousers up and buttoned them. He was surprised that they fit him as before. The food wasn't that great. Either he wasn't getting the same bad chow shipped over from the nearby mess hall or his appetite just wasn't there.

The night before, his appointed JAG attorney, a young, red haired, slinky-built guy who appeared to have just graduated from West Point had briefed him on the strategy based on his decided plea.

After McCullen finished dressing himself, he looked in the mirror. It wasn't actually a mirror, but a reflective piece of metal, bolted to the wall, that reminded him of a fun house mirror. He looked rather "GQ-ish" in a way, if that could be said about Class A uniform. McCullen posed from side to side and front to back. He and the uniform didn't look half bad, he vainly thought. He pushed the thoughts of *Gentlemen's Quarterly* out of his head and reality sneaked back in again as he continued to get ready.

It happened to be a clear sunny day and McCullen looked up and felt the warmth of the sun on his face as the military police escorted him out the front door of the Provost Marshall office. In the front, sitting alongside the manicured lawn with a sprinkling of multi-color annuals for touch, awaited two clean, army green sedans.

The flowers were laid out by the post's civilian engineers but more than likely done by the Officer's Wifes club. Projects like that were usually publicized in the post newspaper, *The Mountaineer*.

The one sedan in the front of the driveway appears to be an escort vehicle with at least two military policemen inside. The second had a driver still seated in the front and an MP posted just outside the passenger door apparently awaiting the escort detail.

The military police went all out as far as McCullen could tell. Each as far as he could see wore the ceremonial black, glossy helmet with individual rank and unit insignias. Both shiny as well.

As the MP in charge of the escort relayed a whisper to one of the MPs in the lead sedan, McCullen stared at the flickering of lights at NORAD, which sat along the mountain at his 3 o'clock position. I wonder how are the personnel inside the complex starting their day, he pondered. "Probably awaiting the news of his hearing today," he muttered.

There wasn't a single cloud in the sky, and it was almost as if nature was mocking him, teasing him, letting him know that there would always be sunny days, even while he was behind bars.

McCullen found himself being ushered to the second sedan and seated in the rear like a mother attending an infant in a car seat. After some brief words with his superiors, the MP in charge of the escort detail was seated next to SFC McCullen and he signaled the lead sedan to leave. McCullen departed the grounds with old glory waving in the wind.

Preacher was now wondering if asking Petersen to have lunch with him was a bad idea. He had been waiting in the car now for about 10 minutes and still no sign of her. With just occasional glances, he eagled the main door.

After changing the radio station from Jazz to R & B, he saw Petersen appear from the main doors of the Replacement Center. Preacher noticed that she appeared a little more refreshed than she did moments earlier. Definitely had a little more pep in her step.

"Sorry about being a little late but sarge had me check a file just as I was grabbing my purse," Petersen told him while buckling up. It was said without any genuine remorse. She knew Preacher would understand. Preacher was annoyed about the delay but didn't show it. He couldn't stand waiting for people and didn't like the thought of someone waiting for him.

"No problem. What would you like for lunch?" said Preacher, while exiting the parking lot.

Petersen paused for a moment before answering, "I thought we were going to the mess hall." Goapele's *Milk & Honey* was coming from the radio.

"What gave you that idea?"

"Well...I...I assumed—"

"What about fried chicken and mashed potatoes. I feel like having a hardy lunch today. But since you're the guest, I will leave it up to you," Preacher said. "Unless you really do want to go to the mess hall for lunch."

"No, no, no...I like your idea much better—-smart-alec," replied Petersen with a grin on her face.

"Okay then, we'll go to that Neon Sports Saloon, if that's okay with you?"

"Oh. Okay, I've been their once. It has some descent food."

The ride to building 6287 was uneventful. Under different circumstances, McCullen thought it would even be boring. His escorts held not even conversations. With the exception of the occasional metal-against-metal that was heard on someone's uniform, not a sound was made inside the vehicle. Only the tire noise impeded the silence of the trip. The silence reminded him of the movie "*Dead Man Walking*" starring Sean Penn and Susan Sarandon.

The news crews were camped out in a roped off section of the Judge Advocate General's parking lot. Some in cars, others in news vans fully equipped with the necessary equipment to beam out their reports to home base. Everyone appeared to be represented: *ABC, CBS, NBC, PBS, FoxNews, BBC, CNN, CourtTV* and some radio stations. Even a Japanese crew appeared among the newsmongers. Everyone sitting and waiting to be the first to get the "big scoop" of the day.

Today, the Judge Advocate General building and lot, building 6287, became host to an Olympics of UCMJ legal jousting. Not since the Aberdeen rape trials did so many of the media flock on an army base. The major networks were already set up for live feeds. Some were even feeding their morning shows earlier today.

Strands of thick television cables and wires circled like worms around JAG. They formed spider webs within the designated area in preparation for the many newscasts, which would use JAG for their backdrop.

The Fort Carson Public Affairs Office had even arranged with JAG personnel to ensure that the media had access to the courtroom during and after hours. This also gave them access to the latrine facilities as well. It was, in part, requested by the major TV media to allow them to broadcast live portions of their nightly newsmagazines. NBC's *Dateline* producers initially made a request to Fort Carson's PA office and were flatly denied. But their request was eventually granted after they pleaded with the Post Commander's staff. Fort Carson had enough problems now without additional bad press from the major TV and print media.

The two-vehicle convoy arrived just two blocks from the JAG building. McCullen couldn't believe what he saw. He could not possibly believe that the reason all these vehicles and people were here to view him. McCullen leaned his body slightly forward in his seat, to the point where his guard used his arm to settle him back. Without a word spoken, McCullen complied. His escorts didn't appear surprised at the entire scene. They acted like this trip had been performed many times before. Perhaps they had done earlier trial runs of this trip, McCullen thought.

If the crime he was accused of didn't sink in earlier, the sight of the media and the attention they brought certainly did the trick. The gravity of his situation now came to light. McCullen's heart was now beating so fast that he was sure the MP sitting arm-to-arm with him felt it. If he did, he certainly didn't give any indication of it. McCullen slowly put his hands slightly above his stomach to feel just how fast it was beating.

He had hoped that this move would not attract the attention of his guard but that too wasn't so. The MP looked slightly towards McCullen without making direct eye contact and politely told him to put his hands down. The MP in charge, seated in the front, heard this as well and turned to look at his guy for a couple of seconds. He turned around to face the attention of Fort Carson's new guests after getting a nod that everything in the back seat was okay.

The convoy proceeded to the rear of the JAG building. After some skillful maneuvering around vehicles and people, the sedans were met by a number of MPs awaiting their arrival. McCullen was once again flabbergasted as the number of people including MPs assisting the entourage with their arrival. He saw a mix of both MP and apparently legal personnel from the looks of it. With the exception of a meager few, the majority of the media were in the front.

The MPs that were posted at the rear of the building had now guided the convoy to their preassigned parking spaces. Before the sedan had made its dead stop, the MP in charge bailed out of the vehicle to meet one of his men who was waiting for him. Brief but precise words were exchanged then he ran back to his vehicle.

To make sure that the transfer of his prisoner from the sedan to the JAG building went as smooth as possible, the two sedans were comfortably surrounded by military police equipped with their trusted sidearm, the M-9 pistol. Unlike at some civilian trials as well as hearings, security of the accused especially of military crimes of this type tend to be very tight. Making sure no harm came to the accused whether by someone else or him or herself. If just being on a military installation wasn't intimidating enough for anyone thinking of starting trouble, being on the receiving end of MP's directives that were now being "barked" in the area to stay away during the transfer would do it.

The MP opened the door to allow McCullen to exit the sedan. "Watch your head as you exit and don your headgear!" were the instructions ordered to McCullen. McCullen complied and was held by the arms by his guards, as he was shepherd to the rear of the building with the final destination being the courtroom within it.

As he was being whisked away to the building, McCullen looked around frantically to see if he could spot his wife and child. He didn't see them as he was arriving in the car, but he thought they might have been waiting in one of the vehicles that were parked.

He looked to his front; he looked to both sides and did not see them. Soon he found himself at the top of the stairs. "They must be already inside," he thought. "They wouldn't want to face the circus outside no more than absolutely necessary. The MPs would have escorted them as well inside away from the media." McCullen had disappeared within the interior of the JAG building.

Neon Sports Saloon was a sports bar located in the "banana belt" of Fort Carson, location in the area of the post that was the shape of a banana on all military maps. Fairly new to the post, it quickly established a reputation for its games, contests and weekend dancing. The name "Saloon" could be a little misleading. It could give one the idea that it's just full of western hicks. The "Saloon" pulled in soldiers of all types with all backgrounds despite its southwest décor, what would one expect to find in Colorado.

Upon entering the establishment, Petersen and Preacher went straight to an available booth. Having someone greet you at the door was rare considering the atmosphere was usually informal and buzzing with military types. The two were seen by a young lady dressed in a blue jean shirt and kaki pants as she was carrying a tray of empty glasses to the rear of the bar. She said, "Sit anywhere you like. Someone will be right there." She was probably the wife of an officer or a high-ranking NCO.

The Civilian Personnel Office tended to give the spouses of military personnel priority to base jobs assuming they met the qualifications and the positions didn't fall under some "bid out" contract.

As the two walked across the main floor and maneuvered around a couple of soldiers shooting darts, Preacher trailed Petersen and couldn't help but notice the fragrance of her perfume. Now viewed without her headgear on, her long hair was now swept back and brooch with a wooden hairpin. Her make up was in keeping with her brown eyes and smooth, bronze complexion. Petersen wasn't like some females who would wear bright lipstick on top of a dark complexion, giving them the appearance of a clown.

The booth, designed for four, gave the two plenty of room to sit their field jackets and headgear. Petersen sat and was about to say something when two people at the bar in civilian clothing caught her attention. They were signaling her to get Preacher's attention.

Preacher's eyes were temporarily occupied by one of four strategically placed satellite-connected TVs in the place showing ESPN highlights of the Williams sisters participating in a doubles match some place warm. "Preacher, I think the two guys at the bar know you," whispered Petersen. Preacher, still locked on the TV was hesitant but did look back to Petersen. She nodded her head to the left with a smile that also caused Preacher to show some teeth as well before looking towards the bar.

The two gentlemen at the bar appeared to have been there for a while. Their beer glasses were almost empty and they had their fair share of leftover chicken wings in front of them. Without apparently asking, the bartender arrived with a fresh pair of glasses complete with beer.

Preacher immediately recognized the two gents. He raised his hands, gesturing a "hello." One of the men even nodded his head forward and winked his eye. Preacher merely chuckled at the hint and that was the end of the man-to-man communication.

Petersen was pretending to be looking around the place until she had Preacher's complete attention. Still smiling, "What was that all about?"

"Those are two young warrant officers I met at the Replacement Center a while back. They made a big stink about their orders upon arrival here and being assigned to our automation section as opposed to running a supply section as part of 7th Infantry Division. I happen to be in the office during lunch when my major asked me to assist him with getting the appropriate documentation from their personnel file downloaded from Army Headquarters to here."

Preacher glanced at them again but tactfully. He continuing, "I mean, you could tell these guys and the major were in a heated argument concerning their permanent assignments. Anyway...about an hour on the phone with his counterpart at Fort Belvoir after getting transferred from HQ, they got everything straightened out. Talk about pressure." Preacher played with a napkin while taking a deep breath. "I'm in this room with three officers waiting for answers after a heated conversation, on the line with HQ and tension you could cut with a knife."

The same young lady they saw upon entering the place stopped at their table. "Are we set to order now?"

"Sure," said Petersen, "I'll have the chicken and rice, please."

"And your drink?"

"I'll take a Coke."

"Will that be all?"

"Yes, thanks."

After final notations in her order book, she brought her attention to Preacher. "And you, Specialist?"

"I'll have the fried chicken and mash potatoes, please." "I'll have a Coke as well."

"Okay, then folks. That should be about fifteen minutes," the lady said while ripping out the order and walking once again to the rear of the bar.

Preacher noticed the beautiful smile on Petersen's face. There were not too many females in the Army that could truly say that they could really look good in ACUs. Petersen was an exception.

Before Preacher's mind began to drift, he was reminded of what he was talking about before they were interrupted. "Oh! Yeah! Before I forget. What some commissioned officer was trying to do was this. Despite the two young warrant officers, I think they're W2s, having their assignment already arranged prior to leaving their former post, the necessary paperwork was not processed on this end when it was supposed to.

This officer, a captain I think, was trying to cover his butt by giving these brothers the shaft by sticking them in an infantry unit. Fortunately, the brothers were smart enough to be carrying a memo signed by a *full bird* colonel along with their PCS orders stating where they were to be assigned. I was instructed to make some phone calls and query a certain personnel database to confirm what they were saying as well."

The story didn't initially stand up and grab Petersen by the shoulders but her interest was now aroused. "The chiefs were not assigned to your section or I would have recognized them. So where did they end up at?"

Preacher continued, "These young chiefs got somebody's attention here because they ended up at the MMC." He quickly picked up from the blank face that had now plastered on her face that she was unfamiliar with HHC/MMC.

Headquarters and Headquarters Company/Materiel Management Center was the center that all of Fort Carson's equipment from paper clips to non-nuclear weapons were ordered through. "Materiel Management Center is housed in one of the older string of white buildings near the McGrath Avenue gate. Its exterior appearance can be a bit misleading to those of us who are aware of the type of work in one of the sections there."

The waitress brought two glasses of water now caught Petersen's attention. Preacher said "thank you" without looking at the waitress or even looking up for that matter. Petersen sipped her glass while Preacher looked on.

"Which is what, may I ask?" Petersen was pretty sure it had something to do with his job or closely related because a glow in Preacher's eyes appeared to be there.

"Inventory Management!" said Preacher. He made a gesture with his right hand now for emphasis. "Basically ordering for the post. Nothing sexy about that. But, it's how they're doing it that impresses me."

"And how are they're doing it, Preacher?" Petersen had now brought herself forward in the booth and rested both of her elbows on the wooden table. With the occasional glances at her glass of water on the table and at the décor, her eyes appear to be in direct line of sight with Preacher's.

Preacher was now caught up in the story. "They have a IT staff." "That's Information Technology—"

"I know what I.T. stands for," said Petersen. "I do read from time to time. Pretty soon I hope to be finished with the Dr. Seuss series before I move on to something more challenging."

"They have a staff of about twenty people. Of--" He had finally got the joke and started chuckling, "You think you're funny don't you? I.T. could have meant 'International Terrorism.'"

Petersen laughed as well but also to how Preacher reacted when he had registered to what she had said. "Anyway, the staff consists of obviously officers and enlisted whose primarily tasks is making sure that Fort Carson's supply needs are taking care of within the constraints of checks and balances. Some of this work is done on windows-based PCs but the bulk of the work is performed on large-scale servers processing applications programmed in-house. All of the applications are uniquely developed by some of these officers and enlisted." Preacher took a sip of water.

"I am told that they go to schools all over the country both civilian and military to hone their existing technical skills as well as learn new ones.

"I found out shortly after arriving here on post that their was a real reason for the existence of that section. About five years ago, some supply clerk at one of the armament units was entering the supply orders in the procurement system at that time. He or she thought they were entering the code for fluorescent lamps but two of the digits were transposed. Nevertheless, the order still went through.

Well, about a month later. A very large item was being delivered on post but the driver wasn't sure where to drop it off despite having the address with him."

"What was the problem?" asked Petersen.

"Well, the problem was the clerk transposed those digits. He or she ordered an anchor for a navy battle cruiser. Can you just imagine how big that thing was?"

"No way!"

"Yep. That's what they ordered. That's what they got. Well, not exactly. That matter obviously got to the highest levels on post and arrangements were quickly made to 'Return To Sender.' After that, the post commander summoned his staff and the key supply personnel on post. He instructed them to make the necessary arrangements so that that would not happen again. Behold! The Materiel Management Center was born. And it all came out of a single mistake from a clerk."

Petersen noticed that Preacher was obviously envious of that crew. "Have you thought about talking to someone about transferring over there? I mean, you certainly got the skills for it--I presume."

"Psst," he muttered. "Are you kidding me? Get transferred from the Replacement!" Preacher now shook his head. "The last time I mentioned to my supervisor about the possibility of being transferred to MMC, I was *asked* to see the major in his office.

He didn't raise his voice or threatened me in any way. But he made it very clear that under no circumstances would he allow me to just transfer out of PAS." Preacher chuckled again as if he had heard another joke from the two guys that were playing darts.

"What's funny?" replied Petersen.

"After I had risen up and was making my way to the door to leave, he said this very smooth but precise: 'There is one way you can get transferred.' I remember I looked at him like a kid getting two suckers but only asking for one. 'And that is to 3rd Brigade.' At the time I didn't know who they were but he clarified it for me. 'Infantry. 3rd Brigade Combat Team to be exact.' With that said, I left the office and I never inquired about that again. I...AM...NOT field material. I can stand going on a Field Training Exercise or FTX for two weeks out of three hundred and sixty-five days. I don't like it but I can stand it. But spending nine months out of the year is another.

Besides, infantryman probably translates into security guard any way according to the *Occupational Outlook Handbook*. I would like to do more than walk around someone's mall armed with a radio and hear rugrats all day."

Petersen was now grinning from cheek to cheek. "I guess he told you, Preacher."

Preacher was now seated back against the fabric-covered back rest within his side of the booth. His arms were extended and fingers interlaced. "Yes, Petersen, he certainly did."

Preacher had almost forgotten about that event until now. The sarcastic way it was delivered. The expression on the face of the major when he said it. Perhaps he was making sure that he "nipped" any ideas of Preacher wanting a transfer out of his head once and for all. And if he delivered it right. Preacher might even tell the rest of his coworkers concerning the exchange about his experience and they two, will forget any ideas about wanting to leave their cushy jobs.

Petersen was now using her fingernail that was glistening with bright red polish to trace the grains of the wooden tabletop. Preacher noticed that now she appeared to be in thought or perhaps listening intently to the sounds of Mariah Carey's *Obsessed* coming from speakers that were strategically placed throughout the room. It was hard to tell for sure which one but if he were to bet, he would say the former. Her eyes with its dead stare would betray her.

"Aren't you afraid that you gonna break that nail?" Preacher paused briefly. "You apparently invested a lot of time on that one."

Petersen looked up. "No. Not really."

Preacher knew that that nail had no more polish on it than the rest but was just trying to get her talking. Petersen was still playing with the grain. Her big smile had faded away. She looked at Preacher eye to eye.

"What do you want out of life, Preacher?"

Preacher was caught off guard. Before he could respond she spoke again. "I mean--I see you, for instance, headed out to school sometimes from the Center after work. Sometimes in uniform, sometimes in civies." She played with the grain. "Despite you soldiering and all like a good specialist, perhaps like even a good sergeant--God knows we need a few of them here. You don't strike me as a 'lifer.' I can see a lot of people in our unit as a lifer but not you."

"I hope that was a compliment," said Preacher, smiling.

Petersen returned the same smile. "It was." She looked around the room observing the people while she took in the music. Then her attention was back at the table.

"I have just been in long enough to know the type. You're smart and seem to have plans that don't include the U.S. Army. Okay. How close to the mark am I?"

"That is a very good observation of me, Petersen. I didn't think that you, of all people, was watching me that close. You don't seem like the type that would be after--."

"Someone like you," Petersen stopped him in his tracks. "The 'hoochie-mama' after a conservative brotha like yourself."

She could tell she really got Preacher off guard. "Relax, Preacher. I know about some of the stuff people say about me. Most of it is because most people don't know me either. I mean the *real* me."

They both took a drink of water. Preacher was sure that he had thought that to himself but didn't know that he had mentioned that word to someone else.

"I know that sometimes when I go out, I tend to dress let's say, 'more freely.' But that's just my way of escaping the restrictions that are put upon us daily." Petersen sat back against her own back rest. "We all have our own way of dealing with life's problems. As far as my dress code and demeanor, I can be a lady when I want to and I can be 'free' when I want." Pause. "As long as it doesn't interfere with my military responsibilities. Wouldn't you say so, Preacher?"

"Yes...Yes...I would say so. You're right on all points. We all have our own way of dealing with issues. Some of us are better than others. I'm not one who is saying that I'm doing all the right things but I'm managing. Military life is different than most people realize. It can be fun and adventurous and it can be darn right stressful."

Petersen mentally noted that he didn't cuss.

"You are right about me also as far as my plans," he continued. "I don't plan to stick around too much longer when I receive my degree from *Regis*. The Denver campus has a branch on 2330 Robinson Street, right off highway 24. That's where my night courses are held. They are eight-week semesters. That's considered accelerated courses. If I'm taking two courses a night, I get out of there around 2200 hours and hopefully get in bed by midnight. If I have one class a night, I could get out by 2000 hours.

I soldier to the extent that I can. And do a pretty good job of it, I think." Preacher let out a sigh. "But there are so many things that come with my cushy job that I just don't like."

"Like?" asked Petersen. "Like the fact that most of the enlisted are forced to live in post-World War II buildings. Even though I currently do not live in them now. I have and I could very well be pulled back in at the choosing of the unit command."

Petersen looked on as her companion talked. "The Army, if you haven't figured it out, is not that keen on 'personnel management' like I have noticed with the Air Force. The Army just doesn't utilize their people and resources to the point of achieving efficiency. For instance, the Center duty roster that's in place there. All the lower ranking enlisted are assigned to the roster at some point in order to make sure that the latrine and hallway are cleaned daily."

Preacher was now getting more and more intense as he spoke. A nerve had definitely been touched. "Now, instead of hiring someone at minimum wage to do this after hours, the Army would rather have soldiers stop what they're doing about an hour before the day ends just to make sure that these duties are completed. Why? Just because." Petersen also detected some tension in his voice and demeanor and she grinned. Preacher noticed but he fired on, "Just because soldiers before us did it and those before them. 'Just because' doesn't make it right. Doing things just because it's always been that way." Preacher took another sip of water.

"The Army can certainly take a few lessons from the Air Force as far as personnel management is involved. I sometimes go to Petersen Air Force base for dinner. 'Just because' it's different. And one day I was sitting at one of the tables in their cafeteria. They don't call them 'Mess Halls' there. And this airman and I started a conversation. It's usually pretty easy to do so because they don't get too many Army types in there. They kinda look at you as a novelty.

"We talked about his job and I talked about mine. When I got to the part about this roster, he started laughing but was certainly not surprised. He told me he had heard a lot about some of the stuff we do in the U.S. Army.

By contrast, contract civilian employees perform duties such as these. To his knowledge, it's been that way forever. Does the Army brass know about this? Sure they do. But if something has been a tradition for decades, why change it?" Preacher cased the room. He pursed his lips and focused on to Petersen.

"Now, you would think that in this day of trying to retain as many smart and educated soldiers as possible, one would concentrate just a little on eliminating extended foreign duty tours, increase in pay, improve the standard of living for the lower enlisted and do away with these menial extra duties because they don't help morale at all."

Preacher let out a sigh again, looked at his half empty glass then back at his lunch date. "Are you finished now? Have you vented for the day? Now tell me what you really think," said Petersen. Both of them had to chuckle at that one. But soon the chuckling had stopped. Petersen looked at Preacher again.

"What do you want out of life?" she repeated. Preacher realized that he really didn't answer her question at all and she knew it. *What is she fishing for?* he thought.

"My needs are basically simple. I would love to position myself professionally and personally to be able to provide for my future family. Be able to support my mate and my mate, support me." He sipped his water.

"Just have a happy life and provide some things to any future children that I didn't have available to me when I was growing up." Pause. "That's it, Petersen."

Petersen looked at her glass of water too and then back up at Preacher, caught up in the moment, totally oblivious as to everything around her. "Speaking of mate. Are you seeing anyone now?"

Preacher still setting back looked up at some lights to the rear of Petersen and back. "No. Not seeing anyone at all. I have some female friends but they are just that. Friends. Not to make any excuses or anything but between work and school, I don't have that much free time. And besides, all of the girls on this post--"

"Excuse me?" snapped Petersen in her most feminine voice.

"I'm sorry. Ah! Women truly know that they beat out the men at least three to one. And some of them say it. Therefore, they can be as picky as they want to be. You have to agree on that point, right?"

"Okay, okay. I'll agree to that but not every woman is ready to just jump on any man just because she can be finicky and the numbers are on her side."

Preacher wondered if Petersen was truly one of these women and whether or not she was trying to tell him that she was interested in him and available.

"Petersen, I have seen young, white girls come through the Replacement Center that I knew were real 'country.' To the point probably that they had to have come from the hills of Tennessee or Kentucky or someplace. I mean, I would have guessed that the only men they could possibly get with would be their daddies, brothers or some of their other relatives. You know they have to be real 'country' if I, a brotha from Arkansas, am talking about them." Preacher giggled a little at his own remarks. "But occasionally I may see them at an EM club. Sometimes I may go there with a couple of friends after work just to chill and listen to lies being passed back and forth. Any how, these same... women can be a real trip. Acting like they're all that just because they were able to buy some mascara and some tight, new jeans. And those white guys are eating that stuff up. Fighting amongst themselves as to who will talk to them and maybe, just maybe, get some that night. I mean you see this stuff and all you can do is laugh."

"I hear ya Preacher. I see the same shit and you're right. It is funny," she said.

"Preacher, you know, for someone who is from the south, you seem to have lost your accent or it comes out sparingly."

"*Whal tank ya maam. I sha nuf appreci' ate them, thos wards,*" stated Preacher, using his best southern drawl. It was sufficient to get another giggle out of Petersen.

"So is it safe to assume that you are available?" replied Petersen.

"I must admit you're not shy about asking about what you don't know are you?" said Preacher.

"No. I am not." "Well...Yes, you could say that. I'm available."

"See. That wasn't hard was it?"

"No. I guess it wasn't."

"And you, Miss Cynthia Renee Petersen?" Petersen was surprised that he knew her middle name. It wasn't easy to get. That would certainly not be on any duty roster.

"Hmmm...It would appear that someone has been checking up on me."

"Da, I am a member of PAS remember." Pause. "Okay," said Preacher.

"Okay what?"

"What do you want out of life and are you available? And you know what I was getting to but you were hoping that my mind would have a memory lapse. Right?"

"Yes, I was hoping."

"I too would like a happy life with my potential companion as well. Like you, that part of my life doesn't involve the U.S. Army. I want to get out as well and work at some corporation utilizing my skills here of course."

Petersen now allowed the smooth rhythm of Maxwell's *Fortunate* to enter her mind and she responded with a little sway as she talked.

"You and I are not that much different." This aroused Preacher's interest a bit. "We both are planning on leaving our current positions to those who truly want them and we both seek a secure but happy life over the horizon." Preacher acknowledged with a couple of nods.

"As far as whether or not I'm available? Well, like you again. Yes." Pause. "I too am looking for that special someone."

"I didn't say that I was looking," said Preacher.

"You didn't have to. I think we all 'look' consciously and when we find a possible match. Someone that may fit the bill. Whether it's at work, at the grocery store or even at lunch we approach them in some way. Some are subtle in doing it. Others may be more direct. But *we* do look."

Petersen looked eye to eye with Preacher when she made those last statements. *She is definitely sending me a line, he thought.*

CHAPTER EIGHT

Nearly all of the one hundred or so seats in the courtroom were filled, mostly with the out-of-town reporters. The historic room was now occupied with both its own soldiers and those whom yearned to cover them.

This room, not to mention the building itself, always stood as a representation of military justice. Other buildings were utilized for different things over the decades but not the Judge Advocate General building.

The historic significance of the building McCullen found himself in did little to impress him. McCullen was totally unaware of such meaning as he was brought within the building and into the courtroom. It was simply the farthest thing from his mind right now.

The lightly gray colored walls with matching bubblers on each end that often signify a government dwelling barely caught his eye. Neither did the bright white ceiling doing its best to reflect the less than bright lamps fixed along the hallway. In fact, the freshly polished hardwood floor did more to reflect lighting than anything else.

Two large doors guarded the entrance to the courtroom. The polished brass handles would be noticed long before they were within reach of a potential guest.

The courtroom itself was not a very large one by civilian standards, but was usually adequate for most military proceedings. It was definitely getting tested with this spectacle.

Once inside and beyond the main doors, the courtroom stood out as a pristine place. The guest seating, defense and prosecution desks, the jury box as well as the judge's throne in the front appeared to be of cherry English furniture. The lighting, though still somewhat dim gave the courtroom a cozier appearance.

But while dim, the lamps somehow managed to highlight the cherry wall paneling around the perimeter of the room. At the center of the ceiling hung a beautiful crystal chandelier accented with electric lighted candles.

Unlike in the hallway, its bright white ceiling appeared to enhance the lighting. It even created some constant snow flake-like visual effects on the ceiling.

Like in the hallway, the hardwood flooring was kept in immaculate condition. When one walked, it sounded like an "old fashioned" church with its occasional creaks. And like the church, the interior had its own smell of distinctiveness.

McCullen sat in the courtroom. His lawyer was seated next to him at their desk. The room with the exception of the front was filled to capacity. Guest seating consisted of a chosen few military higher ups and the press. Only a select few of the media were allowed inside leaving more than a few of them on the outside. Whether inside or out, the news coverage went on.

McCullen's parents, still in South Ozone Park, New York, would have been permitted to enter the courtroom but declined to see their son imprisoned after he was placed in custody early on. His parents took it quite hard and didn't want to see him in that light. They stayed in contact with him via the telephone and other information was from news reports. That was not hard since the "big" military story was hardly confined to Colorado.

The plea by McCullen's mother to his wife to stand by her husband though thick and thin fell on deaf ears. His mother didn't appear to know about all of her son's past "creeping" or didn't care.

All mothers see some good in their sons and daughters regardless of what they do. Sons and daughters could very well commit the most gruesome of crimes but even then a mother will still be a mother. To cut the children loose is not that easy for some.

The number of people in the room gave McCullen more of an indication of how important this trial was to the rest of the people in the world. He looked around and saw some people from his unit. None of any great importance to him.

He scanned the room again, looking for his wife. He didn't see her. As he did so he noticed that he did draw the attention of his media guests and some of them quickly bowed their heads to jot down notes. Photography of any kind was not permitted.

He looked over it again, slower than before, checking every seat, but still there was no sign of her. But she had to be there; he knew she cared for him at least enough to want to find out what would happen to *him*, what would happen to *them*.

A sergeant dressed in his Class As appeared from the front of the room. "All rise." A door to the extreme front of the room just right of the judge's area opened slowly. Walking stoically towards the room's occupants was a "full bird" colonel in his black robe. He passed old glory and rested in his chair.

After everyone was seated, the judge ruffled through some papers on his desk for a brief moment. He looked briefly at McCullen, perplexed as he did so, then faced the papers again. "Will the defendant rise?"

McCullen was still looking for his wife at the rear door hoping she would walk in. He felt his lawyer's hand around his arm, pulling him up.

"You have to stand, sergeant," his lawyer whispered in his ear. McCullen then stood with him. His wife wasn't there. She wasn't there for him so that was more than a hint and a half as to where she stood. There could be no greater statement made than the one she seemed to be making at that moment.

"How do you plead Sergeant First Class Randall McCullen?" the judge asked. McCullen paused as if to wait until his dear wife entered the courtroom and shouted, "Not guilty your honor. My HUSBAND is not guilty!" But such dramatics would not be the case. She was not in the room and as far as he knew, she wasn't on her way.

A flood of thoughts entered McCullen's head. More to the point, how did he let things get this far? What drove him to react the way he did? Was it bad parenting? He searched his soul hoping to reveal an excuse to ease his mind somewhat. Just hoping to place the blame of his current situation on somebody else to relieve himself psychologically. But McCullen knew it certainly wasn't his parent's fault.

Maybe it was his wife? Did she provide all the things a loving wife should provide her man? Was she totally there for him? Of course she was, he thought. He was here of his own accord. But he had to get out of it. If not entirely out, at least place some of the blame on someone else. *Share* it.

"How do you plead?" the judge said, his voice booming even louder than before. McCullen shifted slightly to glance back to the rear of the courtroom. He even looked to the main doors; still there was no sign of his wife. Even his parents couldn't see him like this. He apparently would face this journey alone. But he also knew what he had to do.

"Not guilty your honor." McCullen dug deep down to find whatever strength was available to say the words. He said them sharply and loudly, despite the nervousness of his stomach and the cloudiness in his head.

Malcolm's day was pretty much uneventful after the lunch with Petersen. But he did wonder about her the rest of the afternoon while working at PAS. Although rerunning the images and the conversation in his head, he attempted to have a productive day and was looking forward to class that evening.

Malcolm left work with the majority of the staff in PAS as well as the Replacement Center. Only the major was left in the section.

Malcolm didn't bother to bring any civilian clothing to work in order to change before class. His military uniform would do just fine tonight. He exited the gates of Fort Carson and proceeded to the I-25 on ramp. Heading north, it will take him to the other end of town.

Malcolm's *Systems Analysis* class was let out early that evening. Between his two classes, he decided to go to the school's computer lab to put some finishing touches on a project before the second class started.

The branch campus of Regis University provided a great deal of resources to its students. Especially to the military ones, but amenities like a student union, cafeteria or a study center to kill time or relax was not one of them. A small library and a break room with vending machines, some chairs and a sofa were available but that was about it. The computer lab, Malcolm thought, would do just fine tonight.

Later, *The Foundation of Computer Science* was also let out early. Apparently tonight, the faculty had other things on their mind besides instructing. But that was okay too with Malcolm. A refreshing thought had entered his mind as well.

The traffic on I-25 south was a lot more bearable than it was earlier. A lot less headlights tonight, Malcolm thought. Malcolm remembered the route like the back of his hand. He'd made it numerous times. Turning left on the Exit 141 ramp and left again onto South 8th Street to Motor City Drive.

The name Motor City Drive was pretty definitive. It apparently was named or renamed due to the many dealerships that were lined up along the street. If you are looking for a vehicle then Motor City Drive was the place to be. Other than a speckle of other establishments, dealerships were the dominates.

Malcolm drove around to the back of the establishment. After scanning the lot he proceeded to the back door. Very few cars were in the parking lot. He overlook the multi-color sign, "YOU MUST BE AT LEAST 18 YEARS OF AGE TO ENTER THIS STORE..."

From the time he had went through the doors, he was flanked on both sides by DVDs. Malcolm kept walking. He knew exactly what section to go to.

Malcolm, in his ACU was met briefly with a glance by the black gentleman behind the raised counter. Malcolm thought the gent stood out somewhat in his black and white captain's cap.

Despite feeling a little uncomfortable in the store while in uniform, Malcolm doubted that anyone cared. The gentleman behind the counter was not only enjoying his big cigar but also the video he was watching in the area. One of the perks of working in an adult video store is watching the video or videos of your choice free of charge. Tonight's selection by the caretaker appeared to be one featuring this young lady with pony tails dressed in a red plaid school girl uniform performing several sexual acts on some older guys in a large beach front house. This viewing monitor was located next to the surveillance monitors that monitored the interior and exterior of the establishment.

Malcolm imagined that all kinds come in this place including GIs. *Besides, this is a military town. Right? One more didn't really make any difference.*

As in most adult bookstores, Motor City Video & Magazine's interior was somewhat subdued in the lighting department and plastered on the walls was an assortment of sex toys that anyone could buy for their enjoyment. The store had its books, magazines and videos sectioned off. Whatever one was into, it could be found: straight, gay, bisexual, lesbian, all white, all black, all asian, all hispanic or a combination of them.

To the side of the large display area was another corridor that led to the "arcade." With a handful of tokens purchased from the guy behind the register, one could enter one of many small booths and watch a selection of adult movies just by inserting some tokens in the machine.

As Malcolm went to his display area of choice he noticed a couple of people entering the arcade area. A black curtain that was strung up shielded the corridor, fanning as people strolled through.

It was very dark with only a couple of red lights burning here and there. Music, though faint, could be heard from the area as well. The scene ended with the last person going through and Malcolm concentrated on his own venture.

Despite going through this many times before, not just in this store but in others as well, Malcolm never felt totally comfortable. Colorado Springs was not an extremely large city but it wasn't tremendously small either. He always was on the alert for anyone that might recognize him. He knew it wasn't that unusual to see people in such a store purchasing material. That was certainly okay. But what wasn't okay was if he was caught looking preoccupied in the *wrong* section of literature or DVDs. How that could be explained away?

Malcolm proceeded to the far corner of the room and proceeded to browse. He reviewed the assortment of DVDs in the *New* or *Just In* bunch, but almost never purchased any of the DVDs. He was willing to wait until they were available for renting.

Below them was his preferred section. After reviewing each one of the display cases, two were mentally marked for later viewing. All the cases on display were just that--empty DVD cases. The DVD itself would be retrieved and placed in the boxes by the cashier. A quick scan of the area in front of the room cleared the way for him to retrieve them.

Casually but directly, Malcolm arrived at the counter.

The black man, somewhat chubby, turned to face Malcolm. "Buying or renting?" he managed to say while still chomping on the stogie. He barely looked at Malcolm while he spoke. And that was just fine to Malcolm.

"Renting?" Malcolm's debit card was already on the glass top counter. In fact, the counter not only had a glass top but the front was glass as well to allow customers to view other necessities they may need.

It was just like standing in the checkout line at a grocery store. You had your magazines, candies and other snacks staring you right in the face. But at Motor City Video & Magazine, the snacks were replaced with more adult-geared items like: edible panties, multi-colored condoms, ribbed condoms, oils, lubricants, vibrators and various other sexual-enhancing products.

Malcolm looked up about the same time as his cigar-chewing friend was ringing him up.

The video cases, now with their respective contents were placed in a brown paper bag and were handed to Malcolm over the counter. "Have a good night." That was all the chunky black man said.

"You too," Malcolm responded while exiting the store.

Like a kid who couldn't wait to open his Christmas gifts, Malcolm grabbed the bottom of the brown bag and tilted it over the passenger's seat. The DVDs, *Black Jocks* and *Black Dudes* escaped the bag.

Using the light of the parking lot and not the car's interior doom, Malcolm stared at the front, sides, and back of each of the DVD covers. After about 10 minutes of gazing, he was ready to leave.

Malcolm would take advantage of the earlier than usual school night and go to bed. He had been staying up late the last couple of nights. The videos could wait until later. They were a 3-day rental.

Malcolm was up and about in the morning. When he arose it was about 0330 hours. By now it had to be about 0345. He had already donned his PT uniform and performed his usual bathroom ritual.

As he appraised the contents of his gym bag he thought about how structured his life was now. How every minute was accounted for. And how many of those minutes were devoted to what he wanted to do?

Even while away from the post and even on leave. On any given day, one was often reminded where you are and who you work for. Can't escape the military establishment--even mentally. From the housing units, whether on post or off, to the shopping centers as well as to the surrounding sites in and about Colorado Springs. A reminder of the existing military presence.

From seeing the various uniform military folk, sometimes with their families around town, to the viewing of their military vehicles both in the air as well as on the ground by the respective branches, there was no mental escape from Uncle Sam.

Malcolm often wished he was ready to leave the military with his degree in hand in search of an ordinary life. How he wishes for the day where he could walk into a *Home Depot* and make a substantial purchase for *his* home. A home that carried a mortgage. A home where he could return to after work and enclose himself in its solitude.

It was at that moment he thought of what Oprah Winfrey said on one of her shows before the format was so dramatically changed. When it was a talk show and not one about *Self-Empowerment* and *Being Good to Yourself.*

Malcolm forgot about the topic of the show but in one episode someone asked, "*What is luck?*" And Oprah gave her definition. "*Luck is preparation, awaiting opportunity.*"

After inspecting his ACU for its completeness, Malcolm was reminded of something else. In the living room lying on the coffee table from the night before were the two adult DVDs enclosed in the brown bag. Malcolm retrieved it and placed it on a shelf in his clothes closet. Even though he had very few visitors, he certainly didn't want to take chances. Maybe he would view them this evening.

Later, he would vacate the premises and be one of many commuters this morning on Academy Boulevard.

The pre-PT festivities were pretty normal, the PT itself was the usual and post-PT revelry was nothing out of the ordinary for HHC. So far for Malcolm, the morning was uneventful. He waited his turn for the shower stall. Surprisingly, very few takers were there to rinse their bodies of the morning's sweat.

He often wondered how so many people could accept that sweat and dirt on them all day without the urge to get into some water. Past observations would lean towards the white guys more in violation of this. The very thought would drive Malcolm nuts all day.

There appeared to be a full crew at PT formation this morning but still only a handful here in the latrine to get a shower. Not that he was upset about it; the sooner he got into the hot shower stall, the sooner he got out.

Only Malcolm and a black private first class were now waiting to enter the shower stall. Malcolm knew the young PFC and the two quickly instigated a conversation about him getting his specialist promotion. He wasn't in the military that long and was already antsy about getting more money.

The idea about accepting more responsibility along with the rank appeared to be of no concern to the "young buck." Malcolm decided against pointing this out to the youthful PFC and continued on with the dialogue without interruption.

The exchange was abruptly halted when the two saw the previous occupants, sergeants, exit the shower stall.

One after another, both Malcolm and the PFC entered the shower stall only wearing a towel covering the lower half of their bodies and shower shoes, of various styles and colors.

Malcolm closed the dingy plastic curtain and went to one of two empty shower locations. The PFC claimed the first one. Malcolm found what appeared to be a somewhat dry corner of the stall and placed his toiletry bag there. Upon getting the bar of soap, Malcolm started the stream of warm water. The PFC was already in progress.

He was about 5' 7", 165 pounds with brown skin. He stood under his own showerhead while streams--droplets at a time--would spatter down his body. He closed his eyes tightly and let the water splash over his silky, black, curly hair. The look of gratification was as if he was savoring the moment, the tiny jets of water must have felt like miniature massaging fingertips over his coffee colored, smooth skin.

Malcolm found that not glancing at a shower buddy was once again difficult, if not impossible. These urges were getting more and more frequent.

The man was beautiful. Brown, chiseled chest with no hair on it. The same was for most of his body. Barely any pubic hair, but Malcolm was certain it was due to shaving. It had to be, he thought.

Moving further, the specialist got full view of his eight cut inches between his legs. Fortunately for Malcolm, he had yet to start shampooing his own hair. This allowed him to get a clean unobtrusive view and do so while the PFC was preoccupied with his own shampooing.

Malcolm could see the veins and the big mushroom head on this medium statue of a person. Right at that moment, the specialist's own dick jumped to full attention. Control was further lost even more as the PFC turned as he lathered up. The water continued in a steady stream down the crevice of his muscularly developed back to the tighter crevice of his firm, shapely ass. The vision before Malcolm was just astonishing. The clear streams of water pulsating on this brown skinned brotha's contours under the subdued lighting, was like a marvelous painting in the making.

The specialist knew then it was time to finish his own wash and get the hell out of there. Besides, the PFC was about to rinse.

The shower felt good to Malcolm after experiencing the show he had seen. He also knew that he had to do a better job of controlling himself in these situations.

There was no doubt that this unit has gays in it, right? Mathematically, it would have to considering that the military is just a segment, though a strict one, of society.

Based on the last census, the U.S. has a population of about 293,655,404. Depending on whose survey one may read guesstimates put the percentage of that population who is gay at about 10 percent, or roughly 30 million. Considering Fort Carson had over fifteen thousand active military personnel on it's post--using those figures--that would put the number of gay people at least fifteen hundred.

Yes, there had to be gays in the unit. This didn't make the possibility of the repercussions any easier if he got caught by the wrong person. *I wonder how many of the gay personnel are black?* Malcolm showed no emotions or pondered any feelings toward guys of any race other than black.

While both groups of people--gays and blacks--existed outside the mainstream of society for the most part, relations between the two groups have often been chilly, adversarial, and sometimes unreceptive.

Blacks often have seen the gay community as a group of white privileged, immoral and aberrant men. Even though a substantial part of this group included other races including other blacks.

Gay people, on the other hand, saw the black community as intolerant, homophobic and demagogic.

The warm, moist, stale air of the latrine gave way to a cool, mountainous airway that greeted Malcolm now fully dressed just outside the door. After a trip to the mess hall for breakfast, he would continue his day at PAS.

The room was lit as it always was this morning. Malcolm walked pass the operator's desk but no SSG Hamilton. That wasn't too out of the ordinary. SSG Hamilton would often leave for breakfast after getting the operations running. Sometimes he would go to the nearest AFEES snack bar or to the mess hall.

No one else was here this morning. The officer's area was certainly "clear" in the section. No lights were on. The rest of the enlisted were probably still at the mess hall if they got caught in the rush hour.

The Patton Dining Facility was a fairly large one but it also received a large number of bodies through it as well. The menu items were pretty descent considering the number of people they had coming through and the time they had to prepare them. Breakfast was good. One could get the usual compliment of goods: eggs, sausages, bacon, toast, pancakes, grits, assorted cold cereals, fruit, milk, juices and, of course, the military's life blood--coffee.

Lunch and dinner was another story. Occasionally they could whip up a good meal for lunch and dinner but most of the time, the best way to describe it was "edible." On some days Malcolm would just simply describe it as "nourishment."

Malcolm hated enduring the long lines that came with eating at the mess hall so he tried to go there as early as possible for breakfast and occasionally during lunch.

Unlike most of the other enlisted soldiers, Malcolm did't necessarily have to go to the mess hall to eat. The SPC got BAQ just because he is authorized to live off post. The mess hall was just convenient and inexpensive.

Depending on the time of the month, Malcolm would limit his trips to the mess hall. Soldiers in the army were paid either twice a month or just once. Usually around the fifteenth and/or the end of the month.

It was possible to determine the days of the month based on how long the lines were outside the dining facility. Like a lot of people outside the walls of the military, soldiers too often find themselves with too much month left and only a small amount of money available. This particularly applied to the lower enlisted and was reflected by the length of the lines.

A habitual saver, Malcolm was fortunate enough to have the resources to apply his own strategy concerning the dining facility. When everyone was paid, they tended to stay away from the mess hall as long as they had the funds to eat elsewhere.

This was when Malcolm would go to the mess hall--the place could be nearly empty sometimes. As the funds got a little low in the pockets, the patronage to the mess hall as well as the lines outside the door increased. Malcolm's trips to the facility decreased in contrast.

Malcolm despised the way soldiers waited outside the mess hall sometimes as if they were in line at a soup kitchen. It just seemed to him that another way of doing things should be considered. He was sure glad that he had been in the army a while and was able to move off post so he wouldn't have to endure such a degrading circumstance himself.

Malcolm had now settled in at his cubicle after making sure that all of the automation functions that should be running right now for the users were in fact running. SSG Hamilton, who was really responsible for this usually made sure that these assigned tasks were accomplished first thing in the morning.

By this time, his captain had wandered into the area and he too was getting settled after retrieving a cup of java from the common area.

Hours later the whole staff with the exception of one PFC who was on leave, was here and accounted for. PAS was reverberating with the sounds of chatter among the staff, computer and printers humming away as well as the occasional shouting by the major to one of his subordinates. Usually the captain or lieutenant. Things were normal--for now.

Malcolm was now very settled in his cubicle. The keyboard and the mouse appeared to be moving in unison with each other. He didn't like the task at hand but it was something that needed to be accomplished for the Finance section. He absolutely hated the programming involved in the report writer application that PAS used to create custom reports for the center.

It was different but rather tedious work that had to be done in creating such reports. A possible query solution to a problem he was working on, had just crossed the threshold of his mind when at that very moment his captain appeared rather abruptly behind his chair.

Startled, Malcolm turned around to see who in fact was behind him, frowning.

Most of the time, Malcolm was able to control his facial exhibitions but this time he was caught off-guard. That solution that had entered his head earlier.

CHAPTER NINE

Specialist Hodkins was also at his cubicle, also concentrating on a problem as well as a solution to it. Hodkins was actually thinking about his friend Malcolm. Not professionally, nothing related to work, but personally.

Hodkins was now ready to move forward with things concerning his friend. He had given things a lot of thought since that incident in the latrine that morning assuming it really was something. Malcolm--in his mind--was special. Not like any other brotha he had ever met.

So much so that he didn't want to miss out on the possibility of doing something about it. He heard it time and time again from his buddies and at the bars he frequented: "I should have did this... I should have did that when I had the chance. How different things could be for both of us. Blah. Blah. Blah." Usually it was guys talking about another woman.

Hodkins didn't want to be in their shoes months or years from now saying the same thing. He wanted to act on the situation now--in the present--while he still had a chance to do something about it.

But he first had to figure out something. Was Malcolm gay? Was he bi? He had to figure that minor problem out. But to what extent would he proceed to find out? Was it worth jeopardizing his friendship with Malcolm? Was it worth laying on the line a lot more than friendship? Thoughts of his other friends and their awful encounters with CID ran rampant in his head.

He shook them out. "*I don't giva fuck about that.*" He didn't want to go through life wondering *what if.*

Hodkins stopped staring into the monitor in front of him and turned to leave his cubicle.

He exited PAS, leaving his field jacket behind. Didn't want to take the time to get it.

After walking through the main doors of the center, Hodkins stood outside with his back against the front railings and whipped out his iPhone to press some digits. He didn't want to risk his conversation being overheard and he didn't want his call interrupted by some new lieutenant wanting a salute.

To pull this off he would not only need a friend but a very close friend. When the soft voice responded to the rings, Hodkins presented his request.

Malcolm as well as the captain ended up with the major in his office. Both were seated in chairs about two feet from the front of his desk.

His office like most of his kind had the usual "I Love Me" wall: Paper encased in glass held the presentation of his college degree, various unit awards throughout his career and a sprinkle or two of photos of army buddies.

The desk also held some photos of family members including a black labrador retriever. Also located at the top part of his desk were military mementos he had acquired along the way during his career. Most of them seemed to be from the various German Oktoberfests he had attended. One just couldn't keep some soldiers from their beer. The bottom part appeared to be strictly reserved for working.

Major Balin, dressed in the official black sweater over a lime-green shirt, was at his desk staring at some papers. He seemed to be peering through the bi-focal lens as they sat on the bridge of his nose.

He appeared to be unmindful of the fact that the two were even there. Was he being rude? Of course not. It was nothing personal. When you reach that rank and even higher, you are entitled to treat people with such disrespect. Especially when you are an officer.

Malcolm was seated and with peace of mind until he recognized that the papers the major was viewing were contained in a brown personnel jacket. What was a little worrisome was that the personnel jacket was his.

Usually when someone was looking at a personnel jacket it was either good or bad news. There was no middle ground here as far as Malcolm was concerned.

"There is some *Morning Blend* coffee over there if you two would like some," said the major. He never took his eyes off the personnel papers as he spoke.

The tone as well as the delivery of the message was somewhat comforting to Malcolm considering what he was thinking at the moment. It also gave Malcolm the impression, at least at the moment, that they--the captain and himself--were equal of sorts since they were both getting dissed.

"No thank you sir," they replied in unison.

The major then looked up at them. "Well, let's get down to business then," he grunted.

"Specialist Malcolm, you have an impressive personnel file considering only being in the army a short time." Malcolm gave a surprised look as if he didn't know what the major was reading. He continued, "You worked at a hospital, as a programmer, while attending a two-year community college. After completing college you entered the U.S. Army. Why, may I ask?"

The major leaned back in his gray government executive chair while awaiting a reply.

"Sir, the reason I enlisted was because after completing my associate degree in computer science, I was unable to find a job in my chosen field. Arkansas, as you may or may not know sir is not exactly known for its many high-tech companies. In fact, it has very few." Malcolm took a breath and continued, "So instead of wasting money on a degree and working out of my chosen field, I decided to put the degree to use and get some experience on top of it."

The major put his hand under his clean-shaven chin. "Hmmm. Do you plan on leaving the military once you have acquired this experience?"

Malcolm had a standard reply to such questioning by those other than close associates. The true answer was just the opposite but it was really nobody's business. The major was no exception.

"At this point sir that is still up in the air. I have not decided."

The major just stared at him as he answered the question, but looked back down at the file in front of him as he leaned forward.

"It says here that you have taken quite a few additional courses since you have been here at Fort Carson," the major continued while setting back in his chair.

"Yes sir, I have."

"Working on that bachelors degree I presume?"

Malcolm simply hated the fact that someone would ask a question they already knew. "Yes sir." And he wished that he would simply get to the point of this meeting. Surely the major didn't summon him just to shoot the breeze.

"I would bet that you're gonna be worth quite a penny if you do get out, specialist."

"I would hope so sir. If I do get out," Malcolm added. The major nodded his head.

"Anyway you guys. The reason you're here is because of Specialist Malcolm. The U.S. Army with all its good wisdom has determined that Specialist Malcolm is worthy of being a sergeant in this man's organization."

The captain sat back in his chair and waited for Malcolm's reaction. Malcolm's captain, his direct supervisor as far as the officer ranks were involved, smiled and immediately looked to his side at Malcolm to shake his hand.

Because Malcolm was not as excited as the rest of the personnel in the room, the captain practically had to grab his hand in order to do so.

Malcolm thanked him for his congrats but that was the extent of his excitement.

The captain couldn't quite get why the specialist showed very little expression of the news. His eyes scrutinized the specialist like a surveillance spy satellite scanning a rogue nation below.

He has seen lowered enlisted react more from a fifty dollar raise than what he's seeing now. Perhaps there's a reason for this. Perhaps this specialist had already decided about his career in the army. Perhaps he was getting out once his tour is over.

"You don't seem too happy about this promotion, specialist," said the major. He was still leaning back in his chair still attempting to read the young specialist.

Malcolm wasn't quite caught off guard by this "new" news. He had already had a heads up concerning this tentative promotion.

The enlisted ranks particularly of E5 and E6 are promoted based on what is known as *cutoff* scores. Every month each MOS receives a cutoff score, usually in the high hundreds. Each soldier has acquired some promotion points within their personnel file.

One of the fastest ways of acquiring such points is from college credits. A point is given for each college credit that a soldier acquires. In Malcolm's case, he has acquired quite a few.

Also, each month those soldiers who are eligible for promotion and think they have points close enough often pickup a copy of *The Army Times*, which also lists these cutoff scores, to check.

Unit management will eventually get notified about a soldier's tentative promotion but for whatever reason it hits the paper first.

"Sir, I appreciate the good news and all but there is one more thing that has to be accomplish before I can get my stripes," replied Malcolm.

"Yes, you are correct. After reviewing your file there seem to be a little matter of you going to PLDC first," the major said.

"Yes sir. That is correct."

Primary Leadership Development Course was a school that all specialists or E-4s had to attend if they wanted to get to E-5. They could attend before or after they made their cutoff scores.

Slots for the on post school would open up every month. Only a certain number of slots were available to each unit at Fort Carson so usually the E-4 with the most time in service would be asked to attend.

Malcolm had been asked to attend in the past and each and every time he would politely decline the offer. There wasn't a lot of pressure then but now that he made the cutoff score and a promotion was in arm's reach according to some, he would be getting pressure from his supervisors both officer and enlisted a like, as well as others in his unit.

His answer would still be the same. Malcolm had given this decision a lot of thought and he had long decided that it would be best if the army and he depart when the time arrived.

This would obviously be a decision that would appear unprofessional and disrespectful to a lot of people. No one simply declines a promotion to become part of the NCO ranks.

"So when will you be going to PLDC?"

"Well, that's it sir. I don't intend to go," Malcolm replied in a matter of fact manner leaving no room for any misunderstanding.

"Hmmm. I see."

Even the captain should clearly see that I wasn't interested in a promotion and more than likely would be leaving at my earliest convenience. Why continue this meeting?

The major was certainly not stupid and knew when it was time to quit. He guessed that Malcolm was planning on leaving the army.

Leaning forward, the major's silence had ended. "That's too bad, Malcolm. We need soldiers like you in the army."

Malcolm eyed the officer. *Yeah. Right. The only real reason you even want me to stay is that no other enlisted person in this section knows more than I do about these systems and the operations. I make you look good.*

"I would like to try to talk you into staying but somehow I think that would be futile. Therefore, a waste of my time and yours. Mostly, my time," stated the major.

The last sentence got Malcolm's attention. *Gee, was he being a little brash with that last remark?*

"Yes sir, it would be a waste of time," shot back Malcolm, tactfully.

The major arched his eyebrows. "All righty then. I guess that's all I have. Unless you guys got something for me...this meeting is over."

One after the other, Malcolm and the captain left the major's office.

THREE WEEKS LATER

The atmosphere in the Replacement Center as well as in PAS was a little livelier. There was a little more chatter and most of the enlisted seem to put a little more pep in their step.

But the atmosphere always seemed to be a lot festive around Iron Horse Week at Fort Carson. Especially for enlisted personnel.

Iron Horse Week, no doubt named for the famous division's nickname, allowed post personnel to partake in either viewing or participating in the athletic events. All personnel were encouraged to be released during that week of festivities. Its primary function was for the moral of enlisted persons therefore those units or functions that can close for business, do close. Those units or functions that must be manned did so with personnel from the officer ranks when feasible.

A lot of enlisted used the week to goof off. Most participated in some fashion at some event: play or watch baseball, play or watch track and field, play or watch b-ball and participate or watch weight lifting.

Malcolm was no exception. Malcolm would used the week to steal some study time and prepare a project for class but Hodkins and himself would also participate in a b-ball tournament as part of the Iron Horse events.

Both Hodkins and Malcolm occasionally played ball after work at the gyms with other guys in the unit, but only Hodkins consistently used his "self-described" skills during Iron Horse. This would be Malcolm's first year in doing so. Both Hodkins and Malcolm were about even in their b-ball skills. Neither brags of their future standing in the NBA. Both just did it for fun. It was the second event for Hodkins. He would also participate in his other passion: Track and Field. Especially, the 100 meters. That's about the only event where he has a real chance of winning anything.

This didn't by any means eliminate the attendance at morning formations. In fact, they were still held but they could be attended in civilian clothing and PT was cancelled this week.

Once the brief formation was over, everyone was usually released to attend or participate in his or her chosen events.

With a score of 70 - 50, Hodkins knew that the unit team was going to rack up a win and move up the chart towards the semi-finals. After congratulatory high fives and the occasional brotherly hugs with the opposing team, Malcolm offered a suggestion as everyone gathered their gym bags.

"Does anyone want to head over to Iron Horse gym area to watch some track and field?"

"Where?" said one.

"Hell no, I'm going back to the barracks so I can get some sleep," said another.

"I'm going to my old lady's house off post for some 'quality' time," said the short brotha from the orderly room.

The bags were gathered from along the gym floor and the team, some with drenched jerseys on, walked out of the gym.

Not only did the unit team win but also they won in style. Like most brothas on the court, the NBA attire was truly represented. There had to be about fifteen hundred dollars worth of athletic shoes just with the team. Not to mention the other teams that were there. Then there were the jerseys and shorts. The brothas do have to look good. Regardless of what their doing.

"Short man. Your woman should be at work or some place. It's only about ten o'clock in the morning," said Hodkins. "Shit. What kinda work does she do anyway?"

"She works--"

"Shit. She's probably one of those welfare bitches. That seem to be the only hoes that hang out with this nigga," interrupted one of the guys, which caused everyone to laugh.

Another added, "Nah. Nah. Nah peeps. They call it W-2, now." And the laughter continued.

Even shorty had to laugh at that one but he still had to get the last word on the subject.

"Fuck all of you niggas." That instigated more laughs.

The group approached the parking lot and Malcolm noticed that Hodkins never really responded to his offer. He laughed as everyone else did, but he never really replied.

"What about you Hodkins? I know you're up for some track. A high school star such as yourself. You might even try evaluating some of your competition."

Hodkins kept walking towards his truck. Both Hodkins' as well as Malcolm's vehicles were nearly side-by-side. Despite Malcolm making a lot of sense about the evaluating part, he had to decline.

Malcolm noticed that Hodkins was apparently giving a new guy in the unit a lift back to the barracks. He thought his name was Terrance or Trance or something like that. He looked about six feet three, one hundred and ninety five pounds of muscle. He had hard, muscular arms which were bigger than most of them.

Similar to most of the guys, his attire consisted of a Duke warm-up jersey. He appeared to be quite comfortable with Hodkins. He immediately opened one of the rear doors of Hodkins' Blazer and situated his bags.

"No my man, Malcolm. Not today, I have some thangs I need to take care of," replied Hodkins. He said it without even looking directly at Malcolm. Subtle eye exchanges were made between Hodkins and the new guy briefly then the Blue Demon just took his place in the front passenger seat to await the driver.

Finally looking Malcolm in the face, Hodkins said, "Maybe tomorrow the two of us can catch a track trial. Definitely before my own. You did have a good idea about that. Thanks for watching my back."

With that said Hodkins pounded fists with his friend then he jumped in the Blazer and proceeded off the gym grounds.

Malcolm thought it was rather peculiar that Hodkins would have bonded with the new guy so fast. Perhaps he was instructed to show him around the post considering he was straight from AIT and all. Basically a new recruit. But then again that could have been accomplished almost any time. Certainly not worthy of foregoing a chance to see some of his future competition.

It wasn't worth thinking about it now. Malcolm was eager to get to Iron Horse gym to see some track. It would be Hodkins' loss.

The blazer made it to Hodkins' apartment in record time. It wasn't that surprising since it was near the middle of the day. Both Private Terrance Moore and Hodkins immediately starting stripping off their clothes once they had gotten through the front door.

Moore laid his gym bag near the sofa in the living room while Hodkins proceeded to his bedroom. But he stopped just as he was entering the room.

"Hey nigga. Don't open that funky gym bag up right now and have the whole place smelling like feet like you did last time."

"Ah! Go to hell and take your own musty ass in the shower."

"I had to open every window in the place before I could get that funk out," Moore said before shedding his clothes.

"Fuck you."

Somehow, despite him shedding his clothes after Hodkins, Moore entered the shower first. But Hodkins was there shortly afterwards. The initial contact of the cool water against his body shocked him, refreshing him and stripping away the fatigue and sweat from his muscles. But as he looked Moore over, he realized it did nothing to cool the heat he was feeling elsewhere.

The shower stall they were in was big enough to hold two people comfortably. Right now, the atmosphere was quite comfy in deed.

If you lust over a guy when he's got his clothes on. Nothing describes what you feel seeing him stripped down in front of you. Despite seeing him before, it was like he suddenly saw a whole new side of the young private, like a painting in the works before. It was now completed. Hodkins had felt those feelings before, having got with other guys before, but each time was very different from the last.

The specialist ran his eyes up and down Moore's naked muscular form. He could see his light chest hair, which highlighted the separation between his pecs. Moore's legs were very muscular like his own and his calves were thick and ripped. His skin was light brown and his short black haircut complimented his gorgeous face.

He had the most unbelievable six-pack Hodkins had ever seen. He was completely shredded and his muscular torso made a perfect V-shape into his crotch. The specialist's eyes inevitably dropped straight to his naked groin. Oh yeah! There was that size. He was half hard and already big. It wasn't out of keeping with his well-built body, but it was nicely large, hanging from a thick patch of tight black hair.

Moore passed over a bar of soap he had picked up from somewhere while Hodkins' eyes had been otherwise occupied.

Hodkins took it and started rubbing himself down quickly still looking over Moore as he checked him out with the same thorough eyes. Hodkins' eyes wandered Moore's muscular body as he became accustomed to his exposed genitals. The rest of him was just as beautiful. A lean, mahogany, smooth, muscled; all tight and used to the rigors of high impact basketball.

The specialist eyed again those tight, muscled shoulders and long curving biceps. His gaze followed those flowing, graceful curves, holding a strong athletic power. He hardly noticed the attention Moore was giving him until he looked up into his dark eyes. Hodkins could see his gaze locked below his belly button.

The specialist stood erect and unashamed before him realizing he was approaching the same state.

They silently passed the soap between them, taking turns to soap and rinse. At one point Moore soaped his penis rather roughly, leaving Hodkins standing and watching on silently.

Moore hit Hodkins again with that same old easy smile as he rinsed himself off in a motion that saw his hand run the full length of his thickness.

"Turn around," he said, almost in a husky whisper. "I'll soap your back up."

Hodkins complied, regretting slightly that he wasn't able to give him the same visual attention he was enjoying. Feeling a strong hand on his shoulder, the other rubbing long, easy strokes of soap down Hodkins' body more than erase that quilt. Hodkins' whole body quivered as his spare hand rubbed gentle strokes across his back, washing away soap. His hands felt so strong and good against Hodkins' skin, melting his muscles as Hodkins found his hand slip to Moore's genitals.

The private, new to the military perhaps but not to such intense seduction. He was definitely a skilled veteran in that regards. Maybe more so than the senior specialist. Moore took his time, more than likely taking in the sights too, soaping Hodkins' sides and long thighs before telling him to turn around.

Hodkins saw the same dreaming, lust-filled look in his eyes as he pushed Hodkins gently against the cold, tiled wall of the shower and started soaping his front. Hodkins stared at Moore's muscled body as he soaped his chest. The water splashed off his shoulder, showering them both in the coolness. His hand rubbed easy strokes across his shoulders and chest as he stared Hodkins over again and again.

Hodkins couldn't help notice the heavy erection blazing up, bobbing forward slightly under its weight. It was hard to its fullest, wormed with a number of thick veins. Moore gently soaped around his own member, avoiding touching it, as though on purpose, ultimately soaping his thighs. Nothing physically sexual had happened between them to that point. Hodkins was nearing climax with his hands all over his body.

Moore cussed as the soap slipped out of his hands. "Hey, can you get that?" Thinking it was more than just corny theatrics, Hodkins decided to submit to his shower mate's advances. Hodkins decided not just to retrieve the soap but purposely bend over to get it rather than just a quick squat.

Immediately he felt Moore's hand against the center of his back, attempting to gracefully hold him down but only with just enough pressure to imply that.

"Put your hands against there, man."

Hodkins' heart continued to pound. Whether it was with a woman or a man, the anticipation of sex was always exciting. The private's other hand slipped onto his ass. "I think this is what we both want." Hodkins put his hands against the tile and spread his legs slightly within the constraints of the tub and its available space.

Oh yeah, Hodkins knew what this was all about. And yeah, he wanted it bad, and if Moore wanted it even half as bad as Hodkins then his dreams were about to be made.

Hodkins' whole body was still quivering as the private's strong fingers slipped between his ass cheeks, Moore's other hand still on his back. Hodkins felt the heavy stream of cold water pounding down on his back as Moore's fingers began pushing and rubbing at his asshole. Hodkins sucked in a tight breath, feeling Moore's fingers push roughly into soft places deep inside him. Horny for more attention, Hodkins pushed back against them.

Moore's other hand continued rubbing gently on Hodkins' back, relaxing the specialist to the inevitable as his other probed and pushed and played deep up his passage. Hodkins was panting heavily. His hard on throbbing to new heights of hardness. He tried desperately to relax, so he could loosen up there quicker. Hodkins even rocked slightly.

"You got that soap?" Moore asked. The ranking specialist grabbed it up and passed it back to him quickly. The private's finger was still lodged deeply inside him. Hodkins then felt it slip out quickly and he waited silently as the private started soaping up his member.

Moore decided to bury his face deep in Hodkins' ass. Hodkins, feeling so good there were tears in his eyes. He panted and moaned. Moore took his dick and began to slide it up and down the crack of his target. He nibbled on Hodkins' ear and spread the cheeks apart, lubed his fingers up and began to finger Hodkins' hole. He slid a lubed magnum condom on his dick then he placed his head at the hole. He slowly pushed in. Hodkins began moaning.

The pace was picked up and Moore moved in and out of Hodkins yelling, "I love this ass! I love this ass!" The body banging was hard and rough as before with the two of them. After a passionate kiss behind the neck and some more of his rough love, Moore's body began to shake.

In the middle of the intense exchange, Hodkins quickly realized he had climaxed spilling his seed on the wall. Moore, rather it was due to his youth or just exhilarated, was far less restrained both physically and audibly as he cried out.

Moore was driving in strokes that left Hodkins whole body shuddering as well. His hole was aching with the unbearable pleasure of his 10-inch organ.

Moore's shouts reached a peak as he did. He barely slowed his pace as his thick organ swelled, throbbed and fired his burning fluids.

He even took a few longer strokes, all but pulling out. Not until he had well finished cumming did he collapse. Sweating and exhausted, he leaned against Hodkins as he did his best to savor the moment and brace himself during the assault at the same time.

Moore finally had the strength to pull his softening self out. "Damn, Hotch. That was good!"

They got out of the shower …

Malcolm was snuggled quite comfortably in his bed. He had achieved a level of deep sleep that allowed him to virtually keep the same resting position that whole night.

That was abruptly ended when nature unrelentingly called. He untangled himself from the sheets and slid out of bed, his morning hard-on was now freed from their restraints.

Malcolm staggered into the bathroom, hit the light, and positioned himself at the toilet and struggled to keep from pissing on the floor.

He decided to get back into bed. But the sun peaked in through the blinds, illuminating his face. He had forgotten to adjust them.

What he thought would be some more bedtime would not materialize. He was up for the morning. But despite all that, he still managed to sleep much later than he usually did. He actually needed it too.

Between his ball playing the day before and staying later than expected at the gym, he needed the extra rest. But those were not all of the reasons he was tired.

The two adult DVDs that were rented by Malcolm a few nights before, had finally been viewed. Deciding that last night was as good a time as any to watch, he decided to watch both two-hour videos starting at about 1800 hours. But as far as he was concerned, it was good viewing. And all in the comfort of his home.

In his pajama pants, Malcolm gracefully entered his kitchen area to start boiling the water he would need for his coffee.

Still in pants but with a shirt now, the specialist entered through his patio doors to take in some mountain air as well as the morning scenic view.

His observation was not without its obstacles, he could see some hills and a partial picture-perfect view of Pikes Peak but that was about it from the apartment complex. This late in the morning brought with it a sense of peace and serenity in the complex. The majority of the people in the housing units were military and most were bound to be hard at work by now. Like most, Malcolm would take advantage of the week of festivities on this day and skip morning formations.

He had already dropped hints to his platoon sergeant yesterday that he may over-sleep this morning therefore missing formation. His supervisor, one of many, caught on and stated that he would cover for him.

The grayish clouds that appeared to cap the hills at its highest points seemed to just linger there as if to warm them of the cool mountain air. And on that mental note, Malcolm decided that the short time on the balcony was long enough. He prepared a fried egg sandwich with the usual condiments while he also prepared his coffee.

The specialist entered his living room and after setting down his breakfast, grabbed the remote. His ever-interesting morning duo, "Ken" and "Barbie" were once again on the topic of the year. At least, for the Colorado Springs area.

With them on the *Fox 21* set, was their military law consultant. They had appeared to be discussing where the case went from its present point, but Malcolm apparently caught the discussion on the tail end. The consultant's last word was followed with a news clip by one of the station's reporters.

"At the opening of his court-martial on rape charges, Army Sergeant First Class McCullen was portrayed yesterday as a man who used force to humiliate and degrade female soldiers to satisfy his own selfish sexual needs. McCullen, 28, says the woman consented and didn't know how the Rohypnol or 'ruffies' entered her body.

The sergeant first class is one of two men charged with criminal sexual misconduct at the army post, one of four major military installations in this area. The other, Private Alvin Folster was not charged with rape but of other lesser charges. Mostly due to him not physically touching the victim and his eagerness to testify against his former friend.

The 28 year old army finance specialist, who is married and the father of one, also told the judicial panel that he was unaware that the victim had taken the Rohypnol.

McCullen's testimony was consistent with earlier reports: that he believed that the drug was taken by the victim herself or was given by his former friend, Pvt. Alvin Folster.

Pvt. Folster has denied any involvement of that night's incident.

McCullen has pleaded innocent to the rape charges claiming the relationship was consensual. The Army sees a relationship of that sort as a violation of an Army rule that prohibits relationships between supervisors and their subordinates.

The military prosecutor told the military jury of four officers and six sergeants, all stationed at Fort Carson 'This case is about rape, power, access and control.'

In his opening statement, the prosecutor said McCullen used a combination of fear, intimidation and drugs to compel this young lady to gratify his selfish sexual desires.

Military prosecutors said witnesses would testify that McCullen threatened them with physical attacks and even death if they talked, quoting one enlisted person as saying McCullen said, 'If anyone finds out I'll kill you.'

"That would be Folster alright," said Malcolm.

"McCullen's defense attorney, Captain Leonard Brookhiser, said the case was not about rape but about women who were 'attracted to and willingly engaged in sex with' McCullen.

Women would simply have sex with McCullen either because they were seeking preferential treatment or they were attracted to him, Capt. Brookhiser said."

"Bull shit," barked Malcolm rather loudly. "You first have to be in a privileged position in order to give preferential treatment. He was only an accounting records clerk for God's sake."

"This case is about a sergeant first class who stepped over the line, who engaged in consensual sex when he should not have," the defense attorney said and continued, "But it's also about a private first class who engaged in sex with McCullen and many others and should not have."

Malcolm felt that McCullen's lawyer was really scraping the barrel on this one. Apparently, he didn't have too many cards left, much less "good" cards. He thought McCullen was gonna get some time. Just a matter of how much he was gonna get. He's in a 'No Win' situation on this one. His lawyer was just trying to minimize the number of years.

Malcolm further wondered that if this asshole was running for district attorney in the civilian world he could forget about being elected with this case around his neck.

"The other criminal sexual misconduct charges as well as army policy violations aside, a single rape conviction could mean life in prison."

That was enough for Malcolm this morning. He grabbed the remote to deactivate the TV and proceeded to get dressed.

The Academy Boulevard traffic, partly congested by the various air force, army and a few civilian personnel, was all but normal this time of the morning.

Malcolm was glad that he didn't have to be anywhere in a big hurry this week. He was even going to try to avoid going into the office if he didn't have to.

He was looking forward to spending some time with Petersen today.

During the past few weeks both Petersen and him had been spending a lot of time together. Surprisingly not just to everyone else, but to them as well.

Most people in the unit really did see the two as a rather "odd couple." Malcolm was viewed as a rather conservative, religious as well as career soldier. Petersen, on the other hand, was viewed as a loose, arrogant and someone who would more than likely complete their first tour and leave the army--pregnant.

There was certainly more than a fair share of gossip going around about the two specialists. All of which came from the enlisted ranks.

The chatter from the males, both senior and lower enlisted, were along the lines of, "She must'a wanted a 'quiet' motha fucka to tap that ass." More than a handful of guys wanted to get into her panties.

The women's comments were tamer: "The stuck up guy finally got his nose turned up by someone."

But Malcolm, who used to view Petersen as the gossip portrayed her, didn't see Petersen in this light now. He now saw her in a rather new light.

As it turned out, the two had a lot in common. Each liked to listen to R&B, each were pretty "locked" when they made up their minds about something and each tried to keep a lid on their true inner feelings.

CHAPTER TEN

Malcolm was enjoying the ride to the post. His mind was more relaxed than usual. Savoring the moment. He may even relish this whole week. He knew next week may be a little hectic since not a whole lot will take place this week on post.

He even felt comfortable physically. He had put on a fresh pair of white Jockey boxer briefs, a navy blue Nike knit jogging suit with legs that detached midway which fit his body to the tee, and a pair of white Nike cross-trainers.

All this serenity may have been the catalyst for an idea.

Malcolm utilized the first *"For use by authorized vehicles only"* detour he saw, heading north on Academy Boulevard.

The stores in the Citadel Mall wouldn't have been opened long this morning but at least one jewelry store would have a customer this early in the morning.

After passing by a couple of jewelry stores, there was one he felt comfortable with at least by his observation of their display window.

He went up to the counter. "Excuse me, please," he said to the clerk.

"Yes," she said, "May I help you?"

"Rings," he said. "I'm looking for rings."

"Is there something in particular you're looking for, sir?" she asked.

"Possibly a friendship ring."

"We have some nice friendship rings over in this section." She pointed.

Malcolm checked them out.

When one walked through the jewelry store's doors, it is clear that the owners and staff take pride in the shop. It was neat, clean, brightly lit, and well-organized. The jewelry is laid out in such as way that customers can easily spot what they are looking for.

"Hmmm. I don't know about these," he said.

"Oh, well, how about these?" she asked, as she moved to the other side of the glass case, and in, the process completely avoiding others, which were in the middle of the glass case.

Malcolm checked out the ones she chose to show him, but he didn't like any of them, either. Then, he looked at the batch that was conveniently overlooked by the lady. He spotted a few he liked.

Malcolm wasn't sure if the oversight was deliberate or accidental. In any case, a small commission was better than none at all.

"Hey, what about these?" he asked.

For a brief moment, a disappointing look plastered her face. But just as quickly as it appeared, it left.

"Let me see those two right there," he said.

The clerk slid the door open and got the rings out and set the tray on top of the counter so Malcolm could get a better view.

The jewelry selected were fourteen caret, solid white gold friendship rings.

He placed one of them on his left finger.

Surprisingly, it fit perfectly.

Is this an omen or something? Maybe it is the right time to present this.

Normally, as in the case of his high school ring, some fitting would be required.

He held the other one and examined it very closely. He had hoped that the other would fit Petersen. He had noticed a lot of things about her but the size of her ring finger wasn't one of them.

Luck would have to prevail or at the very least, it could be returned to be fitted. He couldn't really tell if it would fit her, but he went on and purchased the rings, anyway.

"I guess these will do for now," he said, as he placed his debit card on the counter.

"Aw rrrighty, Sir!" She smiled as she turned away to scan the card. She charged his card for the rings and handed it back to him, she asked, "Would you like these rings gift wrapped?"

"Only one of them. I'll be wearing the other," he replied.

She did as he instructed and handed him the cute, red jewelry box.

"Here you go, sir, and have a great day," she said.

"No. Thank you!" Malcolm shot back. Malcolm left the Citadel not bothering to check his favorite men's stores. He couldn't wait to surprise Petersen with her ring.

The front parking lot of Headquarters and Headquarters Company had very few cars. The idea of running into little or no people suited Malcolm just fine. He had already called Petersen on his cell phone while he was on the boulevard that he would be there very soon. Hopefully, that would give her a bit of a heads up in order for her to get a head start on those womanly things that females must do prior to leaving their homes. But somehow, he figured, that would do very little to increase their chances of leaving in a hurry.

Malcolm didn't have a whole lot of experience with women, but even he knew a woman wasn't leaving her domicile until everything was just right. They were totally different animals from their counterparts, he thought.

He greeted a SFC that was roaming the halls of the unit before he got to the stairway that led to the second floor of the barracks--the female rooms.

But surprisingly to Malcolm, someone was occupying the supply room today. Its main door off the hallway flew open and out of it was Specialist Chris Hammond. It was at that very moment that Malcolm knew that a quick in and out of the unit would not take place.

Specialist Hammond is a very nice person but could be very talkative not to mention nosy. Hammond was a two-year veteran of the army, currently married with two kids but Malcolm sometimes wondered how long his marriage would actually last.

It was rumored that the very same home boys he hung out with at his house parties and those away from home, were the same ones who were trying to hit on his wife. Or maybe it was the other way around. "Not all 'dogs' have testicles," Malcolm would sometimes say.

"Waz up dawg? Or should I say playa?" Hammond said in a not so subtle tone. Hammond was known for a lot but tact especially in the middle of the common hallway was not one of them. "I always say—"

Malcolm interrupted, "No. Tell me what you always say Specialist Hammond."

Specialist Hammond was actually in his civies carrying his army-issued backpack in one hand. Apparently he was preparing to leave for the day to enjoy himself. But he motioned for Malcolm to come inside the supply room.

"Before I was rud-a-ly interrupted. What I was going to say was that you really do have to watch those quiet motherfuckas. There is just no telling what *you* guys are up to," Hammond said, smiling. "Dawg, I heard rumors about you and Petersen but I said, 'Not Malcolm,'" the recently promoted specialist said while twisting his mouth and dipping his body. "If it was anybody else, I would have believed it. But not you dawg. Not my homie."

Hammond was from Beaumont, Texas but Malcolm let him vent on.

"Excuse me Hammond but you probably believe most of the rumors you hear anyway," Malcolm said.

Hammond paused as if to really give what he heard some serious thought. "Maybe, but, as in this case--for damn good reason. Some rumors are true aren't they?"

"I wouldn't know," Malcolm stated as he smiled.

"Bull shit," was the Texas native's only response. "I'm from Texas and I know bull shit when I smell it." Even though Hammond was from Texas, it would not be a complete shock to Malcolm if he has never seen an actual bull.

Once the two of them were inside the room and the door was closed shut, Hammond dropped his field pack on the floor.

It was at that moment that Hammond seem to settle down and act like the Hammond one rarely saw. Not the loud mouth, always kidding, never serious but happy person whom you always seem to see when he's around his homies. Both he and Malcolm leaned against the front *May I Help You* counter. The supply room, which received and issued everything from paper clips to small arms, was only occupied by the supplies resting on the various high-stacked bins and the two specialists.

The décor of the spacious room was of the typical dark and light gray of most old army facilities, right down to the floor tile. It was Hammond manning the supply room this week. His sergeant was on leave.

"Malcolm, I was gonna call you or catch you during morning formation sometime today about a matter you've taken care of before," said Hammond while working on a sly smile.

But Malcolm had a good idea what was coming.

"It's about ah... well I'm just gonna come out and say't." His face was now more somber. "I need a little loan. My Kids—"

Malcolm raised his hand to stop him.

"Hammond, I have told you before. I don't want to know why you need it. Just let me know how much. Depending on the amount I will either loan it to you or I won't."

Hammond appeared calmer now.

"So how much?" Malcolm replied.

"Hundred," said Hammond.

"Okay then," Malcolm said calmly while reaching in one of his pockets for his wallet.

Hammond was always amazed how expressionless the face of the person standing in front of him was whenever he would give him a number as to what he needed. No one else he knew would do this without giving him some excuse for not loaning it. If they had it it would more than likely be a loan with weird interest tacked on.

But not Malcolm. If Malcolm said he didn't have it, that usually meant he didn't have it at that moment. He probably had to go to the nearest ATM to retrieve it.

And he would loan it to him without interest. Was he just a nice guy in Hammond's mind? Perhaps.

But what the new specialist didn't know was very few people had the privilege of a relationship such as the one he had with Malcolm. Malcolm deliberately limited such a relationship to no more than a handful of close associates. Not necessarily friends, but associates.

Malcolm trusted the supply specialist. He wasn't sure at first but he started loaning money to Hammond in small amounts and as Hammond started paying him back when he was supposed to, he gradually increased the loan amount.

Hammond wasn't sure what his loan cap was but he limited his loan requests to what he only needed for his short term fix as well as what he could pay back. Malcolm thought this was the case himself and that was one of the reasons why he liked the Texan.

After retrieving the black leather wallet, Malcolm handed the crisp one hundred dollar bill but only after rubbing it firmly with his fingers to make sure that another one was not sticking to it.

"Ah... just give it to me. If another one is sticking to it I'm sure you won't miss it," Hammond said with a big smile while grabbing.

"Yeah. Right," said Malcolm.

It was always difficult for some people to grasp the notion that they too could achieve some spending money as well as a savings of some sort if they conditioned themselves towards their own spending. Even married in the military. It's not easy but it can be done, Malcolm contemplated.

With the money in hand, Hammond was now eager to get out of the room and head for home. "I betta get outta here and hit home before my wife kill me."

"Okay 'young' specialist you take it easy and tell your wife I said hello for me," Malcolm told him.

"I will."

Malcolm opened the door. He turned around and the two bumped their fist together before the senior specialist continued his walk down the hallway.

While locking the door, Hammond told him thanks.

"You're welcome," said Malcolm without turning around. He kept walking and raised his right hand briefly.

But Hammond was still the same old Hammond.

"Was that a hand or your middle index finger, partner," said Hammond in his worst Texan accent.

"It was my index finger," Malcolm said.

"Just checking," said Hammond while walking towards the main door of the unit.

About midway, Hammond stopped and turned around and shouted, "Yo. Malcolm!"

Malcolm had been hoping he could reach the stairway. He turned around.

Neither one really saw a clear image of the other's face in the dim hallway.

"She really does like you." "She likes you a lot." Although Malcolm couldn't see the expression on his face, the tone was one of rare seriousness.

The junior specialist exited the main doors.

Malcolm just stood there in the hallway for a while to absorb what Hammond had said. Someone from the other offices was walking across the hallway when he or she broke their stride. The figure saw Malcolm apparently just standing there down the hall.

Malcolm nodded his head and a smile had even managed to creep in. That's good I guess, he thought.

She was ready when Malcolm arrived at her door and after a few minutes, Malcolm went down the stairs as quickly as he went up them.

Petersen looked more striking each time he saw her, in or out of uniform. But today, she was even more stunning. Petersen was dressed in a simple ankle length beige skirt with a thigh high split on one side. Her athletic top exposed her pierced belly button presenting what appeared to be a small diamond. Her hair, now in curls, flowed to her shoulders.

Malcolm, totally unmindful to his surroundings after viewing Petersen from top to bottom, said, "You look great."

"Thanks," Petersen said. "You do too." Malcolm proceeded ahead of her as they approached the car. He opened the passenger door and walked around to get inside.

Once they were both inside, Petersen reclined the passenger seat and put on her Oakley sunglasses. After making sure her hair would be over the headrest, she leaned back. Although not starting so smooth, Petersen was quite comfortable being around Malcolm now. So much so that there were times when she wanted to share some of her innermost secrets with him but for whatever reason, didn't.

So comfortable that the two often called each other by their first name while away from the military establishment or among themselves. One would think that wasn't a big deal, but it did take some conditioning.

Malcolm switched discs and the two cruised along Specker Avenue with Maxwell's *Lifetime*.

"May I ask you a few personal questions?" Petersen asked.

He was hoping that the start of this beautiful day would not end because of a few personal questions. "Only if I can ask you one," he said.

Petersen turned her head slightly in his direction. "Okay. This is gonna be nice. Answering a question with one, I can handle that." She then paused. "Okay. Preacher, if you could change just one thing about your life, what would it be?"

Malcolm premeditated. Her fragrances enthralled his senses. Not just talking about his nose either. But it was a question as if it was on her mind all morning and was just waiting for someone to ask it.

"That's an easy question, but with a much harder answer. What I would have liked to say at some point down the road in my life is that 'I have truly done and said all I have wanted to do and say.' Not constantly reminding myself later what I should've done or said."

Petersen looked at him again through her shades. He had a look of determination plastered on his face. Or was it? She thought. Was it something he had yet to accomplish in his life or was it something he regretted not accomplishing?

He had a look of being "out of body," but yet mindful that he was driving. She turned away and brought her attention to the various people scrowing, minding their business as they went about their day on Fort Carson. There were male, female, young, not so young, military personnel and civilian. Some enjoying the break they were getting this week and others having to work regardless of it. The figures seemed to breeze by as the vehicle cruised. Soon, what had been interesting outside was overshadowed by what and who was near her. The rhythm of the song was soothing to her.

"Okay, my turn to ask questions," Malcolm said.

Petersen appeared more alert as if she was hearing the lottery numbers from her favorite radio station.

"Are you the type of woman who would hold a man's past relationships against him?"

Malcolm glanced down at Petersen's thighs. The flap of her skirt had formed into a V near her crotch.

"No. What's in the past should be left in the past," Petersen replied while settling back into her seat again. "But if he cannot allow things to remain in the past, we have problems. But I would hope that that would be worked out long before things get too serious."

Petersen looked back at Malcolm. "That shouldn't be too much of a problem. Should it?"

Malcolm quickly glanced at her. She looked at him with such a smirk on her face that she appeared as though she was waiting on a confirmation from him. Perhaps getting away from the theoretical questioning to one of real substance and waiting for a real answer about their own relationship.

Malcolm thought to himself. "No. That shouldn't be a problem," he replied. He put more thought in her response and was about to ask her to clarify some hypothetical points related to her response but decided against it.

Malcolm learned one of many lessons, mostly from others, of how women could sum up your past history based on just a few questions. But he felt he had to add one more response.

"It is important that all things come out from both parties," Malcolm continued while braking for a red light. His fingers, while on the steering wheel, also tapped to the sway of the music. "Lay everything on the table for discussion to eliminate any surprises down the road. In this day and age, you can't expect everyone to be perfect about their choices in life."

Malcolm punched the accelerator. "I know I'm not perfect and I don't try to be. However, I'd rather risk the chance of being single the rest of my life, before I'd be faithful for the sake of making someone else happy or for appearances. This world that we live in dictate so many of our actions for better or for worse."

Petersen wasn't sure what all that was about but it was interesting. She was not sure if it was brought on by her response or whether it was on his mind.

Malcolm turned off the road, searching for a parking space. On a normal day at Iron Horse gym, he could probably park any place he wanted but this was not a normal day. He would have to get back on Specker and park along side it on the gravel some place with other vehicles already there. They could walk to the track & field areas just outside the gym where they would enjoy the events.

The gym's outdoor track field was not the state-of-the-art track capable of hosting events such as the NCAA championships. Nor did it have seating to accommodate thousands of fans, press box facilities to house the needs of national media and network television. Nor a state-of-the-art timing system with video scoreboard. In fact, the five-lane track just had enough room to accommodate the other multi-events: vertical jump and pole vault.

But it was more than accommodating during Iron Horse week. Most of the people who did use these facilities under normal circumstances, did so as part of their annual physical training test or just plain physical fitness. The track could accommodate a whole unit, if necessary, for that purpose.

Rivalry among some units at Fort Carson was just as strong as at some colleges during events such as these, and the crowd was raucous in the bleachers.

Petersen and Preacher found a pair of seats near the top. The sight of a woman baring a little flesh such as the case with Petersen was enough to bring out the "dawg" in some brothas. Malcolm noticed the stares, some on the sly, others very noticeable, that some brothas gave Petersen. He wasn't sure if she was uncomfortable with the glares or just used to it. But Malcolm was not comfortable with it. Even more so when they went by a group of guys. The tongue of one of them eased out of his mouth. Malcolm chalked it up as just immature and kept on going.

The day wasn't too bad for an outdoor event. Not too warm and not too cool. The occasional sun break from the cumulus clouds was a welcome sight to all seated below.

The contestants of the men's one hundred meters seem to be not bothered by the current state of the weather, but not totally unwitting to their surroundings. Fashionably garbed, some of them appeared to be making extra effort to attract attention with their various warm-up routines. No doubt to get some extra female attention.

A few of the homies of at least one of the participants kept riding him.

"Yo peep. Enough with the show. You're gettin' noticed." Similar comments from that part of the bleachers kept coming for at least five minutes until the guy got fed up with his unit buddies and gave them what appeared to be a modified version of the "finger." Supposedly this would somehow escape the scrutiny of anyone who may have seen it.

But that wasn't to be. Moments later, a distinguished ACU-clad gentleman who Preacher recognized as the sergeant major of one of the combat engineer battalions approached the guy on the field.

What happen next was no less than a tactful tongue latching. The race participant was at modified "attention," even in his civilian clothing, and he stared the sergeant major dead into his eyes as the senior enlisted person did all the talking.

Everyone in the bleachers felt the guy's pain.

The sergeant major no doubt reminded the young gent, in a manner he would understand, that this was a family affair and he was to conduct himself accordingly. Afterwards, everything and everyone seem to settle down a bit.

The warm rays of the sun, the antics of the crowd as well as the verbal exchanges with Petersen put Malcolm's mind at ease, taking away of thoughts of PAS, school and back home.

The last talk he had with his grandparents left him thinking that not all was okay despite assurances that everyone was doing fine. He wasn't sure what but something didn't seem right on the phone.

Some who were perhaps natives of the mountainous west, may dislike the warm rays but as a southerner who hated the cold, Malcolm welcomed them.

All of these distractions almost made him forget about a certain task today.

Petersen was watching the guys warm up at the pole vault area.

"I have something for you, Cynthia Renee Petersen," he said, as he pulled the jewelry box from his pocket. He opened it and temporarily paralyzed Petersen.

"What's...what's this, Preacher?" she asked. Her eyes widened. He took the ring from the box and a thought entered his mind.

He grabbed Petersen's left hand and placed the ring on her finger. To his surprise, the ring was almost a perfect fit. Malcolm had a grin on his face as he put the other matching ring on.

Malcolm knew that he could have selected a quieter setting for what he was about to do but he wanted to get it over with and do so while he still had the nerve to do it. Everyone else surrounding him for now would have to take a back seat.

Malcolm placed his right hand on top of Petersen's left and gazed into her beautiful brown eyes. He was now ready to confess his feelings for her.

"Cynthia Renee Petersen," Malcolm said, as her full name was called in a semi-formal tone.

Petersen really was caught off guard which was evident by the surprised grin on her face. *Oh, God, what's Malcolm up to now?* She thought.

"First of all, don't laugh. Even though this may sound just a little trite. I care about you, Petersen. I care about you a lot. It's been only a month, but I feel like it's been much longer. You may even feel that what I'm about to say is foolish and impulsive, but I don't want to take the chance of losing you to some other hard head. You—"

Petersen started to giggle but Malcolm caught her in midstream and quieted her by placing his index finger to his lips. She knew then that he was serious and wanted to get this over with.

He continued, "You make me feel good inside--damn good inside, which is a great feeling to have. I'm attracted to you, and I'm not going to deny it to myself. I know you're attracted to me too, so I'm making a proposal to you, Cynthia."

"What?"

"I want the two of us to be lovers, Cynthia. I guess I'm asking you to be mine--to be faithful to me. These rings," he confessed, as he looked down at their hands. Petersen glanced down as well. "These rings are a symbol of the commitment I'm making to you and they express how I truly feel."

He looked up, again.

So did Petersen.

"Will you accept my proposal, Cynthia Renee Petersen? Will you start a new era in your life with me? We have so much yet to explore with each other. Not just sexually, but mentally, as well." Malcolm smiled.

Then the crowd roared. Neither Petersen nor Malcolm was startled by the outburst as fans cheered their respective contestants during the pole vault announcements. But it was only a little distracting from the seriousness the two were currently embraced in.

Petersen stared into Malcolm's anticipated eyes, speechless. She was all choked up. No one had ever poured his heart out like this to her. The moment was so moving. The strong, sometimes abrasive gal couldn't help that her eyes were a little misty.

She couldn't help but think about the moment that her girl friend in Baltimore left. That moment in her life also left her eyes watery. No, they weren't just watery, they were shedding tears.

But this was a good moment in her life. Just as Malcolm had admitted, she liked him too. But she didn't want to be hurt again either.

But in this case, she threw caution to the wind and flushed her fears and doubts down the toilet. Petersen looked up at the events before her on the field. Just to stare. Then she brought her eyes back to him.

"First thing, Malcolm... You're crazy for doing this, but you're right. I am attracted to you. You've stunned me with this, and quite frankly, I don't know what to say." She looked down at her finger with the pretty ring on it.

Malcolm was tired of the suspense. "There's only two words I wanna hear from your lips, Cynthia... yes or no," he said firmly.

Petersen looked into Malcolm's eyes again. She smiled. "Yes, Malcolm Preacher. I accept your proposal."

The crowd roared again. One of the pole vault participants had just wrapped up his event.

They both laughed.

Soon, Malcolm hoped, they would consummate their new union.

The past week as well as the weekend was no less than amazing for Malcolm. Not to mention refreshing. The sport events were great, he had spent a lot of time with Petersen and despite all of that going on, he seem mentally ready for the week. Or so he thought.

Shortly before the PT session of the morning and right after he arrived at the unit, Malcolm was summoned to the first sergeant's office. Malcolm was informed by the 1SG that one of his uncles had died late last night in his sleep.

"The family had tried to reach you but could not get through. So they notified the Red Cross which notified the unit," he said. *Fuck,* Malcolm thought. *He forgot to re-connect to the cell network when he reset his phone.*

The news was a shocker to Malcolm. His uncle and he were certainly not as close as his grandparents, but still close. It had been a few weeks since he last talked to him in North Little Rock. Like his father, Jarod, a 60 year old, Vietnam-Era marine veteran was not much of a talker on the phone. Both were pretty much "get to the point" type of men.

Unfortunately, the phone was how most of the family members communicated with Jarod these days. For the past year and a half, he has been hospitalized at VA Medical Center in North Little Rock, Arkansas.

Jarod was diagnosed with diabetes about five years earlier which required him to get insulin injections, change his work habits as well as his diet. He didn't do too well on his own and Jarod never quite met the ideal woman for himself.

He had accidentally cut his foot while in the yard (It was never clear why he was barefoot anyway) and because he didn't seek treatment in a timely manner, it eventually led to a trip to the VA hospital.

Jarod thought the two and a half-hour trip to the VA hospital would quickly result in some strong ointment, a bandage and a same-day return. But that would not happen. What started as a cut on the foot would gradually escalate to kidney failure and eventually to regular dialysis. Because of the dialysis attention and the absence of medical facilities that could provide such care in a thirty-five mile radius of Hamburg, he would have no choice but to stay at the hospital, a full one hundred and thirty miles away from Hamburg.

The 1SG, being the perceptive soldier that he was, read the expression that glued on the face of Malcolm. It was an expression of shock and disappointment all rolled up into one. It stayed on his face for about a minute just as Malcolm himself stayed almost motionless in his chair.

At this time, there would be no hugs. No lengthy and mundane words of sympathy given by the 1SG. It was not his place to give it nor did he thought would be needed. Those words were more suited for Hallmark moments on the "outside" in civilian life and this, in his eyes, was not one of them. This would be the case even if Malcolm were a female.

"If there is anything the unit or I can do for you don't hesitate to let us know," he replied stoically behind his desk. "How soon will you be leaving for home, Specialist Preacher?"

"As soon as I let my platoon sergeant and section sergeant know, and pack."

"Don't worry about those two; I'll take care of them for you. Just go and pack and get home." Ending with those words of concern for his trooper, the meeting was over.

"Thanks, 1SG."

"No problem, specialist."

There were a few more matters that had to be taken care of prior to hitting the road. Malcolm needed to get the oil changed in his car but more importantly, he also needed to let Petersen know that he would be leaving town for a few days.

The scenery just outside Colorado was not exactly great but it wasn't that bad either. The stretch between Ranton, New Mexico and Amarillo, Texas, could be rather blah with its flat land, dry brush along the roadside, cattle scattered here and there plus the occasional tumbleweed, depending on the time of the year.

But perhaps it was what was needed right now. The solitude of the trip gave Malcolm plenty of time to think. He had given his section a status of the projects he was working on. Someone else would immediately handle anything pressing. And those buddies that he saw, he told them that he would be out of town for a while.

Petersen told him that he would be missed but kept insisting to call or let her know if she could do anything. She was adamant about this before he left the post and she called him at his apartment prior to Malcolm leaving early this morning.

It was only now when a thought hit him: *Was she trying to get me to take her along? Well I'll be damn*ed.

Malcolm was disappointed in himself for not coming to that conclusion before he left. With Jarod's passing and all, he had a lot on his mind.

"But I doubt she could have left on regular leave on such short notice," he said to himself.

But Malcolm probably would not have allowed her to come along anyway. Their relationship was not that far along to allow her to visit his family at this time.

Malcolm's mind wandered to other things as the cavalier swerved gracefully from left and right down the winding highway.

The road rose and fell through the valleys of New Mexico. Just as it could be found within pictures of a coffee table book of the west, even the rock and, in some cases, the soil displayed various shades of color.

Even way out here as Malcolm saw critters crossing the road, life thrived. Not just the various birds he saw but small and large animals he viewed on the vehicle's side as he passed them. Rabbits and mule deer seemed to be the most plentiful out here.

All part of the circle of life. He thought.

For every mule deer and rabbit he saw, he appeared to see the same number of carcasses of that same species.

That triggered the reminder of why he was even traveling through this part of the country right now.

Malcolm thought about the time his deceased uncle taught him how to properly shoot his first rifle.

It was actually one of the top-of-the-line Daisy BB models. It was obviously a pump action. The more you pump it with pressure, the more velocity you got from the ammo. Back then, there weren't CO^2 cartridges. And the ammo--if you wanted to call them that--came in two forms for that particular rifle: BBs and pellets that were actually balled at the head but flared at the tail.

It seems rather cruel and inhumane by today's standard among people. In fact, most cities have some type of law or ordinance against it, but Malcolm and his crew of neighborhood boys grew quite accustomed to using their assortment of pellet and BB guns against not just bottles and cans but the variety of birds that existed in Southeast Arkansas.

Today, you couldn't carry around a BB gun in most neighborhoods yet alone start shooting birds. Right after law enforcement personnel finish with you then you may have to deal with animal right agencies. But in the day, law enforcement couldn't care less about such things. In fact, the local cops would ride by and might even ask you to let them have a shot with it depending on what accessories caught their eye.

As far as the shooting of birds, if it was a crime on the books, it was obviously not enforced. And to everyone's knowledge, birds just like rabbits, squirrels, etc. were fair game.

It was a cool Saturday morning and Malcolm, around 12 years old at the time, had just finished breakfast and decided to practice his marksmanship on a flock of chickadees that had rested on one of many plum trees in his grandparent's yard.

Malcolm wasn't sure if it was him or the possibility that the sights on the pellet rifle were off but he wasn't exactly a sharpshooter when it came to shooting it initially. Malcolm was sure the problem lay with the rifle. After all, he was just one in a long line of hunters in the family. Therefore, being able to shoot should be natural to him.

As in about 50 percent of his attempts, he missed his feathered targets. The chickadees, startled by the cracking of surrounding twigs and the sound of the rifle, flew away from the scene.

Malcolm took out his frustration on a couple of bottles that lined the drainage ditch between the road that went in front of the house and his grandparent's property. His uncle, who was visiting across the street, was probably viewing the whole thing, at least in part from the inside.

Malcolm had finished shattering the last significant piece of one of the bottles and was debating on whether to walk down the nearby railroad tracks along the woods to spot more birds, maybe even a rabbit. Back then, every small black community was next to or near the tracks.

"You don't seem to be having much luck with those birds lately. Are you blind or something?" asked Jarod, halfway exposed in the doorway of the front of the house that he was occupying.

"Jarod, don't let the flies in here! I have enough trouble trying to get rid of the ones I have now," a voice from within shouted.

"Ah relax. It'ta give ya something to do today," he said.

Little Malcolm who was still miffed about missing those birds thought about not even responding to his uncle or simply saying something *smart* but after some thought decided against it. The last time he did that his behind was almost the subject of a whipping if not for the intervention of his grandmother.

"No," he replied, but with some attitude.

His mind was now made up. He had decided to take a trip down the tracks after all. Whether it was further prompted by his uncle's personal observations, he wasn't sure.

"Where ya' going?" said Jarod.

"Down the tracks."

Pause.

"Wait a minute. I'll go with you," responded Jarod.

Malcolm didn't expect a reply like that and wasn't sure if he wanted his uncle tagging along.

"That's okay. I'll go by myself," said Malcolm.

"No," his uncle insisted, "I will go with you down there and show your butt how to shoot. You should know by now anyways."

There was no sense in arguing about it; his uncle was going.

"Don't worry. You are probably getting low on BBs anyway. I'll bring back some from the store later."

That was all that was needed to convert a frown to a smile. He was in fact getting low on both BBs and pellets.

Lessons of marksmanship wouldn't be the only lessons Malcolm would learn from his uncle. Later it would be about hunting, fishing, cars, women and other life's lessons. Malcolm wouldn't take to heart everything his late uncle would teach him.

Especially about the women since his uncle didn't do too well in that area himself.

He didn't have too many problems getting them. Some his age. Some younger. Some even a little older. His uncle's problem was keeping them. With the exception of one whom he fathered children with, he would just leave them as if he had become tired of them. But even he didn't marry his children's mother. He would keep in touch with the children and sometimes check on their mother when she wasn't shacking with anyone but that would be the extent of their relationship.

Jared had found a lot of joy in hunting over the years, but nothing compared to the pleasure of watching a young person learn his way around the woods, and around guns. Jared's time in the woods with young hunters had been some of the most rewarding time he'd ever spent.

In the woods was where the magic lied. The magic of watching wildlife undetected; the magic of watching a child's eyes when he sees a rabbit or even a bird while hunting with that pellet gun. *The true rewards of hunting with young folks lie in the satisfaction of watching them respond positively to the natural world around them*; Jared thought while they walked along the tracks.

Neither said a lot during their walk. Young Malcolm seemed determined to kill something hence the determination on his face as he looked back and forth between the wood's edge and the edge of the soy bean field. Both edges ran parallel alongside the railroad tracks.

The wood's edge was notorious for housing a large variety of birds in the pine and sweetgum trees and the edges of the soy bean field proved time and time again to show the occasional cottontail rabbit munching or playing in the area.

Jared thought it was always best to start kids where there's a promise of action. This is why rabbit and/or bird hunting is a great way to introduce kids to hunting; there are plenty of them; and kids have a greater chance at bagging a rabbit or bird than something bigger. And, should they miss, it's not a big deal... there's usually another bird waiting on the next tree or rabbit around the corner or at the next big bush.

After a couple of close calls with a red Cardinal and a Blue Jay, the day was really beginning to look promising. Jared and young Malcolm had just past a few large bushes on their left when Jared spotted a pair of ears on the edge and between two rows of soybeans.

Jared tapped Malcolm on the shoulder who was looking elsewhere at the time. But after a quick scan, he too saw the ears and they both stopped walking. The rabbit was oblivious to them being there and was apparently preoccupied with his feeding.

Jared signaled to Malcolm to take a couple steps forward for a clearer view of the head. Malcolm complied. Using the mounted scope, Malcolm "glassed" the head of the rabbit and placed the head on the crosshairs.

Jared noticed that Malcolm was breathing heavy. "Try to control your breathing," he whispered.

With the breathing slowed and the head still in the crosshairs, young Malcolm removed the safety and squeezed the trigger.

The 22 hour trek from Colorado to the southern agri region of Arkansas was near an end. Malcolm preferred the voyage across the panhandle at night instead of day because he would be spared the agony of traveling across the dry portions of Texas and Oklahoma. It could be visually terrible on the eyes as well as on the mind.

He was now in much more familiar territory. Having gone through Little Rock, Pine Bluff, Fountain Hill and points in between, he was only minutes from the Hamburg city limits that would put him even closer to the family.

Fond memories of growing up in such a small town poured into his mind as if a cap within his cranium was released. How simple life was for him as he and his buddies and his classmates carried on with their lives at the time.

They didn't realize it but life was good. It would start getting complicated after high school. Some married right away, others went to college and started their careers and others, like Malcolm did, are doing a stint in the military.

But no matter what order you start living your adult life and making your own mistakes, at some point you start dreaming of just how good you really had it staying at home and going to middle and high school. When your biggest worry was, "Is that home work assignment due tomorrow or next week?" Some of the high-hormone males would have a few more serious problems like, "Did that condom do the trick the night before?"

Those were the days, Malcolm thought.

He was now on the final stretch to his grandparent's house.

He could remember when he was in middle school and that this side road, off Main Street, would actually be gravel. It wasn't paved with black top until he was in high school. There were people he knew back in Fort Carson who probably had never seen a gravel road growing up. But he was also pretty sure that all of those who didn't were city folk.

The neighborhood didn't appear to have changed that much. A few new brick houses here and there but that was about it. Most of the people Malcolm grew up around couldn't afford a brick house but that changed as people started to get better jobs. Not that there were many around the area.

People were moving about in the neighborhood. It was much warmer and greener here than near the mountains. He came upon the house, a sight for sore eyes.

Once he turned off the paved road onto the semi-paved driveway he positioned his car. Relieved that he was here, he looked to the opened porch on his right but saw no one.

His grandparents, who were probably sitting near the window, got up from their chairs to gaze through the plain glass, wooden window of their house. The view from this particular window would routinely allow them to see what relative was coming down the road, as well as what child was misbehaving near their house so they could tell their parents.

Once they realized who it was, a smile came across their face and they started to make their way outside.

Malcolm smiled. He was home now. Maybe for a short time, but home just the same. He parked and shut the engine off.

It was time to see the folks.

Chapter Eleven

The pastor had just finished his final words to the crowd at the cemetery and the casket lowered into the ground as *taps,* no doubt provided by the VA, was played on a DVD player that sat next to the casket.

There were whimpering sounds made by some members of the precession and soft cries by Jarod's surviving daughters but with the exception of watery eyes, no member of the immediate family was very emotional. Not even Malcolm's grandmother made a sound. Of all the folks here, she had to be hurting the most.

Malcolm watched the casket being lowered. He was summoned back a year ago when he last saw his uncle alive.

He had just arrived in Arkansas. The final destination was home. But considering his uncle was in the VA hospital in North Little Rock and he had to travel through there anyway, he stopped by to see him. He wasn't sure when anyone from home had seen him last and it would be nice to give the rest of the family a recent update on Jarod's condition.

Despite the purpose for entering the grounds, Malcolm found the grounds somewhat serene while driving up the looping Fort Root drive.

This time of the year in the south, everything seemed green as well as clean. If you didn't know any better you would mistaken the complex for a historic college. But the hospital personnel in their various uniforms would quickly dismiss that idea.

After finding the right building and the right ward, Malcolm decided to check first with the nursing station to see if it was okay for Jarod to have visitors.

After getting a *go ahead, suga* from the head nurse, Malcolm walked down the hall to the room as he was instructed. After opening the door to the two-person room, Malcolm knocked softly on the heavy door. He wasn't sure if his uncle was asleep despite the TV being on.

"I'm awake," said Jarod. The voice was a little weak, not the usual clear, confident one that Malcolm was used to but he assumed it was Jarod talking.

Getting closer to the second bed, he saw his uncle laying on his back, the bed raised to give him a better angle to the TV. Malcolm could see his feet sticking out from his pajama pants. Jarod was actually lying on top of the bed sheets.

His uncle was happy to see his nephew. It had been about a year and it looked like his nephew had gained a few pounds. Even though one could clearly tell that was Jarod, his face appeared to have loss some muscle mass. In fact, his whole body had lost some muscle mass.

This was, surely Malcolm thought, due to his kidney problems.

"Would you get me some ice from around the corner? I want some water but I would like it a little cooler than right from the tap," said Jarod. Malcolm noticed his frail hands as he was handed the plastic ice bucket.

Malcolm quickly left the room and barely made it around the corner before tears came running down his face. He didn't want his uncle to see his eyes watery and was glad that an opportunity arose where he was able to escape from the room to get his composure.

His weak uncle's condition caught him off guard and he barely held it together in his room. He was sure that the staff was doing everything they could do for him, but Malcolm couldn't help think that his condition was deteriorating.

You got to shake this thing and get back in that room, Malcolm thought to himself. A young candy stripper who appeared to be making her rounds saw Malcolm but continued her way.

While still in the hallway, he spotted an ice machine and retrieved some ice.

Once back in the room but after making sure that his eyes and face were dry, his uncle and him caught up on things. Even got in a laugh or two. They were only interrupted once and that was by the nurse to get some vitals.

They continued on with their discussion, ranging from the type of food he got in the hospital to the calls and topics he got from momma. Even though he talked rather vibrant when he rambled about home, Malcolm noticed that he made no mention of getting out of here. It was as if he was at ease with the possible idea that this would be his last home.

Jarod figured that Malcolm would stay until sunset if he didn't say anything. Jarod turned to him and told him, "It's about time for you to get back on the road before it gets dark."

Reluctantly, Malcolm told him that he was right but in his heart he wasn't ready to leave his uncle.

After some coaching from his ever so persistent uncle, Malcolm rose up from his visitor's chair and gave his uncle a big hug. After making a mental note of the messages to be delivered from Jarod, Malcolm walked slowly out the room.

Malcolm would exit the room without saying the words, "I love you." That was something the men in the family didn't say to each other, they all felt they didn't have to. With a final wave, his uncle and he departed.

Just outside the room and right next to the nursing station, the tears came flowing again.

The nurse who was sitting there saw Malcolm as he walked past but only said, "Goodbye."

What hurt Malcolm the most was that he couldn't help think that he could have just seen his uncle alive for the last time.

That would prove to be true.

With the casket in the ground, the sun was released from the cloud cover. After most of the day being secluded, the sun almost given the appearance of a re-birth finally appeared at that moment.

It seemed so serene. It was at that time that Malcolm's grandmother grasped the hand of her surviving son tightly and began to cry.

"I can't believe he's gone, I just can't believe it!"

"It's gonna be all right, Mamma."

After the pastor said a few last words, Malcolm as well as the family exchanged emotional hugs with friends then he escorted his grandmother over to where the limousine was waiting.

Major Matt Balin was not accustomed to getting his butt chewed by the battalion commander.

If anything, when he had contact with his commander, it was usually him calling and telling him congratulations on him or his crew accomplishing a training mission or about some future officers meeting. But not this time.

The commander told him that he has never in his 25 years of military service heard of anyone turning down a promotion. That usually doesn't happen. And he wanted to know how he was going to correct the problem.

After satisfying the commander with his speedy and simplistic solution, the commander and the major continued their discussion with more important mission matters. Afterwards, the commander felt that he made his point known about the earlier issue and that the competent major could easily put to rest such a minor problem. A subtle threat, in most cases, usually does the trick; he thought. The idea that he even had to go on that level over a trivial matter was still puzzling to the commander.

In any case, the major was not used to getting such calls and he set things in motion to make sure that such a call would not be targeted to him again. Or at least for nothing as petty and chicken shit-ish as not wanting to go to PLDC.

After finishing up his earlier conversation with the battalion commander and after a hefty lunch at the Colin L. Powell officer's club, Major Balin got on the phone with Preacher's platoon sergeant.

He stated to the SFC *their* particular problem and offered possible solution to handling it.

The seasoned sergeant listened to the officer on the phone. At times, the sergeant appeared not to believe what he was hearing, but he wasn't shocked. While going up the ranks, serving with both officer and enlisted, he had seen and heard a lot, both good and bad. By now, he was not surprised how one person could screw another. How one or more people could derail careers or possible lives? And now he was seeing it again. An officer about to shit on his fellow soldier. Like in most companies or agencies, you had those who would get what they wanted at any cost. Regardless who they walked over. But you didn't expect to see that in a *cohesive* military unit. At least not one like here, and not your own troops. But the reality is that every entity, civilian or military, has their bad apples, SFC thought. Now this time his commander was doing so, or about to do so with no regret in his tone.

SFC Miles figured that something had to prompt this. He wasn't sure what it was but something or somebody had to stick a spur up the major's butt in order for him to advocate something like this. He had a sense of desperation in his voice. Perhaps someone told him that he won't get Lieutenant Colonel if he didn't know how to stomp stuff like this out.

The prick, the SFC thought of him as such by this time, even suggested that such a deviance of the system by the specialist may look to some that this unit, the section and its NCOs has a morale and discipline problem. In other words, what may start at the top would eventually roll down hill.

But after hearing what the major said or more so, how it was implied, the SFC came to his soldier's defense.

"Sir," the SFC started off saying. "Specialist Preacher is a very smart but thoughtful specialist. If he told anyone that he has no desire to go to PLDC, then perhaps he did so in order to prevent wasted resources on him since he may be getting out of the Army. If that's the case, then those resources should be going to someone else. If by chance Specialist Preacher changed his mind, which I doubt, then he would simply have to wait his turn."

"Sergeant Miles, you have your instructions. I expect you to carry them out. I want this matter taken care of ASAP," said the major.

On the other end of the phone, the SFC pulled the phone from his ear and cursed it silently before bringing it back to the side of his head. "Yes sir -- I understand," he said hesitantly.

"Good." The line went dead.

"What a real fuck head. Shit really does flow upstream," muttered the SFC.

Really feeling it at the end of the workday, Petersen felt exhausted. Iron Horse Week put everyone behind and playing catch up had to be the word on this Monday. Even though most people appeared fresh and ready to go, there was still a lot of work to catch up with. All sections within the building appeared busy earlier in the day. A few had even chosen to skip lunch, but Petersen wasn't one of them. Keeping her figure didn't necessarily mean passing over meals. At the very least, she was going to leave the office on her lunch break just to get away. Petersen was a hard worker but a workaholic, she wasn't.

At the unit barracks and sufficiently showered, she seemed to have been magnetized to her soft bed.

She was stretched out on it and watching a show. She was so glad that unlike her roommate, she was not on duty tonight. Of all nights, she was happy it wasn't tonight.

Although she appeared to be affixed on the TV, Petersen's mind drifted.

The friendship ring, sparkling as her hands rested on her stomach caught her attention. So symbolic of the friendship that Malcolm and she shared together. She thought about the ring and Malcolm all the time. In fact, there wasn't a whole lot more she did think about.

But all of the potential that may come with Malcolm and her in relationship may be in jeopardy, she thought.

In light of receiving the friendship ring, Petersen decided to meet with Hodkins during lunch break earlier in the day. At the meeting, she had hoped to call off his plans concerning Malcolm.

As it turned out, it was easier than she had thought. She thought he would really be upset with the idea of her receiving that friendship ring. But Hodkins acted as if it wasn't a big deal as far as it concerned his plan. And Petersen was soon back at work.

Petersen stopped staring at the ring and decided to start reading a book of short stories before she got too sleepy. The TV was powered down with the single press of the remote.

It was a Friday and I couldn't wait to get off of work and enjoy my weekend.

I just couldn't wait to get home and hop into a bubble bath and just sit there and relax. I had recently broken up with my girlfriend of three years and really wasn't feeling up to going out even if it was the weekend. When I arrived home I just looked at the empty three-bedroom house and right then I decided that I would go out and have myself a good time. Earlier that day my friend, Catrell, asked me to go out with her just to get out of the house. I turned her down but now I was changing my mind.

I got in the tub so I could get dressed and go out. I called up my friend and told her that I would go out with her. There was no point in me sitting at home just feeling sorry for myself. Catrell and I met at the local club and we just sat at the bar and had a couple of drinks. Finally Catrell went out on the floor to dance with a friend she saw when she came in. Right then a beautiful woman came up and sat right next to me. I mean she was so gorgeous. She had long jet-black hair, brown complexion and had the body of a goddess.

The whole time she was sitting there I wanted to say something to her but I just couldn't. I just couldn't think of what I wanted to say to her but I did know what I wanted to do with her. Of course we said our hellos but that was about it. I really wanted to know her name but I was too shy to ask. Catrell finally came back and asked me was I about ready to go and I said, "Yeah." As we were getting ready to leave all I could think about was the fine sista at the bar. The person whose name I wanted to know so bad.

We were headed out to the parking lot and I started searching for my keys and I just couldn't find them. Just then out of the blue I heard someone call out my name. I turned around and right before my eyes it was my goddess whose name I didn't know, but somehow she knew my name. She told me that I left my keys on the bar. I had a keychain with the name "CJ" on it, which my friends called me. However, I still didn't know her name. I said, "Thank you, but could you tell me your name?" She told me her name was Natasha. Now I had a name to go with the face in my fantasies.

After I got my keys back Catrell went on home and left me in the parking lot with Natasha. She had this soft seductive voice that could turn you on at just the sound of it. We stood in the parking lot and talked for a while. I found out to my disappointment that she did have a girlfriend but things weren't really going the way she hoped. They had been going through some problems. It turned out we had a lot of things in common. After a while we started wrapping up the conversation and God knows I didn't want it to end, but it was getting late. I asked her if she had a ride. She said, "Yes." She came with friends, but she too didn't want to end it on that note. She asked me if She and I could talk some time. I said sure and I gave her my number. On my way home all I could think about was Natasha and her sultry voice.

A week went by without a word. I really didn't think I was going to hear from her. Until one morning I was awakened by the telephone and on the other the end I heard that oh familiar voice. It was Natasha. "I'm sorry for calling you so early. I just wanted to get in touch with you before you made plans. I called to ask you if you would consider having dinner with me tonight."

I said, "Yeah, if you would consider having dinner at my house and let me cook for you." She agreed. "Would seven o'clock be fine?"

She said, "Yeah, that would be great." I gave her my address and she said that she would be sure to be there on time.

Seven o' clock came and she was at my place. She had on a pink silk buttoned down blouse with black dress pants. She looked even more beautiful than when I first saw her. We sat down at the table, ate dinner and talked. After dinner, we washed up the dishes together. "Dinner was delicious," she said.

I said, "Thank you." After washing dishes, we went into the living room and watched television. Well, I wasn't really watching television as much as I was watching her. We talked some more and I just enjoyed being with her.

We were sitting on the couch talking about our relationships and what was going on. She told me that she felt real close to me and felt like she had known me forever. She felt like she could talk to me about anything. She told me she was in a bad relationship but she just didn't have the courage to leave her because she loved her. At least she thought she did. The more we sat and talked the more I wanted to be with her. However, did she feel the same way I did? I could only hope. I didn't want to ruin the relationship we had or were beginning to have.

After hours of talking and watching some television, we both decided that it was getting late and we would call it a night. As much as I wanted her to stay, deep down inside I knew that it wouldn't be. So we hugged goodbye and said our goodnights. I told her to call me when she gets home so that I would know that she made it home safely. I waited up but that call never came. So I called her and a hostile voice on the other end picked up.

"Hello!"

"May I speak to Natasha?"

"Who the hell is this?" she said. I told her my name and then she hung up. However as she was hanging up the phone there was arguing and fussing in the background.

Sunday came and no word from Natasha. I was worried but I didn't want to take the risk in calling and it would lead to another argument. I figured the voice on the phone was her girlfriend. Monday came and it was time to go back to work. When I got home from work I was exhausted and just wanted to crash. Later on that evening Natasha called and apologized for her girlfriend's action. I asked her if she was OK and she said she was but somehow I didn't think so. Natasha and I kept in touch over the weeks, but I still wish it was more to us than friends. Sometimes we would meet and go have lunch and catch up on what was missed, and the whole time I just wanted to be with her. Although I didn't let her know that.

Another weekend came and I decided to go to the club just to get my mind off of Natasha. Catrell and I went to the club and we had a pretty good time dancing and having a couple of drinks. To my surprise Natasha and her girlfriend were there. Natasha didn't look happy. So I went up to their table and said my hellos and introduced myself to her girl, Jackie. Not too long after a few more drinks and a little dancing with Catrell it was about time to go. I had asked Natasha for a dance but she turned me down. Natasha and Jackie *were nowhere in sight when we were leaving. No telling how long they had been gone.*

As we were leaving I saw Natasha and Jackie arguing. Then I saw Jackie slap her and before she could do it again I raced over there to stop it. Jackie and I were about to get into an altercation when Catrell stepped in. Jackie apologized and begged for Natasha's forgiveness. The funny thing about it, she did and I just didn't understand it.

Although I was still mad I couldn't do anything but respect her decision. I offered to take her home but she said she would be all right. So we all went our separate ways but Natasha was still on my mind.

When I got home I had calmed down a little but it was still on my mind. I knew the reason I was so upset. I'd been in love with Natasha from the first time I saw her in the club at the bar and I wanted her to be with me. She was my choice I just wasn't hers. However, I would try to be there for her in any way I could.

The next day was pretty quiet with me still wondering how Natasha was. I just decided to stay home and chill. Evening came and I cooked a delicious little dinner. That's one thing I love to do is cook. I just didn't have anybody to cook for. After dinner I washed up the dishes and ran a bubble bath. After finishing up I went in the living room and watched some television. Somewhere along the way I fell asleep and all of a sudden I was awakened by a knock at the door. I went to the door it was Natasha. She told me she had broken up with Jackie, because she was in love, true love, with someone else. I asked her who and just then she laid a kiss on me that I hadn't experienced for a long time.

She wrapped her arms around my neck while she passionately kissed me and my knees buckled. I didn't know what else to do but enjoy the bliss. I closed the door with my right hand while still holding her with my left and rubbing all over her body. We went to the couch and she got on top of me and started to grind on me so passionately. She undressed me and I undressed her slowly. Our bodies still intertwined with one another. Our clits grinding together I could just feel her moisture. We proceeded to the floor, now I was on top. Although I wanted Natasha this is not how I wanted it to happen. I got up and grabbed her by the hand and led her to the bedroom. I pulled back the silk sheets, turned on some Gerald Levert and turned off the lights. This is how I wanted it. This is how my fantasies were about her and they were coming true right before my eyes.

We climbed into bed kissing even more now, with me nibbling all over her body from head to toe. I wanted this to be special for both of us. I nibbled on her nipples and kissed her breasts gently and slow. She moaned with every kiss. I kissed on down to her belly button and then on the inside of her thighs. I tasted the sweetness and just licked her clit like it would be the first and last time we would ever do it. I took my time in loving her right. I sucked on her clit and she began to jerk. I put my stiff tongue inside of her and just made love to her long and hard. She then started to get louder and jerked even more. When I felt that she was about there I stopped and came back up and kissed her on the lips so she could taste her own sweetness. Now we were both coming close to our climax. I stopped and took out a strap-on and gently slid it into her.

I use long slow strokes while kissing her with such passion. She wrapped her legs around me and that turned me on even more. Her moans were getting louder and our clits were still rubbing together with each inward motion. She started to move her hips with my hips while still kissing me. She nibbled on my ears knowing that that was one of my spots. We started getting faster and faster. She started calling out my name telling me to go faster, and faster, harder and harder.

She told me that she was coming. I said, "Not yet." She begged me to let her come. I said, "No! not yet. I want you to remember this feeling of how it feels just before you climax." She still begged me to let her come while I was still stroking her with long strokes while kissing her deeply. Finally we climaxed together with such intensity and love.

Afterwards we laid in the bed cuddling and talking. She told me that she was in love with me from the first time she saw me at the club and I told her the feelings were the same with me. I'd been wanting her in my arms forever and now she was finally here. We fell asleep holding each other. I was just happy to have her here with me just smelling the sweet smell of her perfume.

Petersen found this book of black lesbian short stories prominently displayed as she was going through *Barnes & Noble* to get to the inner sanctions of her favorite mall.

It was as though the display was deliberately placed were she would see it in her attempt to get to her destination.

Normally, she would avoid going through this short cut of the shopping center but on that day, she was in a hurry. Perhaps, she thought, she was also avoiding any temptation of visiting the gay/lesbian section of this or any bookstore as she had done in the distant past. Apparently, it wasn't distant enough. This, she thought, would keep her on the straight and narrow. Deep down now, she felt that she had failed herself.

With the room lights off, it was time to call it a day. She couldn't help but feel guilty of the feelings she was now experiencing, not to mention anticipating the next chapter of her new book.

Hodkins too was chill'in. Haven't yet gotten his shower and still in his ACUs, he was relaxing watching the Hoosiers and the Badgers go at it. No guests tonight to watch the college game. Just him, the wide screen HDTV and his chips & salsa.

"You're getting your ass spanked, Badgers. Not one of you knows how to play defense."

Hamburg was "The City of Prosperity," according to the sign at the city limits. Prosperity for the Ashley County town of three thousand was needed to keep it viable as a town.

The end of the 90's, some would say the country's most financially booming decade, didn't quite help the area that munch. The Delta area town was seeing improvements, Malcolm thought. But these improvements was slow, a process made more complex by distrust among the races in some cases as well as the reluctance to invest in the area.

The giddy promise of the millennium meant little to the majority of people who resided in the town of over 2900 people. Unemployment was high and pay low for many of the jobs that did exist. With the exception of the jobs that some had at the nearby Georgia-Pacific Plywood and Paper plants in Crossett, Arkansas—about 15 miles away. Other jobs were more in the area of service and tree harvesting sectors. The tree harvesting, obviously, supported the large GP plants.

There was a time when a person, high school graduate or not, could count on working at the Hamburg Shirt Factory or take the 15 mile commute to Crossett to work at one of the plants. But those days were over.

The Hamburg Shirt Factory had long since closed its doors and like a lot of companies, crossed the border to Mexico. But it did this after struggling decades with the US economy. GP was once a lot of people's first choice for employment who wished to stay in the Southeastern Arkansas area. It was also employing people farther south as far as Bastrop, Louisiana. But a bitter strike over a decade ago changed its philosophy about a lot of things.

During that strike the union strongly insisted on getting a bigger share of the company's profits by demanding significant pay raises as well as assurances that senior workers at the Plywood plant be given the opportunity to work at the Paper plant next door which was well known to pay far higher wages for less work.

The strike went into the days and weeks. It had got to the point where strikers were making and setting crude metal tire cutters on the roads leading into the plants to delay the raw materials and "scabs" from producing wood and paper products.

GP eventually brought in its own security personnel from Monroe, Louisiana, 60 miles away, to reduce or eliminate actions such as this. GP's own Georgia-Pacific Lake, used by fishermen obviously but more importantly to provide a water source for its power plants, had to be guarded 24 / 7 at its intake point. Obviously GP couldn't trust anyone in the immediate Southeast Arkansas area to guard its facilities. In diminutive communities such as this, a lot of people were either related to each other or simply had very close relationships with those who work for GP. There was a lot of sympathy for the workers at the plant during the strike and none for GP.

That strike left a bitter taste with both the workers and GP management. Months later, stricter promotion policies were enforced and employment at both plants was dependent on your score from its newly implemented tests. Like most things in life: *Change was a comin'*.

This was a setback for some since only about 72 percent of Ashley County's 24,000 residents were high school graduates and about 17 percent of the county's residents were still below the poverty level. The lack of education was an economic impediment. The area's basic problem was human resources development and it would take a long time to remedy that. The lack of a well-educated, well trained labor force was why there's no Saturn plant in the area. And the absence of such industries was what made many of those who were highly trained leave the area for work or didn't return if you were trained outside the area.

With the Shirt Factory long gone; P.E. Barnes, Hamburg's only lumber yard, barely afloat and stricter hiring as well as some possible layoffs at the GP plants; many felt they had no real future in the area. No area growth, no education on top of that, meant dead-end jobs. Some would even go as far to say that the only way to get a good job was have a friend at the bank or at some other profitable business or plant. As a result, some people just vacated the area.

The farm life, abundant forestry and textile work that kept the region going was gone. Social programs such as welfare that existed decades ago were reduced or eliminated. Generally the people here had been lulled into the thinking or the concept there's supposed to be a slower lifestyle and we don't need to achieve or catch up to the rest of the world. This attitude was a carry-over from generations of the country's inhabitants who supplied labor for the old plants.

The situation drove many into public assistance, dependence and disillusionment. Welfare, or W2 as it is known today has never been much of a living. Welfare reform cut off many sources of income that generations relied upon. Some city residents who'd once believed they couldn't work now found they can not work.

But their may be some encouraging signs of a type of revival in the future. One area was in the type of agriculture. Row-cropping or cotton, soybean and rice farming; which had always been among the staples of the area, had over the years suffered from falling prices in an increasingly competitive world market. As a result, row-cropping had been dependent on government subsidies.

But an alternative crop such as catfish farming was taking hold in this area of the nation we called *The Delta*.

The other area that just may be sort of a catalyst for some change was family ties. Some of the natives were coming back because their roots were here. Some would say a place with unlimited needs in human capital, a stark contrast to what some others might say, and plan to be of some service.

The area overall had a sense of serenity to it, its friendly and life is certainly a little slower here. Malcolm could certainly see himself back here in his later years. But not now.

The sun was signifying that the day was about to be put to rest. The visits with neighbors and friends were wrapped up and Malcolm decided that he wanted to spend some more time with his grandparents before he left early in the morning. Early for Malcolm was about 2 am. By the time he would see sun up the next morning, he figured he would be well out of the state of Arkansas.

Malcolm, narrowly missing a beagle and a spotted hound in full sprint, was approaching the driveway when he also spotted some people setting out back next to the driveway of his grandparents' house.

Getting closer he realized that it wasn't more visitors, which he had feared--he needed a break--but his grandparents, uncle and aunts who were actually sitting outside.

Malcolm's grandparents enjoyed very few amenities, such as air conditioning. They were definitely of a different generation. So as they noticed the sun approaching its setting position and its low lighting, they opted to bring out some chairs and hopefully enjoy the break of the day's heat. But on this day, the setting of the sun didn't necessarily equate to the dropping of the temperature. At least, not drastically anyway.

The grandparents, their adult children and their brats like those before them were simply enjoying some of the great pleasures of life, simply enjoying each other's company as each contributed a story. But with an added bonus.

A treat caught Malcolm's eye. In addition to the friendly conversation and its occasional laughter, most were availing themselves to some watermelon. Not just any watermelon but one they commonly referred to as the "yellow meater" type. Most watermelons were red but some had yellow meat or flesh.

Apparently Malcolm's grandparents had one stashed away in the house and decided that this was as good as any occasion to treat everyone. And everyone seems to be enjoying him or herself.

One of Malcolm's young male cousins finished ripping the last piece of watermelon rind off. He felt a seed inside his mouth and spit it out. It flew a few yards and landed in the grass just short of the pen where the chickens were.

"Hey, that's pretty good," a young female cousin said. "You spit that seed a long way. Can you do it again?" she asked.

The young'in bit off another piece of melon off. This piece had three seeds in it. He spit one, and then the next. Each seed flew through the air, landing in the grass again but still short of the reach of the chickens. Each one went a little further than the one before.

"Here, let me try that," the young girl said. She ate a big chunk out of the watermelon and filled her mouth with seeds. She spit them out, one after another and they soared through the air, landing even further than her male cousin.

They both were now very involved in this watermelon seed spitting contest. Juice ran down the chins of each of the children as each gathered the seeds in their mouths, puckering up and spitting them out.

"We're having a contest to see who can spit the watermelon seed the furthest. Do you want to try to beat mine?" one said to another.

"Wow! That was good. You're the winner so far."

Folks seemed relax. Even the chickens, housed in their fenced area, were not "cackling" as they mingled among each other. But each did strategically position themselves to tackle a watermelon rind once they start flying over the fence. They eyed the festivities as if they had some idea of what was going on.

An occasional hunting dog or two would also make an appearance in the gathering until someone would notice and a "shoo" would be heard. Not every household in the neighborhood would place their hunting dogs in a fenced pen or kennel.

Malcolm always thought it was unfortunate that it sometimes took a tragedy or some major incident to bring folks together. It may be only temporarily but in most cases, they come together and over a period of time life got back to some normalcy. For better or for worse.

But that was of no consequence now. What seemed to matter to all that was sitting and enjoying each other's company if only for the moment. This seemed to be on Malcolm's grandmother's mind as well. She wasn't all smiles and laughs but she seemed to enjoy the presence of the family. It made Malcolm happy.

CHAPTER TWELVE

Nearly all of the 100 or so seats in the courtroom were filled, mostly with the out-of-town reporters. Unlike in the hallway, the courtroom's bright white ceiling appears to enhance the chandelier's lighting. It even created its own snow flake effect up there.

The historic room was now occupied with both its own soldiers and those who wished to cover them.

SFC McCullen was taken to the courtroom. Captain Leonard Brookhiser was seated next to him. The two discussed how today's court martial proceedings would take place, the witnesses that would be called to testify and the full compliment of "he said, she said."

McCullen momentarily broke from the interaction he had with his lawyer. No "excuse me, sir" was even said by the SFC. This was his trial and he could care less if the officer was a little pissed. What could he do? McCullen scanned the room looking for his wife. He didn't see her again. As if he missed her in the crowd, he scanned it again but slower than before, checking every seat, but still there was no sign of her.

Soon afterwards the judge entered the room. All present rose to their feet and sat back down again. The court martial of Sergeant First Class Randall McCullen had begun.

McCullen watched two witnesses, each testifying against him taking the stand giving their version of events. One of whom was Pvt. Folster. The little fucker, McCullen thought, actually told a very accurate account of events but the only two people in the room that knew that for sure was Folster and him. The court would have to prove their case against him.

McCullen knew that with most military trials, the UCMJ was stacked against you. You simply not supposed to prevail in these trials. At the most, he had to do what he could to minimize the damage but there was that hope, that chance that one could get off totally free.

Based on the briefings he had received from the young lieutenant, McCullen assumed the court had to prove that he raped--one of many charges--PFC Muse. This, he thought, would be a little hard considering the haffa had to have plenty of cum between those legs that night. Then it was the possibility of her consenting to having sex with all those drugs *she* took.

The SFC sat there through the testimony, stoic most of the time and even had a smirk on his face at other times but once he was conscious of that smirk, he eliminated it. He would ride this storm out. He had to, he had no choice. McCullen was not about to help the U.S. Army make their case against him. As long as he had a chance, he was going to cling to it.

Every one of Petersen's girlfriends was busy today. They were either tied up at work, out with their boyfriend or, in the case of one, home on leave. Petersen didn't have close married friends.

Preacher was also tied up at work and he couldn't leave early to enjoy the day off with Petersen. Petersen wanted to get away from the barracks for awhile and she needed to get off post. What better way to do it than to shop? After making some last minute touch ups in the room, she got her purse and exited.

Petersen managed to exit the front door without catching anybody's attention, slowing her down from eventually reaching the mall. Surprisingly, there was no one hanging outside near the entrance doors having a conversation.

After walking a few blocks past Post Headquarters and Grant Library with its manicured lawns, Petersen had reached the taxi stand. It was conveniently located near the Fort Carson Bank, Commissary and Main Post Exchange to take advantage of the high-volume traffic area. The walk was quite comfortable. Sunny but the cool breeze coming down from Pike's Peak required those venturing outside to wear at least a light jacket.

The driver in the lead taxi in line noticed Petersen approaching him and immediately got out of his cab to open one of the rear doors. The drive to the mall didn't exactly take Petersen mind totally away from Fort Carson. The driver, an elderly white guy with a somewhat dirty John

Deere Tractor cap on his head, had the radio turned to the ABC Radio Network.

About 10 minutes in the drive, the hourly news came on and after the intro, the lead story was broadcasted:

A military judge ruled that a jury should consider rape charges against Sergeant First Class McCullen who had sex with a subordinate, even if the woman did not resist or state her objections.

The judge issued his ruling in the case against McCullen, who faces counts of sexual misconduct. The defense had sought dismissal of some of those charges. The judge said sergeants have so much power over their subordinates—ordering them where to sleep and eat and how to act—that they are like parents.

This reporter obviously is getting the world of a basic trainee mixed up with life after basic training, Petersen thought.

Because of that authority, sergeants don't need to use a weapon or threaten privates with harm to fit the definition of "constructive force" necessary for a rape conviction, the judge said.

"They are conditioned to follow the sergeants orders," the judge said in his denial of a defense request to dismiss rape charges. "I think there is a sufficient body of law to find there is constructive force in this case."

Angered by the judge's decision, defense attorney Brookhiser argued that "A woman in her own mind can think anything she wants and later claim it's rape. How is a man supposed to defend himself against that? Are the women so weak that they can't even open their mouths and say, 'no'?"

Two witnesses testified this week that McCullen forced himself upon the young female private who was under the influence of a drug without using a weapon, to have sex with him. It was not clear if any of these witnesses struck a deal with the prosecution since we got word that these same two individuals would be having a trial of their own. The Defense argued that any threats were misguided or imagined.

One observer in the courtroom did come to one consensus. "This is the most interesting situation, to have everybody pointing fingers in the same courtroom. The judge will just have to figure this one out."

The defense was expected to call its first witness later in the week.

After the broadcast, Petersen noticed the driver shake his head. She also noticed a hint of body odor coming from the driver or the cab itself smelled with the various body odors of its previous occupants. "It's a shame that happened to that little girl in this community. I could barely make a pickup this morning on post for all those news vans in the way and all," he muttered.

Petersen wasn't sure he was sorry for Muse or that he almost missed his tip. But it didn't matter to her. She refused to pickup on his conversation today. She knew the old fart would probably almost turn around in his seat if he knew that one of the witnesses was sitting in his vehicle. Besides, they were almost to the mall. Traffic was light today.

At 1730 that afternoon a sergeant by the name of John Q. Smith brought the unit commander a manila folder. Once the door to the commander's office was closed, a quick display of the visitor's credentials with shield was shown and the pleasantries were over. The folder was opened. "This is the bio on Specialist Four Preacher," he said. "The picture was taken when he was a PFC, but he doesn't look much different now."

"I know what he looks like, Sergeant Smith, John Q. or whatever your name is," said the irritated captain. The captain couldn't tell what irritated him more. The fact that someone going by the name of John Q. was in his presence or that the person was handing him a folder with the truth, half truth or flat out lies. *What prompted all this?* He found it hard to believe that the failure of a specialist to attend PLDC would be cause for an Army Criminal Investigation Division agent to be in his office.

He would love to tell the agent to get the hell out of his office but he knew that he didn't have the power to do so. The ball was in motion and orders were given. Besides, the person sitting in front of him could have very well been a major under cover. He had heard about guys and gals like these and the work that they do but he had a bad feeling about this. *This is a fucking search and destroy mission.*

"Just give me a minute to look at this." The agent sat attentive and patient. Perhaps he had been through it all before. Most commanders and especially the perpetrators gave him the same "house warming." The agent decided to observe his current surroundings.

The unit CO's office was a large square room, paneled and carpeted, with shelves of legal books lining two walls, a conference table with leather arm chairs and an futon couch. Behind his desk, a steel flag stand displaying the American flag.

The young CO's office wasn't the standard cookie cutter décor. No gray tile on the floor and no visible government gray cabinetry. The furnishings were contemporary but practical. By the looks of things, the agent thought, this CO either had ambitions of becoming a lawyer, was a lawyer or planned on becoming one in his next life after the military. He wouldn't ask. The CO wasn't in any mood for small talk with the likes of him despite being on the same team--The U.S. Army team. But it is possible for one to be on the same team but have different goals.

Frowning behind the horn-rimmed glasses that made him look bookish, the CO continued to read the file and eventually swiveled in his chair to face the window, his back to the agent. What he initially read was of someone who came from humble beginnings and eventually did quite well for himself while in the Army much like himself.

The captain was not a typical rear echelon support officer. He was born in New York City and grew up in Hell's Kitchen, then a rough part of town. It wasn't unusual to see crack vials lying on the sidewalk in his neighborhood. But fortunately for him, high school took him to a very different part of the city. Thanks to financial aid, he attended Horace Mann School in Riverdale, N.Y., a place better known for socialites than for soldiers.

The captain signed up in advance for the Army. On graduating, he went straight to boot camp at Fort Dix, New Jersey. He fought in the first Gulf War and made sergeant in 3 years and left as a scout sniper with two purple hearts and one distinguished service cross. Later, he left the Army and returned to Manhattan. He took night classes at New York University and worked by day as an investment banker for Goldman Sachs. After earning a degree in economics, he cofounded a company that installed satellite TV service to residential markets. He grew long hair and wore flamboyant clothes. He eventually met his future wife and they got married.

Some of the captain's peers and family members would say he eventually got bored with his civilian life and after hinting it around to his wife, the captain rejoined the Army. He was now 30 years old, married and a child on the way. Some would say it had to be hard on his family. His wife, a New Yorker and married to a hunky investment specialist and all of a sudden she ended up with "Rambo" on her hands.

Going back to the Army meant a 75 percent salary cut, but the captain loved it. After a year of officer's training, he was assigned as a second lieutenant to an infantry battalion. The then young lieutenant prepared his platoon by working the men hard. His men grumbled—enlisted men call officers like him "motarded"—motivated to the point of retardation. But he believed that the more they trained, the fitter they were, and the more chance they had of surviving a real war. The effort paid off.

He was later promoted to captain. But it came at a cost. Military life could be hard on families and one night it was believed that his wife gave him an ultimatum: either change his current lifestyle or your family may change. The compromise apparently ended with him eventually transferring from combat arms unit to support. Strings had to be pulled in his case to even accomplish something like that but it happened occasionally. The new captain finally was now running his own company with his family completely intact.

The CO looked at the photo for a minute before scanning the career biography. The photo was that of a very young-looking PFC with the sharp eyes and the taint-skinned face of an athlete. Much like today. The face was composed in an expression of watchful authority that bespoke officer material. Warrant Officer or even Commissioned Officer. His awards and decorations indicated a series of in-services and TDYs for training, commendations for projects completed and time served in West Germany.

He continued scanning the bio. "Likes Jazz and new age music, reads *Black Enterprise* and *ComputerWorld*, like to web surf and IM distance friends, lends money to close friends interest-free ..." The CO looked up from his papers. His glasses eased down the bridge of his nose. "Gee! You mean you don't know what color toilet paper he uses?" sarcastically asked the CO, but he put his eyes back on the file.

Once he started seeing what he viewed as very personal items, the CO barely scanned the rest of Preacher's CID file. After seeing the first paragraph of the second set of papers, the captain quickly surmised that the rest was pure bullshit. The CO spinned back around.

"Am I to understand that you think Specialist Preacher is gay and participating in such activity on and off the post?" stated the commander in a matter of fact manner. "If so, it would appear that you and your agency are throwing a lot of resources at him for an investigation of this type." The CO tapped his pen on his desk. "I have seen rape investigations involving a lot more personnel with fewer investigators than this."

As a matter of fact, why you aren't investigating a rape somewhere, the CO thought. According to some stats, one in every three hundred female service members was raped in the military compared to one in every three thousand in the civilian world. Fort Carson had more than three hundred female soldiers.

Agent Smith was also irritated by the demeanor of the CO. He expected it. "No, sir. At this point, we have no information that Preacher is gay or is involved in homosexual activity."

The CO seemed somewhat surprised to the point where he removed his glasses and placed them in front of him on his desk.

"Then why are you investigating him?"

The agent knew that the CO didn't bother to read the whole file. *It's there in the file I gave you, you prick.* "We are investigating other suspected service members on this post as well as nearby Peterson Air Force Base. Coordinating, of course, with our Air Force counterparts." The agent noticed the CO frowning again and continued his briefing. "Based on our investigation to date, these individuals, including females, all know each other in one way or the other and form a circle of friends around Specialist Preacher." The agent briefly rose from his chair to point to a yellow chart within the stack of papers in the CO's hand. It showed a picture of Preacher in the middle of the chart with lines going from him out to those under investigation. The chart showed that Preacher was the common link.

"This doesn't prove anything as far as Preacher was concerned," replied the commander.

"Enlisted personnel can be very close knit as you may know sergeant."

"Yes, I do sir." The agent wasn't about to get in a confrontation with the CO. Any hesitation by the CO to support the investigation would be dealt with swiftly by those a few pay grades above him within CID. He needed to end this conversation. End this meeting so he could get to work. He cleared his throat.

"Sir, the CID will continue our inquiry in this matter and hopefully get a resolution to it. What we need from you personally is your full cooperation."

"And what would that be exactly," responded the CO.

After about another 20 minutes of more confidential and sensitive details as far as the unit command was involved in the investigation, the meeting was almost over. The CO heard it but didn't won't to believe it. He had no choice but to cooperate. It was his duty to do so. But if there was "blow back," he hoped that it found its way back to whomever started this bullshit. And this had bullshit written all over it.

"You have my cooperation Agent Smith. I have no choice." With those closing words, the meeting was over. "PFC," shouted the CO. In about 3 seconds the CO's door was opened and a young PFC in starched ACUs had entered the room. "Show the sergeant out."

It was a typical day at the mall. It didn't seem to matter if it was a weekday or weekend; the mall was packed with people of all nationalities. Being in a military community can do that for a business. Most importantly every shopper had a bag. *Victoria's Secret. Baby Phat. Apple Bottoms. Target* or as some urban gals and gay guys like to pronounce, *"tar-jhay."*

Petersen grew excited when she remembered the big sale that was going on at *Express*. Petersen started off straight towards the store, and suddenly she stopped short when she realized that her stomach was growling. She had not eaten all day! So she turned around and made her way to *Applebee's*. Her heart started to beat a little faster when she saw the two fine guys standing nearby. One sported intricately styled cornrows, a Milwaukee Bucks jersey and low hanging, baggy designer jeans with *Timbs*. Like many Colorado bruthas of his generation, he projected a youthful, thuggish masculinity. He was the quintessential hip-hopper. Petersen was so distracted that she walked straight into another woman. "I'm sorry. Didn't mean to bump into you like that."

"It's ok. No harm done," she said after brushing herself off.

Now the Specialist was too embarrassed to even look at the guys she had noticed before. As she started to walk away, the woman she had bumped into stopped her.

"Excuse me," she said, "would you mind telling me who did your hair?"

Petersen smiled and told her that she had done it herself. People always complimented her on her hair styles. That day she wore it down and past her shoulders. The stranger looked amazed. She noticed that her hair looked really good too. "Your hair is pretty. Who did yours?" She smiled. She had a beautiful smile. She was really attractive.

Deep inside Petersen felt a knot of jealousy form in her stomach. She knew of course she was attractive, but not that unmistakably attractive. One person could think she was gorgeous and the next person could find her ugly. But with the young lady, there could be no debate about it. She had a creamy caramel complexion, with big brown eyes. They almost looked green if the light was cast a certain way. Her hair was a shade of brown that looked perfect with her skin color.

"What's your name?" she asked. Petersen wondered why she was dragging this out and she started to feel a little unease.

"Petersen," she replied, "what's yours?"

"Marie," she answered, "are you here alone?"

"Yeah," Petersen replied wondering where she was going with this.

"Well, I'm here alone too. Maybe we can just stick together today so we won't be so lonely." She saw the expression of doubt cloud Petersen's eyes because she quickly added, "Please, I really need someone to talk to right now. I'm from out of town. I just left my fiancé because I found out he was cheating on me." She looked like she could really use some support.

"Sure, sounds like fun!" the Specialist said, mustering all the enthusiasm she could. "I was just about to go get a bite to eat from *Applebee's*."

"Oh, me too!" she said. They walked together and took a seat.

Petersen ordered her food, and Marie and she both seated themselves at a table. "I really appreciate this," she said. "I don't know how I'm gonna make it through the week. I've been through so much shit."

"I know how that can be. I got out of a bad relationship myself about a year ago. His name was JaVon, a civilian."

Marie was obviously not in the military or even associated with anyone who was. She wondered why Petersen noted that he was a civilian and not in the military.

"He had the nerve to lay his hands on me."

"Oh no girl!" she shouted and laughed.

Petersen looked at her; she didn't know what to make of her. Was she trying to rip her off or something? They finished eating and went into *GAP* to try on some clothes. Marie asked her for her opinion of how she looked in a mesh, body gown. She looked wonderful. Petersen started to feel jealous again. Not only was she pretty, but she had the perfect body. Nice size breasts, about a 38 C, and a perfect butt! And she was not too skinny, or too fat. Just the right size. Not that Petersen looked at girls in that way anymore, but there was nothing wrong with comparing, was there?

The Specialist all of a sudden did not feel like trying anything on. But Marie literally forced her to try on two dresses. Afterwards, she told her she looked spectacular. "Yeah. Right," Petersen thought. Marie took her dresses to the check out counter, and asked Petersen if she was buying the dress. Petersen said, "No, I can't afford it."

"I got you. Come on."

Had Petersen just heard her say she was going to pay for the dress? This woman had to be crazy. She must have noticed her expression. She smiled and said, "Seriously. You don't have to worry about paying me back. It's my treat to you for giving me company today." Petersen was not going to go along with it, but in the end she persuaded her to let her buy that dress, along with three others from another store.

"What are you doing tonight?" Marie asked as they wrapped up their shopping spree.

"I don't know."

"What are you doing?" For some reason Petersen was feeling extremely close to Marie. It was as if she had known her for years now. "You know I have nothing planned. Why don't you come to my hotel room?" There was a look in her eyes that Petersen could not remember seeing in another woman's eyes before, not directed towards her anyway. Was it lust? No. Petersen did not want to get her hopes up. Deep down perhaps, Petersen really did want to get wrapped in another woman's arms again but never thought it would happen. And she damn sure would not initiate it. "I don't know."

Right before each gave their good byes, Marie handed Petersen a business card-size note. It contained not a telephone number or address, but the words *Yahoo IM* on it. Petersen thought for a minute. How did she know that she even had a computer? Perhaps she had spilled the beans on that during their lunch. The ladies wrapped up their day with a hug and each went their separate ways. Petersen never got her last name.

The waiting was just unbearable for Hodkins. No matter how long he's been in the army, he has never gotten used to the "hurry up and wait" syndrome that is all too prevalent in this life.

The whole PAS section of personnel was ordered to be at the NBC room at 1600 hours to get fitted for the new gas masks that would be issued soon to everyone in the unit.

Hodkins had arrived and arrived on time for a change. But despite arriving 30 minutes early, there was still a line running outside the door from the room and down the hallway. Getting in early and hopefully getting out at a decent time was also on everyone else's mind. But Hodkins took it in stride like everything else.

By 1730 hours, Hodkins had been fitted and a gas mask would be ordered for him. With that done, thoughts of the evening would be on his mind. With a smile on his face and his beret under his arms and ready until he was outside to mount it on his head, Hodkins almost trotted past fellow soldiers down the hallway aiming to get outside. He wanted to do this before someone stopped him with a "hey you" assignment. That was one reason why a lot of soldiers didn't mingle around inside the unit or simply chit-chat down the hallways because of the fear of getting assigned to a last minute "shit" duty assignment.

A female casually walking down the hallway reminded him of an unfinished task. Well actually, it wasn't her exactly but the faint perfume she was wearing that was picked up by Hodkins. Among other things, Hodkins paid close attention to what the opposite sex wore and that included what aroma they were wearing.

The fragrance reminded him of some unfinished business he had with Petersen. The other day at lunch would not be the last day the issue of repaying a favor would be discussed. Petersen may have thought so but a deal was a deal and too much was at stake to allow Petersen to weasel out of it without making an effort to talk her into changing her mind.

The day was still early so Petersen would be at the mess hall, coming from it or simply in her room relaxing before hitting a club with her girls. Petersen was not the type to just stay hold up in her barracks room unless she's broke, sick or had duty that night.

So it would appear that a visit to SPC Petersen would be in order this evening. Hodkins took the stairs to the second floor, passing by a couple of young female privates in the stairwell. *They are getting younger and younger.* Once they had clearly passed him, he managed to tactfully look back and get a view of their asses. Didn't want to get hit with a sexual harassment complaint. One was wearing ACU pants and the shape was not obvious but the other clearly had a nice "onion."

Hodkins managed to clear his head of mannish thoughts and concentrate on the issue at hand. Once on the lady's floor, he managed to find Petersen's room and knocked on the door until it opened unexpectedly.

It was Petersen's roommate. "Is Petersen in?" he said. The roommate was headed out to take care of an errand. Barely acknowledging him standing there, she had managed to maneuver around Hodkins. "Yeah. But home girl is about to hit the shower," she replied without breaking her pace down the hallway. Her roommate was still in uniform. Apparently her errand couldn't wait for her to change. "Go in. Just tell her I told you to do so."

"Cool," Hodkins said. And he did so with another tap on the door.

The room was not as tidy as in the case with most female rooms. Chairs and small tables appeared to have been just placed in the room and clothing was scattered on the beds. But then again it was after duty hours. They were entitled to do so. But with female rooms, Hodkins always observed that a nice lingering fragrance was always in the room. It didn't matter if it was after work, on the weekends or even after PT, the female rooms would always have a nice aroma in them. This one was no exception. The hard heads down stairs—well, that was another story.

Then he saw Petersen, who was apparently sitting at her desk on the opposite side of the room obscured by the tall wall locker. She was in a full pajama outfit. Nothing see through, nothing sexy or anything. Actually it could have been an outfit worn by his mother, he thought. Hodkins also noticed it wasn't even tight fitting but surprisingly quite loose on the Specialist.

After seeing him standing there, Petersen immediately knew what he wanted but asked anyway. "What do ya want?"

Fearing that she would be upset about him coming in the room, he immediately went into defensive mode.

"I got the okay from your roommate before coming in."

"Okay. What do ya want?" Hodkins decided to get right to the point and had already leaned back against the closed entry door. "Petersen you know what I want. We had a deal!" stated Hodkins with a look of seriousness on his face. It was a look of seriousness yet non-threatening. He wanted Petersen to follow through with her promise to help him but didn't want to come across as threatening in any way and give her an excuse to just forget about their deal.

Petersen sat on her bed still in view of Hodkins. "I wished I never promised to help you in that way," said Petersen. "A lot has happened since then."

"I know that." Pause. "But a deal is a deal."

He noticed that Petersen started staring at the floor and she shook her head as if she was in a small battle with her conscious on this issue. *At last she's thinking about it again. Is it possible she might lean back to my way of thinking now?* For about a minute, there was silence in the room. Hodkins allowed her to ponder the thought. She stood up and went back to her desk and retrieved her toiletry bag and large towel and returned in view to Hodkins.

"The answer is still 'No' Hodkins." She said it and barely looked at him standing there at the door. Hodkins had already seen her approach him and he shifted to the side of the door. Petersen was about to take a shower soon and thought that now was as good as any to do it. "I know what I promised. But I am sorry I can't do it," she said as she grabbed the knob and exited the room. Petersen wanted to vacate the room so fast that she didn't realize that she had left someone in her room alone. A guy at that.

"SHIT," Hodkins muttered. He wasn't sure if Petersen heard it or not and he really didn't care.

He paced the room. "Fuck. Fuck. Fuck," he said with such exertion that he thought that one of his facial muscles had pulled a cramp. He kept cussing in the room while staring at the lady's belongings but without realizing he should have left a while ago. It would appear that both Petersen and he weren't quite thinking at this moment. Both had a lot on their minds.

While he stood near the tall locker near Petersen's side of the room, he heard a series of beeps. Familiar beeps. Hodkins walked over to Petersen's desk and it was there he saw her notebook computer. Closer, he realized the monitor was up and the U.S. Army's *eArmyU* website was displayed. *The haffa must be taking some courses with her dumb ass.*

Hodkins was about to turn and walk away until he heard another beep. This time the beep was accompanied by a popup window. He realized it was one belonging to *Yahoo Messenger*. Petersen was in the middle of a chat session when Hodkins arrived at the door. One she had forgot to terminate prior to her leaving.

At the status bar of her desktop it indicated another program was running. Another web page was also opened. "what r your plans 4 tonight" displayed the message. Hodkins was curious about the other web page and quickly closed the popup window and pressed the corresponding program button on the status bar.

Within seconds, the website that was also running in the background on the notebook appeared in the forefront. The web page was a thread from *www.nudeafrica.com* site. It caught Hodkins completely off guard. For about a minute or so he didn't believe what he saw.

The thread of images was of beautiful black females, all nude, but most were non-facial pics displaying breast, ass and pussy shots. Some images were so clear and defined he could see sweat on the asses. Each image or set of images were accompanied by the user, in the form of a sign-on name. Most postings also would include a seductive remark or two. The postings were exclusively *by* females *to* a female audience or viewer.

After navigating back to the home page it was clear that this particular web page was by and for black females since other links on the web site had pages for black, straight and gay male visitors.

Hodkins looked up from the monitor. *What tha fuck! This bitch is a lesbian. Damn.*

Hodkins momentarily stared at the door knob in her room as if he wanted Petersen to walk in so that he could confront her. Instead his eyes went back to the monitor. "A lesbian on the fuckin' dl," Hodkins whispered while smiling. At a different place and time, Hodkins would have grabbed a chair but this room was not the place and now was certainly not the time.

"R u still there. Can we meet tonight?" was the message within another popup along with a beep. Hodkins manhood was slightly aroused by the revealing images he had seen and he tried mentally to reign it in. Hodkins made sure that the notebook computer as well as the desktop was just as he left it and quickly vacated the potpourri scented room. He was not about to confront Petersen now.

I will be talking to you later about our previous agreement after all Specialist Petersen. Hodkins smiled while walking down the upper floor hallway. *Yes, I will.*

CHAPTER THIRTEEN

Marie had rented a room at the Hampton Inn. As Petersen walked up to her room on the second floor, she couldn't help but wonder just what would go down in her motel room. What if they did not have anything to talk about? What if she did want me in a sexual way? Would she be up for the challenge? Once in her room, they chatted about simple things, and watched a little TV. After a couple of hours, Petersen realized with some surprising disappointment that Marie had not had any ulterior motives when inviting her to her room. Petersen was deep in thought when she heard. Marie asking her a question. "Oh, I'm sorry, what did you say?"

"I said have you ever made love to a woman before?"

"Uh, no," Petersen lied. "Have you?"

"Yes.... I was hoping I could make love to you."

Petersen's eyebrows met at the center of her forehead. She could not believe what she was hearing. "Shhhhhh," she said and placed her finger over Petersen's mouth, "don't say a word." She got up from the bed and started to remove her clothing. Like a battle plan, Marie wanted to bring "Shock and Awe" on Petersen before she had a lot of time to think about it.

First she took off her shirt. Then she slowly removed her pants. Underneath, she was wearing a matching black lace panty and bra set. Her breasts were a lot bigger that Petersen had thought. She was speechless, and her heart began beating a mile a minute. Petersen's pussy began to feel warm as she envisioned what was hiding behind the bra and panties. Marie then walked over to her portable radio and put in a CD.

162

Seconds later, *Omarion's* sexually unambiguous lyrics filled the room. Marie started bouncing, Petersen could not believe what she was seeing. She bounced really slow at first, and then she started shake dancing. Petersen was getting extremely wet watching her. Marie started shaking really hard. She pulled down the straps of her bra slowly, until her full breasts were exposed. They looked so juicy and succulent, Petersen wanted to suck them.

Suddenly, the thoughts of that night in Baltimore went through her mind. Marie's breasts looked big, and soft. She moved closer towards Petersen, still dancing. Marie got so close that her breasts were brushing Petersen's face. She placed a nipple on her lips, and Petersen opened her mouth and kissed her nipple.

She came closer, still dancing to the music. This time Petersen licked her nipple, and finally started to suck on it. She put the other one in Petersen's mouth and the Specialist did the same. Marie pulled Petersen's shirt off from over her head, and undid her bra which was clasped at the front. Marie took her bra completely off and she grabbed her hand to make Petersen stand up and dance with her. Petersen got up and started dancing, and she threw her back on top of the bed and laughed.

But Marie continued dancing, and now she turned her back towards Petersen so she could see her booty. She had a nice ass; Petersen got so turned on watching her shake it. She shook it really hard, and it was jiggling. She started pulling down her panties, and pulling them back up. Teasing her. She finally pulled them all the way down and threw them at Petersen. She was so beautiful. Petersen thought to herself that she would not mind eating her pussy. In fact, she wanted to very badly.

Marie moved closer to her and continued to dance. She grabbed Petersen's hands again, and pulled her up. She kissed her on the lips. Marie held her gently and kissed her again, this time placing her tongue in her mouth. "Relax," she said, "I won't hurt you. I just want to love you."

She stopped dancing, went over to the radio and turned it off. She came back to Petersen. "Lay down on the bed." This bitch is a control freak, Petersen thought. She followed her instructions. She lay down beside Petersen. "You're beautiful," she said. "You're so beautiful." She started to trace her finger up and down Petersen's body.

At that moment Petersen felt so special, she really did feel beautiful and *free*. "I think you're pretty too," Petersen said, at a loss for words.

Marie started to unzip Petersen's pants, and pulled them down. She also pulled off the Specialist's panties. Petersen was now completely naked.

Two naked women lying down beside each other. She wrapped her arms around Petersen, and her lips found their way back to her. They kissed passionately for about 5 minutes. Petersen wanted her so bad. Their tongues were moving in and out of each other's mouths, and Marie was holding Petersen ever so gently. Marie pulled away slowly, and started to kiss her mate's neck all over. She moved down to the breasts and started to suck on them. She put her breasts back in Petersen's mouth and she started to suck on them really hard. Marie pulled her breast away, and started to make her way down.

She gently trailed down her stomach with light kisses. When she finally made it to the small, neatly trimmed, v-shaped patch, Petersen gasped. Marie placed her hands on Petersen's inner thighs, and gently opened her legs wide. Marie started to lick her pussy and she felt like she was in heaven. Marie's tongue was so soft and wet. She just kept licking and licking and licking and sucking and kissing.... It felt so good Petersen started to hold her head down.

Petersen came so hard she thought her uterus would burst open. She was so satisfied, all she wanted to do now was go to sleep in her arms. But she knew that Marie probably needed some satisfaction too. Marie removed her stained face from between Petersen's legs. She now rolled over and laid on her back.

"My turn," Petersen said with a wicked smile on her face. Petersen didn't know if she could go through with this. Maybe she should just go now, she thought.

As usual, Marie seemed to be reading her mind. "Don't be scared of me. It tastes real good. She held Petersen's hand and pulled her closer. Petersen licked and sucked her breasts, and kissed her all the way down to her belly button. Petersen slowly pried her legs open as wide as possible. She was now looking directly at her wet pussy. She could not go through with this, she thought.

Just as she thought that, Petersen felt Marie's hand on the back of her head, pushing her down. "Eat me," she said in a sexy whisper. At this point, Petersen couldn't let her down. She stuck her tongue out to get a quick taste. Marie pushed her head down again. Petersen started to lick and lick and lick. Marie moaned and rolled her hips back and forth, pushing her pussy up to meet Petersen's tongue.

Petersen felt good knowing she was making Marie feel so good. She licked her clitoris hard and stuck her tongue in and out of Marie's vagina. Marie was going crazy, and she was pushing Petersen's head down as far as possible into her pussy. She started moving really fast, and Petersen thought she was about to come, *should I stop now*? Marie pulled her head up and Petersen figured she was done.

But Marie laid her down on her back. She was gonna eat her again! Petersen thought with excitement. But Marie had other plans as she lowered her pussy onto Petersen's face. She sat down on her face, with her eyes facing the bed board. She grabbed onto the bed board and started riding Petersen's face. Petersen stuck her tongue in and out of her vagina as she moved her pussy back and forth. She started moving fast and breathing hard.

Then she slowed down and started dragging her pussy back and forth. She was moving in a circular motion. She stopped suddenly, got up, and got back on, this time with her face facing Petersen's pussy. Petersen figured they were going to do a 69. Marie leaned forward and kissed Petersen's pussy, and started riding harder than ever. She was now moaning so loud Petersen was sure there were gonna be complaints. But she kept licking and licking, tongue fucking Marie's pussy until at last Marie finally came. Suddenly she felt a fast squirt of cum shoot into her mouth. After overflowing Petersen's mouth, she got off and let out a long breath. Within 10 minutes they were both sleeping.

The next morning, Marie and Petersen took a shower together. Marie ate the Specialist's pussy in the shower, and the Specialist ate hers. They parted, but they never exchanged addresses or phone numbers. Petersen don't even know her last name. Petersen didn't even know where her home town was.

SFC Miles had just returned from the break room bullshitting with the boys at mid-morning. Like most sections within Replacement Center it was the lower enlisted or the privates, specialists and buck sergeants, that actually did the work in the home. Staff sergeants, sergeant first classes and above merely chit-chatted, bullshitted and walked around the Replacement Center with their coffee cups trying not to get their uniform ruffled.

Once he had entered his personal code in the key pad, he was back in the saddle of PAS again. Most days SFC Miles was bored at PAS and he sometimes killed his boredom by going out on errands both personal and business. Today, he would not be bored.

SFC Miles was greeted by one of the PFCs. "You have this message by the Company CO." Miles read the note and looked up at the PFC. "Why didn't the CO just leave me a voice mail message to call him," he asked.

"Apparently he did sarge while you were patrolling the hallways," replied the PFC with a smirk on his face. The private had delivered his message and he went about his duties.

"Thank you, Pri – Vatee for accomplishing this very important task," said Miles making sure the private didn't get away with that smart ass comment.

Once he was even, Miles proceeded down the short hallway to his office and shut the door. He had an idea that the company commander was going on a rampage about the platoon sergeants letting their preventive maintenance be placed on the back burner.

New significance was now placed on vehicle maintenance since both gulf wars. New directives were handed down and once they got to the unit CO level, it was up to him or her to make it happen.

After checking his voice mail messages, Miles decided to call the CO. The call was intercepted by the clerk just outside the CO's office. After some brief words, the call was transferred to the CO.

"SFC Miles, glad you found the time to call me."

"I just got the message, sir. Things are kinda hectic around here today."

"I bet." The CO was not totally disconnected as some officers were from their non-commissioned officers. He usually had some sense of what was going on at the Replacement Center. He had made a few unannounced visits to the center.

The CO being the CO was a busy man and naturally he got right to the point of the matter. "SFC Miles, do you know why I'm calling?"

Miles thought he had some idea but decided to hold his tongue. "No, sir."

There was a pause on the line.

"Has anyone approached you lately about a matter involving Specialist Preacher?" The pause on the line again told the CO at least one person may have had a heads up on this Preacher mess.

"I don't recall sir," replied Miles.

There was a tap on SFC Miles' door while he was on the phone and one of his specialists showed his head from around it. Miles gave him the hand signal that now was not a good time.

"This will be just between you and me, Sergeant Miles." The CO repeated his question again.

SFC Miles hesitated but answered, "Yes sir. I remember now. A few days ago Major Matt Balin did discuss the Preacher matter with me."

"Sergeant Miles, I don't know if you are aware of this but someone has decided to drop a dime on Preacher and his friends for some reason and what I fear is that in the end a lot of innocent people will get hurt."

He had piqued Mile's interest. "Sir, can you tell me what has exactly happen involving Preacher?"

"I got a visit yesterday from CID about an investigation concerning—"

"Damn!" interjected Miles.

"What is it?" said the CO.

"Major Balin stated that he might do something like this. But only if Preacher changed his mind and decided to attend PLDC." SFC Miles couldn't believe that all this was happening just because a specialist refused to attend training. Which was his right to do so.

"When did you and Major Matt Balin talked?"

"It was a few weeks ago sir."

"Hmmm. So Sergeant Miles, it was your impression that if Preacher cooperated the dogs would be called off. Is that correct?" asked the CO.

"That is correct, sir"

"I see."

"Well something must have caused him to move the schedule up a bit because the wolfs are searching for some prey."

"Is there anything we can do for him, sir?" Miles asked. The sergeant didn't know a whole lot about the CO but rumors had him as a soldiers' CO which was kind of rare. He assumed that he didn't want to see one of his soldiers get the bad end of the stick and would want to help him.

"I have a friend at JAG. I will see what he can offer to this situation," said the commander. That didn't sound too hopeful to SFC Miles.

"I will also run something by 'top' and see what input he can offer as well." "Top" was the nickname sometimes given to the top sergeant in the command. In this case, the first sergeant was the *top* NCO.

"I will be honest with you sergeant Miles. Someone or some bodies are bound to get damaged when this thing is over. It's just a matter of how many will get hurt."

"That I know sir."

"Sergeant Miles, the only reason the affected parties haven't been rounded up is because the investigation is still ongoing. It is a matter of time before those living off post will be forced to move back on post."

"So sir, I am not to do or say anything until otherwise told. Is that correct?"

"That is correct, sergeant. God speed."

"God speed, sir."

The beaming sun light as he approached his car wasn't very welcoming to Preacher. Once in the car he quickly put on his shades in preparation for the drive to class. He had slept good the night before so despite a day of work, he was ready.

He stepped through the main doors removing his shades only to bump into a huge chest. "Oh! Excuse me! Sorry about that. I kinda got blinded by the light adjustment as I walked into the place."

"No problem man. What's up? My name is Taylor."

"Tight man, tight," as they exchanged handshakes Preacher's eye made a mental note up the arms to Taylor's face. The army uniform didn't distort any of his features. Looking at his unit insignia, he was probably a combat engineer. Probably built bridges and drove construction equipment down range on Fort Carson.

A mix of Omar Epps and LL. He had a massive chest and the shirt in which he was dressed, only showed the hard workouts it must have taken to get to that point. His skin was caramel and taut.

Preacher has never taken in a person's look—particularly of the male persuasion—so quickly in his life. "So man, where are you off to? I don't recall ever seeing you around," Taylor said with a smile.

I've been here for about 2 years now and he's telling me that he doesn't recall seeing me around, Preacher thought. "Well, I was going to the break room to grab a cup of coffee. Come with me, if you like."

"Cool."

Taylor followed Preacher to the break room. He noticed that everyone would speak to Preacher as if he was a fixture there. Perhaps like one of the faculties. He noticed that Preacher got the same welcome from both young and old. Black and white. They eventually got to the room and an empty table was awaiting them.

Preacher asked Taylor to grab the empty table as he went to the vending machine for the java.

When the last cup was quickly served by the machine, he joined his new guest. "So where you from man?" Preacher said bringing two cups of coffee to the table.

"I'm from a small town in Arkansas. You probably have never heard of it before I'm sure. Most people don't." This caused Preacher to pause slightly in his actions. It definitely got his attention.

"Try me," he said.

Preacher's professor was in the classroom reading a paper one of his students had written. Among the requirements of Regis University was that each class would incorporate a paper regardless of the type of class, whether it was *Death & Dying* or *Computer Engineering.* The professor taught mostly computer-related courses at Regis University -- Colorado Springs campus.

Like his students he would attend classes mostly Monday, Wednesday and Fridays. By appointment, he would meet with students on Tuesdays and Thursdays. The classes, usually started at 1730 through 1930 hours. Just about right for people arriving after work. For those who had two classes per night, the second class would start at 2000 and end at 2200 hours.

The evening classes were made up of mostly professional adult students. At least half of his students were in the military. Because Norad also had a contention of Canadian military personnel, some of the evening courses at the school had a sprinkling of the Canadian military. And of the military, both officer and enlisted were represented. The professional students in his night classes at Regis tended to listen more and pontificate less, which he rather enjoyed.

The professor's mind tended to wander when he read papers. This, even though the projector was still running. The class was watching or should have been watching a presentation on *Successful & Failed IT projects – A case study.* The lights were low and the sound was not as distracting as some would think.

Right now the professor was wondering why he hadn't gotten into this university earlier. He worked an average of about 20 hours a week, had ample vacation time and was paid $80,000 a year. The grayed haired gentleman had decided he could easily teach into his 70s at this pace and assuming he had his health. His pie-in-the-sky dream was rudely interrupted by the signaling that tonight's class video presentation was near an end.

Preacher thought the evening's classes were interesting but not as interactive as what took place outside of class tonight. His new school mate was interesting and funny. Coming up from similar backgrounds in Arkansas did not surprise Preacher that the two had a lot in common. Both deciding to escape their past surroundings to seek something better. To see what life had in store for them.

Was he buffed? Absolutely. Did he seem to have it going on both in life, being career-minded and in body? Absolutely again. Preacher didn't get a chance to catch up with Taylor before he left his last class. Perhaps he left a few minutes early. In any case, they did exchange phone numbers and email addresses including instant message names. Taylor informed Preacher earlier in the evening when they were in the break room that he didn't always have his cell phone on but usually called back if someone left a message and that oftentimes was a lot easier to reach him via instant messenger on his PC.

With less traffic on the road tonight, Preacher made it quickly to his favorite Chinese restaurant to get some take out prior to going home. Thanks to his cell phone and the restaurant's number in its contact listing, he made it home tonight in record time.

Unlike his friend Hodkins' bedroom which was adorned with posters of hip-hop artists and NBA ballers sharing space with gorgeous swimsuit models from magazines, Preacher's room consisted of a couple of book shelves housing books by *Tavis Smiley, Michael Eric Dyson, Cornell West*, various urban literature authors as well as his share of computer books, reference books and manuals. But like his friend Hodkins, he also had his share of academic achievement awards, trophies, plaques, snapshots of himself with family and friends and pictures of him proudly posing with his high school varsity team. In Preacher's case, a king-sized bed and dressers took up one end of the room.

After stripping off his uniform and devouring his meal, Preacher promptly removed the discarded plate of smelly oriental scraps from his room into the outside garbage. Once back, he sprayed his bedroom with air freshener. Preacher, dressed in bikini-type shorts, was now seated at his desk in front of the computer monitor. It was 2315, his classes were done for the week and he wanted to relax and settle down prior to going to bed. He decided to do some surfing.

Preacher moved the mouse a little to waken the computer which was in "stand by" mode. When the high resolution screen appeared, he was presented with a log on prompt. Despite having very few visitors, Preacher got into the habit of having some kind of password protection on his computer at work as well as at home.

Once logged in, he executed the Internet browser and his web home page appeared. Preacher typed his favorite website in the address bar.

For the last night or so, Preacher had noticed that his Internet connection seemed kind of slow. Despite his indicator lights on his router giving no indications that a problem was evident, he decided to go to *www. dslreports.com* to check the speed of his connection.

But to his surprise, the result page of the site indicated that his speed was typical for a DSL connection. In other words, all was normal. It listed his current ip address issued by his Internet service provider and the test system or remote server that Preacher connected to to perform the test.

After a few clicks on a couple of Internet links, images of all types of nude African-American and Latino thugs slowly loaded within the page onto the screen. Pics of washboard stomach thugs as well as those that were not so muscular from all over the country and even the world posted on this particular site.

They was suppose to be a web site of amateur postings but some of the images being passed on as self pics taken with all kinds of phone cameras, digital cameras as well as film cameras were obviously professional images probably lifted from other web sites. The selection was plentiful.

Preacher stared with lustful eyes, his temperature climbing, his manhood enlarging.

The cursor jumped across the screen, hunting for the right image. Preacher clicked once on the mouse and an image enlarged, displaying a naked, caramel-colored, chiseled African-American brother randomly tattooed and athletic.

He stared at the image growing deeply entranced. He smoothed his hand over his own chiseled chest and slid it down past his belly button, leading to his bulging crotch. He slipped his left hand underneath his shorts and started to stroke himself. He exhaled deeply, each breath becoming more and more intense until a new popup window accompanied by a "knocking" sound appeared on the screen.

TaylorMade: hi. Bro. Sorry I missed you before I left
                 Tonight but I had some stuff I had to take
                 care of.

Preacher almost closed the popup without any interest thinking that someone who he chatted with a long time ago was trying to rekindle a chat session but the name was not immediately recognizable.

Then it hit him. "Taylor – Made." It had to be his new friend.

After removing his hand from his shorts, Preacher responded. He started typing in the message block of the window.

PreacherInCO: Hi to you bro.

TaylorMade:	IC it didn't take you long to get home Tonight.
PreacherInCO:	The wind was at my back. LOL.
TaylorMade:	Curious.
TaylorMade:	What does the "InCO" of your screen name stand for?
PreacherInCO:	It stands for, In Colorado.
TaylorMade:	Oh IC. Anyway, I enjoyed our chat tonight. You seem cool.
PreacherInCO:	I did too bro. U seem cool 2.
TaylorMade:	Curious. Do u have a web cam?
PreacherInCO:	Yes. Do u?
TaylorMade:	Yes.

Preacher was curious why he asked about a web cam since they had already seen each other tonight and to see each other while they chat wasn't that necessary.

TaylorMade:	Turn it on bro and I will turn mine on.

Preacher made sure the web cam was secure setting on top of his desktop which was setting on his desk. Then within his messenger program he selected the "Start any webcam" option.

Momentarily, a popup window appeared which displayed a camera view of Preacher setting at his desk facing the camera. After making some adjustments, Preacher determined that the focus was about as good as he could get it.

He was about to send an "invite" to Taylor, aka TaylorMade when the "TaylorMade has invited you to see his cam" prompt appeared in the chat window. Preacher proceeded in sending his own "invite" then he allowed his PC to view Taylor's web cam by pressing the "accept" button. Now, two web cam views were being displayed on Preacher's PC, Taylor's and his own plus the chat window was still there.

TaylorMade:	You look as good as ever bro.

Preacher was taken a little off guard at his statement. Yes, Taylor looked good tonight and all but he was certain he didn't let him aware of just how good he looked. Maybe he had "gaydar" or something, Preacher thought.

PreacherInCO:	Thanks.
TaylorMade:	So what are you up to now?
PreacherInCO:	Just checking some email and some research-related web surfing.

Preacher lied but he knew that Taylor didn't need to know the real deal.

TaylorMade:	K.

Taylor, who Preacher noticed was wearing a dark t-shirt leaned back in his chair while he sat in front of the web cam and removed it in one smooth motion. It was so smooth; the web cam appeared to have gotten it in a couple of frames.

Taylor's upper body had truly gotten Preacher's attention. He had a nice set of pecs as well as a good washboard.

TaylorMade:	Now we both are shirtless.

Preacher couldn't help himself.

PreacherInCO:	You got a nice bod bro.
TaylorMade:	Thanks. You do to.
PreacherInCO:	I try to workout as often as I can.
TaylorMade:	It shows.
PreacherInCO:	Thanks again.

There was a pause of a few seconds and the image of Taylor appeared to be just staring at his PC.

TaylorMade:	I will be honest with you Malcolm.
TaylorMade:	I am gay.
PreacherInCO:	I'm glad.

Preacher noticed the white teeth behind his big smile when he got the message. Taylor was truly relieved and was very happy he had found a new friend. If nothing else, someone to just talk to about issues that you just can't talk to anyone about. At this point, he also suspected Preacher of being gay as well but wouldn't come out and actually asking him at this point.

After about 30 minutes of chatting about life in each of their respective military units, Taylor wanted to close the evening on a good note.

TaylorMade: I'm enjoying our chat but I have something
                   to show you if you don't mind.

PreacherInCO: ok.

Preacher saw Taylor raise up from his chair and got out of view. 5 seconds later, Taylor reappeared buck naked with a towel and what appeared to be some oil or lotion near him on a desk.

Taylor reached for his web cam and made some adjustments since he was now standing then after reaching for the liquid, squirted the substance in his right hand.

Preacher knew what was gonna happen next. Not all web cammers used their cams to show their parents or grandparents his or her kids via long distances.

Taylor started stroking his lubricated tool. He appeared to do so in some sort of rhythm. As if dancing to music in the background. Taylor slowly turned around to showcase his bubble butt. His butt gave a nice smooth bronze appearance via his high end cam. And Taylor appear to know it looked good too because he was working it just like he was working his dick. He pulled on his nipples as he was stroking himself and that seemed to get him aroused.

Within a minute, the speed of the stroking had increased and Taylor's facial expression had gotten more intense. Preacher almost had forgotten how to breathe. The sight, despite seeing it via web cam was truly a sight to see.

But the scene was coming to a close. With a twisting of his lips and a little bucking, Preacher saw a couple of streams of Taylor's seed shoot. It seemed like he milked himself for 3 minutes. He must have built that up for a few days, Preacher thought.

After he got his composure and cleaned up a bit, Taylor started typing again.

TaylorMade: I hope you liked the show but I should be
                   going now.
PreacherInCO: I did. I did bro. We need to do this again
                   and next time, it's my treat. ;-)
TaylorMade: cool.

Then just as he had appeared online, he signaled that he was leaving. Taylor waved in the web cam and Preacher's view of Taylor went away.

Preacher then closed the view of his web cam as well as the chat window with Taylor. It had already indicated that *TaylorMade* had signed off. The indicator light on Preacher's web cam was off. All Preacher had now was memories of Taylor in his birthday suit. Good memories at that. He sat back and reflected on what had just transpired.

Once Preacher had gotten his composure together, he went back to what he had planned to do for this evening. The image that Preacher was viewing previously had quickly reappeared on his screen after some mouse clicking.

Wasting no time, he pulled his shorts down to his ankles and proceeded to stroke himself. Since he was already hot and aroused thanks to Taylor, the end result came sooner than expected.

It was time to go to bed, Preacher thought.

"Sitting inside ComCore's Network Operations Command Center the command room for servers stationed around the state of Colorado, gives a God's-eye view of its customers' access to the Internet in real time," wrote *Wired* magazine.

ComCore, Colorado's premier internet service provider headquartered in Colorado Springs, was very proud of its newly remodeled NOCC. It boasted receiving 60 percent of the market share in the state and because of their increasing customer base as well as satisfaction, they were forced to invest in their customers by investing in themselves.

Spokespersons were quick to comment on its state-of-the-art NOCC which among other things enable proactive troubleshooting of their network in response to network conditions. The NOCC was staffed 24 hours a day, 7 days a week by expert network operation technicians, providing personal support from such users as grandma installing her DSL connection to fortune 100 companies managing their web content and e-commerce.

The NOCC was impressive by any standards. The large bullpen or "bride" area was molded with the aid of contemporary ergonomic furniture. No doubt influenced by some movie or TV sound stage.

Five huge plasma screens towered the front or stage of the NOCC. They displayed in most cases, the real time health of the ComCore network.

Individual user stations were equipped with multiple flat panel computer monitors for its users. Superb colorful cable management also added to the ambiance of the NOCC. The cosmetics of the NOCC were also created by the dim lighting of the large room on top of the color displays. Some of which included color graphs of sorts indicating various network activity. The design would make the chief engineer of the *U.S.S. Enterprise D*, Lieutenant Commander Geordi La Forge envious.

Not a whole lot happened on the network that wasn't authorized and/or monitored in the NOCC. And special monitoring systems were setup just for accommodating law enforcement, and complying with any court-ordered monitoring.

The monitoring systems were very similar to any hardcore gaming or video editing desktop PC but were configured with special software to look at or "sniff" the many pieces of data as it went back and forth on the network. This data could represent an email, video, audio, text files as well as other data being sent back and forth across the ComCore network.

Only in the case of suspicion of engaging in criminal activities would law enforcement request a court order to view the suspect's online activity. This activity could be in the form of:

Which web site one has visited.

What was looked at on the site.

Whom you send email to.

Whats in the email you send.

What you download from a site.

What streaming events you use such as audio, video and

Internet telephony or *Voice Over IP*.

Who visits your site (if you have a web site)

Any data monitored by these monitoring systems would be copied to a hard disk. Once there, any filtering that was necessary could be done. The captured data could then be processed using special software. If the results, in a format which could be viewed and/or easily printed provide enough evidence; it can be used as part of a case against the suspect.

The assigned monitor specialist tonight at ComCore had just returned from his smoke break outside. The whole NOCC complex was smoke-free.

He had started perusing through the monitor lists of target ids based on court orders submitted to the company. If nothing else got done tonight the monitor list of the targeted customers had to be checked and monitored to make sure the company was in compliance with any court orders. In today's climate of full cooperation with investigations, the ComCore executives did not want any bad PR on their hands.

With the smoke break over, the specialist put two sticks of gum in his mouth to keep his mind off of his bad habit until he could get another smoke break. The rest of the gum and *Camels* were setting on the desk next to the flat panel monitor of the *Sun* Workstation.

Upon logging in the system, the specialist executed the applications maintaining the target list. He quickly determined with a few clicks of the mouse that all targets that should be monitored were activated and were being observed. Due to the court order of the target customers expiring and no renewal was requested, some targets that were on the list yesterday were no longer on it. That would be noted in an automated log as well which was routinely accessed by ComCore's Compliance and Ethics officer. Any and all activity based on the court order would be downloaded and sent in both hard copy and electronic form from the officer to the respective agencies who requested the monitoring.

With a few more clicks, another screen of data would appear in both list and graphical formats—the Recent Activity list. The listing normally appeared with the most recent target activity listed on the bottom of the list.

The night, so far had been slow as far as these targets were concerned, thought the specialist. Only one was listed on the screen and he or she had activity in the last hour or so.

While he smacked hard on the gum he was chewing, the specialist cancelled the screen with the lonely record. In a nanosecond, the record only identified by a case id and ip address: 165.42.227.15 disappeared.

The specialist focused his attention now on a color laser printer on the local network within NOCC. It was off line for some unknown reason. That would need to be troubleshooted. Once that was taken care of, perhaps retrieving a *Camel* would be in order.

Senseless. Tragic. Stupid. Sad. Bad. Those were the words used by both prosecutors and defense during trial on this day during the trial against SFC Randall McCullen.

Lt. Brookhiser argued that his client was in another room while PFC Muse was consuming drinks laced with a sedating drug and was unaware of what had taken place against her much later.

Projecting McCullen's booking mug shot above a photo of the defendant as a professional U.S. Army Non-Commisssioned Officer in uniform, the prosecution began the trial proceedings by contrasting the defendant's public image with the real McCullen, including his infidelity. The prosecution compared McCullen's own testimony with evidence, witness testimony from the trial and the SFC's own statements made to Colorado Springs police who were first on the scene at the home after the gang rape.

Both the prosecution as well as the defense would offer their sound bites for the day.

"The defendant would have you believe that everybody is lying except him," the prosecutor said.

Wearing the classic Class A uniform he wore for the past few days, McCullen often shook his head during the prosecutor's argument. Both military and civilian personnel, whom have filled the courtroom since the beginning looked on intensely as the prosecution attacked several defense claims.

Defense attorneys argued that the prosecution went after McCullen because he was friendly and his career was a promising one in the U.S. Army.

He contended that his client was fond of PFC Muse like most of the specialists and privates in his unit and therefore would not try to harm her. Lt. Brookhiser said that his client did not know that PFC Muse had ingested Rohypnol. If anything, she as well as others at the party, both male and female; may have had a little too much to drink but he kept checking on his guest that night including her. During his checks, PFC Muse was fully clothed.

The young lieutenant asked the jurors to not let the sadness of the tragedy affect how they view the case. "Don't let your emotions he played upon," he said. "Look at the evidence from the witness's testimony as well as other areas."

As if jockeying for position at a horse race, the prosecution was next on the floor. The prosecutor stood and announced his first witness for the day.

"The prosecution calls Specialist Four Cynthia Renee Petersen to the stand your honor."

Petersen tried to use an arsenal of military décor to erase an image defined by high v-cuts, belly buttons and plunging necklines which were customary to her after 1700 hours. Her attire would allow her to at least *appear* to be a credible witness, if not in *content*. Still she imagined the jury seeing her in the scantily clad outfit that she wore the night of the incident.

What would the jury think if they saw me as I looked that night? Would they view me as credible? Or would they dismissed me as they did in rapper Lil Kim's perjury trial? She asked herself beforehand.

The jury, being military personnel themselves, wouldn't see her in her traditional party garb. Some folks always had the view that a lack of clothing or partially clothed suggested sexual control, power and confidence. Traits Petersen possessed and she knew it.

While trying to put the butterflies in her stomach at bay, SPC Petersen approached the stand. After being sworn in she was seated.

The prosecutor asked her a series of questions about that night. They were the same questions which they had previously discussed during their prep sessions. Then it was the defense's turn.

The defense team asked another set of questions. The tone of the questions were a little more abrasive than the prosecutors but then again the defense was trying to get a rapist off the line.

It was hard at times. The prosecution team tried to prepare her for the trial as best they could. They told her just to tell the truth just like she has told them and it would be OK. It would be rough at times. The defense seemed hell bent on getting Petersen to admit to doubts but there would be none.

Petersen kept it together as both the prosecution and defense teams rehashed the events that would change PFC Muse's life. Both sides wanted to give the jury a clear picture from their perspectives to what happen that night using physical evidence and witness testimony. She wanted to tell the truth and she did so, she felt. She wanted to do her part and make sure that the SOB got what he deserved.

Petersen spoke in a soft voice perhaps a little nervous and even elicited smiles from the jurors during some awkward moments. When the judge told the 18 year old Petersen to move her chair closer to the microphone, Petersen humbly apologized and adjusted the chair but made a thumping noise which echoed throughout the old courtroom as if it was empty.

Under more questioning, Petersen conveyed some details of her life. Baltimore, Maryland native; a product of a single parent and who loved to go clubbing at both the enlisted as well as the officer venues when she could get in.

Defense lawyers tried to attack Petersen's credibility during openings. McCullen's lawyers charged that Petersen was upset with his client because he had turned down her advances and her cooperation during this trial was merely payback for her.

In Petersen's opinion that couldn't have been further from the truth. Simply put, McCullen would fuck anything with a cunt. Mammal or not.

CHAPTER FOURTEEN

Petersen was getting ready for her date with the girls. *Where did I put that damn belt?* she thought as she rummaged through her portable closet. *That belt would have gone perfect with this outfit.* She gave up looking.

Petersen took a look at herself again in the mirror. She was dressed in a sharp new bright blouse. Petersen liked designer clothes, but she didn't like them that much. To her most of the time no-name brand clothes looked ten times better than the big designers and cost ten times less.

Besides, she thought, why would she want to be a walking billboard for some filthy rich mother fucka for free? Her cell rang just as she was assessing her butt in the mirror. She stopped eyeing herself and walked over to her cell phone, picking it up on the fifth ring.

Hello?

"Hi Girl. Get your ass out of the barracks so we all can hit the club!" shouted one of Petersen's girlfriends. Three of Petersen's closest girlfriends had just finished some light shopping and a quick meal and decided to visit *Omar's*—one of Colorado Spring's newest and the most popular R&B clubs.

The girls were apparently only minutes from the unit on post and wanted to make sure that their girl was ready to go. "We'll be there in like … 10 minutes, aiight?"

"Aiight, I'll see you then." Petersen's crew sometimes get on her very last nerve but they were her crew and would always be there when she needed them and that was cool.

Petersen pressed the *End* button on the cell and went back to the mirror to take one more good look. After about two more minutes of primping in the mirror, she went back to her closet and took one more look for that belt. She grabbed her *Gucci* bag and walked out the room.

The drive to *Omar's* was smooth since it was after 2000 hours and the rush hour traffic on Academy Boulevard was long gone.

While cruising down the boulevard in a late model Nissan Pathfinder, Petersen and three of her girls—Lynette (23 years old, brown skinned, very pretty and very well-built), Cantrell (22 years old, light skinned, dark wavy, long hair, pretty and well-built) and last but not least—Terrell.

Terrell was the oldest in the group, She was 25 years old, but looked younger. She was a female playa' type who was dark chocolate in color. Once she turned the charm on, she could get practically any brother to pay her bills. She had a body that made most brothas turn their heads in passing to give the sista a second look from behind. And what she was working with from behind was worth a second look.

She kept herself toned by lifting weights and running. Not just with her unit on PT days but on her own as well. Her breast size was proportionate to her body size but her behind was healthy as well. Terrell was the type of gal who knew she was fine and good looking and expected every guy on Earth to fall at her feet. She had attitude.

This was Petersen's crew. They were all happy and appeared to be ready for anything on this night.

As they came to a stoplight at the corner of 76th street and Mill road, they spotted the club. Terrell pulled into the parking lot of the club and backed off the ignition. The crew strutted to the entrance of *Omar's* and walked in as if they owned the place. The dance floor was a little packed as they cased the room.

"I don't know about you ladies but I need a brew," Lynette said. She headed towards the bar. Petersen and the rest followed.

They each ordered Coronas and had a seat at the bar and watched the people dance to the music. Lynette, Terrell and Cantrell decided to feel around the room and make some "scrub's" night by dancing with him.

They squeezed their way onto the dance floor. The dj was mixing it up. The air was steamy with body heat. The scent of soft perfume, spicy cologne and body musk hung over them. The ladies found some brothas and each started off in a hoppy, jumpy move as they smiled at each other. If one didn't no better, one would think their moves were choreographed.

"May I have a seat?"

Petersen thought the voice was familiar but not one that registered as a "friendly," so she didn't turn around.

"May I have seat?" the voice asked again.

Petersen turned around to match the voice with a face. The face was of Hodkins. *Damn. Damn. Damn*, Petersen thought.

"May I have a seat," Hodkins repeated.

"Well, I don't think there's a free stool," Petersen said.

"The ladies may be awhile in this place. They seem to have a lot of energy and there are a lot of brothas in here without a date. They seem to be giving the brothas a nice workout on the dance floor."

Now both Petersen and Hodkins were observing the activity on the dance floor but she turned around to face him.

"Are you stalking me now, Hodkins?" Petersen asked.

"And I would be stalking you because of—what?" he replied. Petersen knew he wasn't stalking her but she didn't have anything else to tell him other than for him to go away. "I'm just here having a good time like you are."

"Well Hodkins I was having a good time until I heard your voice," Petersen said before she took a swag of her Corona.

"You sure do know how to make a coworker feel all welcome."

"What is it you want this time, Hodkins?" It wasn't Hodkins himself that made her uncomfortable but what he wanted. Hodkins, Petersen thought, was actually kinda fine. He was now sitting at the bar wearing a throwback jersey and a fresh new pair of butter-colored tims. He had a nice complexion and perfect teeth.

Petersen didn't think he was knock down gorgeous but he was attractive in his own way.

"You are looking as fine as eva girl," he said smiling over the background commotion.

Hodkins was grinning wide, looking her up and down with a lustful stare along with three other guys at the bar while their dates stared at her with an adulterated hate written on their faces.

Petersen also noticed Hodkins gaze. "Thank you."

When the bartender came over to check on the two, Hodkins ordered an Apple Martini and Petersen got another Corona. The Corona calmed Petersen down a little, Hodkins noticed. They sat, drank and talked a little. At times, it appeared to be a little cordial between the two.

As he talked, Hodkins seemed to concentrate his line of vision on the cross resting above Petersen's cleavage.

"You go to church?" he finally asked.

"Why you asked?"

"Just noticing the cross on your chest."

Petersen finally realized what he was talking about and abruptly tried to turn away a little from her stool buddy.

"I bet you were," she replied with some degree of sarcasm while she sipped some more of her drink. "About every other week. Sometimes on the post and sometimes at a Baptist church here in the city."

"Oh yea, that's good." Hodkins thought for a while about if he had ever went out with a woman or man that got up and went to church on Sunday morning.

Petersen thought the rest of the night would go quite well. The music was perfect, the drinks were nice and the conversation up to now was flowing nicely. This surprised even her. Hodkins was the last person she expected to see tonight, much less have a drink with.

Hodkins noticed that Petersen was getting into the groove of the music. He watched her sway and dip to Usher as she sat on her stool. She was snapping her fingers as she surveyed the people in the large room.

"Petersen," whispered Hodkins. Petersen didn't hear him with all the background noise and music. He tried again with more volume in his voice. "Petersen!"

She then turned around. "What?"

"I saw what was on your notebook the other night."

Petersen thought she heard what he said but wasn't sure. "What did you say?" she told him with a subdued tone as if she was trying to brace herself.

"I saw the images and your instant messages that were on your notebook."

Petersen had turned away from him and looked back out on the dance floor. Seeing other people dance to the music didn't help. Petersen couldn't even hear the music. Small beads of sweat soon appeared on her face and her heart skipped a couple of beats. She was in shock.

Petersen didn't bother to deny it and this point. There was no use. Her secret was out now.

As Petersen stared away from Hodkins, he could see a small teardrop going down her left cheek. Hodkins grabbed a napkin that was on the counter and handed it to her.

Seeing it in her corner of her eyes, she snatched it and wiped her tears from not one but both cheeks.

Afterwards, she turned around and faced Hodkins. "I suppose the new deal now is either I do as we agreed to or you spill your guts. Right?"

Hodkins turned to retrieve his drink and took a sip. "That's right. No more, no less. That's only fair."

With watery eyes, Petersen stood up. "Alright you fuckin bastard!" With that said, she proceeded to leave the bar area when her posse approached her.

"Hey Petersen you still getting your drink on over here? These scrubs in herrrrre was all over my ass," Terrell said as though she had climbed a few stairs.

Cantrell appeared to be the only one who had noticed Petersen's watery eyes. She turned to Hodkins who didn't immediately get her attention.

"Let's go yall. I need to go," said Petersen already heading towards the main door of the club. "I'll meet y'all at the car, aiight."

The ladies looked at each other with strange expressions on their faces. Then they all noticed Hodkins. "What the fuck did you say to her Hodkins?" asked Cantrell.

"Fuck. This is some trifling stuff. I didn't even get a fuckin drink," complained Lynette who then decided to finish off Petersen's.

The posse soon followed Petersen away but still within earshot of Hodkins. "We should go back there and kick his black ass."

Hodkins turned back to face the bartender and motioned him for a refill. Totally dismissing Petersen's lap dogs as he occasionally referred to them. He felt bad about what he had to do to Petersen. He had nothing against her personally but he was relieved that the game plan was back on track. A smile did manage to come across his face.

The bartender noticed as he was bringing his drink. "I see that smile on your face playa. I bet you got that hookup plan for lata?"

Hodkins thought about what he said. "Yes. You could say that."

Now, it was the prosecutor's turn. To erase any doubts about Petersen's intentions and her desire to help PFC Muse by getting her out of a bad situation, the questioning now focus not on McCullen, Muse or Petersen, but on someone else.

Lead prosecutor now standing, started his questions. "Why didn't you get PFC Muse out of that apartment if things were as bad as you say they were?"

Was the courtroom getting a little chilly or was it her, she thought. Petersen sat back a little in her chair. "I couldn't."

"Why not?"

"There were too many guys around the room and Private Folster seem to be guarding that whole area of the apartment," she said.

"So what did you do?"

"I got help by contacting Preacher."

McCullen had moistened his lips as he heard Petersen's testimony. Other than that, he gave no reaction to what he heard.

"Who is Preacher, Specialist Petersen?"

"Specialist Preacher is a guy in my unit who was also at the party. He arrived after I did."

"So, this Preacher didn't partake in that assault that evening?"

"No. he didn't."

"So you contacted Specialist Preacher in order that he get PFC Muse out of that room and eventually out of the apartment. Is that correct Specialist Petersen?"

By now Petersen was tired of all the questions and was looking forward to the ending of them. "That is correct," she replied.

"Did he?" asked the prosecutor. He paced from one side of the room to the other as he fired off his *questions*.

"Yes, he did. Very much so."

"How so?"

"He got to the room somehow and stopped what they were doing to Muse." Petersen turned to the jurors.

"There was a fight and the two were able to get outside and Muse was able to get some medical help."

"Who took her to the hospital?"

"Preacher and myself."

The prosecutor paused as if pondering his next question. "So would you say that without Specialist Preacher's help, it is quite possible that no one else there was able or perhaps interested in helping PFC Muse escape her ordeal? Would it also be safe to say that Specialist Preacher was a hero that night and some would say that he still is?"

That would be the sound bite for the evening news as well as tomorrow's paper.

"Yes. Yes on all three counts. I sure would say so," stated Petersen.

McCullen, trying to be as stoic as best he could, slightly dropped his head as he fumbled around with his pen on the desk. He let out a long sigh as Petersen's testimony ended on that note.

In the same courtroom, where they heard testimony from those who were there on that horrible chilly night, a military jury deliberated for 2 hours in the court-martial of SFC McCullen.

They would review the transcripts of the alleged rape. Stressing that the victim either tried to resist—even if it was just murmuring the word, "no." Or perhaps was too sedated to do anything. Did McCullen create an environment of fear, intimidation and control that allowed him to manipulate all that surrounded him? Was it a license to be mean? To be the company asshole? Was McCullen a mean, arrogant and manipulative person, who used his control over others to his selfish ends? The jury must consider that McCullen did admit to having sex with PFC Muse but he also contends that she was a willing partner.

They also had to consider—which defense tried to hammer in—that the PFC is now lying to protect herself from charges of improper sex with her superior. That the women submitted to McCullen to carry favor with him and testified out of revenge because they did not receive favorable treatment.

The judge told the four men and two women on the jury that they must consider evidence presented by McCullen's attorney that any sex was consensual.

Military law stated that physical force wasn't required to prove rape; "constrictive force," which could include threats or intimidation, was sufficient. Court-martial rules required four of the six jurors to agree on any guilty verdict.

McCullen faced a maximum of life in prison if convicted of rape plus 32 years, a dishonorable discharge and forfeiture of pay and allowances.

With the trial testimony behind him, Preacher was now starting to realize that his ETS date was closer than it seemed.

He reflected how it seemed like a year or so ago when he first went to the unit education center to determine what classes were available to him. Little did he realize that his problem wouldn't be finding schools or classes but determining which of the schools he would sign a degree plan with and finish his bachelor's degree.

He considered himself lucky that in four years stationed on Fort Carson, he had only been in the "field" for about two weeks total. For an infantry post, that seemed a little unusual. But Preacher knew that his MOS had a lot to do with that. There just wasn't a whole lot for a 25B to do in the field.

The trip to the education center today wasn't exactly a waste of time but they didn't tell Preacher a whole lot more than he already knew. He was to stay on track with his current classes. Basically, pass it and he may get his bachelor degree in computer information system prior to leaving Fort Carson. There was still some debate as to whether he needed one additional elective to complete his degree plan after his current course. There seemed to be some disagreement with Preacher's counselor at the school as to whether or not one of Regis University's programming courses were fulfilled when Preacher received a series of college credits because his current job or MOS was closely related to this major.

All indications seemed to side with Preacher considering he had a letter after the MOS evaluations were done that the questionable course credit would be awarded.

Suggestions were made that he should go back home or where ever he was moving to and put in some application. Then there were suggestions that he go over to the Transition Center and brush up on his resume writing skills. But Preacher had a different plan in mind. He certainly wasn't planning on moving back to Hamburg. There was nothing waiting for him there in that town, that county. Not even in the whole agricultural state. He had a couple of cities in mind and would make up his mind very, very soon.

Any number of books from Grant Library or the various web sites could quickly educate one on how to produce a good document. But as far as laying down some job applications, Preacher had a better idea.

Since he had some time before he had to head back to the office from his center appointment, he decided to stop by Grant Library to look over some Sunday newspapers from the various major cities that the library subscribed to, and possibly review the various posted positions on *Monster. com*. Between the two, Preacher had a good idea over the past couple of months as to what areas of the IT field were hot, therefore, allowing him to focus on certain areas on his resume. In Preacher's opinion, his current resume or the draft of it looked really, really good.

Major Balin had been in his office since 0615 hours this morning. It wasn't that unusual for him to do so either. In the military, old habits were hard to stop. He had been an early riser ever since he was a second lieutenant. Back in the day, he had no choice. A baby face, wet nose, brand new officer was often tasked with administrative as well as shit details that were recommended or ordered to start at an ungodful hour.

But with a few years of service as well as a few promotions later, the Major's work schedule was a lot more flexible. Even though everyone had a boss in the military, even the Generals, the major pretty much made his own hours.

In about an hour or so, his driver—a specialist four—will be arriving to work to perform his duties. The first task this morning for him would be a drive to HHC to visit the company commander. The HHC CO was in the middle of one of three weekly meetings with his officers, mostly first lieutenants, concerning troop matters. One of the topics of discussion was about training the troops for "defensive" convoys.

He was just about to tear some officer in charge of one of his platoons a new asshole for poor training stats, when one of the lieutenants saw the major's humvee pull up into the driveway. He immediately, with the approval as well as thanks from the chastised lieutenant, signaled the captain and gave him a heads up. He knew the captain would want to know.

The major had a habit and a reputation of showing up unexpectedly at the worst possible moment and when he thought it was needed, he would get in a "pissy fit" with this officers and senior enlisted to correct a wrong.

Not seeing the humvee, the captain turned around in his chair to see out the window. Momentarily, he saw it too.

"Shit," he spat. *"What the fuck does he want?"*

After the driver made a complete stop, the major vacated the vehicle and after positioning his headgear with gold oak leaf displaying, he proceeded down the walk way. One by one enlisted as well as officers stood at attention as salutes were rendered. Somehow one lieutenant was late with his salute as the major was right in front of him on the side walk but he managed to whip out a salute.

The major saw this and he returned a salute to him but the major did so with eyes staring the lieutenant down as if he was slicing him with a knife.

As the major disappeared behind the double entrance doors and into the hallways of HHC, the soldiers outside gradually went back to their chit chats. The lieutenant that was stared down proceeded along the side walk to his car. He didn't want to meet the major again this morning.

The interior posture was almost the same as outside: folks once they recognized the major immediately made sure that he had plenty of room as he walked towards the company commander's office. Soldiers tried to stick to the walls as the major walked by and seemed to be relieved as they were able to get by without some critizing remarks about them.

The captain had obviously stopped his morning officer's meeting early once he saw the arrival of the major.

The major did indeed thought it was odd that he saw almost all the company's lieutenants spreading out of CO's office area.

Those that were fortunate in coming his way had to greet him and hope that he didn't stop them for any reason. A stop by the major was typically not a good thing.

"Good morning, major," replied one lieutenant as he proceeded down the hallway with every confidence that the major would keep on walking past him.

"Lieutenant, is that the best you can do with a greeting?" shouted the major as he spinned around in the hallway only a few feet from the CO's office.

The young officer was almost startled as he stopped in his tracks to acknowledge the major again. The major now stood directly in front of the officer. "No sir," stated the lieutenant while at attention.

"Then say it like you have a pair of balls!" shouted the major.

"Good morning, major!" bellowed the young officer.

"Well. That's more like it sir," Major Balin stated sarcastically with a smirk.

The lieutenant just stood there, waiting for further instructions.

"You are dismissed lieutenant. Have a great day," said the major.

The lieutenant was relieved. As he stood there in front of the major, he wished he was anywhere else. The same was true for everyone else in the unit before the major walked in. With the exception of the major and the young officer, the unit's hallway was nearly empty. People scattered like roaches.

The exchange was heard by everyone in the CO's office including the CO and he was not looking forward to meeting the major.

After a sharp "Thank You, Sir," the young lieutenant quickly vacated the area and allowed the major to proceed to his next victim. Once the young officer was out of the hallway and out the entrance doors, he let out a big sigh.

By the time the major made it to the CO's office, the occupants knew he was in the area and were expecting him. The major knew this too.

As he walked in he was met by the clerk—a PFC.

"Good Morning, Major Balin. May I get you some coffee?" the PFC stated sharply and to the point.

The major smiled at the private and said, "Not right now. Is the captain in?"

"Yes sir. He is in his office. Please sir, go right on in."

The private knew that he wouldn't normally tell folks to go right into the CO's office but everyone knew that the major was here and the CO had told him already not to keep the major waiting. The major suspected this as well.

The CO's office door was cracked open. The major approached the door and immediately after two quick taps on the door in rapid recession, he grabbed the door knob and entered his office.

Once he looked up and saw the major, the CO stood up from behind his desk. "Good Morning, sir. What brings you here on this fine day?" said the young CO.

Major Balin's official title was battalion commander and though he knew that the line soldiers, senior NCOs, young officers and company commanders called him something else among themselves, Balin was past caring what the little people thought of him.

The major while still standing reached in one of his ACU pockets and retrieved a brown envelope and tossed it on the captain's desk.

What immediately caught the captain's attention was the seal on the envelope—it had the seal of CID on its face.

"Captain, what started as a simple failure to make sure your soldiers attended leadership training has now escalated out of my hands to a violation of 'Don't Ask, Don't Tell.' When the CID investigation is over, all the personnel who currently wear the uniform undeservingly will be out of the U.S. Army. And you. You will get a one-way ticket back to the Big Apple with my blessing," said the major with a slight grin on his face.

"We the jury, find the defendant, Sergeant First Class Randall McCullen... guilty."

The jury foreman's words were met with an immediate, almost deafening silence before a cry broke out from the McCullen family seating area in the packed courtroom.

Wanita and Reginald McCullen sat observing the proceedings while the verdict was read. Wanita was an attractive distinguished-looking woman in her early 50s. Her beautiful auburn hair hung to her shoulders and complimented her bronze skin. As a seasoned marketing executive at one of New York's most prestigious firms and a active member of the city's largest African American Methodist Episcopal (AME) church, she assumed an air of authority and respect.

Reginald McCullen, a tall, stout and handsome man also in his early 50s, was typically a reserved guy although he did have his moments. He wore a lightly shade against his dark skin, giving him a middle-aged sexiness. As a young man, he was a star tight end at Alabama State University. He was also active in the community. Together, Reginald and Wanita projected a uniqueness about themselves as they affectionately held each other.

Wanita could feel the blood pounding in her temples as she struggled to control her fury. "Reginald, they are taking our boy away from us," she hissed under her breathe. Despite her anger, a detached part of her brain observed the scene, cataloging and assigning to memory the smallest detail and reaction among the spectators.

The sergeant first class was found guilty of rape in the first court-martial in the Fort Carson rape trial.

Wanita sat in her seat, the epitome of class, style, and elegance dressed in one of her nicer dress, every hair in place. But her attire and how she wore it was the furthest thing from her mind. She watched the news like everyone else. Newscasts were reporting that her son could get the maximum of life in prison. He already faced a number of years to admitting to consensual sex with lower enlisted—a violation of Army rules. In that context, there was no such thing as *consensual*.

SFC Randall McCullen's mother sat in the courtroom. Her eyes were downcast, fixed on the white lace handkerchief she was twisting into a tight coil in her lap. A single tear rolled slowly down her cheek.

Occasionally her eyes would be drawn irresistibly to the young girl seated directly behind the prosecution team. How young this girl was. Too young to even picture her being in the army if it wasn't for the uniform she wore.

PFC Gwendolyn Muse, the young girl who had shown such strength and courage during her testimony, sat in her seat as well to hear that verdict. As the jury foreman rose to his feet and cleared his throat before speaking, Muse's shoulders had been squared, her back was straight and her head was held high. She now appeared to have weathered the last storm.

SFC McCullen's parents looked impressed by their daughter-in-law's confidence and what appeared to be little or no emotion by what she had just heard.

Not just any female was good enough for her son. She and Reginald had worked too hard and struggled too long for any of their children to just socialize or marry anybody. Reginald and Wanita grew up poor, and still resided in a lower middle-class African-American community, but both believed that each generation was supposed to improve.

But what seemed like confidence and restraint to some could be more like relief to others. Relief on this day wouldn't be reserved just for the young rape victim at the trial.

Mrs. McCullen had everything she needed between her and her husband's job and what monetary gifts her in-laws gave but she was also a miserably unhappy woman. Mrs. McCullen was emotional wreck. She has always known that her husband cheated on her these last few years.

Ignoring the sound of the judge's gavel smacking against wood in his effort to bring some order to his court and muffle the sporadic cries; Mrs. McCullen reached for her handbag, rose to her feet and walked stiffly to the closed double doors at the rear of the room.

This didn't go without the few reporters in the courtroom noticing. The MP assigned to prevent anyone from entering or leaving stepped into Mrs. McCullen's path. Without hesitation, she shot him an ice cold glare and felt no small measure of satisfaction when she saw him flinch in response. But she decided to meet him halfway by saying, "Please."

"Mrs. McCullen," was his only comment as he reluctantly stepped aside and opened the door wide enough for her to slip through.

Just before she stepped through the doors, Mrs. McCullen glanced over her shoulders to find her husband watching her exit. As she met and held his gaze in her unblinking stare, the lips of the precious son of Reginald and Wanita McCullen of Ozone Park, New York, pursed together in a kiss for her benefit.

In order to make her escape from the JAG building, Mrs. McCullen was forced to run the gauntlet of cameras, microphones and by-line hungry reporters who reminded her of a school of piranha in a feeding frenzy. At last reaching the relative privacy of her Nissan Amanda parked in the reserved lot across the street, Mrs. McCullen rubbed the back of her neck in an attempt to ease some of the tension. She leaned her head back against the headrest closed her eyes and began taking deep, cleansing breaths. Reaching up, she tilted the rear view mirror downward so she could inspect her appearance and with a groan of disgust pulled her makeup bag from her purse.

She put eye drops into each eye to eliminate the effects of her sleepless nights, used foundation to blend away the traces of dark circles. By the time she was finished there were no visible signs to betray that this case were getting to her.

She inserted the key in the ignition and started the engine. She now had some decisions to make for herself and the kids.

After the trial, an ad hoc press conference was given.

"If you convict SFC McCullen, you'll be sending a message out to the Army that no sergeant is safe. It's extraordinarily disappointing. It's beyond words, but it is a day everyone knew might come. It's a tragedy for everybody," said a member of the defense outside the courtroom.

"Every woman has a right to say, 'no' to sex. Performing sex acts on the body of an unconscious woman is a crime. It is a crime if the perpetrator is a student, a laborer, an executive or fellow soldier," said the prosecution. "This is a case of the accused using his power, his easy access and his ability to control—an unscrupulous senior NCO--grossly misusing his position to force his sexual attentions on young soldiers."

The sentencing phase of the trial would be held at a later date.

Both the CO and first sergeant were exhausted from the battalion meeting this morning. The company commander got unofficial word that the battalion was being considered as part of a support force for the 82nd Air Borne in about a year.

Pentagon staff had sent us some surveys for each of the battalion commanders as to their combat readiness to support front line units in Afghanistan.

Needless to say, the commander was skeptical as to whether to note a large number of deficiencies in the survey. Too many and the top brass would wonder what the fuck they were doing all this time.

The Battalion CO was being bombarded with stupid ass questions from his company commanders which dragged it along even further such as those pertaining to the additional armor on the humvees. Assuming that they had more armor.

One captain had the nerve to ask during the meeting, "I am currently forced to decide whether to finish installing additional plating on my humvees or redirect those funds toward supporting field exercises."

At the podium, the commander paused and looked at the captain while removing his glasses.

"Lives are being snuffed out over in the Middle East because the *virgin* vehicles were not suited for the current environment over there. Improvised Explosive Devices or IEDs are tearing these vehicles apart. Some soldiers are either being killed outright, dying much later after an insurgency attack or are being mamed from these attacks. Captain, I will give you a few minutes to think about whether you should proceed with installing your armor. You should feel lucky. Some units are resorting to retrofitting used metal plates on their vehicles to minimize the damage a future attack. You sat here in comfort debating as to whether you really need to inform the contractor to proceed with the fittings,"

The commander paused for a second.

"But if you really need me to answer that question for you then it's a strong possibility you shouldn't be wearing those bars you have on your collars." The battalion commander was referring to the captain's rank that most officer personnel had on their collars today.

That exchange set the tone for the rest of the meeting. The commander wanted straight answers to the survey. You were either ready, or you weren't. In the end, lives rest on the decisions made right now.

"What you say we go get something to eat before the lunch rush starts, first sergeant?" asked the CO.

After performing a mental review of his morning and afternoon to-dos, the first sergeant responded. "Don't mind if I do."

As planned, they would have lunch a little out of the way as far as the main post traffic was concerned and far from the media camp. *The Mountain View Tavern* would be known to very few of the personnel here on post covering the rape trial.

There may be a few stragglers here and there, but for the most part it would have just the regulars there and there should be little or no waiting for a table or booth. And that was confirmed as the captain and his "top" walked in the place. They were immediately seated by the young lady and before she had the chance to ask, both gave her their drink choices.

About 10 minutes had passed before the drinks were out to their table. Both were enjoying both the drinks and each other's recollection of events this morning at their "cluster fuck" of a meeting.

The first sergeant had noticed a gentleman walking from the restroom area back to his booth behind them where another gentleman was already seated. The gentleman approaching his booth had what appear to be CNN press credentials hanging around his neck in addition to a Fort Carson Visitor's badge.

The two decided to take an early lunch for a change. Taking advantage of some downtime since the jury was still out deliberating.

Its was a big difference from a few weeks ago when they set things up after their arrival. Between the logistics of working within military protocol and syncing things up with CNN headquarters in Atlanta, Georgia; they were lucky to get dinner by 10 pm.

But still the two pros preferred to be busy than sitting around or looking and recording background footage for future military stories.

The two men had chowed down their course of chicken and wild rice and were now washing it down with a beer.

"This story appears to be coming to a close, oh boy," said Bryan with a thick New England accent. Bryan Mueller has been with CNN since 1995 when the news giant launched its multimedia news arm, CNN Interactive (CNNin). CNNin has become one of the web's most popular sites. Starting back with just 20 people, CNNin has some of the largest websites in the world now staffed with over 200 people and Bryan helped started it as a young multimedia specialist.

Now a full fledge writer, Bryan along with his producer is one of many working on one of the biggest military trials in quite sometime.

"You think so, uh?" replied Jeff.

"Well, maybe you're right."

Jeff started staring at the bubbles escaping to the surface of his beer but he was mentally preoccupied with something.

"Too bad this case and its players are on a military reservation," said Jeff.

"What you mean?"

"I mean that there is something more to this story," said Jeff right before he took a gulp of his beer. Jeff Cabin, only been a CNN producer for the last 5 years but has been in the business for 10 years.

"A local reporter that has been in the *media city* told me that some of the major players that were involved in this case were recently moved or about to be notified of a move from their off-post living accommodations to the regular army barracks. He thought something smelled with that and so do I.

He stumbled across the information as he was trying to get an interview with the Malcolm guy on behalf of this guy's hometown newspaper somewhere in Arkansas. It would be a joint effort between his paper and the one in cotton country."

"So what do you plan on doing about it," said Bryan.

"Not a whole lot I can do about it under the circumstances. I suppose I will pack up and leave Pikes Peak like everyone else once the verdict is read."

Both Jeff and Bryan clinged their beers together for another big gulp.

"Gentlemen, today is your lucky day. I might be able to help you secure that interview you want," replied an army captain as he winked at his first sergeant. The two men nearly choked during their drinking.

Like a toddler "eyeing" the guests in the next dining booth, the captain was on his knees while looking over in the next booth at the journalists.

The two men didn't know how to respond to the captain's invitation and Bryant was still clearing his throat as his beer was going down.

"I prefer not to speak to you here. Let's find a place in the back where we can talk," said the captain.

Momentarily, all four men relocated to a back booth where discussions were held. Where once the media was thought of as the enemy, now were seen as partners. At least in this case.

The captain recognized a golden opportunity to prevent a major wrong from happening against one of his soldiers and he was determined to be a catalyst in its prevention.

Preacher picked up his cell phone and dialed Petersen's number. He stepped onto the small deck of his patio. A cool but comfortable breeze blew from the direction of the distant mountains. A white ring of fog hung on the mountain.

Two weeks had passed since he called Petersen. He had seen her a few times down the distant hallway at work but only had time to wave a "hello" or a goodbye. Preacher was sure that she would get some type of attitude on the phone since he didn't have time for her lately.

The last couple of weeks had been hectic. Between school work, school itself, Taylor at school, Taylor after work and Taylor on the cam, Preacher has had little or no time for Petersen.

He ate his *Swanson* breakfast sandwich with a quick sip of coffee while the phone rang. Petersen had caller ID and he knew that she would check it prior to accepting the call. After the sixth ring, a voice was heard.

"Hello."

Preacher smiled.

"Good morning my nubian princess. How are you?"

"Who is this?"

Let the games begin, Preacher thought.

"Preacher."

"Who?"

"Specialist Preacher. Oops! I meant to say, Specialist Malcolm Preacher."

Petersen had briefly forgotten that she wasn't exactly obtainable the last few weeks either and decided that it may not be a good idea to dog him out too much. Marie, her running buddies and another new friend, were keeping her busy before and after work as well too.

"OK, Mr. Specialist Malcolm Preacher," said Petersen with a smirk on her face. "What can I do for you on this fine day?"

The tone of Petersen's voice seem a little calmer to Malcolm now. Perhaps she wasn't as mad as he thought.

"Preacher, I have spent the past couple of weeks thinking about you. I apologize for not calling sooner."

"I don't know if I want to accept your apology. I've got to go soon."

Preacher could tell she wasn't going to make it easy. He found a clean area on his Resin patio table and sat his coffee cup. He sat down on his lounge chair. "Wait! Don't go just yet! I want to talk to you."

For what seemed like a minute, Petersen didn't say anything and Preacher couldn't think of anything to say. Finally, Petersen let out a sigh.

"Tell you what. Pick me up after work tomorrow. Do you have duty this weekend?"

"No," replied Preacher curiously, "Pick you up? And?"

"If I told you, it wouldn't be a surprise. But I will tell you this much. Pack an overnight bag," she said.

Petersen hoped at a minimum she'd piqued his interest.

Preacher's mind wondered now. Spending the night with my princess while she's house sitting. Or perhaps at a hotel in the area.

"I will be there."

"Good. I will be waiting. Bye, Preacher."

"Bye, Petersen."

Preacher leaned back in his lounger with a bigger smile on his face and finished off his coffee as he gazed at the mountains.

Chapter Fifteen

The drive back to the post was not as bad as the traffic to the apartment for Preacher. Everyone obviously had plans much like him after work. Preacher was looking forward to spending some more time with Petersen.

Within seconds after arriving in his apartment, he was stripped of his ACUs, off to the shower and splattered some baby oil on himself. Pulling on his best low riders and sneakers and a black T and a jacket, he was ready.

It lust as far as Petersen was concerned or did he had true feelings for her. After the last few weeks, Preacher was now more confused than ever about his sexuality.

All seemed so simple for him until he met Hodkins, Petersen and Taylor in that order.

Much like a death row inmate strapped to the electric chair right before the lever is pulled, Preacher thought back, thinking of anything that might have triggered the feelings for both male and female partners.

There was no child abuse of any type. There was no sexual assault at any age. And no, there were no acts of "brain washing." So, he thought, there could only be a few conclusions: 1) Gene defect 2) Simply part of a natural selection of someone who just happens to be of the same sex.

The thought of some of the previous reasons brought out a chuckled from Preacher. Unlike some people including some reverends and other religious groups, he didn't subscribe to the belief that being gay was the result of some defective gene, a life trauma or having to do with your surroundings as one grows up.

In his mind, it was simply natural.

This merely happening now with the trio was simply coincidental. The major life differences, Preacher thought, was the place it's happening at. Fort Carson's military population alone was more than the population of the city of Hamburg. Once you threw in the DOD civilian workers and it's even more.

The military being as close knit as it was, working, living and in some cases eating together would eventually enable some to drop their defenses and allow themselves to relax and be themselves. As opposed to being in a small, country town where everyone knew everyone and about half of the folks were related.

Preacher would have to set aside his internal debate for now; he was at the unit barracks and Petersen waited. Hopefully.

Petersen was dressed in a baby blue sun dress that looked as if it was made from the best fabric in the world. Her hips were hugged by the material and it touched her body in ways that I could only dream of. She didn't appear to have a bra and her nipples were erect through the material. The top of the dress had spaghetti straps. Although he could see that her nipples were erect, he could only imagine what her breasts looked like because the color and the material was not at all revealing. The dress was the ultimate tease. She had such lovely breasts. They looked perky as if she had on a push up bra but she didn't. Her breasts were just perfect.

It almost made him forget her other features. She had long black hair and the most beautiful eyes. She had that same mahogany complexion and her makeup was in a tone that accentuates her African American features.

"You look great as usual," Preacher said.

Preacher felt really good about today as he carried Petersen's bag out the back door of the barracks area. The two wanted to get out as smoothly and quickly as possible which meant that the two had to keep a low profile during their exodus.

"Thanks," Petersen said.

"I'm really curious. Can you at least give me a hint as to where we're going this weekend?" Preacher opened the door and waited until Petersen was comfortably seated.

Once they were both inside, she said, "Relax, I could but that would spoil the surprise. Patience, my prince…"

Petersen reclined the passenger seat and put on her favorite pair of sunglasses. Her fragrance drove Preacher wild. Preacher took the freeway south, then took exit 42.

Preacher continued to follow the directions dictated to him by Petersen and so far, the route was the same route as to someone else's crib.

Within minutes from exiting the freeway, he was at a familiar place. "Is he giving a party or something?" asked Preacher disappointingly.

"No."

"Then why are we in the parking lot of Hodkins' crib? That is where we are going, right?"

Petersen could tell that Preacher was more than a little disappointed. Like her, he was looking forward to spending a little more time with her.

"Come on, Preacher," Petersen said. "Your boiee, if you didn't know was going out of town for awhile. Visit some whore probably."

Preacher could have sworn he saw Hodkins recently somewhere and usually Hodkins mentioned stuff like that to him.

But, Preacher thought, as long as the hard head is not around, it must be OK.

"I hope that boy has the decency to pick up his draws," replied Preacher.

"Yes, that would be nice." They both had a chuckled after that remark.

The sun was beginning to end its tour of duty but Preacher's evening was just beginning.

Petersen was beginning to settle in the apartment. Once her bag was brought in she had prepared to hit the shower.

Preacher never asked Petersen exactly what was on the agenda for the weekend and to be honest at this very moment, it really didn't matter. That could wait.

Naked himself, Preacher stretched across Hodkins' bed awaiting for his girl. If she was sincere about tonight, he didn't want to waste time pulling off clothes, he thought. A flat panel TV was in the room but Preacher didn't have the desire for additional entertainment. He would soon be part of his own.

Hodkins' apartment was surprisingly neat in appearance for once. Other times he had visited the place, there were clothes placed everywhere, dishes in the sink with that musty smell and the smell of weed in the living room.

But that wasn't the case now. Hodkins did a decent cleaning before he left on his trip. He had even vacuumed and used some kind of aroma spray in the crib which Preacher could tell was still going strong.

The bedroom housed a traditional King-size bed with fluffy pillows. The color scheme was of navy blue and egg white.

"Knock, Knock."

When Petersen opened the bedroom door, Preacher gasped. She stood dressed in a silk, black nightgown with spaghetti straps. It was one of the most beautiful sites Preacher had ever seen. Her smooth skin, her sexy brown eyes, her full lips and her melon size breasts were just magical. After a second or two, Petersen realized she wasn't the only one who was excited. Petersen walked to about a foot from the bed and did a simple model pose with her hips tilted to one side with one hand rested on it.

She reached in her top and pulled out a joint. She motioned it to Preacher as if to offer it to him or share it together. Preacher shook his head. In another time and place, it would have been a big turn off for him but he wasn't about to turn Petersen away now.

If anything that stuff reminded Preacher of a *50 Cent* concert he attended a while back. While there with some friends, the headliner at this concert series in Monroe, Louisiana displayed two big fake joints, one on each side of the stage.

Fifty came out prior to his first song and told the crowd to smoke'm if you got'm. And they did. Preacher left the venue with a big headache.

Preacher instinctively rose up from the bed to greet his angel. He reached to grab her firm ass and as he slid his hands up under her teddy, he discovered that she didn't have on any panties. His fingers explored between her legs to discover that he pussy was indeed wet. Not sure if it was from the shower or her excitement.

Petersen stepped back a bit and turned her back to Preacher. She rocked side to side and up and down. Her ass bounced so that the materiel shifted high enough to give him a better glimpse of her tits and rump. The dance seemed rehearsed.

Preacher reached for the remote to turn on the stereo. The radio just happened to be set already to R & B. This show needed some sounds.

Her breasts were swollen and appeared ready to pop out of the smooth fabric that bound them in.

Anita Baker was now singing, "*Sweet Love.*" Back and forth she moved and her ass and breasts. She turned around and began bouncing up and down like a skilled pole dancer from one of the downtown exotic clubs. Preacher wanted to see more, so he reached out to her again. Petersen danced away as if she wasn't quite ready to give the goods to him. Preacher wanted so much to grab her ass.

Petersen walked seductively to him and wiggled back and forth. She stuck her beautiful swollen breasts in his face and lifted each one in her hands. She grabbed his head and placed it in between her breasts as she jiggled them. He breasts smelled good and he grabbed both of them to began kneading and massaging them.

Preacher grabbed her hips. He kissed Petersen deeply on the mouth and cuffed her firm ass. He ran his other hand up the small of her back and ran his fingers through her hair. He kissed her as if it was the very first time.

He then turned her back to him and he proceeded to kiss the nape of her neck. Next, he cupped both her ample breasts and she turned her head to meet his. Both were extremely excited as their hearts were racing. Preacher tried to quickly reach to unharness the *twins* but she blocked his hands, kissed him and danced away from him.

This was beginning to frustrate Preacher as one would guess by now. His dick was so hard that it was hurting. She danced toward him again. Her appetizing sex smelled like fresh fruit. He leaned his head forward and savored the smell, letting out a sigh. He thought he would burst right there after viewing Petersen's body.

"Close the door baby," he said. The light from the bathroom area was intruding on the mood, Preacher thought.

Petersen turned around towards the door with her cheeks sliding from side to side but she went through the doorway. This caused Preacher to wonder what was going on now. About 2 minutes had gone by before another sound had came from the bathroom. From the edge of the bed still, Preacher flopped back on the bed in frustration, his feet still on the floor.

What the hell she is doing, he thought as he stared at the ceiling.

Then he heard some movement in that area and the door creped opened. Preacher slowly rose from his stretched position. "Look Petersen, I like foreplay as much as the next person but this---"

Preacher couldn't believe the image before him in the doorway.

Just standing there in his birthday suit was Specialist Hodkins.

"What the hell are you doing here? What are you doing?" asked Preacher as he instinctively reached for some kind of clothing, but only found his T-shirt near his feet.

"Calm down, bro. Remember, this is my apartment," replied Hodkins with a slight grin on his face.

"You didn't have to cover up for me. After all, we're all friends here." Preacher rolled his eyes. "Where's Petersen?"

Hodkins turned quickly to re-enter the bathroom to retrieve what looked like a breath mint on the counter and popped it in his mouth.

As he did so he felt a stare on his ass but he didn't quickly turn around to confirm instead he decided to look to the reflection of Preacher in the main mirror mounted in the bathroom. It confirmed his suspicions. Preacher was indeed checking his ass out. He turned and went back to the doorway.

"Calm down, bro. and, first of all, I am not drunk," he said. "Your girl has left the building."

"What? What did you say to her Hodkins?"

"She couldn't have said nor done anything to you considering she as well as I, thought you were away for the evening," said Preacher.

"As I said, calm down. She didn't do or say anything."

"Then why did she leave?"

"It's complicated," said Hodkins as he walked around the room still in the buff to retrieve a CD for the player. The radio was not playing anything to his liking tonight.

"Give me the reader's digest version then," stated Preacher somewhat annoyed by now.

Hodkins turned to face Preacher. "OK, then."

"Petersen owed me a big favor." He paused. "I stated to her in a manner she understood that if she would do something for me, we would be even."

Preacher was watching Hodkins the whole time as he tried to explain Petersen's absence.

"What type of favor?"

Hodkins had found the CD he was looking for and proceeded to open the tray to insert it in the player. "What type of favor, Hodkins?" Preacher repeated.

There was a long pause as Hodkins attempted to find the right words to spring upon him.

"To bring you here."

Preacher didn't immediately understand the reasoning. "What?"

Hodkins pressed the play button. "To bring you here, for me," he said, "and it obviously worked."

After a long pause and a stare, Preacher said, "I see."

Surprisingly to Hodkins, the look was one not of anger or sadness but perhaps one of disappointment.

Hodkins sat on the side of the bed behind Preacher. Hodkins stared at the multi-colored volume and bass bars as they danced up and down on the stereo. He did so as though he was waiting for some kind of response from Preacher.

"I asked her to do this big and last favor for me and she did so reluctantly. In fact," Hodkins added, "I doubt if she will ever speak to me again. The deal was," said Hodkins as he finally leaned back across on his bed and stared at the ceiling. "That she would arrange for the two of you to have a get-together here or make you think you were then she would leave and I would stay."

"But I think it was more than she expected."

Preacher turned his head. "How so?"

"After the show and before she snuck out, she gave me a big slapped across the face. She didn't have to say much after that, I knew why."

"Really." Preacher smiled.

"Really. I had it coming," replied Hodkins. "Yes, you did."

"But I tell you what, Preacher. Your girl got some tits and ass on her. I was hard as a rock through my pants."

Preacher quickly gave him a stare that was a knife.

"You looked at her?"

"It was only a peep. I couldn't help it." He paused. "I had to see something."

"And what a sight that was. You got a fine girl, Preach. And the plan, by the way, didn't include her putting on a show like she did.

"Let me guess: you're disappointed, right?" asked Preacher.

"In-n my opinion, she went over the top for you. You should be proud," replied Hodkins.

"Well, I would be... but---", Preacher now motioned with his hands and clearly irritated with the situation. "You are here now."

Preacher removed his eyes from Hodkins, "Right, my girl."

"Well, ... Depending on what happens tonight."

Preacher turned his head again to look at Hodkins, "And what is supposed to happen here. Where is Petersen now?"

"She had arranged for one of her girlfriends to pick her up out front. I had told her that she could use my truck but she basically didn't want anything more to do with me."

"Well, could you blame her?"

"No," replied Hodkins, "I wouldn't."

"Preacher, I want to say something to you now and get it off my chest. If I don't say it now, I might not get that many more chances to do so."

"Well, I'm here. You're here. Shoot?" said Preacher.

"We have known each other for a while bro. Haven't we?" said Hodkins still lying across the bed.

"OK, so."

"Well, you might be heading out soon and I just wanted you to know something before you left the army."

"And what is that," Preacher said as he dropped his head down.

"I love you, Preacher. I always did since the first time we met when you walked into the shop shortly upon arrival on Fort Carson."

If it wasn't for Mariah Carey's "We Belong Together" soothing the room, it would be absolutely quiet.

Hodkins just laid there on the bed. Despite not one ounce of threads on his body, it was as if a flak jacket was lifted off his body. One that was worn for at least 10 years or so. Ten years both girls and gals. But he knew his desires leaned more to the guys.

It was now said to the only person he could ever trust. He wasn't concerned that Preacher would tell someone if he didn't feel the same way towards him. Preacher wasn't that type; he could be trusted just like Petersen. What Hodkins feared more than anything was that the only person he ever bonded with whether he knew it or not, would turn down his advances and move on. But Hodkins had to try.

Hodkins didn't like the silence for long and he was eager to hear what Preacher thought about the situation. "So what do you think, Preacher?"

Hodkins didn't know it but Preacher had started tearing up as he heard his friend speak. All seem to be coming to an end in so many ways. Someone who he also liked had just made a confession to him. He had felt the same way but was afraid to release his true feelings. Hodkins just made it a lot easier for him and the needed to be honest to him as well.

Preacher raised his head and turned around but not so much as Hodkins could see his full face and he spoke.

"I love you too, Hodkins. I always did."

Hodkins laid there as if the words were still vibrating in his ear, over and over again. He eventually turned his head to the side to look at Preacher. He saw what appeared to be a reflection of a single stream of tears coming down the side of Preacher's face. Hodkins felt that his friend also had taken a load off his shoulders.

With the words spoken, instincts seemed to take over between the two.

Hodkins pulled Preacher from the end of the bed into him at the middle and they started to kiss. Hodkins explored Preacher's body with his tongue. He made sure he touched every hot spot of his body. Preacher's body shook with ecstasy as he teased and playfully entered his anal region with his tongue.

Preacher felt so good there were tears in his eyes again. Hodkins waited for him to recover then he lowered his body on him and asked, "Are you ready for the real deal now?"

There was a pause. "Yes," Preacher said in a whimper like voice.

They exchanged a passionate kiss that seemed to suck the breath out of Preacher. He felt like he had entered another world as their tongues wrestled with one another. Hodkins took a brief break to reach under the bed to retrieve a toiletry bag. He retrieved the KY jelly and a condom from the bag. He oiled Preacher's ass and began to finger-fuck him. Preacher was getting excited but also edgy as he thought about Hodkins ass-fucking him. New to the game, he had no problems taking Hodkins' finger. This was totally new to Malcolm and he needed some coaching.

"I won't hurt you, I promise," said Hodkins.

Hodkins parted his legs and began to push his tool in him. Preacher winced as he slowly entered him but he anticipated the ecstasy that would follow. Hodkins' movement was different this time around. It wasn't his usual rough beat it up flow.

He deliberately took his time and worked his friend slow and deep. "I won't hurt you. Just relax for a minute," whispered Hodkins. Hodkins kept his tongue in Preacher's throat and they felt each other become one. Though Preacher felt it, he dared not speak it, at that moment he was in love with Hodkins and from the look in his eyes Hodkins was with him.

Preacher winced and a thin tear ran down his face. There was minor pain but it was tolerable. Hodkins gradually picked up his pace and as he moved in and out of his friend he began to yell, "I love this ass! I love this ass! I love you nigga! I love you nigga!" Both their eyes opened as he spoke those words.

Hodkins stopped his movement momentarily and whispered, "I do nigga, I do." All Preacher could do was smile and cry once again.

Hodkins wiped his tears away and said, "I'm gonna make you love me too." He went back to work.

After about an hour or so, the honey moon was over. Hodkins sensed like times before that the initial pain his mate was getting subsided and the body had adjusted to his rod. The lube also helped he was sure. Hodkins smoothly banged Preacher hard and rough like he normally did. He simply couldn't help himself. After another passionate kiss and some more of his rough love, Hodkin's body began to shake as he orgasmed. He stayed inside Preacher as he released himself.

Preacher thought it was over but Hodkins' tongue entered his mouth and Hodkins was at work again. As he pumped on, he said, "I hope you brought your A game tonight. I ain't gonna be through with this ass for a minute. So enjoy." Then he flipped Preacher over.

"Throw that ass back at me," he commanded. Preacher did what he said and the pleasure of the sex increased as the initial pain all but disappeared. Preacher began to moan and cry out, "Oh shit! That feels good! Work my ass!"

"You got it baby," he said as he slapped him on his ass a couple times hard. They both came up off their knees as Hodkins pumped down into him. Preacher threw his ass up into him. Preacher released a load of white milk without touching himself and Hodkins followed soon thereafter. His was not that noticeable with the condom on. Preacher lay on his stomach as his mate kissed the back of his neck and after a fresh condom slowly worked his still hard dick inside Preacher.

He turned Preacher over and they momentarily shared a sloppy wet kiss. Hodkins' tongue escaped Preacher's mouth and traveled across his face. He nibbled on Preacher's ears and sucked on his neck, and then he found his way to his nipples and worked magic on them. Then Hodkins kissed all over his chest and stomach and he left several passion marks along the way.

Hodkins found his partner's dick and took it into his mouth. Hodkins deep throated him and held his dick in Preacher's throat. It seemed like forever. Preacher whimpered like a baby as the pleasure shook his body and he deposited himself in him. He didn't mean to but he was caught up in the moment. Preacher had never done that before and it kinda took him off guard.

Hodkins lifted his head and allowed the juice to flow down Preacher's dick then with his tongue, he licked away the residue. "Damn nigga! You trying to turn me out," said Preacher.

"Damn straight," Hodkins replied. Hodkins lifted Preacher's legs again and pushed his stick back inside him and as he pumped in and out. They both lifted off the bed.

Preacher put his arms around his shoulders and began to slide up and down on his dick. "Yeah ride my dick baby. Make daddy nut!" As he rode him, Hodkins began to slam his hips into Preacher. A couple times his dick came all the way out but it found its way back inside on his own. After twenty solid minutes of hardcore body banging sex, they both nutted. Preacher glazed Hodkins' chest as he filled Preacher's insides. Hodkins' lowered him back down on the bed and they kissed gently. Still inside him, Hodkins rolled on his back and Preacher was on top.

"You ready to ride this pony baby?" he asked.

"Yeah," Preacher said with excitement as he sat up and lowered himself down on him. They were both possessed. In spite of the soreness in Preacher's ass, he wanted him inside him more and more. He knew he would probably pay for it in the morning.

After another brief exchange of kisses, Preacher began to ride him. Hodkins hands felt so good on Preacher's hips as he allowed him to assist as he bounced up and down on his rod. His hands eventually fell to his side and Preacher had complete control.

Preacher's movements increased steadily until he bucked like he was on a wild horse at the rodeo. "You still love me?" Preacher asked.

"You know it boo," Hodkins said, as he took control again and flipped him over and began to power fuck his boyee. In a matter of minutes he started to explode. As he began his release he pulled out, the condom flew off and shot his load all over Preacher. He then collapsed on top of him. Completely out of breath, Hodkins kissed Preacher and said, "You made this a night to remember."

"Well, not just yet bro," replied Preacher.

Preacher was so hot and desperate now for relief it was not an act of love but sexual desperation that he now pushed Hodkins to the side and crawled on top of Hodkins with a burst of energy. While Hodkins still laid there on the bed, Preacher searched and reached for Hodkins' toiletry bag and retrieved a new condom. After ripping the packaging with his teeth, he wrapped his rod.

Now consumed with lust holding his throbbing wrapped cock in his hands and positioning himself between the fat cheeks, he sank his cock deep into Hodkins. It wasn't hard since there were so much sweat. The more of his cock he worked into Hodkins, the hotter he got. He was being driven almost to madness by the hot lush feeling of his ass.

Hodkins was now offering his body to him and he had taken it. As the feeling of lust soon subsided this new rich feeling of sexual gratification came to him. Preacher still needed more; he wanted that wonderful feeling of his cock slipping down Hodkins' hot throat. Pulling his still hard cock from Hodkins' ass, he began maneuvering him onto his back. Preacher removed the wet condom from his rod. He had now become the aggressor eager to take and on Hodkins to satisfy his own lust. With his legs on either side of him leaning forward, he began feeding his cock into his mouth.

Hodkins looked up in surprise, not sure his boy had it in him. Then the look of surprise turned to passion and finally to surrender. Preacher could feel Hodkins' throat opening wide surrendering to him and accepting his cock as he slide deep into him.

Squatting on his chest now, he leaned forward and began working his cock into Hodkins' mouth. Warmth. Orgasmic, sensual. That was what he felt as Hodkins took him in his mouth. All bets were off at this point. There was no turning back now. Preacher's head reeled back and he let out a gracious moan as he felt the warmth of Hodkins' mouth on his member.

The room was filled with his throaty slurping sounds and also the sounds of his moaning as he gave Preacher head. Preacher grabbed Hodkins' head and helped him to help himself to the throbbing invasion. Hodkins' eyes were sparkling in absolute adoration as he sucked and lapped at his cock.

"Please no… no… more…"

Preacher pulled away from him to keep him from climaxing. Some 20 minutes or so had passed and Preacher savored each minute waiting for him to stop. Hodkins never noticeably tired, never complained and Hodkins stopped pleasing him orally long enough to hear his cry of no more, and then he began pleasing him again.

As his reward, Preacher began unloading. God he thought, this sex was wonderful and he felt like he would never get enough. Sliding down Hodkins' body again and lifting his legs over his shoulders he found a waiting lover eager to surrender to his every desire. He was now getting better and better at wrapping his rod with the condom using one hand. Moving his rod's head toward that puckered entrance to paradise as he slid into his hole, Hodkins' ass just seemed to suck his cock into his body. Obviously experienced, Preacher thought.

Feeling the hot moist walls of Hodkins' ass closing around his cock, he began pumping like an animal driving himself into his ass up to his balls. Preacher was like a young stallion newly come of age.

Hodkins rocked his ass back and forth and up and down with a rhythm that he had never known before. Then without warning he stopped. He brought Preacher's member out all the way to the tip and then slowly allowed him to go all the way back in. When Preacher had penetrated him as deep as he could, he tightened his inner walls. This sent Preacher reeling into oblivion. Hodkins did this motion over and over again.

"You like that?" replied Hodkins.

"Oh shit yeah?"

"You enjoy this boy pussy?"

Preacher have not heard it referred by that name before. "Oh yes baby, damn...what are you doing to me?"

"Shhh...say my name."

"Hodkins."

"Say it again."

"Hodkins."

Hodkins rocked back and forth and Preacher swore to God that he was in love with his boie from this point forward. His toes were tingling, his muscles were tense, and his entire body was vibrating.

Hodkins and Preacher now with Preacher now in the commanding seat, made love for well over an hour. "Slap my ass," Hodkins said.

Preacher obliged him.

"Slap it harder."

He hit it again.

"Harder!"

Preacher smacked his ass like a bad step child.

This did the trick for Hodkins because it sent him over the edge again. "I...I...I'm cumming!"

Preacher felt like he could fuck forever and he just kept pounding his cock into him getting off again and again. Hodkins moaned, Preacher moaned, Hodkins came, Preacher came. The very wet condom slid off. His seed shot out like a sprinkler system until no more would come out. And he cummed harder than he had ever cummed before. Preacher was no longer an innocent virgin young boy; he had now become a fully grown sexual man of the world.

Eventually he simply wore out and needed some rest like Hodkins. There was now a heavy stench of sweat, sex and ass lingering in the room.

Not even he could keep up that pace all night. Finally they just lay there together in that bed with Hodkins cuddled in his arms in completed submission to him. Preacher looked at that soft sleepy face and he knew he should feel some guilt that he'd fucked a man but it felt so good he knew he had to have him again. Anything that felt that wonderful couldn't be bad.

They lay in one another's arms and kissed until they caught their breaths, then Hodkins rose and lead his guest by the hand to the bathroom where they showered together. Hodkins tried to get up in Preacher again but he resisted. "No. I've had enough for now. Maybe later tonight, but right now I got to recuperate." He laughed at him and then Hodkins started to punch and tickle Preacher. As they playfully wrestled under the water with both their dicks hard again, neither of them gave into the pleasure.

After they showered, Hodkins changed to sheets and both got back into bed. "So what's *really* up with you and Petersen now?"

"Nothing, I suppose. Why?"

"Will you continue to see her now?" he asked.

"No, I'm not!" said angrily. "Thank you," Hodkins said. "I appreciate that."

Hodkins now had a smile on his face. "I will cease all contact with my former partners as well. I'm starting over as of now. I hope you will too," said Hodkins.

"I will to but this shit is all new to me. I just had sex for the first time with another guy--with you, and hours before that I was trying to lay Petersen. I liked both experiences, but I don't know. Now that I have cooled down, my head is spinning right now. It's like I got to make a choice about which way I wanna swing."

"Perhaps that was the way you thought until you came to terms with who you really are. I am assuming that you have finally come to terms. If you didn't, you probably wouldn't had allow me to seduce you like I did," Hodkins said. There was silence. "We both remember the scene in the shower stall at the barracks that time. I felt your regret then and I felt the contrast in you now. Just moments ago, I felt like a new Preacher. One that released himself from his own bondage. Much like I did a while back in my life." Preacher looked into Hodkins' eyes now. Hodkins continued.

"There were days I was horny and I wanted a girl, then the next I want a dude. It's like my dick had a mind of its own. It doesn't care where I put it as long as I put it in something when it gets hard."

"Well my situation is a little different. I like dick and pussy. Petersen can throw that ass and keep a nigga hard yet at the same time I like how you make me feel when you got me on my back," responded Preacher. "I felt that too, bro. Brothers like us felt that all the time. You are not alone."

Hodkins kissed Preacher one last time before they both started to make up for the lost sleep. Hodkins rolled off of Preacher and positioned himself on his own pillow. "By the way, Preach. Your girl Petersen is bi bro, she goes both ways too. As I said, you are not alone. Just thought I would tell you, bro," Hodkins said casually as sleep was creeping up on him.

Petersen is bi!, Preacher thought to himself. "Shit!" was the only words muffled out of Preacher's mouth. He simply had no idea.

Hodkins giggled. "Just thought you might want to know, dawg." Minutes later, all Preacher heard was his snores. Preacher laid there and pondered about what just happened in his world. He was happy and had regrets at the same time about what went down.

He concluded, "What's done is done."

CHAPTER SIXTEEN

The phone rang, awakening Hodkins. Preacher was dead to the world, snoring like an old fart, Hodkins thought.

Hodkins decided to let it go to voice mail. It was just after 0700 and nothing in his opinion qualified as an emergency. He figured if it was that important they would call back.

He rolled over to go back to sleep when nature unrelentingly called. He untangled himself from the sheets and slid out of bed. His briefs barely restraining his morning hardon. He staggered into the bathroom, hit the light, propped himself up at the toilet and stabilized to keep from peeing on the floor. Afterwards, he returned to bed where Preacher was still asleep on his stomach with half his body exposed.

Preacher religiously slept naked but now he had briefs on. Perhaps because he was at someone else's house. Clothing at night normally made him feel restricted. Hodkins on the other hand, usually slept in pajama pants but skipped them last night, preferring to feel the smooth skin of Preacher as the two slept.

The sun spilled in through the blinds illuminating the side of Preacher's face. He stirred but not enough to make him conscious. Hodkins noticed that his caramel skin was as smooth as a baby's bottom.

Hodkins snuggled up next to him and gently kissed him on the nose. Hodkins kissed him again. Preacher slowly opened his eyes.

"What are we going to do about breakfast?"

"What? What are you talking about?" Preacher said, still very groggy. The main event of last night's party zapped the energy from his usual bright and early regiment.

Preacher's body was awakening fully to the sound of football coming from the living room.

Hodkins had decided to get up after all and go get some breakfast at McDonalds. While watching a game on ESPN classic, Hodkins munched on a Big Breakfast platter. He wasn't sure what Preacher would want or when so he also got him a platter with a medium coffee waiting for him in the microwave. Preacher didn't strike him as the bagel and coffee type so he figured the platter would do.

After the Friday night activities, Preacher had decided to spend another night with Hodkins so he had gathered some more clothes at his place, including his sleep wear.

Preacher staggered in the bathroom to brush his teeth and wash his face. Afterwards, he seemed awake to see what was in Hodkins' kitchen to eat.

"What do you have for breakfast around this dump?" said Preacher as he walked past Hodkins and slapped him on his head while going towards the kitchen.

Preacher had a gray silk pajama bottom that occasionally clinged to his butt, which Hodkins now admired, as well as a olive T-shirt. The two now had more clothes on than they did all weekend.

"I had brought back a breakfast platter for you but decided that your sleepy ass could do without it and ate it," replied Hodkins while still watching a classic NFL game from the 70s.

While still looking for some cereal of some type, he to see the yellow plastic container through the microwave window. Preacher looked back at Hodkins, who was watching him.

"Lucky for you, you didn't. Hate to top off a nice weekend with an ass whipping," said Preacher.

While Preacher ate his breakfast in the kitchen area, Hodkins stayed on the sofa.

Unlike Hodkins, Preacher was not heavy into sports. He could watch it or not. While Hodkins was definitely concentrating on each play of the game, Preacher delved into a *Black Enterprise* magazine. Surprisingly, not all of Hodkins' magazine collection consisted solely of *Penthouse*, *Hustler* and *Pictorial*.

Hodkins' concentration broke during commercial. "By the way, just in case I don't reach the platoon sergeant in time tomorrow morning, tell the sarge that I got summoned to the orderly room first thing in the morning. They even told me to wear ACUs and not report to PT in PT gear."

"So what did you do now?"

Hodkins looked at Preacher for a second, turned his head back to the TV and gave him the one finger salute. Preacher laughed.

"So what did you do this time?"

"The only thing I can think of is that I am over due for my PM on the vehicle at the motor pool," said Hodkins. "Top and the sarge has been riding my ass lately about the PM on my assigned vehicle."

Preacher thought about that for a moment. It didn't make sense. Summoning Hodkins to the front office to chew his ass out about a PM. If that was the case, 80 percent of the company would be there along with Hodkins.

"So make sure the fucker doesn't mark me down as AWOL this time," said Hodkins with a grin.

"I'll try to remember it."

"Yeah, you do that."

"I don't want to stay inside on a beautiful Sunday like today. So what do you say we hit a movie?"

Hodkins looked up and nodded his head while still smacking his food in total agreement with his partner. Hodkins realized that since the two of them consummated their relationship, "partner" now had a whole new meaning for them even though it will only be known to the two of them—three if they included Petersen.

"That's cool, Preach."

The parking lot of HHC was at full capacity on Monday morning. Even the sick and dying was at formation. There must have been some big wig meeting after PT. It had been months since the parking lot of HHC was this full. There were those in ACUs, PT and civilian clothes.

After double checking his belongings to make sure that all was ready after PT was over, Preacher checked himself out and walked away from his vehicle.

After a salute here, a hello there and some "good morning sirs or ma'ams," Preacher was inside HHC before he knew it. As usual the hallway was shining and the smell of *Johnson's Paste Wax* was wafting down the hallway. People were chatting amongst themselves and zig-zagging back and forth across and down the hallway taking care of brief business before the command to fall in was given.

Preacher's appearance in the hallway did not go unnoticed. Once he was recognized in the hallway, Sergeant Miles approached Preacher and tilted his head for the young specialist to follow him down the hallway. Preacher did just that. They walked till they got near the CO's office entrance.

"The CO needs to see you now in his office," whispered Sergeant Miles. The sergeant was not in PT uniform and he appeared to be ready to report to work in his fresh, starched ACU.

"You mean right now. Like before PT?"

"Yes, right now as in—NOW," said the sergeant. "I will be there too." "I tried to reach you over the weekend but I couldn't make contact with you. But I did leave a message," he said, looking down the hallway as he talked. Occasionally, Preacher noticed Miles waving and nodding his head as he recognized a few familiar faces in and out of the hallway. The bodies became less frequent as the morning PT session got nearer.

"Yeah, sarge. I was kinda out of touch this weekend."

"Well Preacher it wasn't that important other than an attempt to save you the trouble of getting in PT uniform since you won't need it."

"What do you mean?"

"The CO will see you now," the clerk said.

With that said, Miles started walking towards the CO's office and Preacher followed.

"Besides everyone else is there. We were just waiting for you."

"Everyone else?" Preacher asked, while still walking.

But Preacher eventually saw whom the sergeant was referring to.

Just past the clerk's desk in the waiting area just outside the CO's door were Hodkins and Petersen. Petersen was also in uniform.

"And then there were three," replied Hodkin with a grin on his face. His mug immediately glowed when he saw Preacher walked through the door behind Sergeant Miles.

Sergeant Miles walked past the three specialists and made one sharp tap on the CO's door to signal that his young specialists were waiting to meet him.

"You know what this is about, Hodkins?" Preacher asked.

"No, bro."

Preacher then looked at Petersen as if she was bound to know something. But she shook her head in anticipation of his inquiry. At this point, at least, both seemed to forget about what happened over the weekend.

Once a voice was heard on the other side, Miles stuck in his head in for a few seconds. It was back outside the door as fast as it was in.

"The CO will see you all now," said Miles. They walked inside…

The captain leaned back in his chair and started talking.

"A few weeks ago," the officer started talking, "CID paid me a visit and informed me that three of my specialists were under investigation." The captain's eyes wandered from one specialist to the other as he spoke. "Needless to say, I was a little miffed to hear that considering this unit did so well staying off the blotter reports for quite some time now. What troubled me even more was who the targets of the investigation were. Three of my most outstanding specialists—Well, at least two of them anyway."

The captain glanced at Hodkins briefly. Hodkins noticed it as well.

The captain now looked at all three and noticed by the puzzled look on their faces that neither of them had the slightest inkling as to what he was talking about. He whipped forward in his chair and reviewed a manila folder that was laid out on his desk along with the personnel files. "Well to make sure that they prove they actually exist for a reason and to ensure that the tax payer's money are not wasted, CID's investigation of you three have concluded."

The captain looked up briefly and focused back on the papers within the folder.

"An inquiry of misconduct by you three had been started and has now ended."

"Misconduct!" replied Preacher. "What type of misconduct?"

"Yes Sir," added Petersen. "I agree with Preacher. I have no idea what they're talking about. I personally haven't been involved in any incidents."

Both responded to the captain's statement while still at the position of "at ease."

Hodkins didn't bother to say anything. He had been in so much trouble in the past he figured it was just better to stay quiet.

The captain continued while looking at the report, "The misconduct they were referring to is gay conduct."

Preacher stood in disbelief as the words seemed to echo within the room but it didn't. He was in a small amount of shock but he tried not to show it.

It was less than 48 hours since he too had come to terms with his sexuality and he was hoping to deal with it and the military on his own terms and in his own way. Basically, he was hoping to ride out into the sunset without the U.S. Army ever finding out about it.

The wheels immediately started turning in his head. If he was ever kicked out, how would he explain it to the most important people in his life right now: his grandparents? How would they take it? How would they take the news of him being gay? Preacher would obviously have to move up the schedule as far as telling them about his true self.

The shock almost made him forget about Petersen. He had heard the rumors about Petersen a long time ago but thought they were only that: rumors.

This only brought him back as to how they knew about him.

The captain's mannerisms didn't seem to reflect that he was upset. He seemed more disappointed than anything else. But then again the captain had a reputation for tearing someone a new asshole without raising his voice, which was customary throughout the military.

The captain continued, "The CID spared no expense in their investigation."

The captain appeared to be a little sarcastic toward CID as he read the *CID Report of Investigation* to the troops.

SFC Miles, still standing in the corner, just stood there expressionless as the captain read.

"Apparently with the cooperation of your Internet Service Provider or ISP, CID managed to eavesdrop on your communications via ip traffic to support their suspicions and bring the investigations to an end. They used this and other tactics, of course."

Shit. The web cam, Preacher thought.

Fuck. The instant messages. Petersen thought to herself as well.

"I won't pretend to know the significance of this IP stuff but I'm guessing this allowed them to copy what they needed on you," said the captain.

Petersen knew that the chats between Marie and her were quite graphic and denying them or try to misinterpret their true meaning would be futile.

Preacher knew the significance of sniffing the IP traffic between his PC and the ISP. Most Internet traffic was based on this communication protocol.

His entire web surfing, all of his IMs, all of his emails as well as camming would be recorded.

At this point, Preacher thought if the evidence against him was the same or worse as with Hodkins and Petersen, then the only option the three appeared to have was just to reduce the punishment as best they could.

How bad could it be, he thought, it's not like he was PFC Lynndie England of Abu Ghraib fame.

There would be no prison time for this. There probably would be no jail or detention time at all. Other administrative activities could take place for their punishment.

Hodkins like SFC Miles just stood there as if nothing had happen. In his mind, he was probably guilty of something and he just wanted this morning meeting to be over with.

Leaning back slowly in his chair, the captain asked them, "Do any of you have anything to say?"

There was silence. After about 5 seconds, all three responded at least in unisom. "No, sir."

The captain was disappointed as well. Not necessarily at the three soldiers but with this investigation, in general. This, in his view, was a witch hunt. A hunt that didn't find any witches but did find something that was against some military reg.

Aren't we all guilty of something, he thought. *There are a few skeletons in most of our closets.*

These fine soldiers would probably be kicked out of the army not for any abuse or poor performance.

The captain had come to the conclusion that they were probably gay or bi. Neither of them would deny it and their silence spoke volumes. But he doesn't necessarily believe that they deserved to be "outed" and kicked out like criminals. Up to this point, they were all model soldiers and at least one would be considered a leader.

"I really hate to do what I have to do to you all," stated the captain. "The CID Report of Investigation has been passed on to Battalion so they are aware of this as well. I have been instructed to give each of you this."

The captain pulled from the manila jacket three forms and handed one to Hodkins, Preacher and Petersen. The soldiers retrieved it and all three specialists immediately saw the bold, black title at the top of the form: *Homosexual/Bisexual Questionnaire.*

It was the first time Preacher was labeled since his encounter with Hodkins. It felt strange to be labeled this way, standing at parade rest in front of his commander with his platoon sergeant in the rear.

With the exception of some faint noises penetrating the room from the orderly room area, the captain's office was noiseless as the three enlisted read the questionnaire.

As Preacher read his document, he thought about some of the issues that civilian gays or bi people went through in today's society. The issues of invasion of privacy, issues as it dealt with a person's job as well as others which up to now, he only read about.

The document asked questions such as, *"Have you ever stated that you're a homosexual?" "Do you intend to engage in homosexual acts in the future?" "Do you have the propensity or intent to engage in homosexual acts?"*

Preacher and Hodkins stared at the document with disgust. Preacher, at least internally, took it harder than the other two. It was like the questionnaire was actually sounding the questions to him like reading recognition software as opposed to him reading them.

Preacher continued to stare at it and shook his head slightly.

Perhaps tired of sitting down and presenting his specialists with such bad news, the captain decided to stand up and walk to his large window. With his back to the occupants in the room, the captain adjusted the blades in the blinds to view the company grounds as if he was expecting someone.

Preacher looked at Hodkins, still rather curious about the questions on the document and he saw a grin on Hodkins' face. He turned slightly to look at SFC Miles in the corner. He said nothing. Perhaps their wasn't anything for him to say. SFC Miles met Preacher's eyes and he too shook his head.

SFC Miles also was disappointed with this investigation. Here, he thought, were two of his best soldiers being castrated for something that did not prevent them from doing their job, nor was it an issue of national security.

This was something that shouldn't have gotten as far as it did. All this because an enlisted person didn't want to go to PLDC. So instead, U.S. Army resources were geared up for a fishing expedition that only uncovered that three enlisted personnel were in the closet as it was called, he thought.

In the closet but still very capable of doing their job and doing it magnificently. Miles assumed they were guilty of at least some of this and were in fact "in the closet." Considering not one of them denied any of the accusations. Not one of them. But it didn't make it right to do good soldiers like this.

The captain released the blinds and turned around.

"In addition to your responses on the form, some of your fellow soldiers were interviewed and each of your medical files were scrutinized to determined if they can relate any stories, conversations or find any evidence that would suggest you three are homosexual or bisexual."

"I'm straight and personally resent the way I'm being treated and refused to fill out this questionnaire," Petersen said. She handed the form back to her company commander.

After a pause, the captain received the unfilled form.

This apparently was what both Hodkins and Preacher were thinking. They too, handed their questionnaire back to their captain. The captain didn't expect it but he understood their actions. But he too had a job to do.

"If, in the judgment of battalion, the charge of gay conduct is substantiated he will pass the matter up to an Administrative Separation Board which has the authority to order the discharge of you three," stated the captain. "Either an Honorable, General, or Other Than Honorable Discharge will be given. If separation is anything less than an Honorable Discharge, the soldier may be required to pay back the educational grants provided by the military and risk losing eligibility for certain veterans' benefits and even preferred loan rates on a future housing as currently enjoyed by other veterans."

The captain paused for a moment to let his three soldiers absorb all that was said so far.

"So...with all that said, are you refusing to say no more than you already had and provide me with only these blank forms?"

"Yes, sir," replied Hodkins.

"Yes, sir," said, Petersen.

"I agree as well, sir," Preacher said.

The captain went to sat in his chair.

"I hate to do this to you as well as have to place all three of you on restriction until the matter is fully resolved. Either you three will be cleared or kicked out. It's just that simple. I am truly sorry," said the captain.

"I know, sir. It's not your fault," said Preacher.

Hodkins glanced at Preacher at the corner of his eye.

The captain continued, "I would bring you two from off-post back to the barracks but we just don't have the room. Battalion squabbled with me over that suggesting that I place you in one of our sister units until the matter is resolved but I fought that silly idea and won."

"Thank you, sir," said Preacher.

"It just didn't seem right to overburden another unit's barracks space considering living space is of short supply all over this post. Doing that just to appease someone's grudge. Besides, this matter isn't a criminal one and certainly not one deserving of 'barracks arrest.' You are not off-post because of some reward. But you three are all restricted to work, mess hall and your place of residence. So you either will be there or in route to one of three places. Is that clear?" said the commander while eyeing both Preacher and Hodkins.

That task would be easy for Petersen to comply with considering she lived, work and ate on post but the other two specialists would be more tempted to carry on their usual ways because they lived off-post.

"To help aleve any desires to make stops to and from work or a visit to your usual hangouts on the weekends, I have instructed SFC Miles to make periodic checks on you three," said the captain.

There was a long sigh from Hodkins which the captain heard and decided to raise up from his comfy chair.

Looking Hodkins dead in his eyes, the captain continued, "And someone will more than likely be placed on the duty roster a little more than usual."

SFC Miles still stood in his corner. He had heard this bad news earlier with the captain prior to the three specialists arriving. He also knew that his additional babysitting duties would not be too intrusive on the specialists.

The captain had even suggested to him that he should make any physical stops on the troops while leaving work and he *might* want to leave work early to do so which was fine with the sarge.

At other times, he *might* want to just make telephone checks.

The captain knew that these three soldiers were being railroaded and their military careers would more than likely come to an abrupt stop and he didn't want to add to the drama by making their last few days in the military any worse than it had to be. The SFC agreed whole heartedly.

"Is that OK with you Specialist Hodkins?" barked the captain.

"Yes. Yes, sir."

"Good! I'm happy you think my idea was a good one. You remember that the next few days."

Preacher wanted to grin but wouldn't dare while still in front of the captain's desk.

SFC Miles cleared his throat, trying to hold back the laughter himself. The captain didn't plan on making the first sergeant re-do the duty schedule just for Hodkins but Hodkins didn't know that. But for awhile he would be keeping tabs on the duty roster to see if he made the list.

The captain brought his attention to all three.

"If there is nothing else for me then I have nothing else for you. Group! Ah-ten-tion."

The three specialists and their platoon sergeant all went to the position of attention.

"Dismiss!"

After making a left flank by pivoting on the heels of their boots, the specialists walked out of the office followed by SFC Miles.

The punishment was laid down, the countdown to involuntary discharge had begun and thoughts of the future would commence by all three specialists.

Neither thought any jail time would be given but a discharge was certain. It was just a matter now as to what kind. Neither thought of making the military a career but each wanted to leave on their own terms. Each wanted to mature both mentally and professionally on some level prior to escaping a world of heavy discipline to one of more opportunities but on a "looser" reign. Apparently, this was not meant to be.

Now, it was Hodkin, Petersen and Preacher who would need legal counsel.

The very system that was trying to kick him out would be the same one defending him.

But the soldiers had no choice in the matter. The U.S. Army appointed counsel for them and neither Hodkins, Petersen or Preacher nor their parents could afford the counsel that they would need. From the beginning, the deck was stacked against them.

The U.C.M.J., in the mind of many, was designed among other things to keep the military system intact. To detour or eliminate anyone or anything that would attempt to dismantle it. Regardless of the political beliefs, racial factors or rank of the affected.

Perhaps the founders of such a justice system had the foresight to know that the civilian legal system was open to too much interpretation by those who were sworn to work by it and therefore such interpretation over time would change the very foundation of U.C.M.J. thereby possibly changing the military and its fabric which has kept this country secure for decades.

Days went by without any further word as to when the "hammer" would officially come down on the three specialists.

All three were coping with the impeding punishment as well as with their new schedules. Preacher's was simple. Because he still lived off post, he was instructed to come from home to work, lunch and back home again. With permission from his platoon sergeant, he could go to the PX or commissary for necessary items.

Petersen, even though she had a different platoon sergeant, had a similar schedule but not as flexible as Preacher's since she lived in the barracks.

Hodkins on the other hand was having a little difficulty keeping to the strict schedule. After missing a few of Sergeant Miles' "checkup" phone calls, the sergeant emphasized that the situation could be much worse than it is. Despite not seeing how much worse it could get, considering their minor infractions, Hodkins insisted to his supervisor he would once again cooperate with the new arrangements. The suspense of not yet knowing what would happen to him, was really eating Hodkins up inside.

After a rather hectic day in the shop, Preacher was relieved to be heading home from the base. Fortunately for both Hodkins and himself, the personnel in his immediate office were indifferent to his present situation. By both officer and enlisted persons, they were treated no different than before. He was considered the same old Preacher and Hodkins was his same self.

The break area was a little different. The unit as well as the Army as a whole still had personnel with old ways of thinking and don't mind letting people know it.

On one occasion in the break room, Preacher walked in to get sodas when the conversation between two old Chief Warrant Officers "casually" switched from the Post Commander's stat reports to gays in the military.

"They are fucking queers and all suspected of it should be kicked out of this man's army and forced to repay every penny for the cost of boot camp and their AIT including any monies used to pay for the fairy's college," said one officer.

"Bill, it's about $200,000 a piece to train a single person thorough boot camp," said the other. "You throw in the needed advanced training based on the job, benefits, needed travel, et cetera and you can easily reach $400,000."

"That's fine with me."

Preacher suspected that it was no coincidence that the issue just happened to be brought up. There were no big stories on the broadcast news or in the papers that day which would prompt the two to even mention the issue just as he walked in. But like anywhere else the rumor mill was quite active in the military. The word about Petersen, Hodkins and himself couldn't be contained for long. It was bound to be out.

Preacher inserted his coins and retrieved his sodas from the machine without commenting or even looking at the two neanderthals sitting with their cigarettes and coffee in hand as he vacated the area.

A "village"--or a section within the center in this case—is missing two idiots, Preacher thought.

Preacher thought that he had handled the incident quite well under the circumstances and hadn't thought about it much that day.

But he had thought about how Hodkins would had handled the situation under similar conditions. He had thought about it and in no time at all he come to the conclusion that the outcome would be different. Hodkins wouldn't, he believed, cuss them out but he would probably make them aware that he not only heard what they said but informed them that they probably had nieces, uncles, fathers, brothers, sons and/or daughters or even wives that were "queers." And should be the subject of the same mistreatment.

The officers probably would be shocked at what they were told by the young, black enlisted man and proceed to find out who is his supervisor to make a complaint and eventual punishment. Comparing the two, he was glad it was him getting the sodas and not the other way around.

I guess things do happen for a reason, Preacher thought.

His thoughts later went to how his other special friend was doing. It had been a few days since he last spoke to Petersen and wanted to check to see how she was handling all of this at work as well as overall. In fact, Preacher was a little embarrassed that he hadn't chatted with her in awhile despite working in the same building.

But he really didn't want the two of them seen publicly under the circumstances. He didn't want any backslash felt by Petersen because of it. He thought that because she was a female and all, the stress would be handled quite differently than him and Hodkins.

But after talking to her later that day at home, he was surprised by what she had told him.

Preacher was at his apartment and Petersen was in her room. Her roommate, apparently gone for the time being. Petersen, sounding exhausted, told her story.

"I had a one night stand with one of my sorority sisters. After one night of sex, I wanted to become serious but she rejected me. She said that

I wasn't yet mature enough for her. Whether that was true or not, I don't know but I did know that at that time I was in love with her." She laughed. "In any case, I came out to my mom the next day. The night before I had stayed up most of the night preparing a script of what I wanted to say to her."

Petersen paused as if she was recalling that night in her head. "Awakening the next morning was pretty much like preparing oneself for major surgery—it was scary."

Preacher was glad she felt that she could unload on him to possibly release a little stress.

"I prepared a quick breakfast and after reviewing the notes, called my mom when I felt she was wide awake."

"What then?" Preacher asked.

"Gee, slow your roll, Preacher," replied Petersen, "I'm coming to that."

Preacher smiled on the phone.

"Only with my notes nearby was I able to actually talk to her when she came online. I was actually gripping the paper to the point of crumbling and I needed to spread it out again. Mom, I have something to tell you. It was early in the morning and she knew that I normally don't call anyone that early unless it was important and I needed something. There was a short pause on the line then my mom quickly asked, 'Are you knocked up?' I quickly said, 'no' and I decided to prevent my mom from any more guessing and stop the stress on me as well. 'Mom, I'm gay.' After a moment of silence, my mom reacted somewhat strange. She asked a few simple but expected questions and the answers seem to reassure her and me at the time.

I was just glad it was over. But to be honest in hindsight, I'm not sure if my mom was just in shock and wondering which would be better: her daughter being pregnant unexpectedly or she was a 'bull dager.' Using the language of her time."

Petersen continued, "Being like all mothers, I suppose, she did warn me not to tell anybody. Not sure if this was out of my own safety, the family's embarrassment or both."

Petersen sighed. Preacher could tell that after all this time Petersen wasn't fond of reliving the events of that time.

"What was it I read? The first rules of coming out is just to tell the right people. Well, that rule I did follow somewhat at that time. I only told a very close friend and that was it. No other family members. But later, I became a little careless I suppose."

Petersen paused again over the line but Preacher did not push her into telling him exactly what happened. Obviously, it was still painful and he just left it alone.

"Coming out then for me to the extent that I did was just too hard and emotional. Over the years looking back, it has proven difficult for both mom and me. The stress that it puts on you and the fact that mom, I can tell, still has a hard time dealing with it. You know, my mom is from that pre-Internet era and it's not always easy for her, to talk to people about her daughter's lifestyle, go to the gay section of the library or perform a 'Google' for the right books to try to understood."

"But you know what, Preacher?" she asked, sighing.

"What?"

"If nothing else, these last couple weeks have taught me that I have to be true to myself and understanding myself is probably the best thing I can do. As of now Preacher, I am 'OUT!'"

There was a rather longer pause on the phone.

"You are about the fourth person I have 'come out' to. Okay, Preacher you can talk now," she said.

"Okay."

"Well, I guess congratulations are in order. Or my condolences," Preacher said, laughing.

"You are right. It could very well be either of the two. But you know what? I will deal with it. I always have."

"You go girlll," said Preacher.

"The best way, I think, to 'come out' for a lot of people is just to 'be out' instead of encountering all the extra tension of directly telling people the way I did or keeping it to myself. Intuitively, I knew that I don't have to shout it to everyone because everyone doesn't have to know. I don't think it's being secretive exactly as I was before. It's just 'coming out' in a way that works for me. And you know what else, Preacher?"

"What?"

"The last week, despite all us hanging in the wind, has been liberating. There is nothing more fancy-free than accepting an aspect of our humanity that is ridiculed so badly within our race that a segment of our society goes without a loved one to wrap their arms around both day and night. But for me, those days are over. I have started a new life whether or not I stay in the military."

"Hmmm," was all Preacher said over the phone.

"Well, that's my story and if you fuckers are eavesdropping on this phone, well, I guess you got some more to document," said Petersen.

Preacher had to laugh. He thought for a second if it was likely that the phones were tapped but thought it was highly unlikely. If they were, it was over and the investigation had all they needed.

"So what about you, Preach?"

"What about me?"

Preacher knew what she was getting to but wanted to avoid going there. He called to try to comfort his friend. It wasn't suppose to be the other way around. Just because she had been "reborn" because of the CID investigation didn't mean everyone around her had been.

"The stuff that the captain read off in his office."

I really don't want to go down this road with her, Preacher thought.

"Was any of it true?" she said.

Petersen heard a sigh on the other end of the line. The same sigh she heard from her mother each time she tried to explain to her her chosen life after her mother would try to persuade her to find a good boyfriend or find a good church on or near the post in order to change her ways.

After a long pause, she decided to drop it. He wasn't ready, she thought, to talk about his demons. Not to mention any type of "coming out." Assuming that applied to him.

"Anyway, I appreciate you calling me, checking up on me and all but I have to get a few things ready for tomorrow."

"Ok."

"I will let you go for now. You have a good night."

"You too."

"And by the way, Preach," whispered Petersen. "One of these days, perhaps soon. You need to allow me to be *your* shoulder to 'cry on.'"

"Perhaps," he replied softly.

"What was it the great Dr. Seuss once said? 'Be yourself, those who matter won't care and those who care don't matter.'"

That put a smile on Preacher's face. One that Petersen would have loved to seen.

"Good night, sis," he said finally.

Preacher did have a smile on his face. The thought of that evening on the phone with Petersen put a smile on his face.

CHAPTER SEVENTEEN

It was a lovely day in Colorado Springs, with an endless blue sky dotted with clouds. Traffic was manageable and Preacher thought he would be in his apartment in less than 15 minutes.

The humming of the vehicles and the treading of the surrounding road was interrupted by Preacher's cell phone. He answered and after about five minutes on the phone, he would not only get home in record time but will have a visitor bring some dinner for the two of them.

Taylor was coming over for a minute. Both Taylor and Preacher had seen a lot of each other the last few weeks but for the most part met for the occasional dinner or went to see a movie.

Preacher may have invited him over because he didn't want to webcam on his computer tonight or spend too much time IMing. He saw how that stuff could be addictive and didn't want to get too heavily into it.

Preacher walked into his apartment and was greeted by gentle jazz music. He must have forgotten to turn off the stereo prior to leaving this morning. The morning talk show host was long gone and music played in the afternoon.

Since he was in for the evening, Preacher changed from combat mode into his Geoffrey Beene pants with matching top.

He walked around the apartment barefoot as he did his house errands. He didn't want the place to look too sloppy.

Then the phone rang again.

It was Taylor. He was approaching the apartment parking lot and had called Preacher as if they were gonna signal each other to "sneek" into the apartment like kids.

Preacher laughed. "Just bring your butt on up. You know the apartment number."

Taylor walked into the apartment. Preacher offered him a soda from the fridge. He wrapped up one errand before assisting Taylor with the bagged dinner. After Preacher retrieved a set of dishes, the two sat down to a fish dinner. Preacher had the perch and Taylor had the catfish.

"Colorado Springs is a beautiful city isn't it?" Taylor asked as he turned around with a smile full of pearly whites. Dressed in a purple and gold Lakers warm-ups, he was looking good.

"It's ok," Preacher said as he dipped a piece of perch in hot sauce before shoving it down.

"I would prefer a little more color when you get outside the city limits but what do you expect when the whole state has a 3 percent African-American population."

"True," replied Taylor. "What can you do?"

"So what brings you over? Were you in the neighborhood shopping?" Preacher asked.

"Naw. Was thinking about you and decided to check if you were free for take-out or take-in, depending on how you look at it since you were on lock down and shit," Taylor teased with a smile which made Preacher smile too.

The two retired to the living room area after a satisfying meal. Preacher made a detour to the bathroom to retrieve a can of air freshener to sanitize the apartment and get rid of most of the fish aroma.

Preacher sat near but not exactly next to his guest. Even though the TV was on and set to some music videos, Taylor's attention was on Preacher. He would watch a few seconds of a video then would be right back to Preacher's eyes.

Preacher seemed relieved when Taylor asked to be excused to go to the bathroom. "Sure, take your time."

He entered the bathroom and pulled off his warm up top and undershirt, then dropped his pants and underwear. He looked in the waist high mirror and noticed a intoxicated-enhanced glazed look of excitement in his eyes. Taylor was standing in the room with an erection that resembled a foot-long, fully erect jimmie. It was clear that his jimmie was obeying no master but its own mind. He was sure that when Preacher noticed his body, uninhibited sex would come to his mind. After taking a close look at his face and grabbing his rod once, he walked outside the bathroom door and then stepped confidently, and completely nude, into the living room.

Preacher was now engrossed in the *Mariah Carey* video, but when he looked up his facial expression gave him away. He was a little shocked.

"Taylor, what's going on, guy?"

"You tell me, Preach." He stepped closer now holding his jimmie with one hand. It looked like a fist full from where Preacher was standing.

"Taylor, why are you doing this? Do you really want to do this?" asked Preacher in a low, irritated voice.

"I have thought about this for a long time and I do want to get with you, Preach."

"Taylor, you seem like a great guy, and if I wasn't trying to make things happen with a close friend of mine, Hodkins, then I would definitely be interested in someone like you." He was suddenly feeling uncomfortable about being naked. "You got a slamming body, but I can't right now. I would feel too guilty."

"You kidding me, right Preacher? What about all that stuff you said about--"

"It doesn't matter now," interrupted Preacher. "I believe I have found a love of my own."

Taylor was clearly irritated. His nude body suddenly had a thin layer of nervous sweat that was now glistening. "I see."

Preacher didn't think he saw anything but he didn't want to say too much to make things even worse for him.

The pride Taylor had felt earlier along with his rock hard tool, had almost all but disappeared. His eyes were now a blank stare and a chilling emptiness had surrounded him despite being in the living room in the company of a friend.

Taylor wanted more than a friend tonight. He wanted to get physical. He was banking on it.

"I'm going to leave now, but I'll call you in a day or so," said Taylor. Once the Lakers outfit was donned on, Taylor left his friend's apartment.

Shifting on the sofa with a pillow nearby, Preacher was fortunate enough to conceal his own erection from him thereby dousing out any further encouragement. Preacher was truly sorry about what he had to do to his friend. He was sure that Taylor left lonely and rejected. But Preacher wanted to honor his new found relationship—no matter what kind of relationship. And he supposed that meant turning down a handsome naked man in his living room.

Life can be so cruel sometimes, he thought.

Two weeks later...

Preacher did not want to face his coworkers or any members of his unit today. The news of his as well as Hodkins' and Petersen's charges were out. Way out.

The Colorado Springs' *The Gazette* had a front page story on it in bold black letters: **Fort Carson Hero Charged Involving Same Gender Sexual Conduct**.

Today, he thought, would be a good day to take leave. It would be a good "Mental Health" day. He knew it would be only a matter of time before the major mainstream media outlets would start picking up on the story if they hadn't already.

Preacher read a couple of paragraphs of the story and it read a lot smoother than how the proceedings took place days ago. It was not easy standing their in front of all those officers in Class As as charges of this type were being read. Everyone looking all so stoic during the whole proceeding.

The only thing that made it all so bearable for the three specialists was that their direct supervisors as well as the first sergeant and company commander were the only familiar faces there.

He now knew how McCullen might have thought when charges were read to him.

The paper stated, *Three out of the five enlisted soldiers accused of same-gender sexual conduct on and off the post have been formally charged.*

Specialists Malcolm Preacher, Specialists Gwendolyn Petersen and Specialists Clarence Hodkins of Fort Carson's Headquarters and Headquarters Company, pleaded not guilty to charges brought by the US Army after their cases were referred to a special court-martial.

The three soldiers face court-martial proceedings on charges of sodomy, pandering and engaging in sexual acts. The two other soldiers face non-judicial punishment.

A spokesman said the Army considers the investigation complete.

"As far as we're concerned, it's isolated to the unit, and our investigation determined that these five individuals were the only ones," said Major James Mason, a spokesman for Fort Carson.

The charges were made under the Uniform Code of Military Conduct, which retains a provision against sodomy even though the United States Supreme Court invalidated all state sodomy laws in a Texas case it decided in 2003.

Mason said the five soldiers charged had been given military lawyers. An arraignment is scheduled soon.

The two soldiers who received nonjudicial punishments weren't identified. In addition to a reduction in rank, their punishment included 45 days of restriction to the unit area, 45 days of extra duty and forfeiture of a month's pay.

The two soldiers of Fort Carson's Headquarters and Headquarters Company are among the Army's most celebrated soldiers.

The military's "Don't Ask, Don't Tell" policy states that a same-gender sexual orientation is no bar to service. But same-gender sexual conduct is "incompatible with military service," according to the policy, and gays and lesbians are expected to keep their sexual orientation a secret.

Service members who violate the policy are removed from the military. Most receive honorable discharges, but that is all but inconceivable in the case of the five accused.

What a day this is going to be, Preacher thought. The news is out and the gossip mongers will soon start their engines.

Then it hit him.

My grandparents!

He had to contact them and explain the military charges, the process of the UCMJ system as it pertains to him as well as what to expect from the outcome.

Most importantly, he had to calm any fears of him going to jail or prison.

After setting the paper and the coffee down on the table, he grabbed his phone.

Next morning, Bryan Mueller and Jeff Cabin were putting the finishing touches in Atlanta on an article for their media giant.

Bryan was at work in his cubicle while his producer went to the coffee shop for two lattes. They had some time considering he was waiting for an email from *The Servicemembers Legal Defense Network* or *SLDN* for short, which had some good information for them.

"I'm back buddy boy. You now have the fuel you need to keep working well past six today," said Jeff.

Bryan didn't take his eyes off the screen. Instinctly, he reached to his blind side and grabbed the cup.

"Where are we now, Bryan?" Jeff asked.

"Using our previously discussed story outline, we are about halfway with this piece." Bryan took another gulp of his drink. "Once we get the SLDN stuff from your source this morning and do a fact check, all of it should be ready for editor check for tomorrow's *The Situation Room* as well as for the website."

"You know, Bryan, for a second year reporter, that kid from that soldier's hometown newspaper got that background packet in record time."

"Make sure we mention his name if one of us get scheduled for one of our daily shows. You never know. *Anderson Cooper 360°*'s producer may want a piece of this story."

"I hear ya, mate."

"Oh, Oh!" shouted Jeff. "We have mail!" he said after seeing a notification pop-up on his desktop screen.

After reading the From: column, he exclaimed. "It's from them, it's from SLDN!" he said. He spun around to give Jeff a high five.

"Boo-Yah!"

The last day or so was a little draining for both Hodkins and Preacher. For the first time in a long time, he would drive to work not looking forward to anything remotely related to it. Not the work itself or the people.

This day would be no different.

After walking through the main corridor of Replacement Center after morning formation at the unit, it was like Preacher couldn't get inside PAS fast enough.

He was attempting to enter his code so fast his fingers were gliding over the keypad which because he was not pressing hard enough, didn't register in the system. It took him three tries before he was inside the PAS and in his safety zone.

With the exception of Hodkins and another enlisted, most of the personnel including supervisors seem to stand clear of him during the work day, not sure exactly what to say to him if the incident concerning the charges came up or simply not knowing how to react around a possible gay co-worker.

The work took Preacher's and Hodkins' mind off the issue of the military charges.

Chit chat among the soldiers was at a minimum, observed SSG Miles. He would check on the progress of the various projects just to get a feel about everyone's morale not necessarily to get a time table of the projects themselves.

The PFCs he had observed would confer with Hodkins and Preacher as to whether they should take a particular route on an IT issue but only when they had to.

That was a sharp contrast to the usual jovial ruckus that penetrated the interior of PAS.

With very little communication between the two, Hodkins and Preacher were grossly into their computer work. They skipped the mess hall, no doubt due to the large number of soldiers who would be attending as well as the number of stares in the place.

Probably worth skipping today anyway considering it was near the end of the month.

SFC Miles with his coffee cup in one hand and a statistical report in the other walked up to Preacher's cubicle.

"Preach, Warrant Officer Davis told me to give you a big thank-you for that personnel stats report that you quickly put together for him the other day. The General had asked him for the data weeks ago for his next meeting with him and he forgot to give us some notice."

Preacher looked up. "It was no problem. I had wrapped up another report earlier than I had expected and was able to create it for him in about an hour and a half. Well before his meeting with the Post Commander."

"But in my case, he was a happy camper. I do believe he said that buying you lunch wasn't totally out of the question," replied SFC Miles.

"Oh! He did, did he? That must 'a been a good meeting. The old tight wad usually don't even let his pennies get too for away from his pockets," said Preacher.

"That is true," said a smiling SFC before leaving Preacher after a pat on his back. He was now off to see SPC Hodkins.

The drive home was good. The work day was uneventful for a change and Preacher thought it would be a long time before he actually wanted to be drowned in work. That was the case the last couple of days and it did him a lot of good. He was able to focus on the work and not when and what kind of charges would be coming down for him as well as completing and taking a bite full out of his workload.

And based on his short conversation with Hodkins, his work day went about the same. As far as how he was dealing with the impending charges. *Well, Hodkins appears to let a lot of stuff roll off his shoulders—at least on the outside. But one never knows with him. He's human like the rest of us and he may have had a hard time dealing with it all but didn't want to show it, Preacher figured. One day down, many more to go.*

US Army Specialist Malcolm Drexel Preacher, a Information Technology Specialist and until recently a hero to some until the army brought charges against him.

The charges? Same-gender sexual conduct.

At a time when the military is being stretched, the Preacher Case sends all the wrong signals to servicemen. Finding a few good men whether they sat behind a computer or on the front lines will only get harder and harder if overzealous lawyers are permitted to intimidate the troops.

In any army that's a losing formula. Why then is this hero being charged with this? There's seemingly no real good answer.

Spc. Preacher is straight out of some "small town boy does good" story. The 22 year old soybean producing town native in Arkansas statistically should have never left that area. He…

Preacher couldn't believe this was starting all over again. But there it was in the Colorado Springs' *The Gazette* paper. Another front pager.

When will it all stop? He wondered.

But Preacher had to admit that the article was interesting. With the exception of a few untruths about the family, the article so far was right on the money.

Half dressed in his US Army PT shirt and underwear, the specialist sat on the bed with the morning paper laid out and some *Folgers* on the night stand and continued reading.

Unless it can be shown that Spc. Preacher and the others aren't exemplary soldiers; that is, if new facts come to light showing he and the others are doing something criminal in the eyes of the American people despite what the UCMJ states, we call on the Pentagon to drop the bogus charges against the enlisted group.

As far as any outsider can tell and we know that it's not them who count but the military, they are outstanding soldiers who deserve a lot more from their superiors in the way of respect than they are currently getting.

One of the soldiers, Spc. Preacher waived his right to a pretrial hearing and demanded a speedy court-martial.

But a US Army spokesman told CNN the day of the article that Spc. Malcolm Drexel Preacher—whose case has drawn outrage from many veteran, gay & lesbian community and pro-military supporters including a few influential members of congress—still is scheduled to face the pretrial, or Article 32 hearing at Fort Carson, Colorado.

A spokesman said, the US Army has received Preacher's request, but the hearing 'will continue as planned until we announce otherwise.'

Preacher waived his right to a hearing in order to get a Military Judge to sway the prosecution to produce evidence in the case. The formal waiver, filed with the US Army Judge Advocate General office by defense counsel, Army Captain Daniel E. Horner says:

'I hereby knowingly intelligently and voluntarily waive my right to an investigation of the charges and specifications in accordance with Article 32, UCMJ. We have requested discovery (evidence) that has not been produced by the Government absent a court order; and, my desire that I receive a speedy trial in accordance with R.C.M. 707 and the 6th Amendment of the United States constitution.'

This was really getting interesting to Preacher.

'The Servicemembers Legal Defense Network or SLDN, a national non-profit legal services watchdog and policy organization dedicated to ending discrimination and harassment of military personnel, has learned that the US Army Criminal Investigation Division is conducting undercover surveillance operations in the Colorado Springs and Denver gay friendly bars and nightclubs, in an apparent attempt to skirt the letter and intent of 'Don't Ask, Don't Tell, Don't Pursue, Don't Harass.'

Current policy prohibits military criminal investigative organizations from investigating service members' sexual orientation. The policy further allows for all service members to engage in associational activities such as going to gay bars.

SLDN has stated that it has evidence suggesting that criminal investigators are specifically targeting suspected gay service members and, while being unable to discharge them for patronizing the gay bar or nightclub, solicit them to engage in other conduct which may carry administrative or criminal penalties.

SLDN had sent a request to CID headquarters to suspend all surveillance operations at gay-friendly bars and nightclubs immediately, and suspend all administrative or criminal actions resulting from these operations, pending a thorough review of CID conduct in this matter.

According to the transcript of an Article 32 hearing held two day ago obtained by SLDN, US Army CID Special Agent Matthew P. Gibons testified that CID conducts surveillance operations against at least three Colorado Springs establishments having primarily gay male clientele: *Club Q*, *Icon* and *The Spot*.

Special Agent Gibons did not mention any other Colorado Springs Bars or nightclubs under military surveillance, suggesting the CID is specifically targeting gay service members. Special Agent Gibons testified that the surveillance has been running for the past couple of years.

He also testified that US Army Criminal Investigations Division is working closely with the Air Force Office of Special Investigations (OSI) in these operations. The Colorado Springs area houses a number of military establishments such as the US Air force Academy, Norad as well as Fort Carson.

Special Agent Gibons further indicated that the surveillance targets suspected gay service members without any prior indication of misconduct. Special agent Gibons testified, 'when we identify someone who we think is a US military member… we target that individual and then see if the information can be developed.'

Special Agent Gibons also testified that he intentionally selects young informants and undercover agents to go to these establishments during the early morning hours. According to the Article 32 hearing transcript, the covert operatives approach military-looking men, initiating conversations and flirting.

Special Agent Gibons further testified that CID undercover agents routinely trace vehicle license plates of suspected service members.

The CID surveillance has also targeted civilians. Special Agent Gibons testified: '[CID has] identified people in the past that—after we put the person under surveillance and followed them and found out who they really were—they turned out not to be in the military. So therefore we would take the intelligence and pass it to local law enforcement.' It is not known whether local Springs law enforcement officials know of, condone, or follow-up on civilians targeted during these operations.

The sworn testimony raises serious concerns that military criminal investigators are deliberately skirting the letter and intent of 'Don't Ask, Don't Tell, Don't Pursue, Don't Harass' by targeting suspected gay service members at gay bars and nightclubs for disparate treatment. The surveillance operations chill service members' access to resources within the gay community.

Preacher set down the paper. It was time to finish getting ready for the PT session this morning. Preacher restored the newspaper back to its original delivery configuration and proceeded to find his warm up pants, cap, shoes and jacket. After grabbing a bagel from the fridge, he was out the door.

After a heavy PT session, topped off with a 5 mile run, Preacher went to the post gym for his shower. After the uncomfortable faces he got the last time he was at the unit after PT, he simply didn't want to go thorough that again. Those who were waiting to get showers looked uneasy and those who didn't want him to be in the shower stalls with them probably took a shower in record time before existing out. Most of them were guys he really didn't know anyway.

He could tell by some stares at the gym that he looked familiar based on his photo and video plastered on newspaper and TV outlets, but overall he was one of the guys there.

Once showered and afterwards, a stop in the mess hall for breakfast, he was sitting behind his desk ready for whatever the US Army threw at him. After about 2 hours of work, Preacher got a tap on the back from Hodkins as he walked past him headed to the exit door of PAS.

Preacher looked around to his side in the direction of Hodkins, when he got a nod from him to leave with him. He needed Preacher for something. Preacher acknowledged him and after saving a file he was working on, proceeded to "lock" his screen and left behind Hodkins. The absence of both wouldn't mean anything to anyone. They could simply be on break.

Once outside PAS, Hodkins saw Preacher from the main doors of The Replacement Center as he was exiting them.

"Hey. Let's go to the side smoke break area," said Hodkins.

"Okay."

The day was sunny, yet very breezy. Pikes Peak had a haze about mid-point up its sides. It was another typical day overlooked by the Peak.

Hodkins leaned against a railing that ran along the center, paralleled to the road that went alongside the building.

He had a look of his old self back and seemed a little relaxed.

"So what's up?" asked Preacher.

"I wanted to talk to you out of the way of peeps," said Hodkins.

"Okay, what's up?"

"I was hoping you could help me with something important and personal."

Preacher was curious as to what could be so important that it couldn't wait till later or be talked about in the office where it was comfortable.

"Ok—kayy. I say again—what's up?"

Hodkins let Preacher in on the pressing matter. "Since it doesn't appear we are being charged at the moment with anything criminal, I would like to prepare for my imminent departure from Uncle Sam. It's only a matter of time."

Well that is a good idea, Preacher thought.

Preacher didn't want to bust his bubble by telling him that he should have been preparing for that day years ago. Some would even say when you signed up for the US Army. But Hodkins wouldn't be the first or the last to stop and think about life after the army just before the military career ended.

"And how do you hope to do that?"

"Well, that's where you come in. I was hoping you would come down to the Transition Center with me to see what they have to offer and you can help me decide what shit would be to my benefit instead of just merely accepting what ever bullshit the DOD civilians throw at me."

"Okay. I can do that. When do you want to visit there?" asked Preacher.

Just prior to him answering that, a sergeant from another unit passed by in his new Ford Explorer Sport which prompted Hodkins to pause and wave.

"I have an appointment the day after tomorrow at 1600 hours. I was hoping sarge could let us clock out early to go there." Hodkins had now shifted himself and was now leaning back against the railing.

"That should be okay," said Preacher.

Hodkins folded his arms. "I was not just asking you because you are my boy and all," Hodkins said while jabbing his right arm into Preacher's chest and making Preacher flinch some. "But because you seem to have your shit together, I hate to admit."

"Well thanks son. You should be recognizing a brotha."

"Well from now on, I suppose we have to be honest with one another as well as supporting, right?" whispered Hodkins.

"Right," replied Preacher. "I suppose we do."

Hodkins was darn right sincere with those words. If Preacher didn't know any better he could swear he was getting soft.

"You're not getting soft on me, Hodkins. Are you?"

"Me? Big Nuts Hodkins? Never," he said, laughing.

"Okay let's head back in. Some of us have work to do," Preacher said.

"Good idea."

The two headed back inside.

Preacher passed by the building over thousand times easily while stationed at Fort Carson. But until now, never had a reason to visit it and he was sure the same hold true for Hodkins.

The two actually drove to the rear unit parking lot from work and parked their vehicles. They purposely choose the rear one in order to avoid running into the CO or the first sergeant. Even though the two unit leaders had reserved parking in the front, Preacher surveyed the remaining vehicles in the lot to see if he recognized any of the vehicles as belonging to the CO or 1SG. From the parking lot they only had to walk about a block to the Fort Carson Transition Center. The center, similar to others through out the US Army, was designed and set up to assist soldiers with most of their needs of going from the military to civilian life.

This pertain to giving soldiers access to a nation-wide job bank search via computer, assisting with making resumes, job hunting-related classes, etc. They would even help those with a bachelors or above with getting their teaching certificates for possible immediate employment. In other words, the center was very similar to an unemployment office in the civilian sector.

After walking inside, Hodkins checked in with the receptionist and took a seat. For whatever reason, Hodkins looked nervous.

Perhaps it was just being in a unfamiliar place or it was that being here meant that he was getting closer to being put out of a life he has known for almost 4 years.

"Are you alright," asked Preacher.

Hodkins looked away from the civilian marketing posters that were plastered all over the walls of the center for all eyes to see to respond to Preacher, "I'm cool. I'm cool."

Hodkins' eyes wandered from his friend right back to the posters on the walls pushing job offers from such companies as the CIA, NSA, Department of Homeland Security, Lockheed Martin and others.

Preacher saw the propaganda posters that had mesmerized his friend. "They are impressive aren't they?"

Hodkins sighed. "Yeah, but working at companies like that might be a little far reaching for some."

"Hey," Preacher said almost touching his arm but decided against it at the moment. "Don't sell yourself short. You got skills plus all the military schools under your belt."

"So fuckin' what?"

Preacher continued, "The reason you are here is to see what needs to be 'packaged' to make you marketable, right?"

"Yeah, that's true. You know Preacher, when I said that it was far reaching to some, I didn't mean me, I meant you," smiled Hodkins.

Preacher smiled too and tactfully maneuvered his middle finger out on his right hand for Hodkins' eyes to see. They were both grinning when the civilian transition specialist came out from a door and asked for Specialist Hodkins.

Hodkins rose up and said, "Right here." Then Preacher's friend had disappeared behind the door.

A single beverage station was set up for the quests consisting of coffee, of course, and punch. Looking at an empty tray, cookies or perhaps pastries from the morning were also served at some point during the day.

There was a single classroom. Based on the sign posted just outside the door, it was used for resumes, job search and interview classes. Contemporary music also played from speakers in the ceiling. Probably from a preselected soundtrack or satellite radio.

A set of small cubicles to house six closely knit people was also visible by Preacher. These were used for the purposes of Internet access to facilitate with those on job searches and perhaps company research.

Two of the six cubicles were already occupied by two females. Other than Hodkins and Preacher, there didn't seem like a "hard head" in the whole place.

After a day in the Transition Center, Preacher could see how a place like this could relax you. Surprisingly, there was very little of the military world in the place. Very little of the army's décor. This was probably intended to be that way. To mentally take away the soldiers from that environment at least for a while so he or she could focus on preparing his or her life after Uncle Sam.

Instead of just sitting there looking bored while the pretty receptionist type away on her document, Preacher rose from his seat and walked over to an empty table near a newspaper rack. The rack had a sample of Sunday papers from all the major cities.

Preacher saw *The Dallas Morning News*, *The Atlanta Journal-Constitution* and others but it was *The Charlotte Observer* on the table that caught his eye.

His walk from his seat to the table temporarily distracted the receptionist since the place was relatively quiet and motionless but she quickly went back to her document.

SFC Avery A. Joseph from the 3rd Armored Cavalry Regiment walked in the Transition Center. He removed his head gear and looked around as if he had just exited Customs in a foreign country and was in new surroundings. He had the look of "I need assistance" which did not go unnoticed by the pretty lady.

"May I help you?" she said.

"Yes, mam Yes, mam! My name is Sergeant Joseph and I was hoping I could speak to someone about putting a resume together?" replied the SFC in a surprising soft voice.

The SFC seemed to be about six and half feet easy with a athletic built. Perhaps played some football in high school or college.

The tank unit he is apparently assigned to kept him in shape because his ACU was either tailored or "tight" on him. His neatly rolled up sleeves fitted nicely around his "guns" as well.

And the smooth chocolate complexion of a brotha cared about his appearance because his tan "tank" boots were highly clean even at this time of the day.

Unlike support units and some of their sergeants, these guys in tank units worked hard for long hours and days so to see one appearing in uniform such as SFC Joseph did, spoke volumes to Preacher.

"Sure. Do you have an appointment?" spoke the lady.

"No mam."

The young receptionist was still a little embarrassed by these soldiers coming in, some slightly older than her, others younger, calling her mam. This was evident in the way she twisted her mouth as she smiled and checked her appointment book.

"It would appear that we may be able to handle a 'walk in.' Let me confirm that with our staff. Please have a seat," she said.

The SFC turned around and gradually surveyed the center while going to the nearest available visitor chair.

He saw Preacher at the table and when they made eye contact they each gave each other the "brotha" nod.

After about 10 minutes, like Preacher, SFC Joseph decided to do something other than look bored.

He walked up to the table and pulled out a chair next to Preacher.

"Sup, specialist."

Preacher looked up and made eye contact with the sergeant and shook his hand. "What's up, sarge?"

"Not'ta, not'ta bro," whispered the SFC rather friendly.

Preacher thought it was odd and rather funny that when people found themselves in similar situations such as an impending exodus from their employer whether voluntary or involuntary, a bond always appeared to materialize, whether an honest one or not.

Preacher knew that his eventual departure from the military was completely involuntary at this point but wasn't sure about his new "buddy."

"I saw you at the table reading the paper and decided that we both got something in common."

"And what would that be, sarge?"

Preacher then assumed that the SFC was referring to the situation of Hodkins and himself being charged and eventually kicked out of the army. He thought that the SFC had recognized his face.

"We both are being discharged and are now looking for a job."

He's probably one of those who don't watch the news or when picking up a newspaper, go straight to the sports section. Good!

"Yes, we are, sarge. But I'm here right now with my friend. He's in the back with a counselor," said Preacher.

"Cool."

"I assume you are waiting for one as well?"

"Yes, I didn't have an appointment or anything. Just had some unexpected free time today and decided to put it to good use," smiled the SFC.

"Tanker boys just can't walk off the job like you 'garrison bunnies' do," said Joseph.

"Well, we can't either sarge but we don't go down range that much so we might have just a little more time to handle personal business than you guys," shot back Preacher while displaying his finger in a pinching motion.

"Yeah, just a little," said the sarge.

Now that he was interrupted from reading the newspaper, Preacher had decided to get a little personal as to why he was leaving the military.

"If you don't mine me asking, sarge when are you leaving the army?"

"They are kicking me out in about 2 months after 11 years."

Preacher was shocked. "Damn, sarge! That's rough. All that time invested as well as being over the hurdle towards retirement."

"I know bro," said the SFC. Disgust was slightly on his face but he did his best to downplay it.

Preacher's inquiry led him to relive his frustration all over again. Perhaps the sarge's wife was equally frustrated. Preacher noticed the ring on his finger. She couldn't be entirely happy about the situation either. Wives were just as much part of the military establishment as their spouses. They too had to endure the long spans of being away from their spouses. They too had to live in maybe not so nice housing as their spouses make their way up the ranks. They too had to give up a few things while part of the military family.

SFC Joseph leaned back in his chair to get a little more comfortable while his demeanor had changed just a bit.

"I thought I had did all that was asked of me during my stay in the army," said the SFC. His hands, fingers interlaced, were on his stomach now. "I had gone to all the army schools and thought I did my job very well. At least according to my performance evals, I was doing a very good job."

"Then why are you being let go?" Preacher asked.

The SFC turned his head to Preacher and said matter-of-factly that he failed the runs on his PT tests. "Ain't that some shit, bro. Eleven fucking years down the toilet."

The SFC looked straight ahead. The frustration was clearly on his face.

"Kicking me out for not being able to pass one or two runs. That's just not fair. I have given up a lot and my wife has too for this man's army and its just ain't fair."

Preacher decided to console him just a bit. "It sounds to me, sarge, that you were not the problem. Based on some of the stuff I have been reading and not just the propaganda in *The Army Times* but some of the other mainstream newspapers too, the army has been looking for ways to trim their higher enlisted ranks as well as the higher officer ranks as a means to get new funds to bring onboard new blood." Preacher shook his head as he spoke. "You and others are just the start of the initial exodus from the enlisted ranks. Those fat ass officers, and I mean that literally, will be heading out too in exchange for fresh new lieutenants for Iraq or Afghanistan."

Preacher paused for a bit.

"Sarge, neither one of us really knows what the future would hold while in the military. You never know that if you were staying, the future may not be as bright as you may hope. Maybe a blessing in disguise. You stay and get deployed overseas and come back wounded or even worse to your family."

The SFC nodded his head.

"You know specialists, you may have a point. My mother-in-law said the same thing when my wife first told her. She said almost exactly the same thing."

"Well I guess I'm in good company then, sarge," said Preacher.

SFC Joseph looked at Preacher again. "I guess you are specialist," he said with a smile.

Preacher now thought the SFC was feeling a little better.

"You seem cool specialist," said SFC Joseph. He extended the right hand out for a shake.

"You too, sarge."

"Too bad we didn't meet prior to all this," said Joseph.

"But the important thing is that we did meet," shot back Preacher.

"You know bro after listening to you, I would bet it is the army's loss that you are leaving regardless of the reason," said the SFC.

"Right back at you, sarge." Preacher seemed like he was on a roll. "I'm not an extremely religious person but it just may be that someone has bigger plans for both of us."

They both laughed among themselves just as Hodkins was coming out with the counselor.

I wonder who Preacher is laughing with over there, he thought. Hodkins was walking in the direction of the table when he realized that the counselor was still with him.

"Sorry. Okay, okay I will sign up before I leave today. Thanks for your help."

"You're welcome," said the counselor. "Sergeant First Class Joseph! I am ready for you."

"Right here," said the SFC.

Both him and Preacher stood up.

Joseph went towards the counselor as the counselor guided him towards the door to the counselor chambers. "Thanks for seeing me today."

Preacher went towards Hodkins, when Hodkins turned around to see the receptionist to sign up for his much needed class.

After doing so, he looked up at Preacher. "What was that all about, cuz?"

"We were just having a conversation and started laughing about something," replied Preacher.

"Well, I can see that," said Hodkins while searching his ACU pants pocket for his headgear. "Hope you don't mind sharing it with me later okay?"

Preacher retrieved his black beret and looked at Hodkins. "Yeah, right."

They both left the Transition Center and before the glass door closed, Preacher stopped and asked, "Are you getting jealous or something?"

Hodkins pretended like he didn't hear him and continued to walk down the sidewalk.

"Preacher, we both need to get back to our cribs before curfew. Don't you think?"

Preacher believed he really was jealous and wanted to settle down his friend.

"Hey, Hodkins. Relax! We were just talking. You have nothing to worry about."

"Whatever," Hodkins said, continuing on his way.

CHAPTER EIGHTEEN

Two Days Later ...

*C*olorado Springs *mornings can be a very beautiful site. Especially when the clouds are not blocking the view of Pikes Peak. Yes, they can be very beautiful on a day like today? Today is a good day.*

While setting in the lounge chair on his small patio several stories above ground, Preacher was enjoying the majestic view, deep thought.

He imagined how this neck of the woods truly was between 1700 and 1800 hundreds. How untamed the land truly must have been. To travel around in territory that wasn't previously traveled by others. A trek like that could be both satisfying as well as dangerous. Not just in terms of robbers and Indians trying to kill you but large animals such as grizzlies and mountain lions attacking you whether out of fear or hunger.

The early morning solitude was interrupted by the horn reverberation announcing the arrival of some visitors a few units down in the parking lot. Annoyed, Preacher lowered his feet from his out stretched position and retrieved another sip of coffee prior to him leaving to get the morning paper.

Yes, today is a good day, indeed.

"Charges Dropped Against Army Hero" was the headline in the paper.

Even though Petersen, Hodkins and he were informed of the details late last night, it still felt good to read the headlines. Preacher was truly in a good mood.

He returned his legs back to the comfortable position and took another sip of his coffee which he had refilled. Once the large cup was returned to the small table, he continued to read about the good news in his pajamas.

A US Army information technology specialist will not be tried on charges stemming from an undercover surveillance operation.

The decision by the Fort Carson Post Commander ends the prosecution of Specialist Four Preacher and others.

"Down at the unit level, there was never a question about Preacher's conduct on or off duty," citing a source close to the investigation. "It appeared to be up in the higher echelons. People who had never seen or had the privilege of working with any of the three enlisted soldiers."

An Article 32 hearing, the military equivalent of a grand jury session, was held. In a report originating from that hearing, a source or sources recommended that the charges be dropped against all of the soldiers.

More than a dozen soldiers who served with Preacher in his unit praised him in testimony saying he was an able leader who remained cool in tough situations.

Preacher, 22, was never actually relieved from his regular duties and during the whole process was allowed to keep his off-post housing.

This was also the same Specialist Preacher who was praised by the US Army, Colorado Springs police department and a women's group for rescuing a young female soldier a few months ago, from continued gang rape.

"I think (the decision) demonstrates that Preacher and the others acted honorably during their military tour and did nothing wrong to deserve punishment of this nature," said the source.

Sources do also say that Specialist Preacher will be leaving the army in a couple of months when his discharge date approaches.

More organized veteran groups, meanwhile, are outraged that while Spc. Preacher and others are everywhere in the media, there is little coverage of the local wounded and the dead arriving from both Iraq and Afghanistan.

"Am I angry about the amount of coverage he's received rather than the soldiers who've come home and aren't getting proper medical support? Yes," says Robert Marsh, Director of the local VFW.

"We should be focused on Iraq and Afghanistan and how and the hell we get out of this mess. Nothing against Spc. Preacher. He's a victim of circumstances beyond his control."

Sources also tell us that senior military as well as civilian officials in Washington, D.C. now regard the episode as an embarrassment they wish would go away.

Apparently, at least one specialist is taking them up on that offer in the next couple of months.

With the paper on his lap, Preacher couldn't help but just stare at Pikes Peak with a big smile on his face. Even though the glass patio door was closed shut, he could still hear a faint ringing of the phone. He didn't care. Preacher wasn't going to let that device ruin the moment this morning.

By the afternoon, the whole unit knew—in fact the whole post knew—that Fort Carson's own were freed of all charges. The post's Public Information Office had arranged with the unit commander to offer interviews with both local and national media as long as it was okay with the accused and their lawyers.

Interviews with Hodkins, Petersen and Preacher were arranged with CNN, MSNBC, Fox and CBS along with other print and TV media. None of the three knew that when they arrived to work today, they wouldn't actually be working at their usual jobs. Orders from high above were sent below to offer the soldiers free access to the media to get this story behind them, making the most of this terrible, mishandled situation.

Hodkins, Petersen and Preacher were told to go straight to the unit meeting room when they arrived for work this morning. Petersen's supervisor had to drive her back to the unit. By the time word was formalized about the press event, Petersen had already left the unit headed for work at the Replacement Center.

From 0830 hours to 1600 hours, the three specialists were giving interviews with the various outlets. They did manage to get a couple of breaks before and after lunch, but other than that they were troopers straight through.

This despite the fact that neither soldier was used to the hot lights that were projected on them during the interviews and TV makeup was applied to each for the benefit of the tv cameras.

The makeup made all three itch—even Petersen.

By 1600 hours, all was over with the exception of a later interview with NBC's *Dateline*. Preacher has seen various interviews of news pieces but until now, really didn't know for sure what they entailed until today. Not only was it a lot of work for the producers and the interviewee, but it took a lot of stamina for the interviewee as well. Especially when the interviews were back to back like today.

Specialist Hodkins couldn't wait for the whole event to be over. As soon as the last interview was wrapped up, he almost ran to the latrine to wash off the makeup. The itching was getting to him.

Hodkins did as well as the others during his interviews. One of the reporters seemed to lead him in the direction of chastising the army for making the mistakes they made with Hodkins taking the bait. The Army Public Information Officer stepped in to inform the reporter not to lead the soldier down that path and he reminded Hodkins that he didn't have to answer questions along those lines. With the body language used as well as the tone, Hodkins who was not stupid—took that as, "*Unless you want more trouble, don't continue to bad mouth the army.*"

When Hodkins returned from the latrine, he knew that the work day was over for them. It was time to relax and enjoy the rest of the sunny day.

Petersen had already vacated the area but Preacher was talking to a producer while the producer helped tear down the lighting and other photography equipment.

Hodkins went up to the side of Preacher and stopped and waited until their conversation was done.

"Hey, let's go catch a movie," he said.

That sounded real nice to Preacher. It had been awhile since he been to one. "What's playing now?"

"Some sci-fi flick," said Hodkins.

"Cool. You're going home first?"

"Nah. I have a gym bag in the truck with some gear," Hodkins said as the two of them strolled down the second floor hallway.

"I was hoping that I could change at your place when we leave here," said Hodkins.

"That's cool with me," said Preacher. Preacher wanted to spend more time with his friend and tonight was as good as time as any. Preacher saw it as a celebratory night.

After making it to the first floor and giving out some hand shakes and "brotha" hugs with fellow soldiers, both Hodkins and Preacher were through the heavy metal doors of Headquarters and Headquarters Company trying to make their way to their respective vehicles before someone saw them and tried to stop them for whatever reason. Hodkins hurried, a few steps ahead of Preacher. It was then that Preacher noticed the unmistakable swagger of his new friend.

Preacher chuckled to himself while glancing at his friend. Preacher realized that he was noticing his ass even though he was wearing his combat ACUs.

Hodkins happen to turn around for a minute when he saw Preacher smile.

"What are you smiling at," he shot back.

Preacher paused and said, "Just you!"

Preacher entered his apartment and went straight to the fridge for a glass of water.

Hodkins dropped his gym bag at the front door as he came in.

"Nigga get your smelly gym bag out of this room and take it in the bathroom since you gotta change anyway," said Preacher while sipping.

Hodkins without even looking in his direction just grabbed his bag again and extended his free hand out to Preacher in a stopping manner and proceeded to the bathroom.

"I don't necessarily, have to change in the bathroom," he responded while still walking.

Hodkins strode into the bathroom. Preacher had just closed the refrigerator door and entered his room. The bathroom door was wide open when Hodkins pulled out his thick dick and pissed. Afterwards, he unbuttoned his ACU pants and shirt and let them dropped to the floor.

In his navy blue bikini-cut underwear, Hodkins walked over to turn on the shower. With that done, he allowed his underwear to drop too.

Preacher even now still, pretended like he was intensely focusing on laying out his own clothes for the evening enjoyment but he kept looking up at his friend.

Hodkins' runners built topped off with his almost Ethiopian appearance, large brown nipples as big as gum drops and muscled bubble-butt, presented a very nice encore presentation. He was almost as beautiful as the last time they met.

Preacher's own tool grew an additional three inches in his pants. Hodkins reached in the cabinet to retrieve one of Preacher's hand towels and as he faced the shower stall again, he must have felt Preacher's eyes probing his body because he looked at Preacher like he knew their eyes would meet and winked his right eye. Hodkins then went behind the curtain.

Preacher let out a breather. After setting at the foot of his bed, Preacher looked at the dark silhouette behind the shower curtain. The slow movement of the image told him that Hodkins was caressing the soap and towel over every crevice of his body.

The warm water did indeed feel good to Hodkins. The day itself felt good to him. The last few days in fact felt better than he ever felt in a very long time. With the trial, the threat of the punishment itself as well as the media interviews over, a lot of stress seem to just lift away. Like a heavy shoulder pad that was now off his body and he could now walk with a much lighter load.

Being around friends like Preacher was just the icing on the cake, he thought.

More thoughts of his friend was interrupted by an image on the other side of the shower curtain. He thought it was Preacher taking care of business at the sink but that was not the case. The image appeared to be one without any clothes on. One could tell somewhat even through the translucent curtain.

Then Hodkins knew why he had come in the bathroom. "This nikka is about to take a dump," Hodkins thought to himself.

Hodkins' relationship with Preacher had come closer but he didn't know it was this close yet. Hodkins had hoped they would come to this bridge must later in the relationship but he knew it would eventually come. He now had some idea how other heterosexual relationships must have started off. But Hodkins had to put in his two cents in.

"Don't stank up the fuckin' bathroom Preach," he said. Then the shower curtain was quickly drawn back. Standing there naked was Preacher. He apparently tired of just looking from the outside in and wanted to start becoming more spontaneous and aggressive like his friend.

Hodkins stared at the plump outline of Preacher's body.

"Look Asshole. This is my apartment and I can stank up whatever I want," snapped Preacher. "Now step back so I can get in and maybe wash your back."

Hodkins looked up and down Preacher's body before he stepped back and said, "Cool."

The evening had started out very good. Sharing a nice warm shower with Hodkins, enjoying a Denzel Washington movie with his friend and now enjoying a nice evening stroll on a beautiful night. It was unusually warm this time of year, and the Citadel mall was full of people. There didn't seem to be a whole lot of any breeze coming down from the mountain tonight. The leaves barely moved any as they went by a number of Summer Red Maple trees.

Perhaps this was the calm before a storm. The area was extremely dry and rain was over due.

There were clouds in the night sky but they were scarce. It wasn't hard to pick out a star or two. The flickering of house lights wasn't hard to see either on the hilltops and mountain sides. Both Hodkins and Preacher said very little as they walked from the mall, leaving the vehicle behind in the lot, just a block away to *Applebee's*.

Hodkins would admit to very few people just how much he was enjoying the solitude of the moment with Preacher and that he was looking forward to not just spending tonight with his friend but the rest of his life with him.

The sidewalk path was dimly lit, making the walk even more relaxing. Preacher thought about smacking his friend on the butt but quickly got that out of his head. Too much of a spontaneous action was not always healthy. This was perhaps not a good time.

"This is a nice evening. Is it not?" said Preacher.

Hodkins now looked Preacher up and down again. But this time Preacher was wearing a loose fitting Hawaiian-style shirt and a pair of Dockers. He looked Preacher in the eye again and said, "Yes. Yes it is. This is becoming a great evening out."

They walked into the entrance of the restaurant. A hostess who was apparently near the door inside opened the right door.

"Welcome to *Applebees*," she said with a big smile.

"So what did you do today during the little time you had at work?" Preacher asked as the waiter brought over a glass of water for both of them.

"Nothing special. I was with you most of the day remember?" Hodkins had retrieved his glass and made most of its water disappear.

"Can I get you something else to drink until you're ready to order?" asked the waiter. Hodkins sat their staring at the TV. Several of them had a basketball game that piqued his interest but all was set to close-caption due to the noise level.

Preacher ordered a regular iced tea. "And sir, what can I get you?" the waiter asked Hodkins.

"I'll have a Corona."

"Thank you sir," replied the waiter as he grabbed his tips from the previous patrons and left.

When the waiter returned to take their food orders, both Hodkins and Preacher, one after the other, hit the restroom to relieve themselves.

Hodkins and Preacher both enjoyed an excellent battered cod dinner. Preacher stayed with his original ice tea and Hodkins eventually ordered a second Corona.

Preacher looked up at Hodkins as he was also wiping his hands and said, "Hodkins, I have something to tell you."

Hodkins glanced at Preacher and Preacher's demeanor and tone caused him to pause.

"Gee, Preach. If I didn't know any better, I would think that you were ready to cut me loose," he said while laughing.

"Shit. What is it?"

"I have been in contact with a headhunter in Atlanta for a couple of days now and that agency is helping me line something up before I ETS outta here."

Hodkins smiled and said, "Really!"

This was not the reaction that Preacher was expecting. He thought that Hodkins would give him grief but obviously that wasn't happening now.

Hodkins saw that Preacher looked puzzled. "I actually overheard you a few days ago on the phone in the office," said Hodkins. "You do a lousy job of whispering when you're on the phone."

Preacher let out a sigh. He was relieved that Hodkins already knew. It made things a lot better.

"So much so," he said, cutting his food. "That I was wondering when you were gonna let me know."

Preacher just looked at Hodkins with admiration and nodded his head. Hodkins reached for the Corona and raised it in the air.

Preacher did the same with his nearly empty tea. The two containers clinged. "No more secrets from each other?" asked Hodkins.

"No more secrets," said Preacher.

The waiter, passing by noticed a ice tea refill was in order and said that he would be back with one.

Later as the two left the restaurant on their return stroll back to their vehicle, Hodkins asked while straightening out his sweatshirt and a pair of khaki shorts, "So what's the plan the headhunter has for you in Atlanta?"

The rain clouds had dispersed. All in formation were praying that the merging of the clouds just a few minutes ago wasn't an indication that the attendees at this morning's "get together" would get drenched.

The soldiers were all in their respective platoons: The platoon sergeants in front of their platoon. Squad leaders in their own positions and the officers along with the rest of the senior enlisted were in the rear. All in ACU.

The formation was called to order and after a few words from the first sergeant, he signaled the CO that he was finished, and he appeared in the front of the company formation. Rather suspiciously and right on cue, the clouds immediately above the unit cleared even more and blue skies opened up.

When the soldiers were given the order of "Parade Rest" after Top had given a previous order of "Attention," the CO got right down to business.

"It would seem that today is a special day for someone," the CO said while glancing at a folder in his hand. "Despite the daily grime that is after often placed on a soldier today, you throw in a monkey wrench in our lives just to keep us on our toes. Well, some of us can't always handle it and it can be enough to distract us to a point where we can't do our jobs. Distract us to the point where not only can't we do our jobs but make it difficult for those around one to do their jobs. Not just the individual's co-worker but the soldier's family life as well."

"Well, this doesn't exactly describe the recipient of a very important piece of paper. Not only did he jungle military life and work to get it but he also dealt rather well, if I say so myself, the other adversities that were recently thrown at him."

The company commander had paused and nodded for someone in the rear of the company formation to approach the front. The individual came from the rear around to the side and eventually to the front of the formation alongside the captain.

Preacher recognized the civilian gentleman. *What is Mr. Gonzales doing here?*

"Here with me to help me present this is Mr. Raymond Gonzales from the Post Education Center."

The civilian looked left and slowly to the right before he spoke, "Good Morning, soldiers of the HHC."

The heavy accented voice of the DOD civilian was audible but just barely causing some in the rear to whisper, "What did he say?"

Mr. Gonzales retrieved the folder that the CO had and held it up, reading:

"The Board of Trustees of Regis University by virtue of the Authority vested in it by law and on the recommendation of the faculty of the School of Professional Studies does hereby confer on and to whom these Presents may come, Greeting Be it known that Malcolm Drexel Preacher the degree of Bachelor ..."

With all the recent turmoil in his life Preacher had completely forgotten that he had wrapped up his last college course, submitted his final paperwork to get full college credit for his military schools and was awaiting unofficial word from the school that a degree would be awarded.

Standing there along with the rest of the people in his unit, he was taken a little off-guard. He didn't expect this, this morning.

It felt good to have completed his bachelors degree after all the work that went into it. Sacrificing personal time to do homework after putting in 10 plus hours of military time the last 4 years. But almost every minute of the school work felt good. Preacher had entered the military for the most part, just to get some solid work experience, get some college credit and maybe, just maybe, get a college degree.

Now, standing there as Mr. Gonzales read his name, Preacher had accomplished all three. When Mr. Gonzales finished, both he and the CO stood there and clapped their hands. This instinctively triggered a round of applause from the whole unit.

All of Preacher's fellow co-workers nearby reached over to shake his hand. Hodkins looked at his friend and thought he saw the beginning of a tear in the corner of his right eye.

The CO spoke again. "You specialists, privates and yes, even some "buck" sergeants out there. It's not too late for you to get your degree too like Specialist Preacher. If he found the time to get it, so can you. It probably beats spending most of your money every pay period on booze and clubbing."

"But, but what will we do to relax during our downnnn time, captain?" asked a captain.

The CO, by his southern drawl and noticeable stutter, immediately recognized who asked the question among the many heads in front of him. He looked up and said, "By the sound of it sergeant, you have already been in the liquor cabinet."

The whole unit started laughing in formation.

"You are a smart guy, sarge," the captain said with a smile.

After causing the laughter among his troops, the CO brought his men to attention and dismissed them.

Instead of immediately dispersing to spread out to the individual duties on the post, many of the soldiers still congratulated Preacher on receiving his degree. Many of them were officers. One of the Warrant Officers that Preacher frequently interacted with professionally told him that the Warrant Officer ranks could use a little fresh blood. But Preacher only smiled and shook his hand.

Eventually he got a chance to hold the sheep skin item for a while and before he left the area he caught up with the CO once more to thank him.

"Captain. Thank you."

"Well, I didn't do anything involving this. You did all the work," said the CO while still walking towards his office.

"No, no sir. I meant thank you for helping Hodkins, Petersen, myself and the rest of the soldiers in that investigation," said Preacher.

"You are welcome but I wouldn't be much of a CO if I let anybody try to railroad my soldiers." The company commander turned to walk away and when he got about 5 paces away, he stopped and turned back.

"Specialist Preacher. Whether you decide to get out of the military or stay in and work in the private sector, take care of your men or coworkers. It may not always seem like it's the right thing to do or be easy but in the long run, it will pay off and you will thank yourself for it."

Preacher looked at him and smiled. "I will, sir."

Hodkins caught up with Preacher after seeing the exchange between the CO and his friend.

"Preach, what was that all about?"

"What?"

"What was the CO talking about?"

"Ah. He was just congratulating me again." Preacher turned to Hodkins with his sheep skin in his left hand and slapped him in the belly with the back of his open right hand. Hodkins flinched a bit and grabbed his stomach.

Preacher turned towards the parking lot and started walking with a grin of satisfaction on his face. "Let's get to work, lazy."

"Ah. Naw, you didn't," replied Hodkins. Hodkins tried to slap Preacher on the back of his head but Preacher saw it coming and missed. "Don't get all uppity with me just because you got that paper finally. I can still whip that ass." Hodkins looked around, then back to Preacher. "In more ways than one," he whispered.

The rest of the day was more than fulfilling. But despite the continued congrats in and outside his immediate work area, the continued media calls from large and small print outlets and a return call to the Atlanta headhunter, Preacher managed to get some work done and wrap up a big work project on top of it.

Hodkins and the rest of the automation section, mostly the lower enlisted, talked Preacher into going out to dinner off-post after work. Preacher really wasn't in the mood but he didn't want to feel ungrateful and disappoint anybody since they really wanted to do it for him.

But before all that he had a stop he had to make before leaving the post after work. The last talk with the headhunter gave Preacher an idea.

He was wondering exactly what gave them an edge over other employment agencies and whether they were doing anything unique. Preacher had decided to go back to the Transition Center to rummage through their newspapers again. They appeared to have a better selection than at the Grant Library on post.

After parking in its lot, Preacher entered the Transition Center. The same pretty young lady that was there before was at her post again. This time there were more people than before but most were waiting to see a counselor and a couple were using the computers.

This was just fine with Preacher. He appeared to have the recent Sunday newspapers to himself, including *The Atlanta Journal-Constitution*. The paper table was free of people.

The thought of Joseph came to Preacher's mind. This time there was no sign of him.

Preacher retrieved the recent Sunday edition of the paper and took a seat. He went immediately to the jobs section and perused the Professional/Technical listings. He had decided to perform his own search for now, taking notes and copy pertinent contact information of interesting companies.

Later, he would type letters and send out resumes. He didn't want to just sit around and wait for the headhunter to call. For all he knew, the headhunter was getting a big fee from companies for doing exactly the same thing he was doing now: Thumbing through the papers.

Everyone had decided on a nice Chinese restaurant, *Sien Sien* on Garden of the Gods Road for dinner and that was just fine with Preacher. Of the enlisted in the section, all were there except SFC Miles. He couldn't make it but gave Hodkins some money to buy a round of drinks for everyone.

The decision to dine at *Sien Sien* was not made lightly. The group decided on it based in no small part on a fellow PFC's research. Discussion about what to order went quickly as they deferred to the young PFC with some suggestion regarding specific dishes or what sauce might be preferred.

Preacher's mind was sort of already made up. At this point, he was hungry and didn't feel like experimenting now. But at the same time, he didn't want to discourage anybody else from trying something non-traditional. For him, a large plate of shrimp fried rice with two spring rolls will suit him just fine.

The suggestions were made and the orders were taken. A couple ordered lobster out of all things. It wasn't on the regular menu but was featured on a poster in the window so that was the first item ordered. Of the dishes ordered, the lobster arrived first and was quite a tantalizing sight to behold with golden mounds of minced deep fried garlic contrasting nicely with the orange-red shell and crunchy-skinned meat.

Hodkins' eyes lit up when it was placed at the table. It was one of the most colorful presentations he had ever seen. Preacher noticed his big eyes as well and was pleased to see his friend get excited over something that didn't involved panties, bra or another *guy*.

As they ate, laughter was also part of the menu. Stories of the young enlisted soldiers' short time in the gas chamber, ten mile road marches and soldiers pretending to be gay or just crazy to get out of the military were the favorite topics. Even though Hodkins and Preacher had been out of Basic Training for a few years, they could still relate.

Preacher had stolen a piece of Hodkins' lobster with his fork while he was in the midst of one of his stories.

"This is quite possibly the tastiest lobster I've ever had in a Chinese restaurant," said Preacher among the many conversations going on at the time. The garlic exploded on his taste buds.

The kitchen sent out a complimentary dessert of Almond Pudding which was more like a jelly and it made a refreshing end to a very tasty dinner spent in excellent company.

CHAPTER NINETEEN

Preacher returned home to his tranquil domicile. He had walked past his answering machine and noticed the message counter read five messages.

He wasn't bothered about immediately returning calls. They could wait. He sat on the couch and turned on the TV. But after about 15 minutes of CNN's *Headline News*, it was time to take a bath. After soaking in the warm, lavender-scented bubbles, Preacher had started to feel a little more relaxed. Not necessarily energetic but a lot more relaxed.

Preacher could feel his body reacting to the warm, soothing water. His day was more stressful than he thought or was it an accumulation of everything that has been happening the last few weeks.

In any case, things were starting to get better. He wasn't just thinking about now but his life overall. The outlook appeared to be bright on the personal and professional side of things with the exception of one thing. *A lot of what I wanted to accomplished in life after high school, I have accomplished it or have started to. But unless I do one thing, my life will seem not quite complete. Not quite honest and free to all those I love the most in this world: my grandparents.*

Preacher rose up from the tub, dried off with one of his thick, fluffy towels and after lotioning up, he quickly put on his pajamas.

Preacher went to his desk and moved the mouse to "wake up" his PC. He had executed his word processor and he was about to start typing when he stopped moving his fingers on the keyboard.

Preacher thought about who he would be writing the letter to.

It would be his grandparents. Not some company or something. Preacher wanted this letter to come from the heart and not appear to be otherwise. He would not be using a word processor for this letter. He would use a number 2 pencil on notebook paper.

Preacher relocated his mouse and mouse pad to make more room for his notebook. He stared at the paper for a minute, looking at the lines until his writing hand started moving.

It was like the hard point of the graphite and the recycled paper was the only thing making a sound in the room. Preacher didn't want any music playing and the TV was off. He wanted to concentrate on what he wanted to write. He figured that the thoughts would flow and he could better transfer them to paper if there was little to no distractions in the room.

> *I've been trying to write this letter for the last 4 years and every time I start, I stop. Now, I'm able to write because it will help me feel better about myself.*
>
> *Let me start off with a thank you. Thank you for taking me in. Thank you both for being there. Thank you for caring. Thank you for all that you do and have done.*
>
> *There are times when I sit and wonder where I would be today if you were not there. I know it's not easy to raise someone's child as your own even if it is your grandchild but I know you have tried.*
>
> *I began to realize that there was something different about me. I realized that I was attracted to other guys, but I still liked females.*
>
> *I lied to others and myself. Then the last 3 months, I was forced to face the truth about myself and I thought it was time for me to step back and analyze the issue.*
>
> *What it came down to was that I accepted the fact that I am a bisexual: I like both guys and gals. No fad, no craze, just pure and simple me.*
>
> *Yet, now I feel as I get ready to go to Atlanta after my discharge that I should say something. Not just to be finally honest with everyone but to just set the record straight. It would be real awkward if I surprised everyone by coming home with my significant other that just happened to be a guy.*
>
> *I have already told two of my closest friends and they still love me for me. I wished it would be that way every time I told someone new, especially my family but that's wishful thinking.*

You always ask me what's new and how am I doing. I don't feel like I tell you everything, I know I don't tell you everything. I always leave out the parts that I assume will make you unhappy.

I'm sick of hiding important details about my life that my family should know or that I would like them to know. In other words, I'm tired of living a perpetual lie. I hope that you understand everything, I am trying to say, and I hope this doesn't change our relationship.

I have lots of really great people in my life. Some of them are friends and some are more than that. The one that I get along with the best is Hodkins. His first name is Clarence. He is one of the closest people in my life here.

I am happy with my life the way that it is. I am now beginning to realize that I am the way I am because I was born this way.

This new change in my life is not the result of any molestation growing up or any incident in the army. So please don't blame yourself for the way I live my life and the fact that I have "strayed from the path that God has set for me." But I don't think that I'm that far off from what God intended for me, believe it or not.

I will admit that I am not as close to God as I could be. But I have begun to realize that God has an unconditional love for everyone including me.

I think I'm better for coming out. I can now be who I am. I don't have to be ashamed. Sure there's going to be people who don't like it, but that's their opinion and they're entitled to it. I think now that I'm out—out, Grandma, is when you tell folks that you are gay or bi—I can achieve many of my dreams without all of that extra baggage of lies.

You and grandpa helped with part of that dream when you raised me and allowed me to finish high school. Now, I'm taking it to the next level by making a new beginning in Atlanta, Georgia.

For awhile with that witch hunt of an investigation, I wasn't too sure I was gonna make it but with that over; I can make it happen.

Thank you for everything,

Malcolm

The writing, like the music in the room, had stopped. With his pencil still in hand, Preacher stared at the paper. He had finally done it. He had written his "coming out" letter. Preacher just stared at it in silence as if he wasn't reading it but as if the letter was speaking to him. He removed the pages from the pad and folded them on the table. Once he retrieved an envelope from the desk drawer, he placed the letter in it and addressed it.

After some thought, he had come to the conclusion that he couldn't wait to drop this off at the mailbox. *If I wait till morning to mail this I might change my mind about mailing it, he thought.*

Preacher grabbed some sweats and his old jordans from the closet and walked out of his apartment with his keys and his letter. The letter will get mailed tonight.

This is all part of a new beginning, he thought.

On his return back to his apartment, Preacher sat on his bed and while removing his shirt before going to sleep, he started crying. He didn't regret what he just did. It was tears of joy. Mailing the letter was apparently what his mind and body needed.

It was like a heavy load was released from his shoulders and a type of stress was freed from his mind. Despite the tears, it felt good. It felt really good.

Malcolm Preacher knew now that this was what he needed to do for a very long time. With all the lights out in the apartment, the stereo silenced, now stripped naked in bed with warm flannel sheets; Preacher rolled over on his side and drifted to sleep. He had wiped the last of his tears and soon would be in a deep, sound sleep.

With his parents looking on, and without any signs of his wife in the room, the words pulsated as if he was still in the very sterile and open courtroom.

"We the jury, find the defendant guilty of 3 counts of rape, sexual battery, official misconduct and corrupt business influence …"

It might as well been life. He felt that way at least. McCullen was so shocked of the amount of time given that he didn't think about crying. Only the 3 years he would spend behind bars. He merely thought that it was a lot of time for what he actually did. He and others did.

All that time spent away from his family. All that time spent away during the holidays. His child. All that time spent away from life. Leavenworth wasn't Pelican Bay or Fulton, but it would still be hard, straight time. His life as he knew it was dead.

The sudden rattling of the prison bars and his shackles on his hands and feet roused him from his trance. The flight to Leavenworth, Kansas would be his last flight in a very long time. He would be 43 years of old when he is eventually released.

The ride from the airport to Leavenworth Prison was the absolute worst so far. Shocked at his hands and feet being anchored to the bus floor with about fifty others, was just a taste to what was to come.

Looking around the bus, most had the same scary facial expressions. Probably the same as his. It was like sliding down a deep black tunnel. He knew the end was coming but not what was meeting him on the other end.

McCullen was older but most were about his age or a tad younger. They came from every branch of the U.S. military, sentenced for crimes ranging from mail fraud to murder.

Perhaps they were in his shoes too being their first offense and all. Perhaps they had been here before and come back due to different crimes. Possibly couldn't cope with life.

That was certainly possible, McCullen thought, but not likely.

Due to the nature of how the ranking correctional specialist instructed everyone to sit and stay quiet, no one said a word during the trip so far.

McCullen noticed that once the vehicle was outside the city limits, the countryside started appearing right before his eyes. Rolling meadows appeared. Then he saw golden wheat fields dancing with the wind as if they were doing a "wave" like the people at ball games. Sprinkled among them were wind farms and cell towers. But McCullen wouldn't see them for very long.

The trek of the bus down the hot and dusty highway was coming to an end. At a distance the structure appeared small but as the bus gain some ground it grew quite huge.

The bus maneuvered per instructions of the awaiting security personnel. In a matter of seconds after arriving at 1300 Metropolitan Avenue, the bus was hastily unloaded at the US Penitentiary at Leavenworth, Kansas. Otherwise known as the "The Castle" or Fort Leavenworth.

Standing in some sort of a formation, the awaiting correctional specialists barked the appropriate instruction in the appropriate tone to get the occupants off the bus and standing in a military formation as fast as possible to get them processed for their long stay at Fort Leavenworth.

Once the pleasantries were out of the way by the warden, the task of getting the new arrivals situated was resumed again by the correctional specialists. The group was quickly separated by sub-groups and preceded towards the bowels of *The Big Top,* a dome over the rotunda.

One of the first obstacles that McCullen saw was an 8 foot high chain link fence topped with concertina wire. The only way through it was a double-locked gate, where a sign detailed visitor dos and don'ts.

On the other side of the tall fence, McCullen sensed the looming authority imposed by the guards in tight, tailored uniforms, exposed ripped biceps and large chests.

Still in shackles, the federal inmates entered the interior of the huge complex. Like all new inmates, this new class was photographed, fingerprinted and strip-searched. That was really tough on McCullen. He was almost in tears when he had to surrender to a cavity search which included him bending over and spreading his ass cheeks. Like the rest, his personal items were inventoried. He was issued khaki-colored trousers, a button-down shirt and black steel-toed boots as well as a change of bedding and set of towels.

Prisoners were allowed a plain wedding band and a religion medallion, both of which must be worth less than $100, a pair of prescription eye glasses and legal papers. After being interviewed by prison staff and briefed on the institution's rules, the inmates were marched again to their cells.

McCullen was a little "shocked and awed" at the facility he now found himself in. The fact that he would spend years here was about to make him sick to his stomach. The thought of him rushing to his animal cell to keep from puking on the freshly clean floor, made him just as nauseous.

Their wrist and ankle shackles were no longer on their bodies but metallic noise still got their attention.

As the inmates passed by one block of cells to the next, the unnerving sounds of inmates and guards shouting, metal doors slamming, and occasionally restraints jingling floated through the eight story facility. The distinct smell of disinfectant was stinging noses; the eyes adjusted to the sunshine casting cylinder-shaped shadows that filtered through barred windows.

One by one, as they marched to their respective cells escorted by at least two guards, the inmates were introduced to their new home. Each new cell was monitored by way of closed-circuit television monitors fitted overhead just outside the cells.

Prior to leaving, the military police instructed McCullen he will be starting his two-week orientation sometime after breakfast tomorrow and later his work assignments will be made.

McCullen looked around the small cell. He laid all of his current worldly possessions on the bare bed. He stood there in his new uniform and just stared at the interior of his new home.

If things had not sunk in as to just how bad his situation was, it was sinking in now. This was certainly a new low for him.

His new bare room complete with bars brought it all home for him. McCullen, now without his restraints, made up his bed according to the brochure he was given. When he was done, he just sat there again looking out of his cell for about a minute. Staring as if waiting for someone to come and open the cell doors.

When he was finished seeing outside his world, he dropped his head in his hands and started crying. Crying without regard to the camera that was surveying the cell. He simply couldn't contain it any longer.

Inside the central control room of the prison; two military policeman, both sergeants had the duty of monitoring the facility via the cameras. Up until the time the newbies came in, the shift was uneventful. Now, at least for them, things appeared to be picking up.

One of the sergeants had just come back from the mess hall on a snack run. As soon as the door was open, his partner gave him the bad news.

The sergeant had barely sat the pastries and hot coffee down.

"I hate to tell you bro but you owe me 50 bucks," said the sergeant, still watching the monitors.

"Why's that?"

"One cracked."

"Fuck!" said the sergeant barely getting back in his high chair. "I was only gone 15 minutes. Ain't that a bitch."

His partner looked towards him to retrieve his black coffee. "I keep telling you bro once these fuckers find out that Fort Leavenworth is no 'Camp Cupcake' they crack and crack soon."

"Which one of the bunch cried first?"

The sergeant was sipping his coffee while flipping through the new roster. "Ah, it was ...Oh... SFC McCullen."

"You mean formerly a sergeant first class," said the senior sergeant while laughing. "But you have a point. This is no Camp Cupcake or Club Fed."

Building 1280 seemed almost abandoned today. If Preacher didn't know any better, he would have thought he went to the wrong place.

Even though he was sure he didn't make such a mistake, he double-checked his clearing checklist just to make sure. And the paperwork assured him that this was in fact the right place.

It just seemed odd that Central Clearing, Building 1280, was this deserted of customers. *Clearing* Central Clearing was a task that was both welcoming and stressful when you are about to unload your TA-50 field gear. Especially when you are lower enlisted.

Central Clearing was ran by DOD civilian government employees, who could make your experiences quite stress-free or a nightmare depending on how they feel at a particular time of a given day.

All field gear was expected to be cleaned and in a serviceable condition prior to being returned. Even if a given item like the mess kit consisting of the metal fork, spoon, knife and plate is still in its original plastic wrapper. They would expect one to remove the items from its original container; the same one in which they gave to you and clean each item in the kit. It makes no sense but that's just part of the bureaucracy that makes the whole Post Clearing process interesting.

Given up the TA-50 is just one of many areas on the checklist that one must complete prior to PCS, transferring or perhaps ETSing.

Last on the list would be the visit to Personnel Records and Finance. Everyone wanted to get that final paycheck from Finance before hitting the road. But before that happened, clearing building 1280 was a must.

Preacher entered through the steel doors of the complex carrying a leather carrying bag with straps going across his chest and a seemingly heavy packed olive-colored duffle bag strapped on his back.

The interior of the room had the usual dull, gray décor with the usual military propaganda posters stapled about. Even though a buzzer had rung as he entered the door, no one bothered to peep around the bend to see whether Preacher, the customer, was ready for inspection. Voices could be heard but that was about it as far as a presence being detected.

To save time, Preacher proceeded with removing the duffle bag strapped to his back and started removing each of his field items one at a time and placed them on the counter that was apparently used for inspection based on a nearby diagram.

Preacher was halfway done when an old lanky fellow came from around the corner. The gentleman was wearing an old camouflage BDU shirt with some old faded blue jeans. His attire was even tackier with the old black jump boots minus the spit shine.

"Specialist, you may want to reconsider unloading all that before I truly get started!" barked the civilian. "I'm the one in charge of this return session and I will be the one dictating what is removed and when. But thanks for your initiative."

Preacher was hoping it wouldn't be one of those days during this phase of the in-processing. He could truly do without any attitude from anybody much less from a controlling DOD civilian who got his jollies from enlisted personnel who wanted only to turn in their gear without the unnecessary hassle.

"But let's just start with what you have on the counter," said the civilian. By the opened Marlboro pack in his left top pocket of his jacket, Preacher suspected that this guy had just returned from a smoke break outside of the facility.

"And IF they pass my rigorous inspection, you may not have to put them back into your duffle bag for re-cleaning and re-inspection."

The gentleman looked Preacher in his eyes as he spoke but Preacher didn't want to play games with him. He thought that this guy was just looking for an excuse today to send someone back for re-inspection later. Preacher sensed an definite power trip or simply a "wannabe" from this guy.

One by one, the civilian handled the items on the counter. After scrutinizing them, each were thrown into a nearby bin for re-issuing to the next *visitor* to Fort Carson. As he neared the end of the inspection items on the counter, the gentleman would request for more TA-50 items to be placed on the counter. One by one, the items were inspected and surprisingly, the civilian simply did his GS-14 job and the process went quite smooth. The items from Preacher's duffle bag were eventually transferred back to the ownership of Fort Carson.

Preacher was beginning to see light at the end of the tunnel. There were only two items to go, if you didn't count the duffle bag itself and Preacher was beginning to relax.

The civilian held up the winter parka and even spread it out and shook it. Preacher saw a lint ball float down to the floor and he was hoping Mr. Inspector didn't see it. He did almost the same thing to the waterproof poncho. Perhaps this was only for theatrics since this time he did so, he eyed Preacher lightly.

After he snatched the poncho from the counter, it too landed in a bin full of ponchos.

"All seems good. Congratulations, specialist." He motioned for the remaining duffle bag Preacher held. Once it was given to him, it was thrown into a corresponding bin without even eyeballing it. "Give me your paperwork including your orders."

Being extremely relieved that it was over, Preacher quickly retrieved the items from his carrying bag and handed them to him.

The DOD civilian found his department's line item on the checklist and he stamped the sheet and signed it at the bottom in the signature block. He returned the items back to Preacher minus two copies of his orders and Preacher quickly exited the doors.

Just as the door was about to close shut, the civilian shouted at Preacher. "Specialist!" Preacher did hear him but he really didn't want to go back in but he did so anyway.

"Yes, sir!"

Looking straight at Preacher, the gentleman spoke. "From an old Vietnam veteran to another veteran, good luck with whatever you choose to do with the rest of your life."

Preacher was somewhat shocked by his remarks but was grateful for them. The civilian had apparently looked closely at the orders to see they were in fact discharge orders.

"Thank you very much sir," said Preacher just prior to the door closing.

"Don't call me, sir. I work for a living," Preacher heard even with the door closed.

What a day this is going to be, Preacher thought. And what a difference a few weeks can make.

Then, he wasn't really sure whether he would simply be dishonorably discharged with a hefty fine or do some time in the stockade.

Now, resting in his pajamas on the patio, he was mapping his future once again in his head. The therapeutic effects of the aroma of *Folgers* certainly help turn the gears of his mind for a clearer picture indeed.

Things were getting back to normal, not only in his life but on post as well. Now, the only thing of substance in both *The Mountain Post* and Colorado Springs' most read newspaper was of the various units rotating out to both Iraq and Afghanistan. In some cases, units were making four trips back to the war zones.

The few friends and associates he knew in those war zones all wrote or said the same thing when he communicated with them. "I can't wait to do my time in this fuckin place so I can get the hell out."

Preacher looked up and away from the newspaper for a moment. He knew he was very lucky not being over there. He wanted to savor the moment and took another sip of coffee.

Preacher browsed the paper, getting through a few pages until something indeed caught his eye. What caught his eye was true and dear to his profession. A profession he had dreamed of working in since high school. Preacher zeroed in on the article about the state of the IT field.

"It's going to be a tough world for information technology personnel. Demographics will change the new IT workplace. Not the technology as so many expect.

IT professionals will become 'continent workers' who will be brought in to work on a project or to deliver a specific product. If you are not very good, there will not be many places to hide."

This has the smell of India and Pakistan outsourcing all over it, Preacher thought and continued reading.

"Minority groups lagging in IT education and training today such as blacks and Latinos will fall behind. But it is to companies' advantage to tap into this potentially rich but poorly trained talent pool, and the way to do that will be to establish cross-cultural training programs.

But what if companies don't embrace this resource? Certain areas are already seeing disappointed people when the job they were getting $50,000 for can be done in India for $28,000 or less. Software development is being exported at a fast pace.

Large companies will recruit much more aggressively overseas and will establish IT schools in less developed countries."

What a time to see this article. Preacher took another sip of coffee. It wasn't the most motivational article he had read lately but it was informative.

"Those large US companies that don't establish oversees offices or schools will advocate through their congressional representatives that they need more immigrants in the way of H-1B visas. This is a non-immigrant

visa, which allows a US company to employ a foreign individual for up to six years. It is designed to be used for staff in 'specialty occupations,' that is those occupations which require a high degree of specialized knowledge. Generally at least the equivalent of a job-relevant 4-year US Bachelor's degree is required. It is one way that US companies keep down wages of Americans holding the same jobs."

Preacher looked up and folded the paper for easy carrying. Now that he was enlightened with the knowledge that certain sectors of his profession was going down the toilet, he got up from his comfy chair and left his place to begin his morning regiment.

He was not in any hurry to get to the post this morning and it was a good thing because some early morning fog that drifted down from Pikes Peak had caused an accident near one of the Fort Carson Gates.

Traffic on Academy Boulevard near that gate was backed up since the flow was now being rerouted by a state trooper towards another gate. Those who could not help trying to see the accident scene driving by didn't help matters.

Preacher exited his Blazer and after making sure he had retrieved his shoulder bag and head gear, he was headed to PAS. Preacher entered his code on the keypad and the lock disengaged. Seconds later, he was in the office.

Preacher walked to his pod area and everyone was so focused with their own work that he was barely acknowledged coming in. SSG Hamilton could be seen through the glass door of the small server room fumbling with some data backup cartridges. SFC Miles, as well as the officers could be heard in their respective office areas conversating on the phones with their business chatter but SFC Miles did notice for a second, peeping out of his office, that he was in the area.

The rest of the enlisted stayed at their post, in their pod areas, fixated on their flat panel monitors. Once in his pod, he placed both his head gear and shoulder bag in their rightful place. Once settled, he too was in his chair and stroking his keyboard.

Preacher had finished composing his fifth email since he got in to work and was putting some finishing touches on a Frequently Asked Questions document or FAQ that may be handy for the enlisted staff after he departed for good, when he noticed that the PAS was nearly empty.

He didn't notice earlier but one by one, the staff slowly but discreetly had walked out of PAS. First, it was the major and his lieutenants, and then SFC Miles and his enlisted corp including Hodkins had vanished.

CHAPTER TWENTY

The last time it was this quiet was around the Christmas holidays. But this time of the year was kind of strange he thought for a week day.

If it wasn't for the fact that he was working on an important document before his mid-afternoon clearing appointment with the education center, he would get up and do some investigating of his own but he really did want to finish it, go to his appointment and leave early for the day. Like most people in his position, he wanted to take full advantage of his "clearing" time.

Preacher had completed and printed the first draft of the document after about thirty minutes when his desk phone had rang. After a minute of hearing someone complain about the date in a report, the person on the other end of the call had convinced Preacher to get up from his desk to make a trip down the hall for a face-to-face.

"Yes sir," was the only thing Preacher said before hanging up. He had left PAS at a steady pace and his mind was thinking about what line of code could be causing the numbers not to be carried over from month to month. Preacher had spent a lot of time on this EOM or End-Of-Month report so the core of the lines of code was somewhat fresh in his mind still.

It was the downside of taking your work too seriously. One's mind never let go of some problems, Preacher thought.

While walking down the nice shiny hallway which still reeking with the aroma of floor wax, Preacher noticed somewhat that the hallways were clear. In fact, not a sound was coming from areas that noise should be coming from.

Even with the absence of an influx of new arrivals, which were due to start arriving in an hour or so, it was still unusual for the hallways to be this quiet.

Perhaps word of a Replacement Center formation just outside the front door escape his attention this morning. He didn't see anything in his email box this morning and he didn't recall hearing anybody mentioning a special formation.

Preacher kept walking towards his caller's office, just a few paces away at the other end of Replacement Center building. At almost halfway down the hallway and near the classroom, Preacher was hoping during this strut that this problem didn't take too long to resolve since he was still planning on leaving the office early.

He was at the doorway of the classroom walking by when someone said, "The problem is in here, young specialist!"

The voice barking in the near silence had almost startled Preacher as he slowed his roll down the hallway.

Preacher was almost passed the hallway when he glanced to the right and got a sight of all the occupants of the center in the classroom before coming to a full stop.

"Surprise!" everyone said in unison.

Preacher looked around the room and it appeared that most of the officer and enlisted personnel were there which didn't happen too often.

"If you didn't figure it out already there really aren't any problems with reports," said First Lieutenant Vanover with his authentic Kansas accent.

Preacher did indeed figure it out that the people in the room were there to see him off. There, perhaps to say goodbye and good luck.

The major had indeed rounded up everyone with the help of his staff. Everyone, enlisted and officer alike, stood as the major said a few words about Specialist Preacher, his accomplishments as a Information Technology Specialist while at PAS, his leadership for the rest of the enlisted staff whether he knew it or not and to wish him luck during his endeavors after the military.

Preacher in his lightly starched camouflage uniform stood to the major's side now as he spoke. Preacher smiled and laughed along with the rest of the staff as he listened to the major recount some of the events within PAS.

Near the end of his speech, he topped it off by saying that with the exception of the most recent events affecting Specialist Preacher and others; that as long as he has known Preacher he has always gotten his IT projects done in a timely manner, done them professionally and he has yet to hear anyone in the unit say anything negative about him. And that went for both officer and enlisted.

The major went on to say that the PAS will soon miss the specialist, his attitude, his professionalism, work ethic and expertise in his field. But hopefully, he added, some Fortune 500 company will gain due to our loss.

"Here, here!" shouted a voice from the crowd. Preacher looked out and found out that that voice belonged to Hodkins.

"But I have spoke enough for now," said the major. "Is there anyone else who would like to say something?" Three people caught the major's eye. The two sergeants and one officer gave stories of their frequent interactions with the specialist. All were good and positive.

As each spoke, Preacher reminisced. Each story, each scene that led to the conclusion by its storyteller brought him back to a period of time where he was learning the ends and outs of the military. Some would be by formal training; others would be with the assistance of both enlisted personnel as well as officers but most would be by OJT and trial & error like most who wore the uniform. Along the way, he would see friends and associates come and go and hopefully he would learn and keep some knowledge which he gained along the way.

Sure, he thought, there were some bad times but they were certainly outweighed by the good ones.

"... and the colonel who probably worked in the Pentagon staffing and Personnel section said, 'If I want Preacher in my Automation section by the end of the month then unless God himself says No, it will fuckin happen.' At that point, the Post Commander over heard the colonel talking which quickly caught his eye.

"The general walked behind the colonel and said, 'And if God is busy and send me in his place, would that help?'

The colonel looked at the one star right in his face like he saw the reaper himself and turned from pale white to a bruised red.

The general, as if he was late for a meeting started towards the exit when he turned back and looked straight at the colonel and said, 'Oh, colonel. I have been briefed on the Preacher situation as far as a possible transfer to the military's headquarters and after pondering on it for about, ah, three seconds, I have decided that the specialist is needed here a lot more than there at your palace.

You guys can get contractors for any work you want. We here at The Mountain Post don't always have that luxury.

This subject is closed.'

The general turned around with his aids and left the area.

When the colonel realized that he wasn't breathing, he started getting chest full of air and retrieved his black beret with the shiny eagle on the front and left the building as well without muttering a sound.'"

After that the room erupted with both laughter and applause. They laughed not at the senior officer but the event.

When the last story was told, the major, decided it was time to close this ceremony with an award to the specialist. "Okay, okay everyone please settle down," spoke the officer. "We have one final thing to disperse here today.

As the major spoke, he made a few steps behind him to get something that was wrapped and leaning against the corner.

"Also, as a token of our appreciation for all the work you did while assigned to the center, Specialist Preacher, we have a gift for you."

As the major attempted to unwrap the brown packaging from the item, Petersen, Hodkins and young Muse looked on from there spots in the room.

They were all happy to see their friend get his departing gift but there was also sadness too. All thought that they were losing a friend. With the exception of Hodkins who would be meeting up with Preacher eventually, Petersen and Muse knew that they would be losing the friendship of one of the most caring and unselfish people they know.

But they were also very happy to see Preacher leave the army in search of his place in the civilian world. The major finally removed the last piece of paper and tilted it holding the object at both the top and bottom for Preacher while he viewed it.

While everyone else waited to see, Preacher stared at it in amazement as if he was looking at baby pictures. He grabbed the plaque on the side with both hands and another 5 seconds; he maneuvered it around to show everyone else.

It was rather large. Made of a dark wood with a bronze plate covering a quarter of the plaque. Above it, the unit name and post insignias were halfway embedded in the wood. Above it was a large holographic picture similar to the anti-theft ones on computer software packaging. But in this case, the image was that of Specialist Preacher standing in front of a computer system. It was a far cry from the usual government plaques that they handed out.

Preacher had recognized the image in the hologram. It was taken while at AIT in Fort Gordon, Georgia a few years ago.

"Damn!" said the major. "I hope I get something like this when I leave this dump."

"Just so everyone knows," the major continued, "the general and the post sergeant major found out about this little ceremony somehow and they insisted that they chip in on this gift. But then the General went a step further and contacted a friend who works at a graphics design shop and got them to create the holograph. A trophy shop took care of the rest."

Preacher was hoping that this would be the end of it all so that he wouldn't be all misty eyes giving any closing remarks. He was glad to see everyone at the center had made it. That's was thanks enough. Most people, he felt, were there to genuinely say, "Thanks for all you have done, Preacher."

He knew that his time in the front was getting short. And when he thought that he was in the clear, it came.

"Speech! Speech! Speech!"

Damn, damn, Preacher thought.

He couldn't avoid it now. He would have to say something. And by doing so, he hoped he wouldn't lose it in the process and start a flow of tears.

The movers came 2 hours after the start of the appointment window that Preacher was given by Post Housing on the base. After about an hour of hauling and positioning of Preacher's shipment in the truck, Preacher was presented a form to sign off and they were on their way.

The apartment looked strange without any furniture. And obviously looked bigger now. Just like it did when he first moved in.

Preacher decided not to leave the apartment just yet. After some light cleaning, he could have just turned the keys in the apartment manager but he wanted to stay in the apartment for awhile. As he often did many times before, he decided to go to the patio and sat for a minute.

As he walked, his steps echoed across the kitchen floor and throughout the empty apartment. For about an hour and a half, it was just Preacher and his thoughts while he sat outside at the foot of Pike's Peak, staring at the horizon.

Thinking about the past and what the future will hold consumed his mind. But the current thought, he would have to put on hold for now. The knocking at the door seemed a lot louder now in an empty apartment.

Taking his time apparently was too much for the person on the other side of the door because he or she started to pound on it now.

Preacher knew that it had to be someone he knew because no one else would be that rude during this time of the day. He opened the door.

It was Hodkins.

In uniform with a big smile exposing those pearly whites with two catfish plates wrapped in plastic in one hand and a cold six pack of Coors in the other.

"Are you going to let me in or what, Preach?" said Hodkins. Before Preacher said a word, Hodkins started walking forward through the rooms to the patio area. "But then again this is not your place now. Am I right?"

Closing the door and spinning around, Preacher shot back, "For your information asshole, technically it's still mine until I turn the keys in."

"And then, you will technically be homeless. Right?" Hodkins had turned around with the goodies in his hands to see the expression on Preacher's face.

It was tempting, Preacher thought. Should he smack him in the face or in the gut? Then again, it was thoughtful of him to bring lunch over since he didn't have a chance to go out and get anything. Preacher decided to just concede. "Turn around, asshole, so we can just eat."

Hodkins complied and he sat the catfish and drinks on the patio table. Preacher noticed that Hodkins had a satisfying look on his face. He appeared proud to be helping his partner. Hodkins knew that Preacher would be cleaning up and tying up loose ends while waiting for the movers to arrive. Then once they left, he would go back to cleaning up the place until he was satisfied with the job. Hodkins knew that Preacher would either forget or forego lunch to get things done.

Hodkins had even picked up some caramel cake slices for desert. "So are you off the rest of the day?" Preacher asked.

While still leaning over the table preparing the food, Hodkins turned his head looking right at Preacher and made a kissing pose with his lips. "Don't you wish I did?" he said.

Preacher immediately turned away from the patio and went back to the interior of the apartment. Hodkins knew that Preacher hated when he did that.

When everything was ready on the patio, Hodkins peeped into the patio doorway and shouted to Preacher that lunch was ready.

He too, noticed how his voice was echoing within the emptiness of the apartment.

When Preacher had arrived, he had already found Hodkins sitting at the table with his ACU top off. Wearing his brown tee shirt and the rest of his uniform while digging into his plate of catfish fillets. Looking at his current bottle, he had already taken a few sips of his Coors.

"By the way," Hodkins said, "I told SFC Miles that I needed an extra hour for lunch to help you with something. And he said okay. So I'll be going back after I leave here."

After setting down, all that Preacher said was, "That's cool." Despite the mountain air, the catfish smelled good on the patio. "You did well, Hodkins." "The fish was right on time."

Waiting first to put down his throat some more hot sauce—soaked pieces of fish, Hodkins managed to reply, "No problem bro. What are partners for? I knew you would be working too hard to get your ass something to eat." Hodkins continued attacking his fillets and Coors. And the action didn't go without notice.

"Damn, boy. If I didn't know any better, I would swear that you were hungrier than I am." Preacher too started to enjoy the fish as he watched Hodkins' muscles under the brown t-shirt reacting to Hodkins use of the plastic cutlery. At times, Preacher thought, Hodkins was surely a site to see.

He could be just as cute and adorable during times when he's not trying to be. When he ate, he kept his fingers and mouth as clean as when he started. Even barbeque. Hodkins is a trip and don't even know it, Preacher thought.

While glancing up between bites, Hodkins noticed Preacher staring at him. "What!" Hodkins said, like a kid who was just caught misbehaving.

"Nothing, knucklehead," said Preacher with a big grin on his face as he brought his attention back to his lunch.

"Ah! I see. You were checking big papa out on the sly," spoke Hodkins. "That's cool. You are entitled to it now, partner. If you behave yourself, I will treat you lata." Hodkins capped the statement off with a wink of the eye.

With the lunch finished, Preacher thought the least he could do was pickup the leftover scraps and put it along with the rest of the trash that was tucked away in a bag in the corner of the empty kitchen which he acquired while doing some cleaning.

Preacher decided to leave Hodkins on the patio with the cell phone in his ear. He seemed quite comfortable now with his feet propped up on one of the chairs.

Preacher could tell this call wasn't one of his babes or one of his boyz on the other end of the line. The call left an expression of seriousness on his face as he spoke. Perhaps, he thought, there was a minor problem at work that needed his attention.

With the absence of Preacher, Hodkins was considered the "go to" guy now as far as the enlisted personnel were concerned. No more dependence on Preacher for guidance as well as the person for all solutions. Hodkins had to step up to the plate now. With a large black plastic bag in one hand and an old cotton mop that had seen better days, Preacher left the apartment to find the nearest trash bin.

The nearest trash bin turned out to be on the opposite side of the building. It seemed funny to Preach to be walking along the driveway around the building with a mop. This particular bin was not full and he was able to deposit his trash in the almost empty bin.

Now back in his apartment, he heard an unexpected sound. No, it wasn't just the reverberating of the apartment itself. He was getting use to the echo now including the fact that he could now go from room to room in a straight line with all the furniture and fixtures out of the way.

As he walked closer to his bedroom, it became obvious now that the shower was running now. Knucklehead had decided to take a shower after lunch and after Preacher had scrubbed it to remove the soap scrum before the "walk through" by the building manager prior to turning in the keys.

Preacher was not visibly mad but he was kinda ticked with the shower stall getting soaped up again. The water had stopped running and Preacher stood in the hallway, waiting for an explanation from Hodkins.

Hodkins wasted little time drying off and soon the bathroom door opened. He came out still drying himself off with a small towel. Behind Hodkins was the steam coming from the shower stall as he walked out in the hallway and facing Preacher still standing there.

Hodkins noticed Preacher's demeanor as if he was waiting for an explanation. To save both time and trouble, Hodkins merely wrapped the damp, small tight towel around his waist and motioned to Preacher with his right index finger to follow him.

Preacher didn't know why immediately, but he complied. Then he saw it.

Hodkins stopped and stood in front of Preacher's air bed which was inflated and laid in what use to be Preacher's fully furnished bedroom. Now, just a large room with an inflatable bed in the middle.

Now, the expression on Preacher's face was that of "What is this for?" Preacher looked at Hodkins and Hodkins said, "You thought I was kidding when I said I might give you a taste earlier?"

Preacher looked at Hodkins straight in the face and said, "Well, you might as well—-"

"Preach, I'm not taking no for an answer." Hodkins snatched the towel around his waist and let it hit the floor. All the while walking to Preacher to grab him around the waist to give him a big wet long kiss.

Hodkins managed to catch his friend off guard because before Preacher knew it, he was against the wall with his pants down to his ankles. Still off guard, Preacher felt mesmerized by Hodkins' body. His washboard stomach, glistening skin and inches of cut, thick meat between his legs was enough to pause anymore.

Hodkins was beautiful. Accented by his hairless chest, thick neck, thick nipples and a picture perfect waistline. Once Preacher came to, he knew he wanted to service those nipples but wanted to vacate his clothing first. But Hodkins had other plans. Just as Preacher had removed his undershirt, Hodkins had dropped down on his knees to truly service his friend.

The only word Preacher managed to get out of his mouth was a soft, low "No." He wanted to make the next move on Hodkins. But as Hodkins started licking around the mushroom, Preacher's naked body just leaned back against the wall and he tilted his head with pleasure.

Hodkins, down on his knees but with the towel now between the floor and his knees, now started to lick the area of skin between his friend's dick and ass. That was the SPOT.

Preacher knew then that he wanted to be totally relaxed if this was going to go any further. He quickly put his hand under Hodkins' arms and moved him to the side as not to make any sudden movements to hurt Hodkins or himself.

Preacher motioned Hodkins to get on the air bed. While Hodkins positioned himself for acceptance of Preacher, Preacher unleashed his pants around his ankles. Once on the air bed himself, Preacher was totally relaxed. Now with his partner on his back, Hodkins now resumed the tongue bath he was giving Preacher.

For what seemed like a half hour or more, Preacher just laid moaning and even trembling at times from the tongue lashing he was receiving. Then suddenly, Hodkins stopped working his magic.

Hodkins stood and said, "I'm not going to make you cum right now. You need to do something for me." Hodkins leaned over to the side of the air bed and grabbed a condom and some travel-size lube. After giving Preacher the condom, Hodkins started to put lube in his ass.

While Preacher was fitting his rod, he asked, "How did you bring this stuff in? I don't remember seeing the lube."

Concentrating on the task at hand, Hodkins only words were, "Side cargo pockets." Hodkins was referring to the side pockets in his ACU pants.

The room despite being almost empty was now heating up with the body heat and sweat. Hodkins finished his required task and rose up enough for Preacher to make his move. With a devilish grin, Preacher proceeded to lick Hodkins' hard brown nipples down to his rippled stomach and started to the shaft licking up to Hodkins' own little head.

Preacher's treat would be short lived to his disappointment. Hodkins, perhaps for selfish reasons interrupted Preacher's ravaging of him and maneuvered his body. Hodkins just gazed into his partner's eyes with no comment.

Now the bodies had switched places but Hodkins was now on his stomach and Preacher was on his knees near Hodkins' own knees.

Preacher positioned himself close enough so Hodkins could grab his dick to put it in his tight hole. Preacher noticed the twitching of Hodkins' head as he entered. Preacher was sure the initial entry was painful. He wanted to take his time with this and slowly ease in. "Slow down, baby. I'm not going anywhere. Plus, it's nice to know that no one has been in that ass since the last time we were together."

As the lube made his hole wetter and Preacher's dick slicker, Preacher began to feel his dick was now sliding smoothly inside that tight tunnel. Then suddenly, Preacher stopped his actions and pulled out. He pulled out.

"What's wrong?"

"I was about to cum from that tight ass of yours being so wet. I'm not ready to bust a nut just yet," said Preacher. Hodkins was turned on and was not expecting that from Preacher right now.

So Hodkins raised up on his knees and with one hand grabbed Preacher's dick and guided it to his wet cheeks. With very little maneuvering, the wet hard head found the ass like the space shuttle docking at the International Space Station.

All the while Hodkins' own dick was throbbing and dripping precum on the air bed, Hodkins slowly reared back to receive the whole shaft of Preacher. As the shaft was going in, Hodkins would tighten his hole several times so he could feel it. That move, he knew, would drive Preacher crazy. As for him, the pain Hodkins experienced earlier was replaced with complete enjoyment.

Hodkins' eyes rolled back in his head with pleasure, as Preacher was going slow and soon somewhat faster as the ass was loosening up. It was not a pounding on Hodkins but nice long consistent strokes.

They fucked doggie-style for at least an hour. Preacher tried to stay hold of Hodkins' waist for better leverage but with the juices flying and all the sweating, it was tough going. They both looked liked they got out of the shower dripping wet. But Preacher was stroking Hodkins like any other woman. You could hear the wet ass cheeks as Preacher was now ramming it.

Sweat ran off their faces and dripped into their eyes. The air bed below Hodkins' face had a small pool of water on it. Some of Preacher's sweat was simply rolling off of Hodkins' back. The glistening of Hodkins' back due to the sweating merely added to the appeal of Hodkins' sex appeal.

After a while, Preacher's dick was hurting like crazy as it was throbbing with the anticipation of cum bursting from his shaft into the rubber sock. He tried to suppress any loud screams by biting his lips. He rammed Hodkins for the last burst of his seed. Preacher let out a loud moan, ejaculating.

After that intense play, the two interlocked bodies laid there for a short period of time. The bodies glowed with their open pores. Not from a shower or spa treatment but from pure sex play. They were exhausted. Not so much in pain, Preacher during the ramming and Hodkins for the receiving. Both put in their fair share of work in and were just plain tired.

But both knew they needed to get up. Hodkins had to return to work and Preacher needed to turn in his apartment keys. They rolled over. Both Hodkins and Preacher just stared at the ceiling without saying a word.

After a minute, Hodkins eased up and dragged himself back to the shower stall. He couldn't go back to work with a heavy odor on him. The sweat and cum had to be removed.

Once a heavy stream of pulsating water flowed down recreating the mist again, Preacher came in to join him. They just stood there in silence as each soaped and rinsed each other. Each used a small towel to get into all the crevices of the other with the care and love of a couple that was married for years. The towel glided over all the contours of the other. *What an afternoon!*

Preacher had two more days left in the process of "clearing" the post before he would be leaving the post, the army, and this part of his life for good.

Preacher sat on the balcony sipping his favorite coffee. But on this day, it wouldn't be on his balcony that he sat on for the last 4 years. This time it was Hodkins.

Hodkins would get offended if Preacher referred to his apartment and its contents as Hodkins' stuff because even though Preacher had moved in until he was *cleared* and finally left the army, Hodkins considered the two a couple and wanted to start thinking along those lines since eventually the two would be living together in Atlanta anyway.

Preacher, still in his PJs, was determining how best to fill out his day considering he had only two "clearing" appointments left. Medical, taking place this afternoon and Finance, taking place tomorrow morning.

Neither would take long to clear. But both were by appointment and could not get bumped up any further even though Finance was in the same building he had worked for the last 4 years. With Medical, that should be about an hour or so considering he was not located in a combat zone. No injuries were suffered and he was certainly not getting out on medical discharge.

Finance, Preacher thought between sips, should take about 2 hours. Factor in the wait time, due to the number of personnel that must be processed through Finance whether you are arriving on the post or departing. In both cases, travel pay was likely due to each soldier for their journey and that takes time. No one knew that more than someone who worked there. Or used to work there.

This idea of entering all of his professional contacts in a database was a great idea. Preacher knew it was the right thing to do at the time he did it but didn't know just how important it would become.

Preacher was able to hone his database skills towards his contact database, tweaking the data fields here and there, putting the same professionalism and care in his personal project just like he would for a project within the walls of PAS. He designed it to give him just enough information on his contacts but not risking information overload.

Preacher was able to concentrate on his database projects with a little more intensity than usual during his trial. After work, it allowed him to take his mind off the events of the day while preparing him for his eventual departure from the military.

Preacher eventually had a finished product worthy of a place on the store shelves of *Office Max*, *Office Depot* or *BestBuy*, assuming it was professionally burned and labeled to a CD, shrink-wrapped and a decent marketing campaign behind it. The software itself wasn't just functional but it was also visually appealing with smooth, bright aqua-themed data screens.

Preacher had decided to breakout his HP laptop from its case to review his list of contacts. The laptop usually had a fully charged battery. Preacher made it a point to keep it that way. He never knew when an emergency would come up and he needed to whip it out for immediate use.

Once Preacher heard the *Welcome* sound as the laptop fully booted up, he knew that soon his data would be at his finger tips. In a matter of a few seconds, Preacher's desktop was displayed and his database's icon was there to execute.

Preacher took another sip and he savored the taste as if it was his last. He simply couldn't believe how close he was now to getting out of the army.

Working a 9 to 5 was simply just a dream a few years ago. Soon, the 4:30 am wakeups would be just a memory. Preacher licked his lips and moved his cursor with his optical mouse over the desired icon and double pressed its left mouse button.

At first, he didn't realize he had a treasure trove of IT and business contacts. He didn't realize just how many people he had run into during his stay at Fort Carson. And not all of them were based on the scattering of business cards that some handed out like pens at a convention. Some were people he had remained in contact with as the job of an army ITS required it.

He had even remembered some of them telling him to keep them in mind when he left the Army. As he tabbed from screen to screen, his contacts trove represented some of the biggest names in the IT field: *Lockheed-Martin, General Dynamics, EDS, Booz Allen Hamilton* and others but whether he could work out of the Atlanta area was another thing. But he would check. He thought that he might assist his Atlanta headhunter by making a few calls on his own to some of these folks. It wouldn't hurt to put a lot in the pot to see what came out, Preacher thought.

Preacher always hated goodbyes. They were the absolute worst for him. Goodbyes always seemed to make things final. That was especially the case with one of his uncles passing away.

He said goodbye to him too knowing that it was probably the last time he would ever see him alive. As it turned out, he was right. He was also right about his mother. But this was different; he knew but it still didn't stop those depressing emotions from coming in.

No one was ill. No one was elderly and dying this time. Just two good soul mates temporarily separating for a short time. Not due to a dispute or anything but merely because of a search for a new job in a new environment.

It was now 1500 hours. About 3 hours away from the time the sun would be setting in the mountains.

CHAPTER TWENTY ONE

The last small box was loaded in Preacher's vehicle. This time Hodkins stayed in the apartment as he handed Preacher the last load. Hodkins had taken the afternoon off to assist Preacher with his departure. Now, he wasn't sure if that was a good idea or not.

Preacher had never seen him cry before. Not even close. And Hodkins didn't want him to see his tears now. That was one of the little things that separated men from women. Women cried when necessary. Men did so in controlled environments as if someone saw them they might get tossed out of the boys club or something.

While giving Preacher the box in the apartment, Hodkins didn't look him straight in the face and after doing so, found a reason to vacate to the bathroom to pee. In reality, Hodkins' eyes had begun tearing up. He needed to go wipe his face with a cold, wet face towel.

Prior to returning back upstairs, Preacher made one last check of the vehicle to make sure that his shoulder bag was there on the floor in the front passenger side. Among his important papers such as birth certificate, original social security card and diplomas; were his discharge papers including his final clearing form complete with the needed approval stamps on the front.

All this was in the bag. They will be needed as he settled into his new life. The headhunter that made contact with him had made arrangements for several job interviews while he temporarily stayed at a motel.

Preacher also made some phone calls of his own to some contractors who did quite a bit of work for the federal government. And he too had arranged some interviews. Preacher did not want to be sitting around a lot once he got to Atlanta and, as of now, it didn't appear that he would.

With the bag in sight and vehicle locked, it was time to see Hodkins for the last time in a while. Preacher was not looking forward to seeing Hodkins this way and he was hoping really hard that it goes well. He was so in thought that he almost walked into an older gentleman on the way up the stairs to his car.

Preacher looked up at the guy who had by now stopped in his steps and said, "Excuse me." He was apparently not in the best of moods himself. He shook his head as if annoyed and he went on his way.

Preacher didn't notice this and he continued on his way up the stairs to the apartment. Once at the door, he opened the partially opened door, all the way.

Preacher walked into the apartment looking for Hodkins. The search didn't take long. Preacher saw his friend leaning back against the sink counter in the kitchen. With his arms folded on his chest, he looked at Preacher with a smirk on his face.

"So far, so good," Preacher thought. "This might not be so bad after all." Hodkins looked at Preacher as if he was waiting for him to walk through the main door at anytime.

Preacher continued walking towards the kitchen when Hodkins rose up and walked towards him too. Hodkins stopped at the main entrance to meet his friend face to face.

Preacher had stopped in his tracks when Hodkins grabbed him by the waist in a bear hug and kissed him on the lips. Hodkins, by now had removed any moisture from his eyes.

"I need to go in order to make good time before night fall," Preacher said.

"I know." Hodkins release his friend and motioned Preacher out the doorway and out the apartment. This even surprised Preacher. No emotion on his face or in voice. Just simply, "let's go."

Preacher was glad it went like it did and he was able to get away with no drama and get on the highway. By the time they had made it out the door of the apartment, Hodkins had released Preacher's hand.

Once down the stairs, Hodkins was already in front and they both made it to Preacher's vehicle in no time. Preacher walked quite comfortably in his leather-strapped sandals, khaki pants topped with a cuban shirt which was also being beaten by the light breeze of the day.

With the bag checks already done, there was nothing else for Preacher to do but enter the vehicle. Hodkins appeared quite calm and relaxed as

Preacher got seated in. Once ready, Preacher turned the key and the engine was ready to go.

While leaning on the driver's side door, Hodkins gave Preacher a brotherly fist bump showing the pearly whites then he backed away from the vehicle as it was put in reverse to pull out of the parking spot.

Hodkins took a deep breath as he saw his friend send the vehicle forward out of the parking lot and Preacher bumped his horn as he drove toward Magrath Avenue to exit the main gate.

Hodkins let out a sigh and turned around to go back up the stairs. He noticed the moment seem so different. It appeared to him that the breeze that was around them earlier had gone, the singing of the cardinals that sat in a tree above Preacher and him had stopped and the foot traffic that was in and out of the apartment complex had all but disappeared.

Once back in his apartment, Hodkins immediately made sure the door was locked and he headed to his sofa. Hodkins flobbed down on it like he had heavy shoulder pads on his shoulders. He first leaned back then he leaned forward bringing his hands up to his face and buried it. The tears flowed as if on cue.

It was almost as heavy weights were now lifted as Preacher passed through the main exit gates of Fort Carson for the last time.

No more four o'clock wake ups prior to getting to work. No more odd work details by higher ranked officers and enlisted personnel just because they were having a bad day or perhaps something that someone in the platoon may have done or said. No more coming to PT formations in near summer uniform during cold mountain mornings just because that was the uniform of the day. Along with the good parts of the job a lot of bs came with it too and it was finally over.

But for Preacher now, all that was literally not just miles away but hundreds of miles away. That part of his life along with a big chuck of his old military gear was left behind in Colorado.

The caretaker of *The Army Store* on B Street just outside of Gate 4 of Fort Carson was less than enthusiastic about getting more surplus military uniforms from yet another former soldier from another Colorado Springs area military base. His enthusiasm was reflected equally by the amount of money Preacher was given for the equipment. Preacher thought it should be enough to pay for gas to get him out of Colorado and through Kansas, at least.

Preacher drove on Interstate 70 at the center of the United States. I-70 is more than a route out of Colorado into Kansas. It is a path rich history. It was inhabited by Native Americans displaced from other parts of North America from 1830 to 1854.

Between his thoughts of his past and those of his future, Preacher took time to soak up his new surroundings. This was a route he had never taken before. The Kansas landscape was very similar to the panhandle of Texas and Oklahoma. A trip he was very familiar with which frequently took him from Southern Colorado to Arkansas.

Western Kansas has been known to have as many as 300 clear days in a year. The mountains in nearby Colorado block the rain, making this part of the state sunny and dry.

Sunshine was exactly what Preacher got most of his drive today. The highway was hot, as indicated by the heat waves that ones sees on the road ahead. And that is also accented by the occasional tumbleweed and dirt devils to the sides of the road.

Fields stretch mile after golden mile across the state. The flat landscape consisted of carpets of billowing golden wheat fields, bright yellow sunflowers, herds of grazing cattle, humming oil derricks and towering signature grain storage elevators silhouetted against wide open skies. Around each corner of the winding road, Preacher saw a piece of the Old West.

A strong gust of wind against the vehicle brought Preacher back to the present. Out of nowhere, a few dark clouds appeared. Preacher was reminded that just like his old route, when he would often go home, this too was right in the middle of "tornado alley." The endless skies could be an innocent blue, and then, like an unruly child, they could cause havoc to a peaceful scene. Blizzards, tornadoes, hail, and relentlessly burning sun could ride in on the Kansas winds.

With the exception of a 5 minute rain shower, the appearance of the isolated dark clouds were mostly uneventful. Perhaps a big tease to a local farmer but mainly uneventful to Preacher's travels.

Whenever he got too restless sitting for hours in the driver's seat, Preacher started looking for nice travel stop to quench his palate. Not necessarily a truck stop but a nice place to go in and sat for a few minutes. But not too long. Preacher is on a schedule of sorts.

Then in between those pit stops he would stop at the familiar interstate rest areas to stretch his legs and to relieve himself. The first day after

Preacher's ETS was both of relief and enjoyment as it was winding down. Preacher hoped that he would have many relaxing days just like this one.

Kansas too, was letting Preacher know that another of its days was near completion. A solid gold sunset reflected in the summer wheat fields melt into the horizon. Acres of sunflowers and the sweet smell of prairie grass after a brief shower delight each of the senses.

Preacher had now decided to turn off the air conditioner and roll down the driver's side window. As the sun was about to rest, its heat was diminishing and it was quite comfortable as he drove down I-70.

The ever-changing prairie was covered with the colors of its wildflowers; the sunflower, of course, and the buttercup, primrose, wild daisy, gay feather and wild onion—each a different color and each lasting only a few days.

Preacher also noticed the panorama views of river valleys, rolling grass lands, meandering creeks, jutting lime stone bluffs, and amazing rock formations. It was places like that, Preacher thought, that the westward trails of our pioneer ancestors met those of the Native American.

Preacher by now was truly amazed by the orange glow of the setting sun behind the fields of golden grain. Just like this day, Preacher's time in the military had ended and just like a new day would appear over this vast land tomorrow so will a new beginning for Preacher.

One lifestyle ending and another one about to start.

The mild, sunny morning was soothing to the soldiers of the Mountain Post today. The line outside the dining facility was only twenty deep and it moved very quickly. One would be inside the building before you knew it.

The men and women, despite any personal dilemma they found themselves in, any family problems and perhaps whether or not their unit was part of any rotation to Iraq or Afghanistan, were in a jovial mood. But then again the smell of eggs, bacon, toast and coffee did tend to calm some even if it was only temporary.

Specialist Hodkins was in a good mood too. Not because of the food, even though it was hitting his stomach pretty well and not because of the sunny weather, but because his day had finally arrived.

After days of "clearing" the post, arranging the shipment of his household goods from his apartment to Atlanta, and signing off on his paperwork, Hodkins was leaving the military. Today he would be leaving

Fort Carson for good. Today would be his last day as a soldier and by this time tomorrow, he would be a civilian.

Hodkins had come into the facility alone. No other friends. Just himself. Perhaps it was in part because he wanted to reflect back on his time in the military alone while he ate his breakfast of scrambled eggs, sausage patties, pancakes and orange juice.

Whatever anyone thought, Hodkins was able to find a small table in the far corner of the mess hall and he ate alone. But Hodkins did do some soul searching as well as some personal reflection of his life, the past 4 years. He did wish he had invested in himself more by way with some college courses.

He would've liked to put more on his resume besides the job experiences he acquired in the field of Information Technology while in the army even though the experience was quite extensive. But given the exact set of circumstances, he would have done the same thing, which meant not going to school and just having fun.

Specialist Petersen would not miss out on the nice meal either this morning. Along with two of her girlfriends, she entered the mess hall as well. By the time she got there the line outside was gone and she and her party walked right in.

Petersen shifted her camouflaged carrying bag with shoulder strap in order to produce her meal card to the sergeant signing everyone in. Afterwards, the party was in line ordering their meals with trays in hand.

Petersen's two friends skipped the hot dishes, choosing the bagels and fruit cocktail instead before getting their drinks. Gwendolyn didn't want a light meal but didn't want to wait for minutes for a dish either so she got what was faster as oppose to the cook-to-order omelets.

The facility wasn't exactly packed this time of the morning but it was lively, Petersen observed.

She observed Lynette smacking her fruit dish at the table and she couldn't resist. "Damn girl," whispered Petersen while looking at her, "slow down on that food smacking. You can go back and get some more."

With that, all three ladies laughed. But Lynette didn't let her totally off the hook. She paused, looked around to make sure the wrong person was not in ear shot and turned back towards her girl.

"Bitch, I thought we were cool. Lately you been trying to bust me out every chance you get. But it's cool. When the moment is right I will return the favor back to you."

"I'm not sure why I even try to spend time with y'all stifling heifers," shot back Petersen.

That got the attention of Centrell who was focusing on her own meal. "Bitch, who are you calling heifer?" She didn't even bother to look around but kept her voice low at the table. "It is way too early in the morning to have that bra wrapped around your neck."

"Well, at least I have something to fill a bra, missy," said Lynette while gesturing toward her chest with her fingers.

All three ladies laughed. Despite Centrell being the butt of that joke, she took it as just fun.

That last low burst of laughter did get the attention of a group of first lieutenants eating a few tables away but they soon went about eating their breakfast.

"You two heifers are crazy. Know wonder you can't catch and keep a man," replied Petersen. "Y'all betta—"

"Excuse me ladies but could I interrupt ya hackling for moment?"

All of the ladies at the table halted what they were doing at the sudden comment. They were somewhat offended by his remark and tone. The tone was just as condescending as what was said. As if females couldn't have a meaningful and informative conversation like the men who wouldn't be described as "hackling."

Hodkins had appeared suddenly from the rear of the girls and apparently made a beeline to them without being noticed.

Centrell looked at Hodkins with apparent disgust. She knew his rep and wondered why females gave him the time of day. And that was even before all that stuff came out about him and Preacher.

Almost in unison, the females spoke, "What can we do for you Hodkins?" It too was in a tone he would understand.

Hodkins stood there with his almost empty food tray in each hand and his beret protruding from his right leg cargo pocket. He too didn't like Petersen's friends and without even acknowledging them with eye contact, he only focused in on Petersen. "Petersen, I have something for you." Hodkins held the tray with his left hand and reached on the tray to get a small manila envelope. He gave it to Petersen and he said in a very low voice, "You'll know why I gave this to you." And just as quickly as he arrived, he vacated the ladies' space.

After setting his used tray on the conveyor belt with the rest of the trays, Hodkins exit the dining facility for what would be the last time.

Waiting for him was a yellow cab. He managed to arrange a pickup just after spotting Petersen in the mess hall. Petersen opened the envelope while the girls watched. They had managed to finish off their breakfast and now had nothing better to do but watch Petersen.

She had ripped one end of the envelope and tilted it to the side so the contents went on the table next to her food tray. All watched as a set of keys and a note fell out. Petersen looked at the keys then the note and looked at her friends and back to the keys. The ladies looked at the keys then the note and looked at Petersen and back to the keys.

Petersen grabbed the note and leaned back in her chair. Lynette had grabbed the keys. "These are car or truck keys." Petersen took her eyes off the note for a second.

"Gee, what tipped you off? Perhaps the 'GM' stamped on the keys?" snapped Petersen just before bringing her attention back to the note.

> *"Well, Gwen, by now you is probably wondering why I left you these keys.*
>
> *To keep this as simple as I can, they use to belong to my Blazer. It is currently in the unit parking lot for you.*
>
> *I will no longer need the vehicle and I can think of no one better to give it to than you."*

Petersen set the note down on the table to view the keys again in Lynette's hands. But she knew she had to finish reading the note.

> *"That's right the truck is yours--free and clear. I even left the title paper work with your name on it in the vehicle. The only thing you have to worry about concerning the well-maintained vehicle is gas and the women or the men flagging you down as you drive on post thinking it's still me in it."*

That got a smile on Petersen's face which didn't go unnoticed by her two guests. They each looked at each other somewhat baffled by all that was taking place.

> *"I'm starting over now with my life and its time that I set some things right. It's just something I want to do.*
>
> *For starters, I apologize for threatening you in the club concerning Preacher. For what it's worth, I wouldn't have done anything to you*

other than scare you but I couldn't let you know that. Although I wasn't sure what my Plan B would have been.

But in any case, the keys to the Blazer are just my way of saying I'm sorry.

I wish you the best of luck in what you may do in the future and I hope the Blazer serves you as well as it have served me.

Take care, Gwen

Hodkins"

Petersen smiled as she folded the note and looked back hoping to catch Hodkins to say thanks. But Hodkins was now seated in the cab. He was now free to leave Fort Carson for the last time. But he instructed the cabbie to stop by the nearest ATM. In minutes, what money he had at the Fort Carson Bank was drained.

With money in hand, a large red sports gym bag and a folder of paperwork; Clarence Hodkins, former US Army specialist was leaving through the gates of Fort Carson for good.

When the airline crew had announced his flight to Atlanta, Hodkins snapped out of his deep thoughts of his times in the Army. He had plenty of good times and bad but mostly good.

He got up from his seat near his gate and got in line with the rest to board the plane.

When the lady reviewed his ticket and returned his boarding pass, Hodkins tucked it in his shirt pocket and approached the door to the gate.

Hodkins stopped and looked back. He almost felt sad to be leaving friends and a way of life he has known for the last 4 years. But he also knew he too would be starting a new life and not just alone but with his new soul mate.

Hodkins brushed the thoughts of the past aside and now was looking forward to the new. Hodkins had changed out of his uniform into some *Sean John*s and on the interior window sill of one of the airport restrooms near the familiar *United Service Organizations* or USO room, he had placed his clean folded ACU shirt on top of his folded ACU pants. Resting on the shirt facing the front was his black beret. Below all that on the floor was his pair of the tan combat boots. His old army gear was neat in appearance and he had left it there, because he didn't want to just throw it out and he didn't have time to sell it.

Being close to the USO area and knowing how soldiers loved their beer, Hodkins knew some newly arrived soldier awaiting his ride to Fort Carson was bound to find it. He had turned around and started down the ramp to the awaiting plane. He was now about to leave *The Springs* to start a new life in *Hotlanta*.

MILITARY TIME CHART

Civilian Time	Military Time
12:00 am	0000
1:00 am	0100
2:00 am	0200
3:00 am	0300
4:00 am	0400
5:00 am	0500
6:00 am	0600
7:00 am	0700
8:00 am	0800
9:00 am	0900
10:00 am	1000
11:00 am	1100
12:00 pm	1200
1:00 pm	1300
2:00 pm	1400
3:00 pm	1500
4:00 pm	1600
5:00 pm	1700
6:00 pm	1800
7:00 pm	1900
8:00 pm	2000
9:00 pm	2100
10:00 pm	2200
11:00 pm	2300

Common Military Terminology

1LT	First Lieutenant. A company-grade officer with 2-7 years of service. A first lieutenant may be a platoon leader or, in exceptional cases, be a company commander. All officers at or above this level may serve in staff positions
2LT	Second Lieutenant. Also known as a "butter bar", a second lieutenant is a company-grade officer with 0-3 years of service. Usually a platoon leader. These poor souls are saddled with all the important extra duties in a company, like mess officer, morale officer, etc. A second lieutenant is never to be trusted with a compass
5-TON	The Army's workhorse cargo truck since the 1940s
AAFES	Army and Air Force Exchange Service
ABRAMS	The M1A1 is America's main battle tank. The best tank in the world, it devastated the Iraqi Republican Guard during the Gulf War
ACCOMPANIED TOUR	Tour of duty with family members
ACTIVE ARMY	On active duty
AD	Armored Division

ADA	Air Defense Artillery. Also known as 'duck hunters' because they shoot down airplanes
ADVANCED PAY	Payment before [duty performed] actually earned
AFB	Air Force Base
AIT	Advanced Individual Training. Where a new soldier learns the skill he will use when he arrives at his first unit
ALERT	Emergency call to be ready
ALLOTMENT	Designated payment by soldier or civilian employee to bank or individual
ALLOWANCE	Pay and special compensation
ANCOC	Advanced Noncommissioned Officers' Course
APC	Armored Personnel Carrier. A lightly-armored, lightly-armed taxi for soldiers
AR	Army Regulation
ARMY COMMUNITY SERVICE (ACS)	Provides family support services on installation for active duty members and retirees, civilian employees, and their families; Reserve Component members see Family Program Coordinator
ARNG	Army National Guard
ARTICLE 15	Disciplinary action
ASAP	As soon as possible

AWOL	Absent Without Leave. To be away from assigned military duty without proper authorization
BAQ	Basic allowance for quarters
BARRACKS/ BILLETS	Place where a soldier lives
ACU	Army Combat Uniform
BED CHECK	An accounting for soldiers
BENEFITS	Medical, dental, commissary, PX, etc.
BG	Brigadier General. A general officer who is condemned to staff positions until he gets promoted. Also referred to as a "one star" general
BN	Battalion. Two or more companies. Cavalry and aviation refer to this as a "squadron"
BNCOC	Basic Noncommissioned Officers' Course
BRADLEY	The Army's light armored vehicle. More of a small tank, it carries fewer troops than its replacement but has thicker armor.
Brigade (BDE)	Two or more battalions
BT	Basic Training. The training in basic combat and military subjects given to newly inducted and enlisted service personnel with no prior military service.
CADRE	Leadership at training level

CAREER PROGRAM	Grouping of civilian employee positions at grades G-11 and higher in the same career field; Army has 21 career programs
CG	Commanding General
CHAIN OF COMMAND	Leadership structure
CHAPLAIN	Military minister, priest rabbi, or pastor
CI	Counter-Intelligence
CIVIES	Civilian clothing. As oppose to military clothing.
CLASS As	Green slacks/skirt, light green shirt, tie or neck tab, and jacket
CLASS Bs	Green slacks/skirt, light green shirt, and optional sweater without jacket
CLEARING	Obtaining official release from post
CLUSTER FUCK	What results when no one knows what the hell is going on; or when someone can't tell his ass from a hole in the ground is in charge of those who can; or when people are running around like chickens with their heads cut off. You get the idea.
CO or CDR	Commanding officer. CO can also refer to a Company, housing two or more platoons.
COB	Close of business
CODE OF CONDUCT	Rules by which a soldier must live

COL	Colonel. A field-grade officer that commands a brigade.
Also referred to as a "full bird" or "full bull"	
COLORS	National and unit/organization flags
COMBAT SERVICE STRIPES	Stripes for time served in combat
COMMISSARY	Grocery store for military
CONUS	Continental United States
CORPS	Two or more divisions
COURT-MARTIAL	Trial system within the Army
CP	Check Point
CPT	Captain. A company-grade officer with 6-12 years of service. The lowest rank to be referred to as "the Old Man"
CQ	Charge of quarters
CSM	Command Sergeant Major
CTT	Common Task Training. Teaches a soldier's most basic skills --marksmanship, first aid, map reading, etc.
DA	Department of the Army
DAYROOM	Recreation area in soldier lodging

DEPENDENT	The husband or wife who is not in the military; minor children; other relatives who are dependent upon the military sponsor for support
DEPLOYMENT	Soldier or civilian employee sent on a mission without family members
DETAIL	A job or assignment
DINING IN	Formal social gathering for soldiers only
DINING OUT	Formal social gathering with spouses
DIRECT DEPOSIT/ SURE PAY	Soldier's or civilian employee's guaranteed check to bank
DISCHARGE	Departure from active duty
DITY MOVE	Self-movement of household goods
DIV	Division. Two or more brigades. A division has between 12,500 and 25,000 troops
DOB	Date of Birth
DOD	Department of Defense
DOGTAGS	Identification tags worn by soldiers
DOR	Date of Rank
DRESS BLUES	Informal attire with four-in-hand tie/ formal attire with bow tie
DRESS MESS	Formal attire; short jacket equivalent to "white tie and tails"

DUTY ASSIGNMENT	Job/place while on active duty
ESPRIT DE CORPS	Morale within unit or organization
ETS	Expiration of term of service. When you are discharged from the military
FA	Field artillery
FAMILY ADVOCACY	Program that assists with child and spouse abuse problems
FAMILY CARE PLAN	Written instructions for care of family members while sponsor is away from duty station (can include provisions for finances, wills, and guardianship
FAMILY PROGRAM COORDINATOR	Provides family support services to Reserve Component members and families; active duty members and civilian employees see Army Community Service
FAMILY SUPPORT GROUP	Organization of family members, volunteers, and soldiers/civilian employees belonging to a unit or organization that together provide an avenue of mutual support and assistance and a network of communication among the family members, the chain of command, and community resources
FIELD DAY	Designated day for military displays
FIELD GRADE	Majors, lieutenant colonels, and colonels
FORMATION	Gathering of soldiers in a prescribed way
FROCK	Assume next higher grade without pay

FRUIT SALAD	Ribbons and medals worn on uniform
FSB	Forward Support Battalion. An FSB provides the administrative, medical and logistical support to one brigade.
FTX	Field training exercise
FY	Fiscal Year. The military year which runs from October 1st to September 30th
GARRISON	Post or community
GEAR	Equipment used by soldiers or civilian employees
GEN	General. Commands an army, joint command, or one of the armed services. Also referred to as a "four star" general
GI	Government issue; slang for a soldier
GI BILL	Education entitlement
GI PARTY	Clean up duty
GRADE	Corresponds to pay level of soldier or civilian employee (e.g., E-3, 0-1, or GS-4)
GREEN BERETS	Special Forces
GUARD MEMBER	Military member of the Army or Air National Guards
GUEST HOUSE	Temporary living quarters
GUIDON	Unit identification flag ("Flag that troops rallied 'round.")

HARDSHIP TOUR	Unaccompanied tour of duty
HASH MARKS	Stripes for enlisted members' time in service
HAZARDOUS DUTY PAY	Extra pay for duty in hostile area
HHC	Headquarters & Headquarters Company. The unit that controls the lower ranking members of a unit's staff sections
HOR	Home of record
HOUSING OFFICE	Where you check in for housing
HQ	Headquarters
HUMVEE	The military's current version of the Jeep, the HMMMWV (High Mobility Multi-purpose Wheeled Vehicle) is also referred to as a "Hummer"
ID CARD	Identification card issued to legally recognized members of America's Army family
IG	Inspector general
IN-PROCESSING	Officially becoming a member of the post/unit
INSIGNIA	Indicates branch of soldiers
ITT	Information Tour and Travel office
JAG	Judge Advocate General

JODY CALL	Troop cadence for marching or running. At one time they were about inspirational subjects like killing and pillaging. But in a kinder, gentler Army of peacekeepers that is no longer acceptable.
JOINT PERSONAL PROPERTY SHIPPING OFFICE (JPPSO)	They coordinate the shipping and delivery of your personal household items when transferring to and from a post/unit
JUMP PAY	Extra pay for jump status
JUMPMASTER	Person supervising paratroopers on a jump exercise
JUNGLE BOOTS	Special boots for tropical climates
KLICK	Slang for kilometer
LATRINE	Toilet or Rest room
LEAVE	Approved time away from duty
LES	Leave and earnings statement; monthly pay check
LOCATION ALLOWANCE	Allowance received for PCS move
LOGISTICS	Equipment and support needed for performance
LTC	Lieutenant Colonel. A field-grade officer that commands a battalion. Also referred to as a "light colonel"

LTG	Lieutenant General. Commands a corps or a base. Also referred to as a "three star" general
M-16	Fires a 5.56mm round to a maximum effective range of 460 meters. Basically a pumped-up .22, the bullet is designed to tumble on impact -- a Very Bad Thing for those hit by it. This venerable weapon is now in its third incarnation. To conserve ammo, the military reduced its full-auto capabilities to a meager three-round burst
M-203	A single shot 40mm grenade launcher that is mounted beneath the barrel of an M-16
MAJ	Major. A major is a field-grade officer who is condemned to staff positions until he gets promoted. The exception is special operations forces, where a major may be a company or detachment commander
MANEUVER DAMAGE	Damage caused by the military to civilian property. The U.S. actually pays for it. This doesn't occur a whole lot in the U.S. since most maneuvers are done on posts or bases. But overseas, it not unusual.
MEDEVAC	Medical evacuation
MEPS	Military Entrance Processing Station. The military has one of these massive inter-service initial in-processing centers in most major cities. It is where the bulk of your initial paperwork, including the signing of your contract takes place.
MESS HALL	A Army cafeteria

MG	Major General. Commands a division or a base. Also referred to as a "two star" general
MOS	Military Occupational Specialty. A soldier's specific military job skill identifier, the skill your are taught after basic training. The Army may guarantee you the training that does not mean that's what you'll be doing after you finish it.
MOTOR POOL	Area where official vehicles are kept
MRE	Meals Ready to Eat. They are made of meat that is too poor to be put into Spam, so they are also known as "Meals Rejected by Ethiopians". MREs also come in plastic bags, so they are not nearly as useful as the old C-rations which came in cans that could be used as coffee cups, stoves, alarms, booby traps, and whatever else an inventive soldier could jury rig
MSG/1SG	Master Sergeant or First Sergeant. Both are senior NCOs. The difference is that a first sergeant serves as the top-enlisted person in a company. A first sergeant is also referred as "Top" or the "First Shirt"
MWI	A search of the premises for contraband such as drugs, guns and knives. This may also be accompanied with urinalysis tests.

NBC	Nuclear, Biological & Chemical warfare. U.S. policy is that we reserve the right for first use of nuclear weapons, will use chemical weapons only if they are used against us, and will not use biological weapons at all. Chemical weapons are more commonly referred to as "poison gas"
NCO	Non-Commissioned Officer. A fancy name for sergeants – the backbone of the Army
NCOIC	NCO-in-Charge. The highest ranking NCO in a military office or activity
n-DIGIT MIDGET	Double- or Single- depending on the number of days someone has left in the military. A single-digit midget is an object of intense jealousy among other soldiers. The midget's attitude and desire to work is often in direct proportion to the number of day's left on his enlistment. Also known as a "short timer".
OCS	Officer Candidate School
OIC	Officer-In-Charge
OJT	On the job training
OP ORDER	Operations Order. A bulky piece of paperwork that few people read in its entirety. It is the plan that attempts to micro-manage every facet of an operation.
ORDERLY ROOM	Company office
ORDERS	Spoken or written instructions to soldier
PAO	Public Affairs Office

PCS	Permanent Change of Station. Reassignment of military personnel from one permanent station to another
PFC	Private First Class
PINON CANYON	An area outside of the main garrison but still on the post that is used for training by the soldiers and their equipment. This equipment can range anywhere from a M16 rifle to heavy artillery.
PLATOON (PLT)	Several squads within a company
PLDC	Primary Leadership Development Course
PMCS	Preventive Maintenance Checks and Services. Every piece of equipment in the Army inventory has an associated PMCS. A PMCS can be daily, weekly, monthly, before, during or after operation. The inspection, cleaning and minor repairs are intended to prevent accidents or major breakdowns
POLICE CALL	Clean up
POST EXCHANGE (PX)	Army department store
POV	Privately owned vehicle; your car
POWER OF ATTORNEY	Legal document permitting a person to act on behalf of another
PROTOCOL	Customs and courtesies
PROVOST MARSHALL	Military equivalent of a police department

PT	Physical Training. Everything from exercises, to ruck marches, to sports. The PT test consists of pushups, sit-ups and a two mile run. It is scored by age and sex, with women receiving a tremendous advantage
PV2	A private who has graduated from basic training and AIT. Being promoted to PV2 is referred to as "getting your mosquito wings" because of the way the inverted-V rank insignia appears
PVT	Private. The only soldiers who are privates are new recruits or convicts doing hard time in Leavenworth
QUARTERS	Government housing for married soldiers
RANK	Official title of soldier (also, relative position within a military grade such as sergeant or captain)
READY RESERVE	Units and unit members soldiers of the reserve component and individuals liable for involuntary call to active duty in time of war or a national emergency as authorized by law and declared by the Congress or the President
RESERVE COMPONENT	Army and Air National Guard and U.S. Army Reserve (and equivalent in other Services)
RETREAT	Bugle/flag ceremony at end of day. Normally a tape played over speakers at post headquarters

RE-UP	Reenlist
REVEILLE	Bugle call ceremony at beginning of day. Normally a tape played over speakers at post headquarters
ROSTER	List of members
ROTC	Reserve Officers' Training Corps
RUCK	Short for "rucksack", it is the military word for "backpack".
S-1/G-1	Administration and personnel
S-2/G-2	Intelligence and security
S-3/G-3	Operations
S-4/G-4	Supply and logistics
S-5/G-5	Civil affairs and psyops
SD	Staff Duty
SDO	Staff Duty Officer
SEPARATION PAY	Pay for unaccompanied duty

SF	Special Forces. Also known as "Green Berets" due to their distinctive head gear. SF can perform a variety of unconventional warfare missions, but their primary use is to train indigenous forces in foreign countries. The Holy Trinity of SF are JFK, John Wayne and "Colonel" Maggie Raye. JFK gave SF its impetous; the Duke made the "Green Berets" movie; and "Colonel" Raye was one of the few USO entertainers who went deep into the 'Nam bush to entertain the teams where they lived
SFC	Sergeant First Class. A senior NCO with 10 or more years of service. A sergeant first class is the top enlisted person in a platoon
SGLI	Servicemen's Group Life Insurance. A low cost term life insurance program
SGM/CSM	Sergeant Major or Command Sergeant Major. Both are senior NCOs. The difference is that a command sergeant major serves as the top-enlisted person at battalion level and higher units. To a private they appear older than the Earth
SGT	Sergeant. A junior NCO with 3-8 years of service. Sergeants are usually responsible for several privates and specialists
SHORT TIMER	Person with short time left to serve on active duty
SHORT TOUR	Unaccompanied tour

SICK CALL	Specific block of time for medical attention
SOP	Standard Operating Procedure
SP4/CPL	Specialist Fourth Class or Corporal. Both receive the same pay, but a corporal is a junior NCO. At one time there were specialists all the way up to SP8, the same pay grade as a First Sergeant
SPACE A	Space available
SQUAD	About a dozen soldiers. Smallest tactical unit in the Army
SSG	Staff Sergeant. A junior NCO with 6-12 years of service. Staff sergeants are usually responsible for a squad or one armored vehicle
SUBSISTENCE	Food allowance
SURE PAY/DIRECT DEPOSIT	Soldier's or civilian employee's guaranteed check to bank
TA50	Field gear
TAPS	Last call of the day
TDY	Temporary Duty. Many times in conjunction with travel to a different training site
THE MOUNTAIN POST	It's the nickname of Fort Carson as well as the name of the post's newspaper.

UCMJ	Uniform Code of Military Justice. The internal laws that govern the military. See also, Article 15
USAR	United States Army Reserve. A federal force, consisting of individual reinforcements, combat, combat support, and training type units. The Army Reserve is organized and maintained to provide military training in peacetime and reservoir of trained units and individual reservists to be ordered to active duty in the event of war or a national emergency.
USAREUR	U.S. Army Europe. A shell of its former self, the dubious payoff of the misnamed 'peace dividend', since the Berlin Wall fell
XO	Executive Officer. The second-highest ranking soldier in a unit

FLAG ETIQUETTE

SALUTING THE FLAG

Salute the flag...

When it is six paces from the viewer and hold it until the flag has passed six paces beyond. Salute the flag at the first note of the National Anthem and hold the salute until the last note is played. Never use a flag as a decoration – use bunting.

When in civilian attire...

MEN remove hats and hold at left shoulder with hand over heart; without hat, place right hand, palm open, over heart. WOMEN should place right hand, palm open, over heart. When in athletic clothing, face the flag or music, remove hat or cap and stand at attention; a hand salute is not given.

CARRYING THE FLAG

When marching...

Carry the flag on the right in any procession or parade. If there are many other flags, carry the flag in the front center position.

If you are carrying a flag...

Hold the flag at a slight angle from your body. You can also carry it with one hand and rest it on your right shoulder.

DISPLAYING THE FLAG OUTDOORS

On a vehicle...

Attach the flag to the antenna or clamp the flagstaff to the right fender. Do not lay the flag over the vehicle.

On a building...

Hang the flag on a staff or on a rope over the sidewalk with the stars away from the building.

Over the street...

Hang the flag with the stars to the east on a north- south street or north on an east-west street.

Above other flags...

Hang the flag above any other flag on the same pole.

Other flags, separate poles...

Hang all flags on equal poles. Hang the U.S. flag on its own right, hoist it first and lower it last.

In a window...

Hang the flag vertically with the stars to the left of anyone looking at it from the street.

Half-mast...

This is a sign of mourning. Raise the flag to the top of the pole then lower it to the half way point. Before lowering the flag, raise it to the top again at the end of the day.

Upside down...

An upside-down flag is considered a distress signal.

DISPLAYING THE FLAG INDOORS

Multiple staffs...

If you display the flag on a staff with other flags around it, place the flag at the center and highest point. Crossed staffs - Keep the flagstaff higher and on its own right.

Behind a speaker...

Hang the flag flat on the wall. Do not decorate the podium or table with the flag. Use bunting for decoration.

Next to a speaker...

Place the flag in a stand on the speaker's right. Use the same placement for a religious service.

In a hall or lobby...

Hang the flag vertically across from the main entrance with the stars to the left of anyone coming through the door.

On a casket...

Drape the flag with its canton at the head and over the left shoulder of the body. Do not lower the flag into the grave.

www.ingramcontent.com/pod-product-compliance
Lightning Source LLC
Chambersburg PA
CBHW032232010726
47494CB00002B/466